THE BLIGHT OF MUIRWOOD

Legends of Muirwood Trilogy

The Wretched of Muirwood

The Blight of Muirwood

The Scourge of Muirwood

THE BLIGHT OF MUIRWOOD

Legends of Muirwood

Book Two

JEFF WHEELER

47NORTH

The characters and events portrayed in this book are fictitious. Any similarity to real persons, living or dead, is coincidental and not intended by the author.

Published by 47North
P.O. Box 400818
Las Vegas, NV 89140

Cover illustration by Eamon O'Donoghue

ISBN-13: 9781612187013
ISBN-10: 1612187013
Library of Congress Control Number: 2012943331

To Emily

In every era there comes a moment when the collective thoughts, whims, and motivations of a people become so self-absorbed, so malignant, so unheeding that nature itself revolts. Man scars the land such that it finally rebels against him. As thoughts can spread despair and death like seedlings of weeds strewn by the wind, so they eventually draw the Gardener to pluck them out. The vetches must be pulled, roots and all. When this happens, the Medium ceases to bless, and instead, it curses. Instead of healing, it spews poison. It happens swiftly and terribly. The ancients gave it a name, this culling process that blackens the world. They named it after a wasting disease that occurs in once-healthy groves of trees. They called it the Blight.

—Gideon Penman of Muirwood Abbey

CHAPTER ONE

Whitsunday

Someone threw a stone or a spoiled fruit at the man perched atop the maypole, and he nearly lost his balance. After ripping his cap from his head, he shook it at the offender, probably a young man dashing through the crowd. Then grumpily, he planted the cap back on his head, made a gesture of frustration, and continued tying the sashes to the rings crowning the maypole. One by one, the colorful sashes tumbled down.

"He almost fell off that time," Sowe said, wincing.

Lia could not help grinning. "Every year someone tries to knock him down. Every year. What would happen if they did? He would probably break his neck, and then there would be no dancing."

"Maybe that is why the boys do it."

"Not all of them hate dancing. What color sash do you want, Sowe?"

"It does not matter," she said, looking down. "No one is going to ask me to dance." Her shoulders drooped. Dark hair veiled part of her face.

"Only if you hide up here in the loft. If you go to the maypole, someone will dance with you. I know it."

"I do not think so."

"Thinking that will surely make it so."

Sowe just shrugged and looked back out the window to the maypole in the middle of High Street. "What color do *you* think I should choose?"

"Blue," Lia said. "It matches your eyes as well as our dresses." She also looked back. The maypole was taller than the walls surrounding Muirwood's grounds. It was a tradition of sorts, these many years they had spent in the kitchen together, to watch it hoisted up and festooned with decorations. But this year was different. They were both old enough to dance around the maypole. The thought brought giddiness and jittery nerves. Both Duerden and Colvin would ask Lia to dance, so she did not have Sowe's fear of being a girl lacking a partner. But she did not want to embarrass herself by tripping on her hem or squashing someone's foot as they skipped around the circle, holding hands. As she imagined the dance, a sudden pang of sadness struck her. The man who had taught them the maypole dance was dead, and it was her fault. Even the smallest things reminded her of Jon Hunter.

"What is wrong?" Sowe asked, seeing the expression on Lia's face, studying her with concern.

"Just remembering when Jon taught us the dance."

Sowe's smile wilted. She reached out and gripped Lia in a tight hug.

Pasqua's voice bellowed from below. "How long does it take to fetch a bag of milled flour, I ask you? Stop watching the window, the pole will still be there when your chores are finished. Do you smell the honey cakes in the oven? Mind you, do not forget the sugarplums, the tourtelettes, the sambocade. And I need you to carry out the Gooseberry Fool before you change. If you spill and make a mess of yourselves before the dance, you will regret it. Get down here, girls. If I have to come up there, I will bring a switch. I will. Or a broom."

Lia and Sowe grinned at each other through their tears, for they both knew that Pasqua was totally incapable of climbing the loft ladder. They hugged each other fiercely a moment longer, saying nothing, then brushed their eyes and hurried down, moving through the kitchen as if preparing for battle. Every open space on the tables was crammed with trays already spilling over with sweets and delights that only emerged the week of Whitsunday. Lia snitched a tiny Royal cake and stuffed it into her mouth. Sowe looked shocked and then tried not to giggle.

Pasqua's sleeves were rolled up, and she was everywhere at once, stirring pots, poking loaves in the ovens, cracking eggs, and ladling honey. Lia balanced the trays on barrels and chests, while Sowe scrubbed pots clean so that other dishes could be started.

"Lia, take the pizzelles to the manor house," Pasqua said. "They are for the Aldermaston's guests this afternoon. Hurry back, girl. Do not dawdle and gawk! There is much to do."

As Lia approached the door with a tray of pizzelles, it opened from the outside. Sunlight blinded her for a moment, and she did not recognize the man in the doorway. Though she did not know him, he walked in as confidently as if he had entered the kitchens a hundred times.

He was shorter than Lia but as old as the Aldermaston and Pasqua. He had a cropped beard that was well salted, matching the rough tangle of hair atop his head. The leather hood was pulled down about his dirty neck and shoulders, and he wore stained leathers beneath a rough-looking tunic black with sap spots and a sheathed gladius belted to his waist. The sight of the weapon struck Lia like thunder. If that did not, the bow sleeve around his shoulder would have. The wild look of him, the oil and leather smell of him, reminded her fiercely of the man she had buried in the Bearden Muir.

"Who is barging into my kitchen on Whitsunday?" Pasqua said, her voice building to a roar as she turned around. She was dumbfounded a moment. "Martin?"

His voice was loud and thickly accented. "It is a good reason, Pasqua, and I will beg you not to raise your voice at me again. Even these many years have not dulled the ache from hearing you rant, by Cheshu. Tell me where the Aldermaston is, and I will be on my way as quickly as I came." He turned his fiery eyes to Lia. "Do not stare so, lass. That will not do. Not at all. The rudeness of children these days. I will relieve you of several of those since the tray looks so heavy." And with dirty fingers, he snatched three pizzelles and started eating one. Crumbs clung to his beard.

Lia looked back at Pasqua. She stood silently, her mouth gaping open, staring at the intruder. "Martin," she said again, almost whispering. Then her eyes blazed with white-hot heat. "Out. Now. Out!"

He leaned against the doorframe and cocked his eyebrow at her, waiting.

"Get that tray away from him, Lia. Do not let him steal another bite. Where is that broom? Sowe—the broom! Out, Martin. Out!"

"Huff and holler all you like, Pasqua. Just tell me where I can find the Aldermaston, and I will go." He wandered over to a nearby barrel with a perfect dish of sambocade. Not a slice had been cut into it yet. "I always did fancy this dish of yours. I just might have a taste of it."

"If you touch it, I will have your finger in a stew!"

He stood over it, eyeing it hungrily. "Just a little. I will use a spoon."

"Do. Not. Touch. It!"

"The Aldermaston is in the manor," Lia said, nodding to the man respectfully and nudging him with her eyes toward the door. "I will take you, sir, as I was just on my way."

"Kind of you lass, but I know the way. Much has changed since I last roved these grounds. Much indeed, including yourself." His eyes burned like blue fire. "Why, you were but a mewling little thing. It was I who found you in a basket that night, lass. I who brought you to Pasqua, if she has sense enough to remember your first taste of milk. I left Muirwood when you were but a seedling, but how you have sprouted! You have the same look about you. Why, you are even taller than me now. On our way then. Pasqua, I will have some of that later, mind you. You *will* save me a slice."

And he said it in such a way that Lia felt the tingle of the Medium thread through his words.

***

"You wanted to see me when the guests left, Aldermaston?" Lia said, clenching her hands as she stepped into his study. "Astrid said they were gone."

The Aldermaston's voice was leathery and out of breath. "You may go, Martin. Enjoy the festival. I will speak to her. Alone."

She had interrupted a conversation and paused, looking about the room. Lia had not seen Martin in the shadows on the other side at first. He blended in well, his features still and brooding. With a sour-faced shrug, he rose from the window seat and crossed to the door, staring intently at Lia all the while, his expression growing sterner and sterner, as if he found something very distasteful about meeting her a second time.

Even with the conversation unfinished, Martin obliged. "All in due time, Aldermaston. Aye, all in due time. Enjoy the festival. As if I would enjoy myself watching for sneaky cutpurses or learners getting too cuddly under the eaves instead of eating finch pie. Enjoy myself, by Cheshu." He gave Lia one final scorpion look and then shut the door behind him, hard.

Lia turned and found the Aldermaston reaching down and lifting something heavy to the table. She recognized it instantly as Jon Hunter's gladius, except it was polished, and the leather scabbard smelled of oil soap. Next, he set down two leather bracers, a shooting glove, a tunic girdle, and a quiver of arrows. Each item had been painstakingly polished. Finally, the bow came next, and the Aldermaston set it on top of them all. Slowly, deliberately, he pushed them toward her.

Lia swallowed. "I do not understand."

"The Medium weighs heavily on me tonight, child. Concerning you. The feelings have persisted, and I am too old to bother ignoring them. These are yours now. Tomorrow, after Whitsunday, you are the new hunter of Muirwood. I sent for Martin to train you. He is not pleased with the choice, as you could tell, but he will obey. There is no one better than he that I could trust to train you. He is Pry-rian, actually, which makes it all the more interesting, considering our discussions since the death of the old king at Winterrowd. Your training begins tomorrow, as I said."

Years before, Lia had stumbled off the ladder steps carrying a heavy sack of flour. She had fallen on her back, the sack spewing flour dust all over her, nearly choking her to death. She felt like that now, her world turned upside down, her head aching and mouth too full of questions to even know how to start speaking.

The Aldermaston slowly stood and walked to another chest. He gently opened it. "You say nothing?" he asked.

"I am too…I am too startled to speak. What about my duties in the kitchen?"

He looked closely at her, squinting. "You will be replaced with another helper. It happens often enough. It would not be possible for you to do both duties, Lia. You must learn to fight, to hunt, to handle animals." His gaze penetrated her soul. "You will memorize the secret tunnels beneath the grounds for errands that I will send you on. Be one of my advisors, like Prestwich and Pasqua. And Martin. You are to be one of the Abbey's defenders now. Since you are so talented with the Medium already, you will even handle some of the outer defenses, the stones that warn us of danger. The stones that defend us. That is a duty that Jon could never fulfill because the Medium never heeded him. You are different."

Become a hunter? Her? The thought of leaving the kitchen made her ill. Leave Pasqua and Sowe again so soon? Her experience with Colvin in the Bearden Muir and Winterrowd was hardly a fortnight ago, and she finally felt safe again. Now the Aldermaston ruined it with his words. Yet at the same time, she was excited, thrilled that he trusted her despite her youth. That he needed her. That the Medium needed her.

Her mind was so full, her question came out a little foolishly. "Has there ever been a girl before?"

"Pardon me, Lia?"

"As your hunter—I mean, as the Aldermaston's hunter. Has it always been a boy?"

His eyebrows furrowed. "Does that matter?"

It was difficult to explain her feelings. "What will everyone say? They will wonder why you chose me and not someone strong like Getman Smith, or some other wretched like Asdin, who you trust with messages." *They will mock me*, she thought, her eyes boring into his.

He was quiet a moment, his expression beginning to twist into annoyance.

"Fools mock," he answered gruffly. "Tongues wag. Babies cry. And goats bleat." He reached down into the chest he hovered near and pulled out a bundle of soft blue fabric. "They would fuss and fret no matter who I set in that position. Many did the same when Jon became the Abbey's hunter. But only because they do not understand that I did not choose him. Neither did I choose you. Muirwood is guided by the Medium, not by me." He paused and studied her face. "Tomorrow, the training begins. Tonight though, you must dance." He approached and handed her the bundle, which she discovered to be a new cloak and dress.

His voice was thick with emotion. "I cannot believe you are old enough for the Whitsunday festival. I knew this time would come. I always knew it. The night of the storm when you stole the ring. I was so angry with you, that you stole something valuable from my chamber. A gold ring. Yet the Medium forbid me to reclaim it from you or to chastise you. You still wear it around your neck. The Medium was aware that you would need it. And you did, in the Bearden Muir. Just as it is aware that you need this experience now. Here, take these. Your old cloak and dress are fit for rags now. Pasqua has been telling me for some time that you are still growing. And since tonight is the maypole dance, we thought it best if you and Sowe had new dresses and girdles. Go child. Return in the morning for the sword and the rest instead of bringing me my breakfast."

Lia bit her lip. "Does Pasqua know?"

The Aldermaston shook his head. "Not yet. She will know tonight, as I will tell her."

Lia took the soft bundle and hugged it to her chest. Her feelings swarmed, threatening her with tears, but she clenched them back, refusing to cry in front of him. For a moment, for an instant, she had hoped he was going to tell her that she could become a learner at the Abbey. Colvin had promised her that. Would he not have made the arrangements for her to start when the new first years arrived? More than anything, she wanted a tome of her own and the implements of scriving. She wanted to read about the mastons of the past and how they had learned to tame and be tamed by the Medium. That was what she wanted, not becoming a hunter. The experience in the Bearden Muir still haunted her dreams at night. She never wanted to go back there.

Closing her eyes, Lia nodded and turned away from the Aldermaston, uncertain what she should be feeling toward him. Gratitude? Dismay? Trust? Betrayal? Why were her feelings always so tangled and confusing with him?

She hurried out of the manor house to the kitchen. The sun was low in the sky and sinking fast. The festival would begin soon. Everything in her world was about to change.

Desperately, she wanted to talk to someone, to spill her feelings and know she would be listened to. Someone who knew about facing their fears and rising above them. Her heart wrenched with confusion. It was not Sowe she wanted to tell. It was Colvin. She was grateful that she would see him soon. For word had spread all day that many knight-mastons who had received their collars and spurs at Winterrowd had come to celebrate Whitsunday at Muirwood.

***

Sowe clenched Lia's arm, walking so close their feet almost tangled. Her voice was soft and frantic, her breath fragrant from the mint leaves Pasqua had given them. She had also tried to tame Lia's curly hair, but that was always its own challenge. "Tomorrow? You are leaving tomorrow? That is not fair, Lia. You are my sister, not just my friend. How can he separate sisters?"

Lia kept her voice low since there were so many others crowding through the gate, trying to leave the grounds for the village beyond.

"The Aldermaston said he would tell Pasqua tonight. But what can she do, Sowe? He is committed to doing this. When has she ever been able to change his mind? Look, do you see Reome over there? Look how she has braided her hair. She is too beautiful. It makes me ill."

Sowe squeezed her arm even tighter when the maypole came into view, illuminated by torches and rushlights. "I have never been so nervous. We should have practiced more. What if I stumble?"

"You will not stumble, Sowe."

"What if I do?"

"If you keep thinking about that, it is bound to happen! Just breathe deeply. This is our first year, no one is expecting us to dance all that well."

"Who is that young man who just asked Reome?" Sowe whispered. "His arms are enormous!"

"The local blacksmith, I think," muttered Lia jealously. He was a head taller than the other boys. "Ugh, there is Getman. Pray he does not see us."

"He is coming our way, Lia!"

In an awful moment, she realized Sowe was right. They had just exited the gates with the flow of the crowd, and Getman appeared from their left and cut a course directly barring their way to the maypole. Lia's stomach shriveled, and she searched the crowd for a sign of Colvin. Where was he?

"Will you dance with me?"

Lia looked at him scornfully, hating even the thought of touching his sooty hand. But she realized with some surprise that he was not even looking at her, but at Sowe, who squeezed Lia's arm so tightly it hurt.

Sowe mumbled an answer, but the crowd was so boisterous that Lia knew he had not heard her.

"Will you?" he repeated, his eyes blazing, daring her to humiliate him with a rejection.

Sowe released Lia's arm and extended her hand. A look of victory filled Getman's eyes, and he snatched her hand and tugged her after him, for the first circle was forming around the maypole already. Looking back, Sowe met Lia's gaze, pleading with her for rescue; there was nothing Lia could do but watch them. Watch them twirl and dance. Watch the torchlight glisten on Sowe's dark hair as they circled around the pole, back again, swirling, dancing.

Everything seemed to slow like thick honey. It was as if Lia saw her friend for the first time, even though she knew Sowe's face better than anyone's. But it was the unforgiving look in Reome's eyes that spoke the truth. Reome also watched Sowe as she danced—and it was the look of utter jealousy. The look that sprouts from a proud woman's heart when it realizes someone else is more beautiful. Sowe was completely ignorant of the scathing stare. She was shy with Getman, but that only added to her appealing qualities. They twirled, and they danced the other direction. Around the pole and back, weaving the ribbons until the entire maypole was sheathed in silk. Lia stood aloof, with some other girls who did not have partners.

When the song was finished, the dancers were given a reprieve while the coiled ribbons were untangled. Sowe left Getman graciously and started away when another young man, the Tanner boy, appeared breathlessly at her side and asked for the next dance. He claimed her hand and tugged her back toward the newly gathering circle. Sowe looked over her shoulder, searching, but their eyes did not meet.

Lia stood there, her stomach twisting into knots. There were learners dancing with learners, their fine cut gowns and gold-threaded tunics dazzling with jewelry, their skin spicy with the scent of costly perfumes. But on Whitsunday, even the wretcheds were their equals. No one was forbidden to dance around the maypole.

A band of knights emerged from around the almonry, and Lia's heart nearly burst with relief. They were dressed in the same uniform, each wearing a gleaming collar and chain, the same she had seen around Colvin's neck. She bit her lip, searching their faces. They were young, all of them, and quite sure of themselves. But none of them were familiar to her. They approached a gaggle of beautiful learners, whom Lia had known and served dinner to, and then escorted them to the circle. Lia watched them dance, again from the sidelines. As soon as the round was finished, Sowe was beset again by another youth—this time, a learner in fine clothes who had been watching her. An ugly feeling began to bloom in Lia's stomach. She crushed it down, unwilling to let the feeling coalesce into an envious thought. It was Sowe's third dance already.

Where was Colvin? He had promised he would dance with her. Where was he?

"Lia?"

She turned, expecting to see him, but it was Duerden. He coughed, trying to work up his courage. He looked so young and small, even though they were the same age, for she was much taller than him. "Lia, would you…would you do me the honor and dance with me?"

Anything was better than the agony of standing alone for the third dance. She looked down at him. In the back of her mind, she remembered being teased about his height.

"Yes, Duerden. Of course I will. I would be pleased to."

His hand was sweaty. He led her awkwardly to the maypole ring. Reome saw them, sizing them both up, and could not be bothered to conceal a smirk. Sowe stood across the ring from them, holding hands with the learner who had claimed her.

"It is lovely this evening…you look…lovely this evening." It was a gallant attempt, but it felt forced. Everyone in the outer circle held hands, the girls on the left of each boy.

"You do not need to praise me, Duerden," Lia said. "We have been friends for a year now. Are you excited to see your family before starting the second year? Are they staying in the village?"

"Yes, at the Swan. They are over there, actually, by the booth where Pasqua is selling her treats. My father is the one stuffing his face with a tart." She saw him. He was short as well. His mother was taller, more Lia's height. She cringed inside.

"Will he mind seeing you dance with me?" Lia asked in a low voice as the circle began skipping around the maypole.

"No, Lia. It is not your fault you are a wretched, after all. I have never looked at you that way. I would like…you to meet them. My parents. After the circle is done."

Lia closed her eyes, grateful to be dancing, but uncomfortable. Duerden was a good-natured boy. He had always been friendly to her, but she had no other feelings for him.

"I would like that," she said, but it felt like a lie on her tongue. She glanced back at Pasqua's booth, which was brisk with business as it was each year. A year ago, she had watched the maypole dance with hungry eyes. So much had changed.

"Have you heard the latest news about Winterrowd?" Duerden asked as the circle stopped and began rotating the other direction. "The old king was killed by hired archers, they say. Pryrian archers. Do you know about Pry-Ree, Lia? About their mercenaries?"

Her stomach did flip-flops as it had every time he mentioned the battle of Winterrowd. So much of what he told her about it was untrue, nothing more than gossip. She knew the truth for certain, because she was the one who the Medium had used to loose the shaft that killed the king. She had only told the Aldermaston what she had done—no one else—and how the Medium had commanded her to do it. No one else knew. Not even Sowe.

"I know little about Pry-Ree," she said, glancing through the throng surrounding the circle for a sign of Colvin.

Duerden kept going as if he had not heard her. "Pry-Ree was defeated before we were born, Lia. It used to be its own kingdom, but now it is a vassalage of the Crown. They have always hated us. Some are saying that Demont did not win Winterrowd because of the Medium, as the mastons claim. They say that there was an ambush and a slaughter to avenge the death of Demont's father and the overthrow of Pry-Ree. They say Demont was in Pry-Ree before crossing with his men. Now that he controls the king's Privy Council, we may never know the truth. Strange days, Lia. So very strange. I am not sure what to believe myself."

They danced, weaving the sashes and avoiding stepping on each other's toes. Smiles, cheers, and claps heralded them, but Lia's heart was dark. She knew the truth, but she could say nothing of it. Not of the murderous sheriff of Mendenhall and his death by the Medium's fire. Of Colvin and his fear of a battle where Demont's men were hopelessly outnumbered. There were no Pry-rian archers there except for herself, and she was not even trained as an archer. Duerden held her hand and wove the sashes with her, but there was a gulf between them now, of secrets that could never be shared.

After the dance, Lia met Duerden's family, and they were gracious to her. Pasqua embarrassed her by giving her a crushing hug in front of everyone and mumbled incoherently while weeping about losing her again. Sowe was asked to dance every time and had blisters on her feet by the end of the night and a smile on her face that shone like burning oil. As they limped back to the kitchen sometime after midnight, carrying empty platters and trays from Pasqua's booth, Lia's heart grew heavier and heavier with those secrets and with disappointment that seemed to mount with each step on the grass and each trip back.

For Colvin Price, the Earl of Forshee, never came.

CHAPTER TWO

Jon's Leering

Lia wrestled with her emotions, even though she had determined in advance to master them. The Bearden Muir was different, yet the same—oppressive, haunting, thick with memories that could not be banished or tamped down. Standing over Jon Hunter's grave, she fought down the urge to sob, to scream, the desire to undo everything she had done so long ago. It was a year since his death, a year since that awful Whitsunday fair. A year wearing hunter boots, hunter leathers, dealing in a hunter's errands. She bit her lip, willing the memories to dull, the emotions to fade. Jon had died because of her.

Leaves and brush choked the small glen where she and Colvin had buried him beneath a pile of rocks. Had he died at the Abbey, his bones would have been interred in an ossuary and laid to rest with the Aldermaston's blessing. She stared at the Leering stone the Aldermaston had carved, a stumplike block hewn with a man's bearded face on it, reposing, silent. She and Martin had finished digging a small hole for it at the head of the rock mound and set it firmly in place, kicking dirt in to fill the gaps. Their mule would have an easier journey back to the Abbey now that its weight was gone. At least the beast was relieved of its burden. Lia wondered if she ever would be.

"He was a good lad," said Martin sternly, brushing his hands together. He sniffed and grimaced, controlling his emotions. "We will greet him again, you and I. In the next life. In a fair country where no knaves can do him harm. Where no blood is ever spilt." He stopped and wiped his nose, but his eyes were dry and full of fire. He brooded with anger constantly, his temper shorter than even the Aldermaston's.

Lia fidgeted with the leather bracer tight against her forearm. "I will be ashamed to face him."

He snorted. "Did you loose the arrows that slew him? No. Did you murder mastons and spill their blood? No, by Cheshu! There are debts we all owe, Lia. But you owe him nothing for what happened. You paid your fair share in recompense, learning the ways and doing his work, which he can no longer do himself."

Lia closed her eyes. The memories were still bitter. "If I had known then what I know now. The mistakes we made crossing the swamp. The risks we took without realizing it…"

He grabbed her arm and forced her to look at him. His finger jabbed near her nose. "It is a cruel fact, child. Wisdom comes after the moment when it is most needed. I have warned you of the doom of Pry-Ree. We failed to learn from the changing times. Failed to act when we should have acted. Instead, we were crushed, our princes butchered like hogs. So what have you learned from this journey? Hmm? If you were Jon in that moment, what would *you* have done differently? Knowing what you know *now*."

"I do not know, Martin," she answered, jerking her arm away from his crushing grip.

The blue fire in his eyes blazed hotter. "You *do* know."

"He trained with you for much longer."

He snorted and spat.

Anger flushed her cheeks, but she kept it from rising to her voice. "What do you want me to say?"

He pointed at her again. "Only the truth. He was a hunter, yes. He was trained, yes. But you know as much as he ever did. I have never trained a boy or man who learns as fast as you do. From rabbit snares to naming all the little insects in the wood. You know them all and remember it the first time."

Lia wanted to shut the door on her thoughts, but she could not in time. The whisper was there. It was always there. The pulsing of the Medium, giving her thoughts and teasing hints. It probably frightened others how quickly she knew things. What they did not know was how the Medium taught her with silent whispers. She gritted her teeth, because she did not want to speak it.

"Say it, Lia!"

Her body trembled, flushed and overflowing with emotions. She was afraid of the truth. Which was perhaps the very reason the Aldermaston had sent her back into the Bearden Muir to settle the Leering and face the past.

Martin stepped even closer, his nose poking up at her. Even though she had grown more in the last year, and he only came up to her chin, his force of personality towered hers. "Say it, Lia. Cast out the shadows you cringe behind. Say it."

Her voice was barely a whisper. "He was careless."

"Careless? Yes! Can you taste that word? It tastes like ash in your mouth. It should. Have I not taught you this when you first started to train with me? The hunter is patient. The prey is careless." He stormed away from her, stamping his boot in the muck. He spat. "An elk returns to the same place of water because it is the place of water. A patient hunter waits in the bushes. Waits until the elk is thirsty. That way, he has a clean shot. The closer he gets, the better aim. But a man is not an elk." He tapped his finger on his forehead, then pointed to the mound of stones. "He was careless."

Lia sucked in a strangled breath. Her body ached, her spirit suffered. Yet she knew Martin was right. Jon had misjudged the sheriff's ruthlessness. Instead of hiding the trail, Jon could have waited to catch them by surprise. A single archer with a full quiver and a steady aim was deadlier than charging knights, for he could kill those knights at a distance.

Martin paced in the woods, waving his arms with his emotions as he typically did. "He could have created false trails with the horse and let you two sneak into the woods on foot. He could have taken another path back to the trail to throw off an ambush. Or he could have waited for the sheriff and his ilk, and the three of you could have fought together. Greater odds fighting alongside a knight-maston than by himself."

Lia bit her lip. "He was not a knight-maston then."

Martin snorted and waved his hand in annoyance. "We honor Jon's grave today, Lia. You said this maston dedicated it already, so there is nothing we can do to hallow it further. The Leering is here so that the Aldermaston can pay his respects when he is no longer bound to Muirwood. Let us return home. You know your lessons. Now let this experience be a teacher to you as well."

Lia nodded and knelt down by the Leering. She brushed her hand across the face, staring into the silent visage. A year had passed. A year of scornful mocking from Reome for dressing like a boy instead of a woman. A year wandering the woods and valleys and ditches surrounding the Hundred. Of tunnels and passwords, of memorizing faces and messages to be delivered to the Aldermaston's allies in nearby Abbeys. Her world was a bigger place. Part of her longed to be making Gooseberry Fool in Pasqua's kitchen where life was simpler.

Looking up at Martin, she reached into the pouch at her waist and withdrew the Cruciger orb, her special talisman—her only birthright. She wore it on every journey. She was the only one at the Abbey, other than the Aldermaston, who was strong enough with the Medium to use it. It was found with her when she was abandoned as a wretched, and the ball and spindles could be summoned to point the direction of places or people. "I would make one more visit before we go home. There is another Leering nearby. Another memory I need to face."

He scowled but nodded to her. "Lead the way, lass."

With a thought, the spindles on the orb began to whirl.

***

Lia gazed down at the bed of grass, thicker now and still clinging to the damp of spring. The orb in her hand tingled, and writing appeared across its immaculate surface. She could not read it. This was the spot where Colvin had carried her after the blazing fire she summoned with the Medium had destroyed the sheriff and his men. Nearby, the scorched thicket of trees remained. The wood was dead, black, and skeletal. The gorse was thriving again, but the thicket had been ravaged and would take years to recover.

Take me to my Leering, she thought, and the Cruciger orb spun lazily toward the thicket. Martin followed, coaxing the mule again. As she entered the dead place, she ran her fingers across the twisted, blackened trunks as she passed, hearing in her mind the jangle of spurs and armor, the chuckling threats of Almaguer's men. Part of her recoiled at the memory of the soldiers beating Colvin, and how she had flung herself over his body and used the Medium to keep them away from him. She frowned, wondering why Colvin had never returned to Muirwood. No messages were ever sent. No explanation ever given.

She knew that he was alive.

The Earl of Forshee held great favor with Garen Demont and was known to all. Garen Demont, Lord Protector of the Realm, who controlled custody over the young king and ruled the kingdom in his name. The victor of Winterrowd. Oh yes, she had heard Colvin's name mentioned excitedly after being elevated in rank as an earl. For his service in the battle, he was recognized and rewarded with additional lands. He was part of Demont's inner circle, a member of the Privy Council, where only knightmastons were admitted.

Whitsunday, he had whispered into her ear. A broken promise to a wretched.

Ahead, through the screen of dead trees, she could see smoke rising from the boulder as if the fires from a year ago were still smoldering. The feeling was wrong. She held up her hand to Martin, alerting him that something was amiss, and he quietly clasped the hilt of his gladius and tethered the mule with one hand. All of the trees within a dozen paces of the Leering had been charred to ash, so only the budding greenery gave color to the place. The Leering, with the carved side facing east toward the sun, was no longer shaggy with moss.

A smell hovered in the air, mixed with the aroma of charred oaks. The scent of man. Lia shuddered. All around her, she could feel them. The snuffling shadows that loped like wolves and stared at her but could not be seen with the eye. The Myriad Ones were thick around her.

Martin's voice was flat and wary. "This grove is wicked now."

Lia stuffed the orb back into the pouch and withdrew her bow and nocked an arrow, which she kept in place with her finger as

Martin had taught her so well. The air was full of sounds, of buzzing gnats and cawing ravens and the twitter of insects. There were no sounds from other people, but holding absolutely still, she could almost feel the muzzles of the Myriad Ones sniffing about her legs. Cautiously, patiently, she waited—watching the woods for the sign of movement, the sound of intruders. The feeling in the air clung like smoke to her skin. Biting her lip, she focused on the source of the feelings and realized, to her shock, that they were emanating from the Leering itself.

One step closer. Two steps. She ducked around a tree, keeping low to the ground. A single quail flew overhead that might have made a tasty meal, but even the thought of food brought revulsion. Fear filled the blackened grove to the brim. Sickness and disease stalked the woods. As she came closer, even the plant life began to alter. The charred trunks of the oaks were wreathed in vines with bronzed leaves of a shape Lia had not seen before. The leaves were moist and colorful, which was strange. She touched one gently, and the oil stuck to her fingers.

The mule brayed, and Martin hushed it with an apple, his muscles taut as he continued to listen to the surroundings.

Lia grimaced, feeling the oily wetness on her fingertips. "I have not seen this plant before," she warned. Bringing her pack around, she withdrew her gloves and an empty pouch. With her short knife, she cut off a small segment of leaves and stuffed them in the pouch.

"Let us depart, Lia. This is no place for the living. The dead linger here."

"No, something is wrong with the Leering," Lia said. Carefully, she stepped through the tangled vines that tried to grope at her and entered the clearing surrounding the boulder. The vines grew everywhere and wrapped around the base of the boulder. Martin had never seen the depth of her potential with the Medium. If she could get close enough, she might be able to stop the rock from burning. The Aldermaston would want to know as much as possible since he could not travel beyond the Abbey borders.

She crossed around to the side where her face was and stopped, fearful at what she saw. The Leering was alive, seething with power. The face had once been hers. Now it was unrecognizable as even human. The eye sockets blazed with a red heat, but the expression had been charred completely off. The entire face of the rock shimmered with waves of heat. She knew that if she tried to summon water from it, it would only come out as steam.

The entire boulder was pitted with cracks, as if the stone were about to burst from the force of the Medium's power.

Is this my fault? she asked herself. In her memory, the power of the Medium had abandoned her after the fire had destroyed Almaguer and his men. She remembered it ending and feeling weightless. What was causing the Leering to behave in such a way?

Martin's voice was worried. "Lia, come away from that stone."

"I know what I am doing, Martin," she said, trusting her willpower. The boulder was blackened, charred. Lia closed her eyes and reached out to it tentatively. At the Abbey, she could summon water from the Leering at the laundry. She could mix it with fire to warm it. She did not really understand how it worked, only that they responded to her thoughts, as Colvin had taught her.

She quietly willed it to stop burning so she could touch it.

It refused.

Fear bloomed in her stomach. The Leering knew she was there. It defied her.

Stop, she told it in her mind.

"Lia, come away." The mule brayed again.

Again, it resisted her. A mewling sound filled her ears. The Myriad Ones crowded against her, drawn to the stone, to its powerful summons. They fed on the fear it exuded. Some hissed at her.

Obey me, she thought fiercely, pushing her will against it.

The rock groaned. The mewling turned into howling. A breeze blowing through the grove turned into a gust, then into a gale. Lia's mass of hair whipped about her face, along with tendrils of vines coiled around the boulder like little snakes. She held her thought firm. A sensation of illness wrenched through her, making her head spin, and she nearly collapsed into the bed of oily leaves.

She heard Martin shouting, but she could not hear his words through the blast of winds. Her thoughts focused. She could see in her mind the stone's heat quenching. Another groan, another furious storm. Dead oak branches crashed to the forest floor, unable to cling to the trunks. A memory came to her mind.

"The rains have plagued us enough. They will quit. Now."

As the memory of the Aldermaston's words filled her mind, she mimicked the force of his will. *Now*, she told the Leering. *You will stop now.*

It did, but grudgingly. The burning withdrew. The flames were tamped. But she could feel it hunkering deep inside the stone, diminished but not quenched. But that was enough for Lia. The rock cooled enough to touch it.

When she did, an image came to her mind. Soldiers camping around the stone wearing blood-spattered armor and shivering. Not the sheriff—for it had happened during the winter months when snow covered much of the Bearden Muir. A man, devoid of speech and clutching a snail-shaped medallion, had touched the Leering and summoned the flames to warm them. He communed with it in his mind, for he could not speak, and the Leering had told him who last had touched it. It had shown him her face. Lia's stomach clenched and twisted, for she recognized the man and knew his name.

A desire to be observed, considered, esteemed, praised, beloved, and admired by his fellows is one of the earliest, as well as the keenest, dispositions discovered in the heart of man. My advice to new learners is to squelch it all their days, for those desires lead to ruin.

—Gideon Penman of Muirwood Abbey

CHAPTER THREE

Blight

Lia stifled a sob of joy as they crossed the final ring of oaks and entered the grounds of Muirwood. Splotches of violently itching sores covered her face, hands, and legs and had plagued her the entire way back. Washing the plant's oil from her hands did nothing to ease her suffering or prevent the poisonous sap from spreading to other parts of her body. As she and Martin wove through the treacherous marshland, the itching inflamed her hands and face and then spread further. Martin drove her hard, hardly stopping to rest, warning her to stop scratching, but she could not stop. The itch was maddening and unquenchable. They reached the Abbey a day earlier than expected. The sunset colored the sky a rich violet, and the first stars began winking into view.

Martin coughed to clear his hoarse throat. Their water had run out earlier that day. "I will find someone to stable the beast. You hurry to the Aldermaston, lass."

The air was warm with spring, and the Abbey seemed abuzz with life. Lia raised her hood to hide the blistering skin on her face and dug her nails into her ribs to keep from scratching her arms.

Laughter bubbled from the yard by the cloister where the learners were gathered. She kept her head low and walked quickly, not even glancing at the kitchen until she had passed it and entered the manor house from the rear. The housekeeper would be aghast that she had not brushed her boots before coming in, but she did not care. Was the poison killing her? Would it kill her?

She grasped the handle of the Aldermaston's study and yanked it open.

"Lia?"

It was the Aldermaston's voice, but the sound came from behind her. Turning, she saw him approaching down the hall. When he finally saw her face, his eyes widened with shock. "Prestwich! Send for Siara Healer."

Her jaw hurt from clenching it for three days. The itching burned across her body. Its persistence nearly made her scream. She turned to look at the Aldermaston as he motioned her inside his study and shut the door.

"Lower your hood." She did, and he examined her face without touching her. "Is it across all your flesh as well or just parts?"

Lia bit her lip to keep from crying out. "It itches, and it burns. My hands and arms. My legs too. It is…it is everywhere. It came from a plant. Martin does not know what it is. I cannot bear this itching! I brought some…to show you." She fumbled with the pouch and set down her pack. With palsied fingers, she struggled to open it and withdrew a small cluster of leaves.

The Aldermaston looked at it carefully but did not touch. "Where did you find it?"

"In the Bearden Muir at the boulder with the Leering that had my face. The grove was choked with it. The Leering was burning—burning since winter."

"Burning?" he asked, his voice low and concerned. "With no one near it?"

"Not a soul. But someone touched it in the winter. I saw it in my mind."

"Was the stone itself pocked? Was it discolored?"

"Yes. The stone was sick. The Leering's face was nearly burned all the way off. Only slits for eyes."

He looked shocked and concerned, and his expression sent chills through her. He was worried. He was deathly worried.

"Am I going to die, Aldermaston?" she asked.

"The Blight," he whispered. Then seizing control of himself, he faced her. "Put that weed away, Lia. Kneel. Shut your eyes."

Lia obeyed and dropped to her knees, and he placed his heavy hand on top of her head. The fiery itches made her tremble, but the weight of his hand brought a trickle of comfort. She felt the Medium strongly within him, a lake of power lapping at the banks. He was full of it—so full of its strength.

"The poison is not mortal. I rebuke it within your body. Be comforted. Be still." The itching flared up even worse, a spasm that made her gasp. The Aldermaston's voice grew firmer. "Be comforted. Be at peace. I rebuke the poison. It will not afflict you." The words no sooner left his mouth when the itching became even worse. Her skin burned as if afire. Tears came down her cheeks, and she started to sob and tremble. She clenched her eyes, clenched her jaw again to quell it. His other hand came down on her head. "By Idumea's Gift, be comforted. Be still. Be cleansed from this affliction."

A rushing sound filled her ears as the Medium jolted through his hands into her. The pain and itching vanished away, leaving her gasping for breath and weeping with relief. The feeling of well-being, safety, and comfort returned. Slowly, shakily, she drew in a fresh breath and was not tortured by it.

Lia opened her eyes as the Aldermaston stepped away from her and noticed Martin in the doorway, his eyes wide with wonder. Her nose was running, and embarrassed, she covered it with her sleeve.

Martin's voice was thick with accent and emotion. "I warned you about the calling. I told you the work was too dangerous, by Cheshu!" His eyes glittered with anger. "How is she?"

The Aldermaston walked slowly to his chair and settled in it wearily. He looked aged by the ordeal. "The poison will not kill her. Considering her penchant for dangerous circumstances, is it not wise to train her the best we can?" He looked to Lia. "Be wary not to burn the plant," he said hoarsely. "The smoke can carry the oils into the air. It would be harmful to breathe those vapors. It has no roots, so bury it outside the Abbey grounds tomorrow. Touch it not, for even the stems are poisoned."

Martin shut the door and came inside. He went to help Lia stand, but the Aldermaston held out his hand.

"Do not touch her, Martin. Her clothes are soiled with it. You may need to bury them as well if they cannot be cleansed at the laundry. Some strong soap. Wood-ash lye should do, you can get it from the lavenders. Bathe everything, including yourself."

Martin hovered near her. His voice was low and tender. "I worried for you, lass. More so than I declared. That plant, Aldermaston. I have not seen its breed before. I have not seen it in any of the woods I have traveled. Not here or in Pry-Ree."

The Aldermaston massaged his temples, his eyes squeezed shut. "No, you would not have seen it before. It did not originate from this land."

Lia looked down at her hands. The rash and sores were still there, but they were no longer itching.

As if reading her thoughts, the Aldermaston said, "Your body will heal now. In a few days, the remnant of the poison will be gone. Siara Healer can give you a salve to aid the blisters in healing."

"Is it the Blight then?" Lia asked. "This plant?"

"No, the Blight is not a plant or a plague, but it can bring either. We will speak of it tomorrow. You are both wearied from your journey. Eat, and rest, and see me at first light. We had visitors while you were gone and expect more before Whitsunday this fortnight. The Queen Dowager is coming to Muirwood."

The Aldermaston and Martin exchanged a look—a look full of dread.

***

The smell of the salve was horrible, and it stung Lia's nose. Her body throbbed, as if she had been trampled by a stallion, and looked the part. She was grateful it was fully dark when she left the apothecary and started toward the kitchen, anxious for a crust of bread to sate her hunger and a place she could hide her face and rest. Pasty, chalk-colored salve decorated her arms, legs, and face, and she walked with her hood up to hide the white splotches from the few still wandering about. Whatever news the Aldermaston had, she wanted to hear it, especially if it involved the Queen Dowager—the woman whose husband Lia had killed with an arrow at Winterrowd.

Smoke drifted from the bread ovens, and Lia inhaled it. Her stomach was in knots with hunger. It was late, so Bryn was likely still with Sowe instead of back at the village with her family. Lia liked Bryn and was pleased the Aldermaston had chosen her to fill Lia's place in the kitchen to help Pasqua. Usually, that was something left to a younger wretched to learn, but the Aldermaston had chosen someone nearly their own age. It also meant that Pasqua was likely bedded down and the crossbar in place.

Lia scratched her neck, longing for a bath. Siara had given her some special salts to bathe with that would also help with the healing. Thoughts jumbled through her mind. If she had time the next day, she would seek out Duerden and ask what he knew about the Queen Dowager. She had avoided the learner lately because he was so enraptured with his studies about the Medium and wanted to boast to her what he was learning. He did not realize that she already knew it—that someone else had already taught her the basics he was struggling to comprehend. It was so frustrating having to keep secrets from him, to pretend she knew nothing about it. That the Medium obeyed her in ways he could not even imagine.

As she approached the kitchen, she noticed the lights in the upper windows were full, so she realized Sowe and Bryn were still awake. Exhaustedly, she pulled at the handle, and it opened easily, filling her with the breath of baked bread, some roast in the spit, and fragrant cloves and spices. A man's voice was telling a story—a voice she recognized instantly—and it caused her stomach to drop down to her toes.

It was Edmon's voice. They had met at the battlefield of Winterrowd in Colvin's tent. "…No, it is true! Do not laugh. It was the most perfect depiction of stubbornness you could imagine. Picture this—the king's council, and there was Demont, red-faced and shouting…" He stopped suddenly, turning to the opening door.

Lia stood for a moment in utter shock. Edmon, the Earl of Norris-York, was telling stories in the kitchen—*her* kitchen—as if that were completely normal. There was Pasqua, grinning and serving up a bowl of tarterelles. Sowe and Bryn were hanging on his every word, their eyes lit by the lantern light.

Then she heard another voice as he emerged from the shadows beneath the loft. "Lia?"

There was Colvin.

It was too much. All eyes fastened to her standing in the doorway. Could they see her ravaged face in the shadows? She was completely overwhelmed. Colvin approached, wearing clothes elegant enough for a prince of the realm. His maston sword was belted to his waist. She looked at his face as he approached, saw the little scar near his eyebrow, and her blood began pounding inside her ears. Not tonight. Not like this! She was ashamed at her appearance, her muddy clothes, the rash and salve. She could not swallow. She could not breathe. She could not even think properly.

"Lia?" Edmon asked, straightening and then smiling. "Lia! You returned early!"

She slammed the door and started away, walking briskly, then started to run, but she was so tired, she only made it a few steps before walking again. The kitchen door opened, and she heard his boots on the grass behind her. She was mortified beyond anything. This was worse than Reome teasing her about Duerden over and over. Worse than Getman's contempt toward and his grinning leers at Sowe. She kept walking as fast as she could, but he caught up with her before she made it around the corner of the kitchen into the shadows where the moon could not reveal her disfigurement.

"Lia, wait!"

His voice. She had starved to hear his voice again. For nearly a year, she had waited for him to return to Muirwood, to explain himself. To apologize. For weeks after Whitsunday, she had prepared little speeches in her mind. Not a single word from any of them came to her.

Fool, fool, fool! she cursed herself. She was a hunter! She should have noticed the signs that something was different. Careless. So careless in her exhaustion. Stopping suddenly, she turned in time to see Colvin reaching out to grab her cloak.

"Do not touch me!" she screeched at him. She flung her cloak behind her, knowing it was still infected with the sap's poison. She took two steps backward and swallowed heavily, trying to find her voice through the humiliation. He stopped, stunned, his eyes widening with shock and hurt.

"Please…please do not touch me," she said and groaned at herself.

His voice was stern. "Show me your face."

She shook her head violently and backed away farther. "Go. Please go."

"What happened to your face?"

"I cannot see you. Not like this."

"I do not care what you look like! You have seen me at my worst before."

She said nothing.

"Can I see you tomorrow?"

She nodded lamely.

Pasqua's voice bellowed from the doorway. "Lia! Child! Where are you? Lia?" She sounded frantic.

"We are guests at the Abbey," Colvin announced. "There is so much I have to tell you. So much to explain. I am sorry, Lia. I truly am. I will see you tomorrow."

He hesitated before leaving her, his hand slowly clenching and unclenching. She had seen that gesture so many times during their moments together. Then he turned and walked back to the kitchen, his voice low when he spoke to Pasqua. "She is around the corner. Edmon. We must go. Now."

Lia crumpled and leaned against the kitchen wall, unable to stop tears from burning her eyes. She hated crying! She buried her face in her hands and wept, struggling to understand her feelings. For though she was embarrassed and humiliated and undone with tiredness and shock, Colvin had finally returned to Muirwood. He had come as he had promised. She was not prepared for how strong the relief would feel.

That he had not forgotten her after all.

CHAPTER FOUR

Colvin

Lia wrung water from her crinkly damp hair as her friend began coaxing tangles out of it with a comb; Lia regretted that its color was not as fashionable as Sowe's. It was always a battle taming her hair. Bryn brought over a tray of bread, cheese, nuts, and a cup of cider. Lia's body was still wet from bathing, still stung from the scrubbing of the lye soap, but the spare dress was warm and soft, and she felt less constricted without her hunter leathers, which were in a basket waiting for her to purge them the next morning. With a thought, she caused the Leering by the ovens to flare hotter, helping fight the evening chill. The other two glanced at the sudden spurt of flames, but were used to her doing it.

Lia ate quickly, for she was starving. She looked up at Bryn and said between mouthfuls, "How long are they staying?"

Bryn did a bouncy step and a twirl. "A year. Maybe more. What Pasqua said is that we are to feed the Aldermaston's guests until they leave. They are not going to eat at the learner kitchen. Since they will be staying at the manor, we are to prepare the food ourselves and let no stranger into the kitchen. Ever." She stopped amidst another twirl. "With the battle won and the old king dead, should we be so worried? Sowe told me that the sheriff stole in here once and hurt you, Lia. Do you think something like that might happen again?"

Lia gulped down some of the sweet cider before replying. "You should always fasten the doors at night, Bryn, even if I am not back. I can always sleep elsewhere, and I know how hard it is waking up Sowe. Besides, there are still survivors from the king's army wandering the Bearden Muir, living off the land. Martin and I have seen their tracks, but they have stayed away from the Abbey so far. Still, it is best to be cautious." She wiped her mouth. "So explain this to me. How did Colvin and Edmon…"

"The *Earls* of Forshee and Norris-York," Sowe said, interrupting her. "They have titles, Lia. You are supposed to use them."

Lia snorted before continuing. "They came yesterday, unannounced, and said they would be staying at the Abbey for a year? You said they brought two young ladies with them?"

Bryn nodded and twirled again. She was always practicing her dancing since it was her first year to attend the Whitsunday festival, and she wanted to be sure she had it memorized. "One is the Earl of Forshee's sister. She's a second year learner from an Abbey in the north. Not only is she Colvin's…I mean the Earl of Forshee's sister, she is also the companion of the Aldermaston's secret guest—the niece of Garen Demont. The two earls are her protectors. Or maybe *more* than just protectors."

Lia chewed on a handful of nuts, trying to understand what was going on. Pain from the comb made her gasp. "Ouch, Sowe!"

"I am trying to be gentle," Sowe said, tugging another tangle loose.

"More than protectors?" Lia asked. "What do you mean?"

Bryn twirled again and skirted around the edge of a flagstone. Honestly, the girl could hardly hold still! "At the laundry, they say the girls are each *promised* to the earls. That the Earl of Norris-York is to marry the Earl of Forshee's sister. That is so complicated. I hate using all those titles. Besides, they said we did not need to address them as nobles. Edmon is supposed to marry Colvin's sister, Marciana. And Colvin is supposed to marry Ellowyn Demont."

For a moment, Lia's heart raged with disbelief, but she stamped it down. He had delayed coming to Muirwood because he was out wooing a girl?

Bryn clearly did not see her burning face, for she kept on talking. "Reome says that Colvin is too old not to be married or at least promised to someone. She thinks that he should have found a wife before becoming a maston. Do you think he is too old? He is only nineteen. My father and mother did not marry until they were twenty, and five and twenty." She stopped and turned to Lia. "Tell Lia about the girl, Sowe. About Ellowyn!"

Lia sat still while Sowe finished with the comb. She had so many questions she wanted to ask, but only Colvin knew the answers she sought.

Sowe's voice was soft. "She was a wretched, like us. The king kept her hidden in an Abbey since she was a baby, and so she did not know who she was. The earls brought her out. Not many know her story. The Aldermaston said we should not tell anyone that she was raised a wretched. We should only say she is the niece of Garen Demont, and she is to stay for a few seasons."

The niece of Garen Demont. Questions like buzzing flies swarmed around and around in Lia's mind. She had seen Garen Demont following the battle of Winterrowd. Graciously, he had given credit for his victory to the Medium and forbidden anyone to boast of the battle where none of his soldiers had been killed. Such a thing had never been heard of before. Afterward, he had seized custody of the young king and became Protector of the Realm. Many of the earls and barons revolted against the change and refused to swear homage to the young king with Demont controlling him. Many did support him, so the kingdom was dangling between peace and civil war. Some defied Demont, but there were others who had hated the old king and his ruthless acts. It was a tottering pile of dishes that could come crashing down. She remembered something the Aldermaston had told her.

"Finished," Sowe mumbled and put away the comb.

Lia sat forward eagerly. "The Aldermaston said tonight that the Queen Dowager was coming to Muirwood. Did you...?" She stopped, seeing their surprised faces. "I guess you did not know that. She is coming for Whitsunday."

Sowe looked serious. "The king's widow? Why?"

There was so much happening so quickly. Lia rose and started pacing. "When I left, everything was its usual boring self. Now look at it all. I do not know whose side she is on, but I would guess she supports the side of her son. Colvin would know, if he will speak to me again after tonight," she muttered. She wanted to talk to him desperately, to apologize for screaming at him and crying.

Sowe gave her a hug. "Lia, when they came, they both asked to see you right away. That should please you. The Earl of Forshee—Colvin—was very kind to me. He said that he still owed me a gift. You remember, for the time when I helped. You did most of the work. But he remembered his promise. I wonder...I wonder if he came all this way for a reason. That his sister is going to study here for the next year, at least. He is a maston already, no longer a learner."

Lia looked at her.

"You know...to teach you himself," Sowe suggested.

The burning in Lia's heart nearly choked her.

***

At dawn the next morning, Lia retired to the laundry to clean her gear. The water gushing from the Leering's mouth was scalding hot, but Lia kept her mind on the heat and scrubbed at her leather tools using gloves and the wood-ash soaps. She cleaned the sap-stained hunter equipment first—her girdle, bracers, shooting glove, quiver, scabbard—and then set them aside and bundled up the damp dress. She heard voices and footsteps approaching. Angry to be interrupted, she willed the Leering to stop. The eyes of the Leering cooled, and the water ceased flowing.

The morning was cool and misty, and the grounds were veiled. Martin was always up before dawn, and she did not want to miss the Aldermaston's news, so she hurried to gather up her things as the lavenders approached, but the clutch of girls entered the roofed shelter before she could leave.

Reome had a way of scrutinizing with her eyes that made others feel mottled and ugly. With her voice, she could cut as efficiently as a fruit knife. "Look at your face, Lia," she said with a tiny smirk. "What disease are you suffering from?" She clucked her tongue. "Right before Whitsunday, too. How awful."

Lia hefted the basket and tried to walk past without answering, but the other lavenders unfolded like a wall, blocking her path. They all had daggers for eyes and carried their wicker baskets in front of them.

"Let me through," Lia said impatiently. "The Aldermaston is expecting me."

"What happened to your face?" Reome asked, squinting and looking revolted and delighted at the same time.

"It is none of your concern. Let me pass."

"Are you really so anxious to see the Aldermaston? I doubt it. The new guests must be luring you. Treasa says the Earl of Norris-York is the prettiest man in the Hundred. She has offered to help with his laundry, and he accepted. The brooding one said he will not, that he would only trust you."

"Me?" Lia asked, startled.

"Not you, specifically," Reome said, and Lia could tell she was trying to draw out information from her. "Only that one of the Aldermaston's girls would do it. You are still the Aldermaston's girl, Lia. Are you not?" Her smile was sickeningly close to a leer.

Lia's cheeks went hot, but she controlled her emotions. Reome was eighteen now. After Whitsunday, she would leave Muirwood and either marry the local blacksmith or have to find work in one of the bigger towns. She was a beautiful girl and would no doubt find little difficulty convincing a boy to marry her. But in Muirwood, and for most of her life, she had been seen as the most beautiful, the most desirable, until the last Whitsunday when Sowe had emerged and taken Reome's place, without ever trying and without saying a mean-spirited word to anyone. The sudden attention had bolstered Sowe's lacking confidence, and her timidity shrank when she realized that boys would stumble over their tongues just to bid her hello. But unlike Reome, she had not used the situation to belittle others or set the lads fetching things for her or making other girls do her work for her. It was a festering sore to Reome, and Lia could see it pockmarking her soul.

"Move aside," Lia warned.

"I asked you a question."

Lia's patience with Reome's taunting ended. Gritting her teeth, she shoved her basket into Reome's—not hard, but enough to throw her a little off balance. "I *am* the Aldermaston's girl," she said firmly, confidently. In her mind, she pushed the thought at Reome: *Stand aside or you will regret it. Move aside, Reome, or I will humiliate you in front of these girls. I am a hunter.* The tingle of the Medium coursed through her.

Reome stared at her, shocked. She hesitated. For a moment, Lia thought she would have to fulfill her threat. But then Reome took a step backward and moved out of the way. The wall of lavenders crumpled. Holding her basket with one hand, Lia reached into the basket of another girl and took a bunch of purple mint to hang with her leathers while she dried them. "Thank you," she said stiffly as she walked past them, heading back to the kitchen invisible in the mist ahead.

"I hate her," came the low-throated voice behind her, but Lia kept walking.

As she went, she realized she was scowling, her heart pounding, and the wicked temptation arose to go back and shove Reome into the trough. She pictured it for a moment, savoring the image of dunking her head into the water. What would the other girls do if she did?

She caught herself, realizing the danger of her thoughts. Martin had trained her to fight—how to grab a man by the wrist, twist him around, and trip him. How to disarm someone with a dagger. How to hobble someone by breaking their foot. She even knew a dozen ways to injure or kill a man quickly, though she never had the cause to use her knowledge that way. It was locked up tight in her mind, coins she hoped she would never have to spend. But thinking ill of Reome and the lavenders was dangerous. Those thoughts could emerge as actions later, in a moment of weakness when her self-control faltered.

The grass was soft beneath her feet. Smells from the flowers and grass surrounded her, as well as snippets of sounds as the learners rose to begin their studies. Geese flew overhead, splitting the stillness with honking. Lia approached the kitchen to ask Sowe or Bryn to hang her leathers by the fires to dry so she could make it to the Aldermaston quickly. Another sound caught her ears, coming from the opposite side of the kitchen. Curious, she followed it and went around the corner to the rear of the kitchen, the side most hidden from view. Her approach was quiet as doves roosting. She peered around the corner, and there he was.

Colvin.

She paused, watching him, for his back was to her. His sword was out, and he was practicing with it. He moved through a series of intricate maneuvers, as if he fought off ten different men at once. Each thrust and parry was controlled—precise. Memories flooded her. They were so long ago, but she remembered the details precisely. For months, she had fallen asleep each night forcing herself to remember everything she could about the days when he had been abandoned during a storm on the floor of the kitchen, bloody and unconscious. One night, he had practiced with a broom and had misjudged the distance of a table and clacked the handle hard. It made her stifle a giggle.

He heard the laughter and turned sharply. The expression on his face was pure annoyance and hostility. She had seen that look a hundred times in her mind. Impatient. Demanding. Wary. Petulant. The look melted when he recognized her. He sheathed his knight-maston sword in the scabbard and approached her.

She stared at him, clutching the basket to her stomach, and wondered if the mist meant it was only a dream. It seemed she noticed every detail. The silver starburst studs on his scabbard belt, the buckles holding the dark leather jerkin closed. The long pale sleeves matching the cuff emerging from his neck. His face, his hands. The scar. Yes, the scar at the corner of his eyebrow. He was close enough now she could see its tiny little pucker, and she remembered mopping blood from it.

"Were you laughing at me?" was all he said in greeting. His voice was warm.

It had been a long year—a year of pain and worry and sadness. All of that vanished like a drop of sizzling water on a hot skillet. The look he gave her bespoke friendship and admiration. He was glad to see her, not nervous. He wanted to see her. That made all the difference in the world.

Lia flung down the basket and gave him a fierce hug to prove once and for all that he was real and that she was not stained by poisoned sap any longer. She was nearly as tall as him and could feel his cheek against her hair. He smelled of leather and sweat, but also himself. She had forgotten what he smelled like. That sort of memory was too much like smoke to grasp.

"Yes, you idiot," she said, squeezing him hard and then pulling back, embarrassed a little at herself for hugging him, but unrepentant. She looked at his face. "I was laughing at a memory. There are many of you that make me laugh. Others that have made me cry. You did not come when you promised. I am upset with you about that. But here you are now, and I am told you are staying a season or two, so I suppose I could learn to forgive you."

His expression was thoughtful. He seemed a little uncomfortable by her hug, but not displeased by it. "Contrive your best punishment, Lia. I submit to it. But I must be allowed to explain myself."

"Of course you can explain yourself, but not right now." She reached to pick up the basket, but he got to it first, and she almost touched his hand. He handed it to her.

"Why not?" he asked, scrutinizing her.

"Because the Aldermaston has instructions I must hear, and he hates repeating himself. I am a hunter now, not a kitchen girl, so I have duties to attend to."

"When can I see you today?" he asked, taking up the bunch of purple mint from her basket. He smelled it, then set it back down.

"When I am free," she answered stiffly, looking down at the flowers in the basket. "Where can I find you?"

"I have been anxious to read Maderos's tomes, and there is little else I am allowed to do apparently, while the learners study."

"Ah, the forbidden part of the grounds! As the hunter, I could forbid you to wander there. But as the rule is only to prevent other people from finding it, I will give you permission. So, I will bring the apples when we meet?" Lia offered. "The blotchy ones are the sweetest."

He gazed at her face, seeing the blotches there. "I remember. I have craved those apples since I left. I remember this place differently now." He looked around at the mist-shrouded trees. "There is no sign of Blight here yet," he whispered. "I am glad of that."

We should live as if we were in public view, and think, too, as if someone could peer into the inmost recesses of our hearts. The Blight which assails us is not in the localities we inhabit but in ourselves. We are more wicked together than separately. If you are ever forced to be in a crowd, then most of all you should withdraw into yourself. Never trust another to do your thinking. Even a maston.

—Gideon Penman of Muirwood Abbey

CHAPTER FIVE

Scales

The discussion had already started by the time Lia reached the Aldermaston's study, but only by a few moments. Martin was nestled in the recessed window, surly as usual, his arms folded across his chest, his chin jutting. His was a cantankerous presence. Prestwich sat near the desk, organizing stacks of parchments and seals and sealing wax, forever patient and precise. A fat candle lay dripping nearby. His crown of white hair looked like fresh-fallen snow. He was older than anyone else in the room, his age showing more each day.

The Aldermaston paced by the mantle, glanced over at Lia's entrance, but did not stop the thread of his conversation. His voice was soft yet gravelly, as if he were always slightly straining for breath. "The third report from last month. The fourth and fifth from the last fortnight alone. Where were they from, Prestwich?"

The steward lifted his head and poked his earlobe with the stylus. "From the Abbeys at Caneland and Sutton. The latest arrived from Billerbeck with Earl Forshee."

Lia sat next to Martin at the window seat, listening intently.

"The Blight is spreading," the Aldermaston said. He rubbed his mouth. "It ravages Dahomey, Paiz, and Hautland. Few mastons travel alone these days. They come in pairs as the earls did. I have not heard of an Abbey succumbing to it yet, but it is only a matter of time. It weighs on me heavily, this threat we face."

Martin stood, his voice nearly a growl. "Who is infecting the stones then, with this Blight? Who is spreading the taint? Is it the Myriad Ones? When Pry-Ree fell, it fell without a whimper. Without burning Leerings and noxious saps. The princes were betrayed by those they trusted. And when trust fails, so does law. When there is no longer law, there is only war and murder."

"War is only one manifestation of the Blight," the Aldermaston said. "Sometimes it kills with plague. Sometimes with drought. Sometimes even, Idumea forbid, with water." He paused and looked at Lia. "I am sure you are confused. Prestwich understands the significance of the events. Martin does as well, for he endured it previously and witnessed his country succumb to the Blight. You are very young, Lia. You have not lived through this awful season before, the foul ripeness and bitter harvest. This will be your first, so I will attempt to explain it to you. Those of us older than you have seen it repeated like a waterwheel churning in a river."

He turned and went back to his desk. "Prestwich, find the one from Hautland. There it is, with the copper seal. Yes, that one. Thank you." He opened it and squinted. "In this one, the Blight came as a plant with poisonous sap. It started around a Leering in the woods, and the plant spread quickly throughout the forest, inflicting everyone who touched it with itching boils. Attempts to burn it caused smoke to carry the poison inside the victims." He handed the parchment back to Prestwich. "Strange, is it not? That a plant that is not native to this country can appear from nowhere and begin its work of destruction so rapidly. What brought it? When did it start?"

Her stomach twisted and lurched when she thought about Colvin being in danger. "Aldermaston," she said. "I know who ruined the Leering in the wood."

He paused, cocking his head and stared at her in disbelief. "How, child?"

"When I calmed the stone, I touched it. When I did, I saw them in my mind. There were soldiers from Winterrowd—the king's men. They slept near the stone during the winter for warmth. I could see the snow around them. One came and touched the stone, and he is the one who made it start burning. I recognized him because he is the man who tricked me. He brought Colvin to the kitchen and then went to find the sheriff." She paused, taking a deep breath. "When I returned from Winterrowd, remember, I told you of him. He is called Scarseth, and he has the sheriff's medallion. He cannot speak, but he knows about me. He knows I was at that Leering. He knows what I did to the sheriff's men there."

The Aldermaston's face darkened with anger. "Martin, he must be found. The medallion he wears is dangerous. He may not yet realize its powers or what he does with it. But one Leering can lead him to the rest and compromise the Abbey if he penetrates the boundaries I put in place. Find him, Martin. Bring him to me if you can. If not, then do what you must. He must be stopped."

Lia stood firmly. "I can find him, Aldermaston. The Cruciger orb can lead us right to him."

He shook his head, equally firmly. "No, Lia. I cannot afford to let both of you leave. I am in need of two hunters right now." He held up his hand before the protest escaped her lips. "Hush, child. Do as I say. I act with reasons you do not always understand. Have faith in me a bit longer. I need you and your orb here because of the guest the earls brought to Muirwood. Her name is Ellowyn Demont, the niece of Garen Demont and the heir of Pry-Ree, the daughter of the prince of the Pry-Ree, who died shortly after she was born. The birthing killed her mother. In the customs of that land, children are named after their mother's family. Her mother was the only daughter of Sevrin Demont, who died at Maseve, and she was Garen Demont's young sister. It is no secret that the king's entire family still hates the Demonts. The child was reared in Sempringfall Abbey as a wretched. After Winterrowd, her location was discovered. Pay close attention, for this is important. To the Pry-rians, she is the legitimate heir to their kingdom. They have petitioned Demont to have her returned and to study at their Abbeys. So far, he has not consented. There is great fear that they will attempt to abduct her."

Martin snorted, and Lia noticed his eyes were burning with anger. "Abduct, Aldermaston? You mean *return* her to her rightful place. She was *abducted* from Pry-Ree and treated worse than an orphan instead of given her due right. It is wrong to say otherwise."

The Aldermaston's face hardened. "I will not argue the point, Martin. I certainly do not have the authority to determine her whereabouts. She resides at Muirwood for a time, but then we will move her again to another Abbey. The rumor is spreading that she will linger here for a year. The utmost secrecy is required in this matter. When it is time to move her, we will assist. No one must know where she is going or when. As I mentioned, the king's family hates the Demonts. While her existence was primarily forgotten, by design, it is in the open now. Friends of the old king may seek her life. That is why, Lia, you must stay here. You are needed to protect the Abbey, protect the earls, and protect this girl. I trust Martin's abilities. If Scarseth is still lurking in the

Bearden Muir, he will be found. But I feel impressions that you must stay near the Abbey."

Martin leaned back, his arms folded. "You should send the girl to Pry-Ree. There are too many dangers in this land. Too much blood. She would be safer among her own people."

"Thank you for your advice, Martin. You know I trust you, and I respect your wisdom. It is not the time for such a course at the moment."

Martin muttered under his breath and shook his head. "It is not right. It is not right to play such games with the life of someone so young."

"Martin," the Aldermaston warned, his voice growing sterner.

"I have heard you. I will obey. But I do not agree. I cannot agree." He rose from the window seat. "Pry-Ree grovels for crumbs now when she used to feed princes. That ill-made king destroyed us. He is cold under the soil now, and no one mourns him. This girl is the last chance to make Pry-Ree bloom again, by Cheshu. She is the key to its rebirth."

The Aldermaston's gaze was icy. He said nothing, only waited for Martin to finish.

With a sigh, Martin returned to the window seat and sat next to Lia. "I speak my mind, Aldermaston. It is no secret I have my opinions. But I will obey as obediently as Prestwich. You can trust that." He waved his hand at the Aldermaston. "I have interrupted you. There is more you had to say."

The Aldermaston motioned to Prestwich, who withdrew another scroll. The steward's voice was thick and cultured. "This letter informs us that the Queen Dowager will be attending Whitsunday at Muirwood this year. We expect her arrival in a fortnight. Her retinue will be joining her as well, and we have been asked to provide lodging for them at our expense."

Lia looked at the Aldermaston in alarm. "Does she know that Ellowyn is here?"

"I do not know. I can and must presume that somehow she does know and that her retinue will be prepared for many possibilities. They may try to abduct her, poison her or the earls, or determine what they can about our defenses—to plumb the depths of our commitment to protect her. They may test the strength of our thoughts. That is why the earls are staying here and not in the village. That is why they will only eat from my kitchen. And that is why my own hunter will be responsible for their safety while they are here. If any threat emerges, you are to flee to the tunnels, and use the orb to find a safe haven for them. Martin, you do not have long to find your quarry, for you must return before the festival so that I have both of you here when the Queen Dowager arrives. Remember, she was the slain king's wife. I understand that she has been visiting the towns and Abbeys in surrounding Hundreds in recent months. She is a…cunning woman. Be on your guard with her."

Martin leaned forward. "It would be safer to move the girl now then, Aldermaston."

He shook his head. "I would rather she stay under Muirwood's protection while it still is strong. We have time yet, Martin. There is still time."

Lia's mind was burdened with too many thoughts and worries. She folded her arms and looked down at her lap, feeling the weight of her responsibility.

The Aldermaston's voice intruded on her thoughts. "So you see, Lia. I have not sent Martin on the harder errand after all."

CHAPTER SIX

Promise

Lia smoothed the linen napkin enclosing the foodstuffs and carefully packed it inside Martin's baggage. She included some small pouches of spices that she knew he liked and then cinched it closed and held it out to him. Martin gave her one of his rare smiles. His bow was strung, the two quivers full of brightly-fletched arrows, his hand resting casually on the gladius pommel in a way that made her worry. Anything involving the work of death and war made her slightly sick. The nightmares of the battlefield of Winterrowd still haunted her, though not as often.

She gave him a hug, which always made him scowl and shoo her away. "'Tis you who need the comforting, lass. By Cheshu, I get the joy of wandering again in the fenlands and smashing little bloodsucking flies. Your work is more dangerous." He looked at her sternly. "I have taught you well enough if you had the mind to listen. The hunter is patient. The prey is careless. You are a good lass. Be wary. Be wise. Be cautious. I will return within a fortnight." He reached out and smoothed a lock back over her ear. It was a tender gesture, a subtle showing of affection, and it made her swallow.

"I will have Pasqua save you a slice of sambocade," Lia said. "Maybe a whole dish."

He shook his head and pounded his stomach. "It would not settle right to eat the whole thing. But a slice—that would be worth returning to. Keep an eye on the learner quarters. I think there are several of the first years who are getting a bit daring now that the year is finishing. I would not scold you if you dyed some of their hair blue if they wander at night. Woad is a useful plant for that."

Lia laughed and gave him another hug. Then she opened the pouch at her waist and withdrew the Cruciger orb. He peered at her, his eyes suddenly fierce and penetrating. The scowl was still there beneath the bushy cropped beard that was mostly silver and black. He grimaced, his teeth showing. It was as if he wanted to say something, but could not.

"Show me the way to the man known as Scarseth," Lia whispered, unnerved by his gaze.

The orb twirled and spun in her hand and pointed northwest, toward the Bearden Muir. He looked at the spindles, at the writing that appeared on the surface of the orb, but he could not read it either. He nodded to her and then departed, tugging up his leather cowl to shade his face from the noonday sun.

After he was gone from sight, she looked down at the orb again. *Show me Colvin*, she thought, and again it directed her, pointing toward the Cider Orchard, where she expected him to be. Carefully, she placed it back in the pouch and headed off toward the orchard. So many thoughts collided in her mind, she nearly stumbled as she walked. Of the many threats and dangers, it was difficult untangling them all. Mastons were still being murdered. The

Demont girl had enemies. The Queen Dowager would be arriving soon at Muirwood. How could she, one person, handle it all? Part of her had been dreading Whitsunday for weeks, and that had turned to excitement when she learned Colvin had arrived. But instead of enjoying the dance, she would be worried about him.

"Lia!" called a voice from behind. She turned in annoyance and saw Astrid running toward her. He was eleven years old and very short with spiky dark hair.

She stopped, frustrated. "Does the Aldermaston want to see me?" she asked.

He shook his head when he approached, out of breath. "I thought you should know," he said, then stopped, panting. "I overhead Getman Smith talking to some of the stable hands. He did not see me. He warned them against dancing with Sowe around the maypole. He said…he threatened them, Lia. If anyone asked her but him, he would thrash them." His little face bunched up in distaste. "He really is a coxcomb. Tell her, Lia. It is not fair that he should be the only one to dance with her."

She scowled and nodded. "Thank you, Astrid. I will tell her."

"What happened to your face, Lia?"

"Nothing. It is healing. Thank you, Astrid." As he ran to his next errand, she continued on, worrying about how ravaged her face looked before seeing Colvin. The skin was peeling and coming off in flakes, especially her nose. At least the itching was gone.

She entered the orchard from the south side, crossing the even rows toward the Leering guarding the trail downward. But before she reached it, she encountered Colvin partway. The orchard trees were thick around her, forcing her to duck and weave beneath the clawlike branches.

She tried to keep her voice light, to not betray her excitement at seeing him. "I did not bring you any food this time. If you are hungry, it is your own fault. But there may be some apples in the higher branches."

He held up his hands, and she saw he was holding two. "Muirwood apples suit me now. I have not tasted one like these since I left. The ones that grow elsewhere are either red or yellow, sometimes juicy, sometimes mush—but never this blend of colors, and never this particular taste." He tossed one to her. She caught it, noting the blemishes and blotches around the stem.

She smelled it first, inhaling its subtle fragrance, noting the way he watched her. There was a look in his eyes that she could not make out. No anger or impatience. He seemed very calm and self-assured.

She bit into the apple and enjoyed the burst of flavor. "It is a pity you did not arrive in the spring," she said, "when the whole orchard blooms. It is my favorite season here on the grounds, when all the oaks are budding, and the apple blossoms fall so thick you think it is snowing. I think I told you before," she said seriously, regarding the bitten piece of fruit. "That we must be near the garden where the First Parents met. It was probably the garden where we found Maderos, remember? Imagine if that was it."

Colvin shook his head. "That has not changed. You still mock subjects that you know little or nothing about."

With a sweet smile, she asked, "How could I know all that, if no one will teach me to read?" She took another bite. "We know so very little about those ancient days, Colvin. What would have happened if our First Parents had not bitten the apple together, at the same moment?"

"You presume it was an apple. The tomes only say 'fruit.' There are, after all, other things they might have eaten."

"Yes, but there is something less than forbidding to the imagination about biting into a pumpkin. What would have happened if they did not eat it at the same time? What if Father ate it first?"

"There still would have been a punishment," Colvin countered. "That is the point, Lia, not who ate it first or what fruit it was. Maybe in another world, *she* took the first bite and suffered the first punishment. But you did not come all this way here to talk about the fruit of knowledge and what it means. Sit down at that stump. I owe you an explanation for my actions. You may not believe me, but I do regret that it happened. You probably believe I was a faithless knave. I am sure you did. Please, sit while we talk."

There was a patch of grass that looked much more inviting, so she sat there, enjoying another taste of the apple and the fact that Colvin had climbed a tree to find it, and then waited for him to speak. Because of what the Aldermaston had explained that morning, she thought she knew most of it already.

He did not join her on the grass, but stood nearby, examining a branch crowned with leaves. "The day I left you, I told the Aldermaston that I would pay for your learning. He knew I was to be invested as the Earl of Forshee. It was not because of an issue of money that he refused me. He said he did not want to draw attention to you more than had already been done. After Winterrowd, I thought it would be safe, but he warned me that I was mistaken. Other earls would oppose Demont and rise in rebellion. It came to pass just as he said. He warned me not to reveal what you had done for me to anyone, not even Demont. It was for your protection and the protection of Muirwood. The only exception I negotiated was my sister. She knows."

Lia frowned. "Am I forbidden to see you?"

He looked down at her and shook his head. "No, the prohibition is over. I am a guest now, a personal guest of the Aldermaston. It is only natural that his hunter would be asked to accompany me or be seen with me. It is not an uncommon practice among my peers to hunt and hawk. I enjoy it myself. There is more, though. When our little army returned to Comoros with the young king for the coronation, Demont gave me a formidable task. He had depended on me during the battle and knew that my father had sworn, at one time, allegiance to his father. He told me about the existence of his niece—a secret that I knew from my father. I had been told of it as a child. You see, when the old king destroyed Pry-Ree, he wanted to ensure that no prince would rise in the future to unite the people against him. Years ago, the lord prince of Pry-Ree married Demont's sister. They were husband and wife when the old king began his invasion. She was great with child at the time, and he had to leave her to defend his lands. During the war, the child was born—a daughter. Sadly, the birthing killed the mother." He looked at her seriously, and Lia swallowed, unable to keep eating.

Her heart burned inside her.

Colvin's voice was soft. "Much we do not know. Those who survived say the lord prince was so bereft losing his young wife that the Medium ceased aiding him. He fell into an ambush and was killed by the king's men. His head was fixed to a spear in Comoros. The Pry-rians were crushed. The child was taken into the king's custody and hidden in an Abbey. She was to be raised a wretched." His eyes were intent on hers. "Lia, I was asked to find this child. I believed…I truly believed it was you. You were about the right age. The orb spoke to you in Pry-rian. I did not think it likely that they would put the child so near Pry-Ree as Muirwood, but that alone does not invalidate it. You do bear some resemblance to the Demont family. Not your hair but your face, your countenance—it is hauntingly like that family's."

It took a moment for Lia to swallow. "Almaguer thought so," she whispered.

"Demont told me that I needed incontrovertible evidence. He sent me to the archives. I was not to tell anyone of my mission, only to search the records to find out what happened to the prince's daughter. I knew the year when Pry-Ree was lost. I found a tome written in the king's own hand after much searching. The child was taken by the king and banished to Sempringfall Abbey."

Just as the Aldermaston had said, Lia thought.

"It is a small Abbey, noteworthy of nothing, in the eastern part of the realm, near the sea. Demont was already dealing with rebels, and so he sent Edmon and I to the Abbey for the girl. She was there, living by another name. The Aldermaston had lived there when she arrived and knew her true identity, though he had never spoken it for fear of the old king. He released her into our custody with a warning. He was told by the king's men that if she ever escaped, his Abbey would be burned to the ground. The king's men swore they would find the child and kill her and any of her offspring. He charged us to protect her, and we have kept that charge. The Pry-rians want her back, naturally, as she is the only surviving heir."

He crouched near her, so close she could see her reflection in his eyes. His expression was almost painful to look at. "I thought it was you, Lia. I had hoped that by not keeping my promise to you, I would be able to bring you far better news. I am sorry I abandoned you. For the last year, I have been at various Abbeys while Ellowyn was taught to read and scribe in our language, Pry-rian, and Dahomeyjan. Three languages, instead of one. Her head nearly burst! My sister, Marciana, is her companion. It has been a...difficult transition for Ellowyn. She was a lavender at Sempringfall. When I met her, she smelled like that bunch of flowers I saw you with this morning. The scent reminded me of you."

He stopped and breathed deeply, staring down at the grass. "Knight-mastons are being murdered, rebels are skulking in the woods, the Privy Council has threats of war from three other kingdoms, and I...I must coax a girl to read who is terrified of learning, who is terrified of the Medium, and who would rather be washing clothes in a trough." He looked at her, being open with his disdain. "When the latest threat to her life came, we were at Billerbeck. I suggested we come to Muirwood. This is the oldest Abbey in the realm. Your Aldermaston is very wise and may help her to master her fears. But most important, I wanted to be able to tell you in person why I could not come earlier and apologize for neglecting you. The Aldermaston will not let you become a learner in the cloister. You must continue to serve until your obligation is fulfilled. But my oath to you still binds me. It is a duty that I will, for once, enjoy. I am forbidden to teach you now how to read and engrave, Lia, but I am not forbidden to share with you what I know and what I have scribed in my own tome."

Lia took a deep breath, trying to keep it calm and even. So much had happened in so short a time. Of all her feelings, it was jealousy that tormented her. She was jealous that the other girl, who had once been a wretched, had been found. She had been allowed the privilege of enjoying Colvin's company for a year. The privilege of learning to read *three* languages and practicing the Medium openly. What Lia would not have given to have had that opportunity! It was a petty feeling, and she crushed it in her mind, unwilling to let it fester or take root.

"What about your other promise?" she asked, glancing down as she twisted the apple stem and plucked it out.

"The other promise?"

"The one you whispered in my ear when you left?" She glanced up at him.

A knowing smile crossed his mouth. He rose and wandered a few steps, leaned back against the trunk of a tree, and folded his arms. "Well, I never said *which* Whitsunday I would ask you to dance."

"So you *were* going to ask me to dance? That was your intention?"

"You had said it was to be your first year to dance around the maypole. It was also an opportunity to meet you. It did not come to pass as I wished. But patience is the companion of wisdom. It is also a trait you need to practice, Lia."

"If I were not so *patient*," she said, tearing another bite from her apple with her teeth, "I would have broken your foot when you surprised me last night."

"Break my foot? Ample reason to avoid dancing with you this year."

"You were very kind a moment ago, Colvin," she said, pleased he was teasing her. "A year past, you could scarcely speak ten words without insulting me. But it did not take you long to fall back to your bad ways."

He gave her a self-mocking smile. "Much has changed in a year. Including yourself. But I have been working on my manners. My sister is in charge of improving me. She will undoubtedly solicit your help. She would like to meet you tonight."

Lia shrugged. "It is probably a hopeless quest, but we must try. I have not changed that much, really. I am still as filthy as when we left the Bearden Muir. My dress was in tatters from wandering the hills, so I wear these clothes now. My skin is falling off like a leper because of a dangerous plant sap I stumbled into a few days ago. My clothes were blotched with it, which is why I screamed at you last night. I am even taller now, if that is possible, and it can hardly be called an improvement." She licked her lips, trying to match his self-mocking smile. "If you were too ashamed to dance with me, I would understand. You are a knight-maston from Winterrowd and an earl, no less."

His smile faded. "I have three earldoms now, actually. But I do not care what anyone else thinks, Lia. I had not even noticed any of those things. To me, you could never be ugly."

Imagine, if you will, that the sum of all human thoughts could be represented on a measuring scale. The thoughts of a powerful maston, one enabled by the Medium to his fullest potential, could each be represented by a gold coin on one side. Imagine then, that all of the evil, uncontrolled, vengeful thoughts have the weight of chaff and try to tip the scales. The world is a granary of ill-bred thoughts. There is enough to weigh down the world, to bury each one of us alive. Yet if we have enough of the good, it balances it out or keeps it firmly in the cause of right. Imagine, then, scales the size of a kingdom. How many gold coins are there compared with chaff? Enough—just enough. There is enough weight and enough strength to keep the scales balanced. But if you begin to remove the gold coins, one by one? Then every seed of evil matters. Every little seed begins to tip the scales. As long as the scales are balanced to the side of the mastons, the Medium blesses everyone—both the evil and the good. But if the balance is altered, if the weight of the wrong begins to exceed the weight of the right, it triggers the Blight to purge the chaff. It is a warning from the Medium. There are curses that follow.

—Gideon Penman of Muirwood Abbey

CHAPTER SEVEN

Marciana Price

Lia's curiosity about Colvin's sister was intense. Since he had told Lia that she would meet her that night in the Aldermaston's kitchen, as she went about her duties that day, she wondered what Marciana would be like. Wondering made her worry. Most learners were wealthy and spoiled, and only the rare ones, like Duerden, treated wretcheds with any respect. Each year, only a dozen or so new learners joined the Abbey and even fewer fully completed the training. Fewer still earned the rank of maston. Was Marciana selfish and spiteful like Reome? Was she timid like Sowe? Was she like Colvin when she had first met him, always on the verge of anger and never bothering to mask his contempt? She hoped not. But still, she worried.

As evening came, and though she knew they were waiting for her in the kitchen, she had to finish walking the grounds. With Martin gone, she walked in measured steps, patiently, looking for any sign of passage. She checked the nearer shore of the fish pond, skirted the Cider Orchard because she had already checked it after visiting with Colvin, then came around to test the gate locks before returning to the kitchen. Her stomach was a hive of bees by the time she approached the door to the kitchen. What had Colvin told Marciana and Ellowyn about her?

She paused for a moment at the threshold, took a deep breath, and pulled on the handle. The moment would linger in her memory. There was Pasqua, in the middle, teaching everyone to make Gooseberry Fool.

"Whip it harder, like Sowe is. Yes, firm strokes. Yes, the sugar makes it sweet. There is the cream. Like Sowe, faster. Where are the spoons? Edmon, the spoons. Over there. We can share from the bowl."

The opened door revealed both Sowe and Bryn in their aprons and each clutching a bowl. Bryn was trying to match the strokes of Sowe, but could not do it without spilling. Two other finely dressed girls were nearby, watching the mixture happen.

"There she is!" said one of the girls, a smile brightening her face. The girl who approached was as tall as Sowe, as slender and graceful as a swan. Her golden hair was crowned with a braided coil and her dress—it was as richly textured as the best in Muirwood, a deep green—like a velvet forest in the spring. Instead of a girdle, she wore a vest with thin lacings up the front. The sleeves were wide and pointed, barely covering her arms with an intricate stitched lining for the trim. There were no jeweled chokers or rings or necklaces, only a pendant with a deep azure stone set into it. Her arms and wrists were thin, her fingers delicate. She was beautiful, and the beauty also shone from her eyes.

She approached swiftly and embraced Lia as if they had known each other all their lives. Lia was taller, slightly, and felt filthy compared to her, having just walked the grounds.

"I am Marciana," she said, taking Lia's hands in hers, as if she could care less about the dirt and brush clinging to her hair. "Colvin has told me so much about you, I would have recognized you without the hunter's garb. Please, you must be famished! Pasqua has been teaching us one of her naughty desserts. I love Gooseberry Fool. Did you find the spoons, Edmon?"

"At your service, as always, Ciana. Hello, Lia. I am a fool for Gooseberry Fool myself. There is something about the fruit in this Hundred. The gooseberries are only slightly tart. You can eat them by the handful. And the apples! By Idumea, they are delicious! I had never tasted Muirwood apples before coming here. Had you, Colvin?"

Lia glanced at Colvin, feeling overwhelmed by Marciana's exuberant welcome, and their eyes met. Muirwood apples had been their only food in the Bearden Muir.

"They are quite good," he said simply, their eyes flashing with the shared secret. But he said nothing further.

The other girl hovering near Colvin had reddish-bronze hair and could not have been a starker contrast to Marciana. Colvin's sister had all the confidence of a girl who had been raised in privilege, part of a Family who adored her, and with the good looks and charms that had never failed to impress. The other girl, Ellowyn, was dressed in clothes every bit as fine as Marciana's, but she looked like a wretched. Her eyes were slightly downcast, her manners timid, yet not as timid as Sowe's. It was as if she wanted to join the fun in the kitchen, but did not trust herself to leap in. She stood in Colvin's shadow, as if he were a rope that would keep her from drowning in a sea of memories. A year before, she had been serving in an Abbey. For the last year, she had been close to Colvin. Something dark twisted inside of Lia at the thought.

Pasqua's voice strained with impatience. "Bring the spoons, Edmon, over here! Come have a taste. With the sugar and cream, the berries are even sweeter. You can mix in blackberries as well.

And cake. A little cake is also good." She grabbed a spoon from his hand and served him a dollop of Fool.

"It is amazing, Pasqua!" His face lit up with enjoyment as he tasted it. "And so fresh. How lucky you all are, to have it so fresh. You could sell this at the festival!"

Bryn and Sowe both burst out giggling at that remark, and he turned to them, confused.

"She does!" Bryn said, covering her mouth while laughing. "Every year."

He smiled, chagrined. "I remember now. You already told me that. Colvin, you must try this Fool!"

They were also very different, Lia observed. Colvin and Edmon. Both wearing knight-maston swords at their belts, along with collars from Winterrowd. Both wearing the same jerkin and padded shirts. Edmon was more at ease—one who could mix company gladly and care not whether he was with nobles or wretcheds. When Lia observed him, she saw Duerden's traits of kindness and compassion. A few more years and he would have all the girls giggling at some brainless remark. But Colvin was different. He was reserved, aloof, but always watchful. More circumspect and guarded than Edmon.

Lia watched as Colvin dipped his head and whispered to Ellowyn, motioning subtly toward the bowl and offered spoon. Ellowyn smiled enthusiastically, as if deferring to his judgment in the matter of whether she should taste it. He served her himself. Sowe and Bryn joined in, as did Pasqua.

Marciana clung to Lia's arm, as if she could not stand to be apart from her for a moment. Subtly, she led Lia away from the others. "So this is where you have lived your life," she said softly. "I am sure you begrudge not having a family, Lia. I know I would. But Muirwood is a beautiful Abbey. I love it here already. I was so excited to come, especially knowing that it would bring us together at last. If there is anyone in the world he speaks more highly of, I do not know who it is." She stopped prattling, her eyes seeking out Lia's. "You must know that I love my brother, that I regard him more than any other man. *You* saved his life, Lia. It was here, on these very stones, that you tended him. It was up there, in the loft, where you hid him. He says I must beg your permission before he can show me Maderos's lair, for that ground is forbidden to learners, and I am a learner. I know what happened in the Bearden Muir. I have told no one else, not even Ellowyn. I shall keep your secret as you kept his when that cruel sheriff hunted him. I must tell you how indebted I am to you." She patted Lia's hands and then kissed them. "Thank you, Lia. You saved his life. I owe you something for that."

"I was not sure how I would feel meeting you," Lia answered, overwhelmed with emotions. She kept her own voice low. "I thought, before the battle, that I might have to find you and tell you of your brother's death. That would not have been a pleasant introduction. It makes me grateful to the Medium that it did not happen that way."

"I agree! Colvin did tell me that you are adept with the Medium. Another secret I will keep hidden. Poor Ellowyn—she is so frightened of it. There was a Leering at the laundry where she served." Her eyes glittered wickedly. "Colvin hates it when I call them that, but it is far more fitting than *gargouelle.* Why use a Dahomeyjan word when we are so far from that country? Some learners at her Abbey used to torment the laundry girls by making it spew water while they were washing clothes. And you know how fear hampers the Medium. Poor girl. I wish it had been you instead, Lia. I would have loved being your companion, your friend while you learned. But Ellowyn is a sweet girl. You will like her. She is shy, like Sowe. But you will help me draw her out?"

"Of course. You are not afraid? Of those who hate her Family?"

Her smile was infectious. "I do not fear, Lia. It does no good. First, my brother is a wickedly good swordsman. He trains every day, never satisfied with himself. Second, Muirwood has two hunters instead of one. And third, one of my Gifts of the Medium is the Gift of Warning. I have a sense for trouble before it happens. It is true. When I was a little girl, I was playing in the gardens. Two shepherd boys who worked our estate thought it would be silly if they tripped my ankles with their crooks. In my mind, I could hear their thoughts and felt them sneaking up on me, though I could not see them. When I glanced back and caught them in the act, I ran screaming to my brother."

"Did he lose his temper?" Lia asked, eager to hear the story. *This is dangerous,* she thought. *Marciana can tell me stories of his childhood!*

"He was all of twelve years old, but he acted like he was one and twenty. He warned those shepherd boys. He always warns first. You like hearing stories about him? Good! There are many he would not want me to tell you. And you must tell me your stories, Lia. I want to hear them. I want to know you better. I am jealous of Sowe that she knows so much about you, but she is too loyal to you to share anything interesting. From what Pasqua has said, you were a very naughty child. But you and I are alike, I think. I hope we can be friends?"

"Lia! It is almost gone!" Pasqua said. "Hurry over lasses, or you will miss it."

"Here I am, stealing all your attention when you are probably starving. Come over and eat. We have the Aldermaston's permission to be with you."

Lia joined the others, and Edmon approached gallantly with a spoon for her. "It must be excruciating torture for you to live in a kitchen like this with such an excellent cook. And she has taught you all her secrets, has she?"

"It has been a year, but I have not forgotten them all yet," Lia said, tasting the Fool and enjoying it. It was always a favorite of hers. "You should try her sambocade, too, Edmon. That will make you drool on yourself."

"Posh, lass. Do not be making any promises to him for me," Pasqua said. "When Whitsunday comes, he will get his chance to taste it all. If he can stop dancing, that is."

Edmon rubbed his hands together. "I must be a fool, but I have always enjoyed ring dances like the maypole one they do here. It never took much coaxing to get me to try it. And with such lovely partners as all of you make, it would have to be a tempting display of desserts to draw me away." He bowed his head dramatically to each of them, smiling like a blazing candle. "I hope you will all save a dance for me. You included, Pasqua."

"Me? Dance on Whitsunday?" Pasqua chided, beaming at the handsome young man. "When pigs fly, lad. When pigs fly. But I will save you some sambocade for the kind words."

His gallantry reminded Lia of what Astrid warned her of earlier. "I would like to see the look on Getman's face when you ask Sowe," Lia said softly after another spoonful.

Sowe's eyebrows crinkled, and she looked at Lia curiously.

"Who is Getman?" Edmon asked.

"He is the blacksmith's helper," Bryn said. "Strong as an ox, but he is rude and jealous. Everyone is afraid of him except for Lia and Sowe. Lia hates him...well, maybe that is too strong, but she cannot abide his company, and everyone knows he dotes on Sowe."

"He does?" Edmon asked, appraising Sowe again. "And you consider him as well-mannered as a surgeon's leech?"

Sowe grinned, and they all laughed.

"He is that obnoxious then?" Edmon said. "Well, if dancing with you will spite him, I will gladly risk his enmity. Even if he is as strong as an ox. Probably reeks like one as well."

Lia liked Edmon immensely. He had a boyish charm that was disarming. "It will definitely thwart his plans. You see, Astrid told me today that Getman promised he would thrash anyone who dances with Sowe except for him."

Edmon glowered. "Did he now? Well, that is no surprise considering Sowe's great beauty," another bow to her, "But surely only a knave would deprive his fellows like this. Where can I find the great boor? I think Colvin and I will have to kill him. Or at least cut off an arm or a leg. Could he still work as a blacksmith with a stump, do you think?" He performed the impression of a man with a gimp and had everyone roaring with laughter. Except for Colvin, who constrained his expression to a smirk and said nothing. When Ellowyn noticed that he was not laughing, she stopped, too.

"I, for one, will not be intimidated," Edmon declared, gazing at Sowe. "Let him bluster, but he will not deprive me of the opportunity of dancing with you on Whitsunday. Unless you would rather I not dance with you." His eyes grew more serious, more focused, as if willing her to say the words.

A little smile came on Sowe's mouth. "I would like that," she said, then looked down at the bowl, her cheeks flushing.

"I have witnesses then to your consent. You will vouch for me, Ciana? Ellowyn? Lia? Bryn? What a selfish oaf, claiming you for his own."

"Pasqua," Marciana said. "Lia needs to eat something. Where was that plate you were saving for her?"

"I had forgotten, child. It is over by the oven. No, the other corner. Edmon, stop torturing the poor girl with flattery, and fetch a sack of flour from the loft as I asked you when you arrived. Be quick, lad, it is getting late, and I must escort you back to the manor house soon."

Marciana tugged on Lia's arm and led her to the oven. "You must be starving, but I do not want to waste a moment with you. There is your meal." As they approached the oven, Lia saw the Leering near it and felt a prickle from the Medium. The eyes glowed red, giving off heat into the oven. She had not done it and glanced at Marciana.

"Not as impressive as what you can do," she whispered, seeing Lia's look.

Lia took the bread, looking over her shoulder at Sowe and then at Colvin, who was talking softly to Ellowyn. "Colvin taught me so very much," she answered, memories flooding her. "You are lucky to have him as a brother."

"Instead of Edmon?" Marciana asked wryly. She gave Lia a knowing look. "Who is handsome and gallant, but…how can I say this tactfully—he is also very shallow. His moods flit from this to that so quickly. Colvin is steady. That is what I admire in him. Poor girl, Edmon already has Sowe dazzled. Warn her when we are gone. He means well, but he craves attention. He is uncomfortable unless everyone is laughing at something he has said, or unless the pretty girls are blushing and dizzy with giddiness. He knows he is handsome, poor devil. Warn Sowe about him, Lia."

"Warn her?" Lia said, grabbing some fruit from the plate. "He would never do anything dishonorable, would he?"

"He is not dangerous or vicious," Marciana said, rolling her eyes. "No more than any man is. He would never dishonor her. How can I put this? As Colvin has always told me, we are slow to believe that which, if believed, would hurt our feelings. He would never deliberately *try* and make her love him and then scorn her. But he may do it inadvertently. Warn her of that. He pretends more than he feels. Having spent a year with him, I have grown weary of his little gallantries. Sowe will probably be as well after she has gorged on them as I have. Look at how she reacted a few moments ago. Whether they give or refuse, it delights a woman just the same to have been asked. She was delighted. You could see it on her face as well as I could."

Lia looked at Marciana probingly. "You observe people."

Marciana offered a twisted smile. "I ignore most people. But there are some I pay close attention to. Having been born in a Family under such circumstances as I was, you cannot blame me. My mother died giving me my life. Ellowyn and I have that in common. My father never married again, he loved her so much. That is the kind of love I want. The kind I want for my brother. So you see, my gift of observation, if I have any, is only about those who toy and flirt and scheme and envy and stumble in a thousand ways to fall in love. And in the last two nights of being here, I have seen all the subtle clues that exist in Sowe. Warn her, Lia. He is a knight-maston and an earl. But he is also a man with a heart and is easily distracted by beauty. And she *is* a beauty."

Marciana gazed at Sowe for a moment, then turned back to Lia who took another bite from the bread. She nearly choked on it when Marciana said, "So who is this boy you care about? The one you had promised to dance with last Whitsunday! When you were lost in the swamp, Colvin told me you regretted that you would miss the maypole dance because of this boy. What is his name? Is he a learner? Do you still like him?"

CHAPTER EIGHT

Jealous

The only people Lia had ever truly been jealous of during her life were those who came to Muirwood to learn how to read and engrave. The embodiment of that jealousy became Ellowyn Demont. She was like an uncertain dancer at the maypole, watching and imitating everyone else, but always a skip and a twirl too late—one so preoccupied with getting the moves right that the shuffling steps could not be referred to as dancing. Lia's thoughts were cruel, and she recognized that. The problem was that she could not help herself. The deeper problem lay in the fact that she was jealous of Ellowyn for another reason as well. The nub of it—Colvin's constant attention to her.

When he was wounded and hidden in the kitchen, they had argued about Lia's outspokenness and her ability to keep secrets. Colvin had praised Sowe's shyness and reserve as qualities worth admiring. She remembered the conversation vividly. Ellowyn was that kind of girl. The deference Colvin paid to the Demont girl was obvious, tender, and—truthfully—infuriatingly sensitive. Every time she watched them together, it made her ill. The feeling was so strong, sometimes she wondered if she needed valerianum tea to calm her stomach. She understood the emotion. It was jealousy, and it tormented her.

For example, after a visitor arrived from nearby Wells Abbey, Lia was commanded by the Aldermaston to speak to Ailsa Cook about a meal. She spied Colvin and Ellowyn together near the laundry, deep in conversation. Colvin looked animated, his hands gesturing. Ellowyn was completely engrossed, taking in his every word as if it was honey. The feeling in Lia's chest was so powerful, so painful, she went another way, afraid she would be noticed, that the Medium would betray her thoughts to him. How humiliating that would be!

The evenings in the kitchen were especially difficult, and she found herself coming back later and later. The talking and laughing were enjoyable. But it was as if her private domain had been intruded upon, that the kitchen was no longer her refuge but theirs. Every night, Marciana wheedled more information from her. Every night, she did everything she could not to stare at Colvin too much, to keep Marciana from suspecting that something was wrong. Sowe and Bryn had grown closer over the year, making Lia feel as if her place was usurped. The depth and intensity of her feelings were so strong, she began worrying that the Medium would stop working for her altogether.

A week passed since Martin had left. She missed him and his surly advice, his bluff manners. He was always practical, always one to force an issue, never hide from it. He would cut to the quick. What was tormenting her? What was it that truly bothered her? She pondered the question, seeing Martin's scrunched up eyebrows, the angry jut of his jaw. Was it that Colvin was treating Ellowyn with respect when he had treated her so angrily? Did she fear he was forming an attachment to the girl? Was that it? That they would marry? The nagging thoughts were subtle—quick to dodge her attempts at confining them so easily. It was not knowing *Colvin's* thoughts that bothered her. Was she seeing too much in his deference to Ellowyn? Was his politeness no more than that? In the Cider Orchard, she had assumed he felt contempt for the girl. But his manners belied any trace of it. How she wished the Medium would let her see into his mind again!

"Lia, wait up!"

She was so engrossed in her thoughts that she had not seen Duerden's approach from the duck pond. He hefted his tome in one hand and arranged the flap of his leather bag so he could stuff it inside. He had grown in a year, but still barely came up to her nose.

"Hello, Duerden," she said, slowing her pace so he could join her.

"I was…hoping I would find you about today," he said, bringing the bag strap around his shoulder. "I can see you are in a hurry. I will walk with you. I do not want to keep you from your duties."

That was thoughtful. She liked that about him. "I was on my way to Martin's lodge. Are you finished with your studies for the day?"

"I am. Do you mind the company?"

"No." As they started walking toward the western grounds, Lia noticed him fidgeting. "What did you learn from the Hodoeporicon today? You are still engraving it?"

He nodded excitedly. "I am hoping to finish engraving before Whitsunday. I have been burning through dozens of candles at night to work. The other learners think I am daft, but I would really like half of it scribed before I finish this year."

"Any sage bits of wisdom from it?" she asked playfully, bumping into him to knock him off balance. He staggered a bit, grinned, and kept up with her.

"Several. From today—you will like this one. 'A burden which is done well becomes light.' Another good one. 'He who is not prepared today, will be less so tomorrow.' Every learner should be forced to memorize that one. Rather obvious." He started fidgeting again. She could tell he had been rehearsing. "My favorite from today was this one—'What is allowed us is disagreeable, what is denied us causes intense desire.'"

The truth of that statement burned in her mouth. It was so true. Her craving to read was only made more desperate by the Aldermaston's refusal to let her. Would she find as much pleasure in it, were it suddenly given? She hoped so. "Why Duerden, have you been *practicing* that one all day?"

"I just…I thought you would like it, Lia," he said, stammering. Sweat glistened on his forehead. The day was cool. She wondered if he had shared it with any of the other girls. "Have you heard the Queen Dowager is coming to Muirwood? What do you make of it?"

Lia kept her eyes on the trees ahead, keeping the pace steady. "I know she is coming, but I do not know much about her, really. Actually, I do not know *anything* about her. I imagine she is very old?"

"No, she is young," Duerden replied. "She is eighteen, I think."

Lia stopped, staring at him. "Reome's age?"

"The old king's first wife died when we were children. I was eight, I think. I remember when it happened. Three years after her death, he married the Pearl of Dahomey of the royal house of Mondragon. *Pareigis* is how you say her name in Dahomeyjan. Most call her the Queen Dowager. That means the young king is only slightly younger than his stepmother. She will surely marry again, as they had no children together."

"That is disgusting," Lia replied, cringing at the thought. She started walking again, and he followed. "How old was the old king when he married her?"

Duerden looked puzzled and thought quickly. "Nearly sixty, I think. She was fifteen when they were married—our age. Yes, he was an old man when he was murdered."

The accusation stung her conscience. It always made her angry when he doubted the truth of what happened at Winterrowd. "He was not murdered, Duerden. He died during a battle."

"That is not what I heard," he replied skeptically, ducking beneath an oak branch as they crossed the row of trees. "I am not certain there even was a battle at Winterrowd."

It was just at that moment, crossing the border of oaks, that she saw Colvin. Beyond the screen of trees on the other side of the duck pond was the hunter's lodge. Just to the west of it grew a field of purple mint used by the lavenders for scenting clothes and the apothecaries for remedies. She saw him crouching amidst the flowers, with a stem broken off in his hand. As they had not concealed their approach, he lifted his head and rose when he recognized her. He started toward them, and her heart hammered with surprise. There was no sign of Ellowyn.

"That is Colvin Price," Duerden muttered in awe. "He is the Earl of—"

Lia interrupted, "He is the Aldermaston's guest, and he was at Winterrowd. I think I will ask *him* if there was really a battle, or if…"

"That is impertinent, Lia. He is a stern man, does not suffer fools…"

Colvin twirled the stem in his hand and crossed the maze of purple flowers to reach them.

"I am going to ask him," Lia whispered.

"Lia, do not!" Duerden whispered back.

"Good day, Lia," Colvin said. He looked at Duerden and an expression clouded his face for just an instant. She did not understand what it meant, but she noticed it. "I do not believe we have been introduced," he said to Duerden. "I am Colvin Price. I bid you good day."

Duerden stared at him as if some thunder had exploded in his ears and he could not hear a word.

Colvin waited for an awkward moment, patient.

"This is Duerden Fesit," Lia said, tugging at his hand. "From Fath Court Hundred." His palm was sweaty and cold. "He is the friend I told you of."

Colvin was composed. Duerden looked as white as an eggshell.

"We were just talking," Lia went on, patting Duerden's hand in sympathy. "About all the rumors involving Winterrowd. You were there, were you not, Lord Colvin? At the battle?"

The look he gave her had the sheen of amusement. "Yes."

"Well, Duerden was just telling me that some are saying there was not a battle. That Garen Demont could not possibly have defeated the king's army, not losing a single man, without some treachery. It is said that the old king was murdered. Have you heard these rumors?"

Suddenly, Duerden's mouth was working again. "I was not saying that…what I meant is…that is what some are saying, not what I myself believe. I trust implicitly in the power of the Medium, but for the sake of reason and argument, I cannot vouch for what I did not myself witness, since I was here, as you know… learning." He took a gulp of air. "I apologize for bothering you,

Lord Price. It will not…happen…again." His complexion went from white to green.

Colvin's tone was measured, but his eyes flashed with annoyance. "If I were in your position, I would feel the same. The story is truly incredible. But as Lia said, I was there. I witnessed it. We were outnumbered, surrounded, and had to fight for our own survival. I was one of many knights who earned a collar that day. There was a battle, and the Medium was with us. And it is true—not a single man of our company died, though each of us bears the scars of our wounding. Those of us who were there are…uncomfortable…speaking of it. It was a singular moment in my life. Hence, the whispers and the rumors."

Duerden's mouth quavered. "I pray I did not offend you," he mumbled.

"If you are Lia's friend, you cannot offend me," he replied. "Tell me, what studies do you prefer? Which tomes of the ancients do you scribe?"

"I have read many, but I have studied more particularly the tome of Aldermaston Willibald."

"The Hodoeporicon?"

"That is the one."

"I found it rather tedious. But there is wisdom in it. I bid you both good day."

With that, he gave a graceful nod and started back toward the Abbey. Lia felt a gush of unease, wondering what he thought of them. It was so difficult pretending in front of others, forbidden to reveal that their knowledge of each other went well beyond what anyone expected. No one else *knew* that Colvin had hid in the Aldermaston's kitchen except for a few. No one else *knew* that Lia had stolen the Cruciger orb to find their way through the

Bearden Muir to the battleground. No one else *knew* that she was the one who had toppled the king from his saddle with one of Jon Hunter's arrows. No one except the Aldermaston and Maderos.

She watched Colvin pass by when he stopped and turned around. "When you have a moment, Lia, there is a passage from the Tome of Soliven you would be interested in. I thought of you when reading it."

A different feeling spread through her stomach—warmth and giddiness. She looked back at him, saw his fingers absently twirling the stem of the purple mint.

"I have an errand to run for the Aldermaston at the Pilgrim first. When I return, I will find you."

He nodded and went back through the trees.

Duerden let out a pent-up breath. "He is…intimidating. Like the Aldermaston."

Lia smiled at the description. "He is just a man, Duerden. Like you will be when you finish learning at the Abbey."

He shook his head. "I doubt it, Lia. I doubt it." His expression soured. "I do not think I will ever be that tall."

Just as the lamp burns bright when wick and oil are clean, so is it with our minds. All things can corrupt when minds are prone to evil. A soft word of praise benignly intended can wreak havoc on one whose ears itch to hear it. So often, we are pulled and strung along by our feelings, led to this mischief and that because we crave a fleeting emotion. Our simmering anger needs but a nudge to flame up and scald everyone around us. Yet when our thoughts are pure, we become a light by which others learn to read.

—Gideon Penman of Muirwood Abbey

CHAPTER NINE

The Pilgrim's Leering

Colvin's presence at Muirwood made it difficult to concentrate at times, Lia decided. She wondered if every casual encounter with him would have such a distracting effect on her. It had just happened with Duerden, and Lia wondered how many more times it would occur. There were words they could not say because they would reveal too much knowledge about each other. He had offered to share a passage with her—an invitation to seek him out. What was it that he wanted to tell her? Imagining the possibilities tortured her.

Normally, Lia enjoyed traveling the tunnels beneath the Abbey grounds. Using a lamp for light, she would make sure the secret entrances were still hidden and free from cave-ins or flooding. She had memorized the passageways and knew all the markers from above ground that would locate them. But at that moment, she did not want to do her duty and seek out Siler at the Pilgrim Inn and relay a message from the Aldermaston. Instead, she longed to be with Colvin, poring over a tome she could not read and learning something clever from him.

She reached an intersection of tunnels and paused a moment, choosing the shaft that went to the Pilgrim. A web of tunnels crisscrossed beneath the grounds, but they exited in only four places. One was the Pilgrim Inn. Another, Maderos's lair. The other two went farther in opposite directions and exited the grounds in the woods surrounding the Abbey. The tunnels were cold and damp, and she had to stoop to avoid the netting of roots that sometimes grasped at her hair. The air was thick with the smell of burning oil and earth.

She repeated the message again in her mind as she approached the Leering that blocked the way into the Pilgrim's cellar. She reached out and laid her hand on the stone, bringing to mind the maston word that would open it. Only by speaking it aloud would the Leering door open.

As soon as her hand touched the rock, the Medium seized her violently.

In her mind's eye, she saw him clearly, vividly—could even smell his onion breath. Scarseth. His fingers caressed the stone Leering, his eyes white-silver. *Open the door*, his thoughts whispered. *You must help me. Open it!*

The force of the Medium stunned her. She started to speak the word, then clenched her teeth shut as it started mumbling out of her mouth. Her hand was fastened to the stone, tethered by invisible bands. The weight of the Medium was crushing.

Say the word! I must speak with you. I know you can hear my thoughts, girl! A year without speech. You can help me! You will *help me! Say it!*

The force of his thoughts crammed into her mind. She feared opening the door. She feared seeing him, smelling him. There was a wild, desperate look in his eyes. He would do anything to get his voice back. He would kill her if that would help. Wave on wave of fear and desperation engulfed her. If she opened the door, it would be over. She would die.

Away from me! she screamed in her mind, shoving back with the force of her will.

The hold snapped, and she fell back on the ground, dropping the lamp and guttering the flame. It was black. Pure black. All around her, she felt the Myriad Ones sniffing at her. The eyes of the Leering burned red, tiny slits in the dark. Warm, wet oil oozed across her hand, and she jerked her wrist away from it. Rising, she stared at the pinpricks of red and backed away from the Leering. The Medium was gone, but she could sense part of it howling after her. She clenched the haft of the gladius in her hand, trembling like a leaf in a fierce wind. She gulped down air, trying to master her fear, trying to keep tears from blinding her. A dungeon shaft was not a place to confront Scarseth.

Where was Martin? As she hurried away from the Leering, she began to worry about him.

***

She found the Aldermaston coming from the cloister, his head bent in conversation with Prestwich. He looked up at her and then stopped, his look darkening. "What has happened?"

"Scarseth is in the cellar of the Pilgrim. Right now," she said, with more firmness in her voice than she felt. "He wears the medallion and used it against me. He tried to force me to open the portal."

For a moment, he looked thunderstruck. He glanced toward the Abbey gates, then back at her.

"Where is Martin?" Prestwich asked, his face florid with anger.

"I do not know," Lia said. "What should I do? I felt him on the other side of the Leering, but I did not open it. He commanded me…he wanted me to open it."

The Aldermaston's face turned as stormy as any expression she had seen on him. "I have felt something…wrong…for days now. My thoughts kept turning to the Pilgrim, which is why I sent you there with a message." He reached out and gripped her shoulder. "You are my hunter, Lia. Go to the Pilgrim, and bring him to me. I must not…I cannot leave the grounds. Not even for a moment. Not even for this. As the sheriff did, he will use the kystrel to make you fear, to subvert your thoughts with his twisted ones. Lia, you are stronger in the Medium than he is." His eyes burned into hers. "You are stronger than anyone at the Abbey. Believe it, for it is true. Go there, and bring him to me. Take the orb with you. It will protect you and warn you. And your weapons. If he will not come…" He paused, his wrinkles furrowing even deeper. "Then bring the kystrel to me. Do not let him roam free with it around his neck. Do what you must, Lia. Quickly now, before he escapes."

"I will, Aldermaston."

Prestwich looked hard at her. "Send someone with her," he said.

The Aldermaston shook his head. "She is enough. Quickly, child. Before the sun sets."

Lia hurried to the kitchen, her heart hammering in her chest. For a year, she had trained with Martin on hunting, trapping, tracking, but more important, how to kill a man. She knew how to hunt men, how to trick them, how to elude them. But this time it was real. Her throat was parched, her hands sweaty. Her only comfort was the look the Aldermaston had given her. He was certain she would succeed. That degree of confidence gave her courage. After pulling open the kitchen door, she rushed inside, shocked to see Colvin and Edmon there. Edmon was in the middle of one of his stories and had Pasqua and the girls enthralled. He paused to smirk at her, then went on with his story while she fetched her bow sleeve, a full quiver, and shooting gloves from her chest beneath the loft.

"Lia, have you eaten anything yet?" Pasqua called. "The day is getting late. You must be hungry."

"Later, Pasqua. The Aldermaston asked me to hurry." She pulled the shooting gloves on snugly and went deeper behind the stores of barrels, candles, and tubs of fat. She crouched low, out of sight, tugged loose a brick in the wall, and pulled it free. Behind it was the Cruciger orb in a leather pouch. She fastened it to her girdle and shoved the brick back in place.

"Do you want some bread?" Pasqua said, coming over. Sowe and Bryn giggled at something Edmon said. She offered Lia a stubby loaf, which she took gratefully. "Are you all right, child? I can get some cheese, too, if you give me a moment."

Lia smiled tersely. "More chores. I will be back soon." She kissed Pasqua's cheek and slung the quiver and sleeve around her shoulder as she walked back out and stuffed the loaf into her walking bag.

Colvin followed her out.

She glanced back at him as she started toward the gates. "I will not be gone long. I have not forgotten..." The look on his face made her stop. "What is it?"

"I will go with you."

She shook her head. "Stay at the kitchen, Colvin."

Anger brooded in his eyes. "I am not deaf to the Medium, Lia. Something is wrong. I see it in your eyes, and I feel it seething inside you. What happened during your errand?"

She clenched her teeth. "The Aldermaston said…"

"Hang what he said!" Colvin snapped. "You are frightened and pretend not to be. Can you not trust me with a secret, Lia? As if idling my time in the kitchen will benefit anyone?"

"You are stubborn," she said impatiently. "I do not have time to argue with you. Walk with me. I will tell you on the way."

He matched her stride easily.

"I was to deliver a message to the Pilgrim Inn through the tunnels below ground. There is a Leering…would you stop flinching every time I say that! It is just a Leering! It blocks the tunnel, and only a password will open it. When I touched the stone, I felt Scarseth on the other side. Yes, our friend. He has the medallion I snatched from the sheriff, and he used it to try and force me to open the door."

"Sweet Idumea," Colvin muttered, his face glowing with anger. "I should have killed him."

She gave him a sidelong look. "You may get your chance now. The Aldermaston told me to bring him inside the Abbey grounds. I do not understand why. But if Scarseth will not come willingly, then I must bring the medallion with me. I imagine he will not want to give it up, but there you have it."

"And he is sending you?" Colvin said in disbelief. "By yourself?"

"I am his hunter, you idiot. Who else is he going to send? I am the only one with a sword."

He looked at her as if she were the idiot. "There are two knight-mastons here by my count," he said through clenched teeth, gesturing at his sword pommel. "I am sure you were given excellent training, Lia, but have you ever killed a man before?"

His words startled her. The answer was yes, but she had never told him that. When she thought about it, it made her squeamish and guilty, even though she knew she had done the Medium's will. Her victim was not just one of the many nameless corpses in the battlefield of Winterrowd—it was a king. She yearned to tell Colvin, but it was not the right moment for such a secret confession.

"As I said," he went on, obviously interpreting her silence as proof of his argument. "He could have asked Edmon and I."

Lia gave him a harsh look, remembering that the Aldermaston had charged her with their safety. "But I am strong with the Medium, Colvin. Stronger than you."

"I already knew that, Lia."

They reached the gatehouse, which was opened for them. The streets were full of people and carts, the traffic of buying and selling that Lia loathed so much. The people of the village were rude, and getting ruder still, as they usually did before twilight. A few looked askance in her direction, but she ignored them. Several whispered behind their hands and then pointed at Colvin. The wind scattered leaves and dust, and Lia looked up and saw clouds rushing in from the north. That usually meant a sea storm.

The Pilgrim Inn bustled with stain-splotched travelers and weary helpers. She looked for any indication that something was wrong. Siler was talking to some guests, but waved to her. The children were playing at the main table with the guests, one of which was an older woman who fawned over them. Lia approached Siler.

"Is anything wrong?" she asked him.

He looked at her in confusion. "A storm blowing in, by the look of it. I have Brant up fixing the roof right now. Did you see if he was using a rope? I hate it when he forgets to use a rope. Does the Aldermaston need anything?"

"Is Maud in the kitchen?" Lia asked.

"Yes, I believe so. She was when I last checked. At least I think so. I am not sure."

So Lia and Colvin went to the rear of the inn and entered the kitchen. As Lia opened the door, she tested the air, feeling for Myriad Ones. Maud was by herself, preparing a stew and bread hastily. Maud looked over as they entered and grabbed a tray of loaves.

"Lia!" Her face looked worried, but she brightened. "I was thinking about you a short time ago and worried. Are you doing well? How are Bryn and Pasqua?"

Lia looked around the kitchen, searching for anything out of place. "Why are the children playing in the common room? They normally play in here."

Maud's face clouded. "They do not want to play in here anymore."

"Is something wrong, Maud?"

She bit her lip. "No, not really. It is just…well, I told Siler we should tell the Aldermaston, but he did not want to trouble him. It is the Leering down in the cellar. It has been acting…strangely. The children are frightened to go down there now. You know children, and how they can imagine things. But even I have been a little nervous about going down myself. It is probably nothing."

Lia shook her head. "It is the reason I am here. Go with Siler, and do not let anyone in. Wait for us. It will not take long."

Maud dried her hands on the towel and rushed out of the kitchen. Lia turned to Colvin and nodded to the trapdoor near the far wall. That trapdoor was the last place they had seen each other before his return to Muirwood. He walked over and pulled on the heavy iron ring, heaving it up effortlessly. Lia walked around the other side, hand on hilt. Colvin's jaw was set—as tense as any time she'd seen him. He drew his blade.

"The cellar is not very big..." Lia started to say. She did not feel the presence of anyone below.

"How large is it?" Colvin asked. He looked nervous.

"Not very large. Shelves and stores mostly. The Leering is on that side," she said. "I will go down first."

But he was already ahead of her, jumping into the pit from the ridge, landing with a thud.

Angrily, she started down the ladder and entered after him. It felt wrong—foreboding. The feeling came from the Leering carved into the stone door, and she silenced it with her mind. After untying the strings, she withdrew the Cruciger orb from the pouch, and it flared brightly, casting away the shadows. Colvin looked behind some barrels and then motioned her over. His jaw was clenched.

From the position of the barrels, a space had been cleared away. There were chicken bones, crumbs, and holes in the barrels, spilling food. Boot prints were all over the floor and milled grain.

"He is not here," Colvin said. "He knew you were coming."

"True, but he does not know that I have this," Lia said, holding up the orb. In her mind, she focused on his face, the image and smells of him that she remembered—scruffy chin, bloodshot eyes, the stink of sweat and onions. The spindles on the orb began to whir.

CHAPTER TEN

Storm on the Tor

Thunder rumbled in the distance. Gusts of cold wind knifed through Lia's cloak, chilling her skin. An occasional drop of rain splattered against her face, but the brunt of the storm was still looming in the sky. Her cloak flapped behind her with the wind, as if it would be torn away, so she clutched it at her throat and marched on. Colvin scowled, not wearing a cloak himself, his arms folded tightly across his chest, his look determined.

The orb was clear in its direction. It led them out of town, where she found matching boot prints in the dirt that quickly left the road into the scrub and trees. The spindles and the mashed ridges of dirt both pointed toward the Tor, the lopsided hill that could be seen from the Abbey, the highest point of ground in the Hundred.

"I have a question for you," Lia said, closing the gap between them so she would not have to shout.

"You always have questions," he replied.

"The Aldermaston called Scarseth's medallion a *kystrel.* Is it named after a falcon breed then?"

"You have it right."

"Why is it, though?"

"What is peculiar about a kystrel when it hunts its prey?"

Lia looked down at the orb, saw that the spindles had not changed, and thought a moment. "I have no idea why it would be named after a bird. It obviously does not help him fly. I can see his trail clear enough."

"If you have ever hunted with a kystrel, especially when there is wind ripping at you like this, you will notice they hover and wait for their prey. Most falcons like to soar and then swoop down, but kystrels are smaller, more patient, and they hover and wait. When they find their prey, they swoop down suddenly and quickly." He stopped, shielding his face from the wind, then turned to look at her. "Those who force the Medium to obey with a kystrel tend to be subtle, crafty—wary and watchful for someone's weaknesses before they attack. They are dangerous because of their ability to influence your feelings. That is how the Myriad Ones deceive us. Through emotions."

"Scarseth is good at deception," Lia said wryly. "From the moment he banged his fist on the kitchen door, he deceived me. How he wore your maston sword so that I would think he was something other than a thief. Do you remember that night?"

"Yes. I am struggling with the memories. How the past haunts you. I treated you cruelly that night, and you were only trying to help."

Lia bumped into him on accident when the wind shifted and shoved her. She corrected her footing. "At least you admit it now. I often wondered since what you were thinking at that moment. How difficult it must have been to wake up like that, in a place full of strangers, knowing the sheriff was hunting for you. That you would be killed for treason."

"What made it worse was worrying whether or not I could trust you. I had to make a decision quickly. Were you trustworthy or not? I use anger as a shield to protect myself. You recognize that tendency. Your Aldermaston shares it. I tried to offend you on purpose, to see if you would betray me. When you did not and then saved me from the sheriff's men when they did come skulking in the Abbey for me, I knew I could trust you."

Lia glanced at him. "You were testing me?"

"I had to know, Lia. That was the only way I could find out."

Another gust of sharp wind brought several stinging pricks into their faces. The Tor rose ahead of them like a subtle bulge in the earth, a dome that was bald and looked as if it did not belong with the terrain. That was still the direction the prints were going. It was unmistakable.

"You can see the trampled grass clearly," Lia said. "He is not far ahead of us. We need to catch him before the storm catches us. When we fled into the Bearden Muir, I wish I knew then what I know now. I have slept many nights out of doors since then. I am sorry I was so useless."

"You handled yourself well considering the circumstances. Regretting the past serves no purpose."

The light was beginning to fade as they started up the slope. It would not take long to reach the summit of the Tor. One face of it was far steeper than the other. A bright flash of lightning came from the northern sky, followed by thick crackles of thunder.

"It is going to be a beautiful storm," Lia said, admiring the tremors.

"Only you would call a cold, wet, miserable day a thing of beauty," he muttered, digging deeper into himself as the rain began pelting them in continuous sheets. It came in a rush, surprising them with its intensity.

"It is why I wear a cloak, Colvin," she said. "See if you can keep up."

The two marched up the hillside, following the trail as the rain began turning the slopes muddy and treacherous. Before long, her curly hair was wet and clumped, which kept the wind from blowing it around so viciously. Partway up the hill, she lost her footing on some wet grass and stumbled, planting her elbows in the mud and jarring her knee. She wanted to curse, but Colvin grabbed her arm and helped her to her feet. His touch warmed her. He tried to conceal a smirk at her stumble but failed.

Up they went as the surge of rain thickened around them. She held up the orb, watching in fascination as the rain dribbled down its surface, but the pointers continued to direct toward the summit. Writing appeared in the lower half of the orb. She wiped water from her eyes, staring at the words greedily, unable to understand them.

"It says something," Lia said, stopping. The summit was just ahead, but there was no sign of Scarseth. Lightning lit up the twilight, streaking between the scudding clouds. Booming thunder shuddered in the heavens.

"I cannot read Pry-rian," Colvin said, hands on his hips. He scowled with frustration. "Is it a warning?"

The hunter is patient. The prey is careless.

Martin's words came back to her in a whisper. She stared down at the orb, then back at the summit.

"Why would he not bother to disguise his trail?" Lia asked.

"Maybe he thought the rain would hide his tracks during the storm. How could he know when we would follow him?"

"True, but why come to the Tor?" Lia wiped her face, staring again. A feeling rose from the pit in her stomach. "It is not a good place to find shelter, especially during a storm. There are no trees on the summit, you can see for leagues in every direction. There really is not any place you can hide…up…there…"

She stopped and stared at Colvin. He stared back at her.

"We are outside the Abbey's protection," Colvin whispered.

Lia stared down at Muirwood, seeing small pinpricks of light coming from it as night shrouded the valley. Deception—Scarseth's greatest talent.

"A trap," she said, realizing it might already be too late.

***

They charged back down the hill, struggling to keep from slipping, and Lia wondered if they were being fools. The slick footing, the squish of the mud, both threatened to send them both tumbling to the foot of the Tor with broken ankles or worse. Was their mad run justified? The only sounds were their gasps, fresh thunder, and the hammering of her heartbeat in her ears. The storm only muffled, but did not hide, the sudden thudding of hooves from the hilltop behind them.

"The Abbey is too far!" Colvin said angrily.

"To the woods," she answered. Holding the orb in her hand, she thought, *Guide us to the nearest tunnel!* The orb flashed brilliantly, the spindles turning and pointing to the right.

"Put that away, Lia! They will see it!"

"I need it to find our way! There is a tunnel entrance in the woods over there. An old oak and a Leering guard it. We can cross back to the Abbey underground if we can get there. The woods will throw off the horses, too. If we can…"

The hill dipped suddenly, and her foot met open air before she started to fall, gasping with shock.

Colvin caught her beneath her arms and brought her back up before she twisted her leg. "Careful, Lia!"

She wanted to snap at him, but did not. What she needed was time to pull her longbow out of the sleeve and string it. Every moment in their escape was precious. With the storm clouds smothering the dusk, the darkness would help thwart their pursuers in the woods. They reached the bottom of the hill and started toward the woods at a dead run. Lia glanced back at the Tor and saw half a dozen horses coming down at a gallop. The riders were crazed to attempt it, but that fact only acted as spurs to her and Colvin.

"Hurry!" she called, chuffing. Her heart battered inside her chest, her breathing came in gulps of fire.

A horrible animal scream sounded from the hillside. She had no time to look back, but imagined one of the horses had stumbled and went down. The weeds and tall grass slapped against them as they ran, the rain coming in a torrent. Lightning danced across the sky, revealing Colvin's clenched jaw, his locked expression. The wall of oaks stood in the distance, offering the false promise of shelter. Neither spoke, for it was all they could do to keep their legs moving.

The sound of the galloping closed in behind them. There were no words spoken—no calls or threats. Only the thick thudding of the hooves, the snorts and frothing of the steeds. The silence of the men riding them made her tremble. They were being hunted. No mistaking the intent.

Lia's mind raced with ideas. They were close to the woods. Right now, every lightning flash made them stand out against the grain. Dropping to the ground would hide them for a while, possibly confuse their pursuers, but the woods would cloak their movements better. Earlier, the wind had made her shiver with cold. Now she was sweating and hot, pressing as fast as she could. Colvin barely kept up with her. His face was haggard.

One of the horses screamed again, close enough that she thought it was over. With a final surge, they reached the edge of the woods and darted inside. Lia grabbed a fistful of Colvin's drenched shirt and pulled him after her to dodge between the trees. She led in a twisting pattern to disguise their trail. Beneath the crown of massive oak branches, dripping from the storm, they found shelter from the howling wind. The darkness made running too treacherous, so they slowed. She let go of his arm and pulled the bow sleeve off her shoulder, untied the end and then stopped.

"Thank you," he whispered, hanging his head and bending over, gulping air.

Lia's breath was harsh in her ears as she hurried. She fished the bowstring out and fitted it around one tip, then pressed the bow into a tree root to flex it and fit the other end. After tying the empty sleeve to her girdle, she tested the string and was satisfied with the strength of the pull.

"Keep going, and try to be quiet," she whispered back, walking this time and listening for sounds from those hunting them. Thoughts came quickly. If the pursuers separated to find them, it would increase the odds of being discovered, but reduce the numbers to their favor—two against one. If the pursuers were wise, they would comb the woods like a net, keeping within sight or whispering distance from each other.

A crackle from the woods on their left caused her to slip an arrow from the quiver and swing the bow around, changing their course again. Were they seen, or was it an animal instead? The darkness made it difficult to see beyond much of the trees, the shadows smothering all movement. She could hear the soft crunch of Colvin's boots and bit her lip. Hopefully, the sound would not carry far and reveal them.

With the tangle of woods and their deliberate evasions, Lia quickly lost her sense of direction. She had never tried to find a particular tree in the dark. She could hear the sounds of pursuers in the distance. No one called to each other, just the steady, oppressive crunching of hooves as they dragged the horses into the woods to search.

"I need to use the orb again," Lia whispered. "Help me shield the light." She pulled her cloak tightly around and crouched down in the earth, setting down the bow. Colvin knelt in front of her, so close she could feel the heat coming off his face as it bent near hers. Cupping the orb in her hands, she willed it to guide them. The orb lit up, spindles turning slightly, and she saw it.

In the sprawl of oak trees surrounding Muirwood, a single tree dwarfed the rest. The oak was so massive that its lower limbs, each the size of a tree itself, bent low and rested on the ground, as if it were some multilimbed giant so weary with age that it could only droop. The base of the trunk could be encircled by five or six people, linking hands all the way around it. And the upper branches were so twisted and long and vast that no other tree could grow within its shadow. When Martin had showed her the tree, he had said he had named it Sentinel, after the creature created in the dawn of the First Parents that guarded a sacred tree whose fruit granted immortality. The Sentinel oak was over a thousand years old, Martin said. It was part of the grounds of Muirwood. A part that few other than the Abbey hunters knew existed.

"This way," Lia said, as she slipped the orb back into the pouch and took up the bow and nocked arrow. She knew the path now and went toward Sentinel, keeping within the woods surrounding it.

Lightning flashed in the sky, revealing movement in the trees, men in black tabards with swords drawn, skulking through the grove. Lia bit her lip, wondering if they had been seen. Myriad Ones began sniffing around them, drawn by their thoughts. A subtle whining sound filled Lia's ears. She did not know if it was the keening of the wind or the smoke shapes shifting through the forest. Lia tugged at Colvin's arm and kept moving.

On the far side of the Sentinel, she found the mark she was looking for. A shattered stump, long since razed by lightning and fire. From it she marked the steps to a small gully, choking with scrub and swollen with churning water.

"Down there," she whispered, putting the arrow back and kneeling by the edge. She handed him her bow to keep her hands free and slipped down into the chilly waters in the gully. The waters were icy and deeper this time. Normally, the trickle would barely cover her feet. She reached up and motioned for the bow, which he handed to her and then slipped down into the water, gasping with the shock of cold. Carefully, she waded against the current a short distance and found the outcropping of a hunched tunnel, covered with brush.

She could feel the Leering inside it, emanating a feeling of warning. Even though she was used to it, even though she knew it was there, she could feel it throbbing against her mind, whispering of dangers and evil lurking inside the shadows. Parting the scrub, she poked inside with her bow, feeling nothing. The feelings only intensified. It was dangerous. It was a place of death. Gritting her teeth, she crouched and stepped inside, plunging into pure darkness. Her breath rattled in her mouth as she started shivering again. The tunnel Leering was tolerable during the daylight, but at night, it made her afraid, even though she knew it was controlling her emotions.

Reaching out to quell its warning, she crept forward into the small cave until her hand was stopped by the cool, rough stone of the Leering.

"Here," she whispered, turning back and noticing that Colvin had not followed her in.

I do not need a friend who changes when I change and who nods when I nod; my shadow does that much better. Know how to listen, and you will profit even from those who talk badly. Sometimes silence, at the proper season, is wisdom and better than any speech.

—Gideon Penman of Muirwood Abbey

CHAPTER ELEVEN

Fears

"Colvin?" she whispered.

Silence.

The Leering tangled her feelings, so she quelled it with a thought. A pair of deep-set eyes, with the expression of torture, winked once with blue light. She went to the edge of the opening and felt the prowling swarm of Myriad Ones thickly about. Colvin leaned against the gully wall, sword out, staring up at the woods.

"I hear them," he whispered.

"The door is right here," she said. "They do not know the words, so they cannot pass. Follow me quickly."

His breath was ragged. "I cannot."

"What?"

He was trembling. "I…I cannot go in there."

"It is just a Leering. I silenced it. The fear is not real but warns away others. Come, it will be all right."

He closed his eyes, shuddering. "It is not the Leering."

He was afraid. She could feel it bubbling out of him like a seething stew. Something about the dark, crouched hole terrified him. From the woods above, she heard the snapping of branches, the crunch of dried leaves. Several sets of boots, heading toward them. Stepping out into the gully water, she grabbed his arm, felt the knots of muscles quivering.

She pressed her mouth against his ear. "If they find us, they will kill us. Come, Colvin. The Abbey is just past those trees." She tugged gently on his arm, whispering soothingly. Another crack snapped, and lightning lit the sky again, painting his face with shadows. "This way. Come with me."

Somehow, her urgent whispers lured him into the gloom. Keeping watch on the gully hole, she felt her way farther in, pulling Colvin after her. Her hand touched the stone, and she pressed close against it. "*Eveleth Idumea*," she whispered and felt Colvin flinch at her using maston words.

The Leering swung away from her, filling the air with the musty smell of oil and mold. Deeper into the darkness she pressed, tugging Colvin after her until they were in. Something splashed in the water outside. Lia shoved Colvin ahead and turned back to the hole. A man leaned in the tunnel, his eyes glowing silver, sword in hand. She could not see his expression, just the baleful glow of his eyes, reminding her of Almaguer. She swung the Leering shut and willed its defenses back to life, feeding it with her strength. As the doorway sealed, the noise from the storm and gully vanished, replaced by their harsh breathing. The darkness penetrated to their bones. His teeth were chattering.

She paused a moment, appreciating just how close they had been to being captured—or worse.

Lia set down her bow and tugged open the drawstrings to the pouch. She removed the orb, and it began to glow, illuminating the narrow tunnel. The orb was brilliant in the dark, revealing their mud-spattered clothes, the twigs and leaves and grime.

She sat down suddenly, exhausted. "You are afraid of confined spaces," she said softly, though knowing her voice would not carry beyond the thick Leering. "Sit, Colvin. I tested this tunnel recently. It is safe. Here, share my bread. I almost forgot Pasqua gave it to me." She opened her leather sack and withdrew the small loaf. Twisting it in half, she broke it and handed a portion to him.

Colvin sheathed his sword and slouched against the wall apart from her. He looked pale, streaked with sweat and rain. Reaching over, he took the bread and bit into it, shivering.

"At least your eyebrow is not bleeding," she said, nibbling her share.

It was quiet, and they both ate slowly, enjoying the sweet crust of the bread, the fresh doughy center. After the run, she was starving and normally would have wished for a warm bath, a clean dress, and a table stacked with treats. But a moment trapped alone with Colvin was worth any deprivation. She waited for him to talk, enjoying Pasqua's bread, giving him time to master himself.

His voice was ghostly. "Why is it that you must always be witness to my most humiliating moments," he said darkly, staring at his lap. He sighed, his whole body trembling.

"I thought I was the only one who humiliated myself," she answered. "Give me your hand."

"What?"

"You are freezing. Give me your hand."

"I know it is cold. We should get going."

"Colvin, you are being ridiculous. I would like to explain something to you, so give me your hand."

The third time, he finally obeyed. She tugged off her shooting gloves and clasped his hand between hers. His skin was ice cold. Chafing his skin, she leaned closer to him in the cramped tunnel to share some of her body warmth. “Martin taught me, you see, that when we lose heat in our bodies, it can harm our thoughts. Did you know that? If you are lost and wet and cold, it makes it difficult to think. Goodness, your hand is cold. Give me your other, so I can warm them both.” He obeyed, which surprised her, and she took both of his hands and rubbed them between hers. She had never touched him so intimately before. Being huddled near him, with all the earthy smells surrounding them, was making her light-headed and very warm. She breathed on his hands, and he stared at her, his eyes curious yet guarded. As she chafed his hands, his expression slowly changed. The expression was grateful that she was not mocking his weakness, but seeking to comfort him. The tender look made her swallow.

“So you see,” she said, glancing over at the orb, “your fear of the tunnel was made worse by being so cold. By warming you just a little, you will be able to master that fear again. Like you did at the cellar of the Pilgrim when you jumped right in, even though you were afraid to.” She had finished warming his hands but did not want to let them go yet. She nestled them on her lap and kept a grip on them. “How long have you had this fear?”

“I am ashamed to confess it,” he replied, his voice thick. She could hear every breath he took. He was calming down, the panicked look beginning to fade.

“You can trust me with your secrets, Colvin. I should not need to remind you of that.” She gave his hand a little pat.

He leaned his head back against the wall, sighing deeply. “I have always been cursed with an imagination. Of imagining details that do not exist, but that I secretly fear. When it happens, I cannot stop it. It has been that way since I was little.” He looked down at his knees. “When my mother died, I was young. I watched the Aldermaston lay her in a stone ossuary. I was a child but old enough to realize she was dead. But when they started sliding the lid closed, I imagined that maybe she was sleeping. That after they buried her, she would revive." He shook his head, his expression turning sour. "I had nightmares for days that she was trapped in the ossuary and could not get out. After the first night, I begged my father to check. The look on his face—his grief so fresh." He breathed out deeply. "Ever since then, I have been terrified of being trapped below ground. I thought I had mastered that fear. Until tonight."

He looked at her, then a little smile tugged at his mouth. "Do you remember when you first showed me Maderos's cave?"

She nodded brightly, glad that he was talking to her and not snatching his hand away. That he was *letting* her comfort him.

"You said that you and Sowe would play down with the ossuaries at the base of the hill. You cannot imagine what that did to me. That a little girl would hide in one…deliberately."

Lia grinned. "I never would have guessed by your reaction though," she said. "You do so well to veil your thoughts and expressions, Colvin. I wish I could. People know what I am feeling by looking at my face most of the time. With you, it is always hidden unless you are angry. I always wonder what you are thinking."

"Why wonder when you can ask? Did you not accuse me of that as well? I treated you rudely because I did not know how old you were. You seemed sixteen at least. Nearer to my age than you really were."

"I will be fifteen on my nameday this year. So strange. It was not that long ago—those memories you have. But it feels like ages have passed."

"You said you wonder what I am thinking sometimes. Like when?" He leaned closer to her, his eyes showing curiosity and interest.

It was her turn to feel uncomfortable. "Well. I am probably not supposed to ask, which is why I did not."

"You can ask me anything, Lia."

Their relationship went beyond words. The shared suffering in the Bearden Muir and at Winterrowd gave them a bond that others did not have.

"I wanted to ask you about Ellowyn," she said, looking down. "How you…felt about her."

She glanced up as a lazy smile twitched on his cheek. "You sound like Ciana. She wants so much for everyone to be happy, she is constantly giving her opinions and advice."

"She wants *you* to be happy. Is that wrong of her?"

"Very true. She quotes Aldermaston Ovidius, who wrote a great deal on the heart and the emotions. He wrote: 'Someone who says o'er much I love not is in love.' And so she uses that to surmise that either I have no heart, or I conceal the source of my affection."

"And the truth is?" she asked, looking up at him.

"The latter, of course. As a maston, I recognize that I cannot achieve my full potential—that my *family* cannot achieve its full potential—until I find someone. It is a commitment, you understand, that the knowledge of the Medium must be passed on to a new generation. It is part of the oaths we take, as mastons."

"Why are you reluctant to tell your sister that you care for Ellowyn then?" Lia asked, her heart nearly bursting with pent-up hope. Hoping that she was wrong, that her question would be denied.

His eyebrows bunched together. "Why do you say that, Lia? Why do you think I regard her that way?"

Lia shifted uncomfortably, but kept pressing on because there was no other choice. "I see the way you are with her. You defer to her needs. You are very courteous. I know she is shy, and that suits you. You once told me you found Sowe's deference admirable. So many times, you accused me of not being able to hold my tongue…"

Colvin chuckled softly.

"You find your past insults humorous?"

"I laugh because you have noticed all my particular behaviors, but have ascribed the wrong motives. I will tell you something no one else except my sister knows, and she does not even believe me, though she knows I never lie. But it is the truth." He leaned forward, so near she could feel his breath on her cheek. "I told you about Ellowyn before, that I have known her story practically all my life. I have been in love with the…the…*thought* of her for years. A poor wretched, from a noble Family, living in obscurity in an Abbey. Not knowing who she really was. As a young man, I put a thought into my head that *I* would be the one to find her. That *I* would be the one to free her. I know this is sounding silly to you, but let me finish."

Lia stared at him, swallowing, very aware that she was still holding his hands in her lap. "Hardly silly, Colvin. Go on."

"When I met her at last, when I went to free her from Sempringfall, you can imagine my intense desire to meet her. It was the moment I had been waiting for." He paused, as if lost in the memory for a moment. "I cannot find words to describe to you how disappointing it was. I felt nothing at all for the girl. Nothing. She was kind. Polite. Deferential, as you said. Everything a wretched should be. Not a wife. Not someone I want to share every part of myself with. Someone who wants to read from the tomes, to try and improve herself. To learn languages, to travel. To banter and argue with. I was keenly disappointed, Lia. During the last year, I have watched her struggle with the very basics of her own language. She was not raised in the Aldermaston's kitchen, as you were. Her ability to communicate higher thoughts was very limited. Her thoughts never rose above the mundane tasks of the laundry."

He shook his head, looking down at their hands, still entwined on her lap. "I care for the girl and mourn what has happened to her. She will be a political pawn for the rest of her life. Or murdered because of who her father and mother were. Even if I desired to marry her, and I do *not*, I cannot dismiss that there would be insurmountable barriers to that union. The Pry-rians want her. Let them have her, I say. But because of who she is, because of who her parents were, she will be a prize many will fight over with drawn swords. One of the reasons Demont trusts me with his niece, I think, is because I am not trying to win her for myself."

He looked down for a moment, then met her eyes. "So there… you see? The rumors about our impending nuptials are idle tales and nothing more. But I am sure you already knew that." He squeezed her hand gently, and it made her jolt. Slowly, he pulled away. "We should get back and warn the Aldermaston."

Lia stood and shook off dirt and leaves. "If you ever find yourself trapped in an ossuary, be sure to remember that warm hands help." She paused, wanting to say something but not sure if she dared. "In the kitchen, with everyone around and all the laughing at Edmon's stories…it makes it difficult…to…talk like this."

"I agree," he said and rose slowly, needing to stoop to keep from brushing against the roots. She stuffed away her shooting gloves and unstrung the bow before they crossed the tunnel back to the Aldermaston's manor. Walking crouch-backed the whole way did not make it easy to talk, but they did. She shared with him some of the history of the tunnels and how they had been excavated at the beginning of the Abbey's founding, that it was one of her duties to ensure they were repaired and kept up.

When they reached the ladder leading up to the cellar, she went first, shoving open the trapdoor. It opened into an anteroom, leading to the Aldermaston's study. As she climbed out, she heard voices in the other room.

One voice she did not recognize. A woman's voice.

The Aldermaston's she recognized. "Yes, Queen Dowager. I understand your meaning perfectly."

CHAPTER TWELVE

Pareigis

There was something in the Queen Dowager's voice that was familiar to Lia, and the hint of recognition disturbed her. It was not her accent, her decidedly foreign way of speaking, but the intensity with which she spoke. Words with unspoken loathing lurking beneath, but sugary and soothing on the crust.

"My meaning, Aldermaston? You think you know my true meaning? As you say, I am welcome here but without my servants? Without my, how do you say, men-at-arms? This is dangerous country, Aldermaston. My lord husband was murdered in this Hundred. So you ask me to trust my protection in such lawless lands? Certainly, these times say otherwise. Prudence, as you say. Yes, that is the word. *Prudence.* It would be prudent of you, Aldermaston, to grant my servants permission to enter the Abbey grounds."

The Aldermaston's voice throbbed with anger. "I beg you to excuse me, but I cannot allow that. When I last permitted the king's men to enter these grounds, my hospitality was egregiously violated. You understand full well that these lands do not fall within the jurisdiction of the Crown. Your late husband understood this."

"Then why has there not been an inquest into my husband's murder? To see that those who brought it about are punished severely? It is wickedness to murder an anointed king. Your lack of interest in this matter, as you say, is of great concern to me."

The Aldermaston's voice became raspy. "Only the sheriff of Mendenhall has the authority to investigate the matter."

"What sheriff of Mendenhall? There has been no word from him since he came to this Abbey! He was last seen in Muirwood!"

"Correction, Queen Dowager. He was last seen riding the road with plans of joining up with the king's army, which was converging on a battlefield. In all likelihood, he was never numbered with the dead, or he joined the marauding survivors and is one of them. The young king has not named a successor, and what have I to do with that? I have not seen the sheriff since that moment. To insinuate that he met an ill fate here in Muirwood is preposterous. I must bid you good night, Queen Dowager. Your unexpected arrival this evening has caused added concerns for my cook, as well as those I am responsible for. There are orders and instructions to be made."

"I will not be troubled with your inconveniences. As you say, I am unwanted as a guest at this moment. We are waylaid by a storm, that is all. Our destination is the village of Winterrowd. I travel with my men-at-arms because this Hundred is lawless—a situation that you do nothing to prevent." Her voice sounded dismissive.

"This is an Abbey, Queen Dowager, not a garrison. I have no resources to speak of, nor do I have jurisdiction in this Hundred."

"Then best you remember that, Aldermaston. You have no garrison here. You too are at the mercy of these roving bands of thieves and mercenaries from Pry-Ree. I should be loath to hear of any treachery disturbing the peace of your domain."

His reply was cold and even. "Then we understand one another, Queen Dowager. I bid you good evening. Prestwich, show her to her rooms."

The sound of a door closing and voices heading down the hall could be heard. Lia gently prodded open the antechamber door. The Aldermaston was in his chair, brooding, his face a maze of wrinkles and crags.

"Come in, Lia," he murmured, raising an eyebrow when Colvin followed. "You were unsuccessful in finding Scarseth." It was not a question.

Lia shook her head. "We followed his trail to the Tor when the Cruciger orb warned us of danger. Men on horseback, dressed in black tunics, chased us into the woods. We just came through the tunnels."

"As I feared," he whispered. "There are a dozen of her men-at-arms at the Pilgrim. I have refused them entry, except for one bodyguard and two ladies of the chamber. I dared not let the rest inside."

"With good reason," Lia said. "One followed our trail, in the dark, to the tunnel entrance. His eyes were glowing."

The Aldermaston muttered darkly under his breath. "She has no mastons in her employ. Her husband hated them, too. She comes from a strong Family, from the royal line of Dahomey. Though she is young, she is trained in the cunning of statecraft. Be on your guard with her or any of her servants. They may try and befriend you to learn more about the Abbey's defenses. Be wary. I do not know how long this storm will last, but I need you to be vigilant this evening, Lia. She may try to abduct..."

There was a rapping at the door.

Before an announcement could be made, it opened, and the Queen Dowager entered, with Prestwich looking flustered.

"Aldermaston, I warned her that—"

He held up his hand. "What is it now, Queen Dowager?"

She looked at Lia and Colvin, at their mud-spattered clothing. "I was going to ask for fresh horses for our ride tomorrow. But I am told, as you say, that Muirwood does not have sufficient stables? What guests are these, Aldermaston? More arrivals from the storm?"

"You will recognize the Earl of Forshee, I am sure," the Aldermaston replied, his eyes glinting with anger at the sudden interruption. "The other is the Abbey hunter. They were indeed caught by the storm."

The Queen Dowager looked at Lia, her eyes running from her tangled damp hair to her muddy boots. Lia had never met someone so darkly beautiful before. Raven hair spilled down her back. She wore a black dress threaded with silver weave and a bodice cut so low that it was shocking. She had earrings made of diamonds and ropes of jewelry around her neck and throat, with a large spiderlike medallion showing a family crest set against her pale olive skin. She looked amused by Lia's appearance, her full mouth smiling, but her eyes disdaining.

"A very strange choice in hunters," the Queen Dowager said mockingly. "I had heard he was an old man." Then she looked at Colvin, and a wicked glint came to her eyes. "So it is Lord Price. I hardly recognized you. I have gratitude to be returning in time for the Whitsunday festival. A quaint tradition in this country. I shall look forward to dancing with you."

***

The sunrise came through a break in the clouds, painting the heavens in orange and gold. The thunderheads loomed over the Tor, and another blast seemed destined to arrive shortly after, turning the already muddy grounds into an impassable mess. Lia and Colvin walked side by side from the gatehouse toward the kitchen.

"Thank you for walking the grounds with me tonight," Lia said, trying not to yawn. "Right now, Pasqua and the girls have been awake for a while getting ready to feed all these guests. Pasqua will be in high dudgeon because it was unexpected, and the ovens will be hot. Which means I will get a warm bath. And since she is awake and I have not slept, I will sleep in her bed in the manor house instead of up in the loft." She smiled at him.

"A bed is better than sleeping behind barrels and listening to Pasqua in high dudgeon. I understand you completely."

"Get some rest, Colvin. If you leave your clothes with Prestwich, I will clean them when I go to the laundry later."

"That is thoughtful of you. May I join you there?"

She looked at him. "Washing clothes is not very interesting work."

"But I enjoy your company. I wanted to share something with you as well, if you recall, and preferred to wait until daylight."

The words sent a thrill through her heart. "What about now?"

He smiled. "We are both exhausted. Later, then?"

"Very well. I will be anxious to know what it is. When it comes time for you to move on to another Abbey, you will be tired of me. I have not had anyone I could talk to like this…before. I enjoy being with you." A question came to her mind and before she could think better, it blurted out. "A few days ago, I saw you and Ellowyn by the laundry. What were you talking about?"

He looked thoughtful, his gaze ahead at the sunrise. "The Medium. I tried to explain it in terms she could understand. That the Medium can channel anything—that the Leering nearby could summon water as well as mix with fire to warm it." He looked at her smugly. "So really I was teaching her something that you taught me. I thought that by putting it in a familiar setting that she would understand better—water and scrubbing and purple flowers—that it would help her."

"Did it?" Lia asked, already suspecting the answer.

He shook his head. "She is still so frightened by it. You would make a better teacher than my sister or I. That the power of the Medium is already inside of her, just waiting for its freedom. But the Aldermaston forbids it. He does not want anyone else knowing about you."

Lia was grateful to be spared that. Oh, she pitied Ellowyn's inability to muster anything with the Medium. But considering her advantages—her noble bloodline, her training in languages and tomes—Lia had difficulty rousing much sympathy for the girl.

They reached the manor and parted ways, Lia waving to him as he entered while she went on to the kitchen. Already, the separation from him began to torment her. The memories bonded them together in ways that did not exist with others, not even Sowe. They had shared hunger and thirst, slept on the same prickly ground, witnessed the burning of a grove by a Leering with her face carved in it, buried a man under a pile of stones. They even shared a blood-stained battlefield. There were no forced words between them. No inward questioning about what to say next. And he had something he wanted to show her, something written in his tome. She pulled open the kitchen doors, anxious to clean herself before seeing him.

As she had predicted, the kitchen was in an uproar. The smells struck her like a fist, and she realized how starving she was.

"Another egg, Bryn. Over there—no, over there! Do not be wasteful." Pasqua massaged her left shoulder, looking out of breath. She glanced over at Lia and shook her head. "Look at you, child. The Aldermaston had you out all night in that storm, did he? Another flood, I suspect? And here we have five hundred loaves baking, just like before." She smiled, kneading her shoulder. "We have been busy, but Sowe and Bryn are good girls. They were working before I arrived, and I came early. Let me help you wash your hair. It is a thicket as always. You do not want to look like that in front of Colvin and Edmon. Not my girl."

Lia almost told her that she had spent the entire night walking the Abbey grounds in the storm with Colvin, who insisted he accompany her in case any of the riders entered the borders of the Abbey grounds. She was so exhausted, she accepted Pasqua's help because it would bring sleep faster. She hid the Cruciger orb and stowed her hunter gear and garb, while Pasqua went to the changing screen and started fetching warm water from the kettle.

"You heard about the Queen Dowager from the Aldermaston, no doubt," Pasqua said. "I got a good look at her last night. She is a dangerous one, she is. The cut of her dresses. It is shameful, this being an Abbey. Poor learners will not be able to concentrate at all while she stays. Let me hold up your hair, child. Oh, this is filthy. Like you were crawling through brambles and mud on purpose." Warm water drenched the crown of her head and dripped brown from the muddy ends. With a cake of soap and a good scouring, Pasqua helped clean her hair and neck and talked about the visitors, the food they would serve, wondering how long they would stay, while Lia listened to the chatter from Sowe and Bryn.

It was the softness of their voices that attracted her interest. They were trying not to be overheard.

"I think he will come earlier today," Bryn said softly. "Earlier than yesterday."

"It will likely rain all day. He is bored and likes telling stories."

"You know it is more than that. He likes you, Sowe."

Sowe was quiet a moment. "He is very kind, but he does not care for me, Bryn. He is just friendly. Lia told me."

"That may be what Ciana said, but I have eyes! You should see the way he looks at you. He does not look at me that way. Not at Pasqua." Their voices fell even softer, and Lia strained to hear. "How long was Colvin gone before Edmon even realized it? He enjoys coming here. Being with you."

"Being with *us*," Sowe corrected. "Besides, he is nearly finished with all his maston training already. He is bored."

"I do not think so. And stop pretending you do not care, Sowe. I see the way you look at him when he talks."

"You are acting like you are six," Sowe muttered, quoting one of Lia's favorite sayings.

"And you are not acting like you are nearly fifteen. Sowe, this is the year that the older boys start to notice us. Not the ones our age, but the older ones, like Edmon."

"And Getman," Sowe said softly.

"What I am saying is that you should watch for signs from him. Look for those little clues. He wants to be here in the kitchen instead of in the cloister with Ciana and Ellowyn. That says something. You should see his eyes light up when he makes you laugh. As if he craves it each time."

"You laugh at his stories, too!"

"Of course I do! All I am saying is watch for it. Will he come earlier and earlier each day? How many times will he ask you to dance at Whitsunday? Will we—"

"He will dance with me once. Just like he said. He will ask us all."

Bryn did not sound convinced. "You think so. But I have eyes. Tell me you do not care about him."

"I do not care about him…not in that way. He is an earl, Bryn. I am a wretched. I do not love him. I do not love anyone."

Lia remembered the quote Colvin had taught her. *Someone who says o'er much I love not is in love.*

As the warm water dripped from her chin, her thoughts turned to Colvin, and she winced. It was absurd. It was totally, completely absurd. She enjoyed his company. She had shared with him all those experiences that bound them together in mutual affection and caring. But as she had listened to Bryn's words, she began to wonder if she had been blind. Was Colvin telling her things with his eyes that he dared not say with his mouth? There were many hints. He found Ellowyn's quiet demeanor attractive in a wretched, not a wife. He craved companionship, being equal with a woman. He wanted to spend time with Lia instead. He wanted to meet her later by the laundry to show her something in his tome. Just the thought of it sent a crushing feeling inside her chest. She could not wait until the afternoon.

You can learn from anyone. Even your enemy.

—Gideon Penman of Muirwood Abbey

CHAPTER THIRTEEN

Earl of Dieyre

The rains paused midmorning, but thick thunderheads shrouded the grounds and smothered sunlight. Thunder rumbled ominously. There was so much commotion in the manor house with the guests and retinue that Lia's sleep was interrupted many times. Tiredly, but with excitement, she made off toward the laundry to get away from the noise. She was surprised to find Colvin already there, twirling a stalk of purple mint, eyeing its color, and breathing in its scent. He rose from the bench when she arrived.

"With the harsh weather, everyone is indoors," he said with a frown. "Did you sleep?"

"Not well," she confessed, summoning the gush of steaming water from the Leering with a thought and setting the basket down next to it. "I have always been a light sleeper. The slightest little noise wakes me."

"Someone dropped a platter of dishes," Colvin said. "I tossed after that and finally came here to listen to the rain."

Lia withdrew his shirt and dunked it in the trough. She remembered the last time she had washed one of his shirts, and the memory made her swallow against the tingle in her chest. "You seem fascinated by our purple mint. You were roaming in the herb field yesterday."

"I intend to have a bush sent to my manor at Forshee. This is a different variety from what grows in my Hundred. Like the apples…there is something unique about Muirwood."

Lia scrubbed the shirt against the ribbed stones and smacked it with a cake of scented soap. "Is it much different from Billerbeck Abbey, where you studied?"

"There is not much to compare," he said, coming up behind her. He stared at the giant Abbey with a look of awe. "This is the oldest Abbey in the realm. Billerbeck was finished in my grandfather's time. We do not have the rich history. Each kingdom has an Abbey of prestige. I am proud that ours is so…humble. It is not as ostentatious as Dahomey's."

Lia wrung the shirt, rinsed it, and wrung it again. She wanted him to tell her what he had been saving, but decided to draw out the conversation. "To be honest, I do not even know where Dahomey is. The Queen Dowager is from there, but that is all I really know about it. And that the word *gargouelle* is from their language."

"I am proud that you remember the word still. There are dozens of other kingdoms beyond our shores. Hautland. Paeiz. Mon. Dahomey is south, but we are separated by the sea. Our two kingdoms have fought for many generations, but now is a season of peace because of the old king's marriage of Pareigis. It is likely the young king will marry her niece to extend the alliance. The marriage negotiations are underway, though she is still quite young."

Having finished the shirt, she started on her soiled clothes. She thought it interesting he wanted to discuss marriage. "Is it true the Queen Dowager was only fifteen when she married the old king?"

"That is not an uncommon age for girls to marry."

Indeed, Lia thought. She spoke aloud, "Yes, but not to men so old. Or do they? It seems that in most of the marriages that I have seen here at Muirwood, there is not such an age difference."

"You have seen an Abbey marriage?" he challenged in a bemused tone. She could not discern his expression, nor mistake the tone of interest.

"Inside? No, never. The only time I went inside the Abbey was when I rescued you from the Pilgrim."

"You are not allowed inside..."

"Obviously it was not with anyone's permission, Colvin. The orb led me there because of the tunnels beneath the grounds. Which is how I found you and made it past the sheriff's men. There was a room lower down, with rows of benches and a stone table. The Medium was very strong in there."

"Speak no more of it," Colvin said, looking at her with the twist of a smile, as if he could hardly believe what he was hearing. "It is forbidden for someone who is not a maston to enter. Or at least someone who is trying to become one."

"So you cannot teach me what it meant? Those benches, the table?"

"Do not ask it of me."

"Is that why many girls do not become mastons? Because they marry before they finish their studies?"

Colvin folded his arms, looking into the distance. "Yes, it happens often. My sister swears she will be a maston before she marries, though."

Lia squeezed the moisture from the sodden mass of clothes, glanced sidelong at him, and then started cleaning it again. "She chooses this to please you?"

"Being the sister of an earl, she would be an advantageous match to any man of rank. If something happened to me, she would inherit my earldoms. Many of her suitors seek to hold her hand and shed my blood. But she has told me that she will marry a maston, and I am proud of her decision."

Lia laughed softly. "A maston would be less likely to want you dead. Do you have anyone in mind for her?"

"Why are you curious to know?"

"Is it Edmon?"

Colvin smiled at the suggestion, and she could see in his eyes that it was well off the mark. "You do not think she would be happy with him, do you?"

"She is trusting you with her happiness, Colvin. What sort of man would you consider for her then?"

"She is a second-year learner. I have not begun to search in earnest."

"That is not what I asked you. What will you look for?"

He was quiet a moment, his expression grave. "Lia, now is not the right time or…season. The kingdom is on the brink of civil war again. It could arrive at any moment. As long as Demont's influence holds sway, there will be peace. But these are dangerous times."

She continued with the laundry, glancing at his face, at the worry crinkling his eyes. "Tell me more."

"I do not wish to frighten you."

"I am not frightened, Colvin. The world is so vast. This kingdom is so vast. Help me appreciate some of the burdens you carry. Is it about the Blight? Is that why the season is not right?"

He looked at her for a moment, then nodded. "It is happening throughout the kingdoms, and not just ours. We do not know what shape or form it will take, but the Aldermastons all fear it will be devastating when it comes. A Blight greater than any other that has come before. Often, it takes the guise of war, but this time might be different. At least my Aldermaston believes so. The rulers of the kingdoms are not listening to the Aldermastons. It has been many years since a king-maston graced the throne of any kingdom. Even our current king does not have the inclination, the patience, or the humility to study and earn the rank. He wants to be a knight, not a maston. So the threat of the Blight grows, and those who lead men because of their birth are blind to it."

"I do not understand."

"The Leerings are all beginning to fail. And with them the protection they provide. There are students in Billerbeck who cannot command them at all. It requires even more strength of will now, to make one obey. Not here, not in Muirwood. But at other Abbeys it is different. It is a sign that trouble is coming, and devastation awaits us in the future. Rather than acknowledging it, there are many leaders who are focusing on power and land and wealth. The biggest one right now is the Earl of Caspur. Have you heard of him?"

Lia thought a moment. "I have heard the Aldermaston mention him. He has come here before, I believe, years ago. He is the richest earl, is he not?"

"And the most arrogant, the most greedy, and the most powerful magnate of the realm. He does not lack for lands, honor, wealth, or inheritance, but he is fighting Demont, demanding more grants of land and refusing to reconcile. On his side are the earls of Werrick and Andrel. We hear they are raising an army to fight Demont for custody of the king." His face twisted with disgust. "They want control of the king to add to their possessions and wealth. They are resentful that the patronage is now under the domain of a man who is honorable and…"

A voice interrupted from the rain. "Mother of Idumea, Forshee, I cannot believe you are trying to woo the girl with boring political tirade. Let her alone already. You are completely bewildering her!"

The man behind the voice appeared from the walk, his mantle wet with fresh rain, his hair damp. He was Colvin's age and bearded around the chin only, his face handsome yet sardonic, as if he found the entire world a jest that only he understood. His hair was long, his tunic studded with twinkling gemstones. A sword was belted at his waist, but it bore no maston symbol.

On hearing the intruder's voice, Colvin stiffened, his eyes turning with recognition and shock to the newcomer, who joined them to get out of the rain.

"I apologize lass, for the Earl of Forshee's bad manners. Here you are performing labor for wages, and he is blabbing on about such idle things. Really, Forshee, you have no common sense. Girls love being flattered, not preached to."

Colvin's jaw tensed with anger. She recognized it also in the pale sheen of his eyes—tightly controlled anger, murderous anger. "*What* are you doing at Muirwood, Dieyre?"

"I am with the Queen Dowager, simpleton, obviously. I ride with her to investigate the old king's murder. I am her protector in these lawless lands."

"The old king was killed in a battle, Dieyre. Leading an army of superior forces."

"You were there, so you would know. All we have to believe is that mastons never lie." He chuckled with an edge of mockery in his voice. "I do not need to ask why you are here. Tending

Demont's little kitten? Or did you find some wise speck to scrawl in your tome that you missed in Billerbeck?" He looked down at the tome near where Colvin had sat. His gaze turned to Lia. "We studied together there, lass. We have known each other a great long time and cannot stand each other. I apologize if he is boring you."

Lia squeezed the garment hard, wringing it out. For a moment, she could think of nothing to say. Colvin was flustered and angry, his hand slowly clenching, as if he wanted to draw his sword.

The words came to her with a flash of insight. "It was rude of you to interrupt our conversation," Lia said, looking him in the eye.

Her bluntness took him aback, and he looked at her in surprise, then laughed. "Why, that was my very intent, lass. You picked right up on it."

"Is there a reason you are walking the grounds right now?" Lia asked, twisting the clothes again to get the rest of the water out. "In the rain?"

"I was looking for the Aldermaston's hunter, actually," he said, gazing at her with an amused smile. "I was told to look at the laundry, but that is…"

"Exactly where you found her," Lia said, standing. "What can I do for you?"

He looked shocked, then pleased and burst out laughing. "That makes slightly more sense that you should be discussing politics with Forshee instead of haggling a fee for bathing him… or his clothes. I completely misjudged you. Here I thought you were trying to woo a lavender girl, Forshee."

Colvin's eyes went flat with hatred.

"Easy, Forshee. I am only jesting."

"Are you?" Colvin asked softly.

"When am I *not* jesting, that is the better question! As if you would ever woo a girl. Well, lass—my pardon for interrupting then. I had heard the hunter was short and bearded. My information was obviously very wrong, because you are quite tall, and you do not, in fact, have a beard."

The way he said it struck Lia as witty beyond words—more amusing than anything she had heard come out of Edmon's mouth since he had arrived at the grounds. It took deliberate focus not to startle with laughter. She swallowed. "If you know a cure for being tall, I am glad to hear it," she said.

"Another clever retort," he said, complimenting her. "My, you are a surprise. So, my purpose for trudging out in the muck was to find another way to humiliate and infuriate the Earl of Forshee, which I have mostly succeeded in doing, and my second purpose was to seek the Aldermaston's hunter and tell you that the Queen Dowager would like to hunt in your grounds later this day. The roads are too wet to ride, and Winterrowd is terribly far away, so we are postponing our departure by a day. Shall I advise her of your coming now? Or when you are finished bathing the earl…?" He paused for effect, "The clothes, I mean?"

"I must ask the Aldermaston first," Lia said, rising.

"Of course you must," he agreed, smiling. He turned back to Colvin. "Is Norris-York here as well? Good. Did you hear that Caspur offered me one of his earldoms if I take his side?"

Colvin shook his head, his face still livid. "He would never give one up willingly, Dieyre. He is just as likely plotting to take yours as he is to give you one."

"He does not have an heir, you see. And neither do you, and neither do I. Well, no *legitimate* heirs, that is. Interesting. Well, I will dismiss myself back to the rain then. I will tell the Queen

Dowager you are coming later. The hawks will not like the rain, so all we will need is a sturdy bow."

"If the Aldermaston allows it," Lia answered, nodding to him.

Another smile twitched on his mouth. "No one denies the Queen Dowager what she wants. Not even him."

He went back into the rain, walking hastily away. Colvin and Lia stood under the shelter, listening the rain tap on the damp shingles.

"That was the Earl of Dieyre," Colvin said softly, seething, staring at the matted grass his boots had left behind. "The best swordsman in the realm. Of any realm, for that matter."

CHAPTER FOURTEEN

Arrowmaker

Lia sought the Aldermaston first in his study, but Prestwich informed her that he was with the learners in the cloisters. She trudged back into the rain and crossed the murky grounds, adjusting the quiver around her hip and gripping the bow sleeve tightly. The meeting with the Earl of Dieyre had left a swarm of new thoughts, especially related to Colvin. She was struck by Colvin's discipline regarding practicing his swordplay. One night in the Bearden Muir, he said he practiced in case he ever met a better swordsman. *If I hope to defeat a man who has more training and experience than me, then I best drill and drill and drill harder than that man.* He must have been referring to Dieyre.

Another occasion—she recalled his blatant discomfort when speaking about Leerings and what the word actually meant. He had said that a leer was not a look of love, that he had seen wretcheds and knights stare at each other in that way. Another reference to Dieyre and their enmity at Billerbeck Abbey? Dieyre did not wear any of the maston symbols. It seemed an obvious conclusion that he had never passed the tests. Colvin had tensed the moment his voice startled them.

When she reached the cloister, she rapped firmly on the porter door. The porter, Guerney, answered it brusquely.

"It is wet enough to flood and chilly to boot, Lia," he said with a wince. "You are sopping. Be a good lass, and dry off in the kitchen."

"And while I am there, fetch you a tart?" she replied with a grin. "You are a lazy man. Tell the Aldermaston I need to speak with him."

"I will. You can wait indoors here out of the rain, but do not sit on my chair. That would leave a mark on the cushion." He unlocked the door and let Lia inside the small porter room and withdrew a ring of keys. He locked the porter door, then unlocked one of the two gates leading into the inner grounds, exited, then locked it again. Passage within the cloister was limited to the learners and the teachers because of the value of the precious aurichalcum they worked with. A single tome was worth a hefty ransom in gold, which was why only the wealthy could afford to be learners. The ancient tomes of the Abbey were stored in the vaults within the cloisters, behind iron gates protected by keymasters and the porters. Lia peered into the gardens at the center of the cloister, watching Guerney traverse beneath the protected walkway at the edge of the square garden. He unlocked a door at the far end and went inside.

There was a square fountain in the center of the garden, with a Leering in the center in the shape of seven maidens kneeling before a knight-maston. She wondered what it symbolized and determined to ask Duerden if she could remember it later. Within a few moments, Guerney was shuffling back toward the porter gate, shaking his head. His hair was streaked with gray, and he was missing a tooth in the front.

The keys rattled in the lock, and he shook his head, muttering to himself. "On with you, lass. The Aldermaston will see you."

"What?" Lia said, surprised. No wretched was allowed inside the cloister.

"Do not gawk, lass. I asked twice to be sure. He is the Aldermaston. Go on, we do not have all day."

Lia followed him into the cloister, unsure how to feel about the privilege or the fact that she was sopping wet. All her life she had walked by the cloister, staring at its windowless walls. Sometimes, she heard laughter from the garden or the fountain splashing. But she had never ventured inside before. The Aldermaston had never let her.

"Strange days," Guerney said. "That Queen Dowager—she is a beauty, is she not? Have you met her?"

"I did," Lia replied. "She arrived last night."

"That she did. What a stir she is causing. Everyone is gawping at her, especially the learners. She is with the Aldermaston now."

Lia thought that was interesting and felt her stomach flutter with anticipation. "Is she?"

"As if the Abbey is her domain. I do not like her mother tongue, though. Those Dahomeyjan cannot be trusted despite their fair looks. A fair face and a foul soul, is what I think. Like Reome. Reminds me of her."

They reached the inner door to the cloister, and Guerney unlocked the door. "I will let you out when you are done. Blast the skies, there is someone else knocking at the porter door. Cannot folk tell it is raining today? The nuisance. Be a good lass, Lia." He held the door for her as she entered and then shuffled back the way they had come.

Lia stood at the threshold of the study room and was surprised by the shocked expressions that met her. But she quickly ignored the few faces and stared in awe at what she beheld. The cloister was a series of interconnected square rooms that formed a larger square around the garden. Leerings for light were engraved into the stone walls at each corner, the walls and ceiling filled with sculpted friezes and paintings, including the ceiling. On each wall were giant oak shelves, massive and sturdy, with ladders fitted with hooks to reach the higher shelves. The walls glittered with golden tomes, eight stacks high. Interspersed throughout each room were big alterlike tables, also made of polished oak, where learners stood to study the tomes and engrave in their own. How many tomes did the cloister contain, she wondered. How many hundred?

"What are you doing here, Lia?" Marciana asked, suddenly at her side. Lia stared at the walls, the paintings, trying to fill her eyes with the sight of it all. If she had felt jealous simply walking around it, the feeling inside her was keener, more like starvation. The value of the rooms astounded her. The sheer magnitude of it dwarfed her comprehension.

"I know wretcheds are not allowed," Lia whispered. "But the Aldermaston said I could. Is each room like this?" she asked, seeing past the archway midwall into the next square room.

Marciana nodded, her eyes alight with eagerness. "There are far more tomes here than at Billerbeck. I am scribing lines from Ovidius today. A different translation from the one I read last year. Though Colvin is impressed with Muirwood's collection, and that is not easy, he chooses to study elsewhere." She frowned. "Here comes the Aldermaston and the Queen Dowager. I will speak with you later. I am with Ellowyn at that table."

Lia dared not move past the threshold of the doorway, completely bedazzled by the countless stacks of tomes, the glitter of the aurichalcum, the immense collection of wisdom pervading the room. The feeling of the Medium was rich in the air. The collection had been growing for hundreds of years.

"There you are," the Aldermaston said, his eyes intense with anger. "I was just telling the Queen Dowager that it was a foolish idea to hunt today, and here you arrive fitted to weather a storm. It is madness hunting in such foul weather. Madness."

The Queen Dowager's voice was silken. "Your hunter is not afraid of a little wet, Aldermaston. It is always raining in this Hundred, no?" Pareigis was dressed in black velvet still, another design than the gown she had arrived in, with silver trim and a wreath of jewels around her throat. The bodice of her gown was scandalously low-cut.

Lia knew the Aldermaston's thoughts. She could tell by his expression what he wanted. "My lady, I came to tell the Aldermaston of your request, as given me by the Earl of Dieyre. I will go if he commands me, but I would not trust horses in weather like this. And with the mud, we will not get far afoot."

"In Dahomey, we ride in weather worse than this," she said, her voice hardening.

"As I said, I will go if the Aldermaston commands me. But I do not recommend it."

The Aldermaston's eye glimmered. "I agree, Lia. I do not advise it. It is not safe to venture far beyond the grounds now."

"Safe?" the Queen Dowager demanded. "What do you mean?"

"My hunter informed me of riders prowling the woods behind the Abbey proper. They may still be out there. Obviously they could not be your men, Queen Dowager. That would be in defiance of my authority since the grounds extend a great distance beyond the walls, as you well know. They extend out as far as the Bearden Muir. I trust these marauders will move on, but why tempt them with a highborn target such as yourself? It would be safer to remain in the Abbey until the rain clears."

Lia almost smirked at the Aldermaston's subtle message. It was clear to her that he suspected the riders she and Colvin had discovered were Pareigis's men. If she took responsibility for them, he could claim she was in defiance of his authority and expel her.

Her nose flared, and she studied him with a calculating eye, measuring her response carefully. "It is surprising that you trust your defenses into the hands of a young girl, Aldermaston. Should these roving thieves and bandits grow bold, what would happen?"

The Aldermaston smiled threateningly. "You have not heard then, Queen Dowager, of the history of the Abbey's defenses? There is a hill nearby as a reminder of what happens to those who trespass this ground."

"I have heard of that hill…and its *stories*," she replied charmingly. "I do not believe them."

"You may believe what you will. But I would not risk your safety or any of your men's wandering outside the grounds. She does know how to use the bow, after all."

"I imagine she was trained well by her master." The voice was silken but full of venom. She turned to Lia. "What wood do you use for a bow?"

"Ash," Lia replied.

"You fletch your own arrows as well? Or does someone in the village?"

"We do our own."

Pareigis's eyebrows lifted with admiration. "May I see one?"

Lia glanced at the Aldermaston, uncertain what to do. He nodded subtly. Slowly, she parted her cloak and withdrew a single arrow. The Queen Dowager looked at it closely.

"The best fletchers are Pry-rian," she said, turning the shaft slowly, examining the feathering. "The threading ties like this, the way yours is. Are you Pry-rian, girl?"

Before Lia could respond, the Aldermaston said, "The hunter who trained her is. Why do you ask?"

The Queen Dowager's eyes met the Aldermaston, and an impish smile came across her mouth. "My lord husband was killed by a Pry-rian arrow. The fletching was like this."

"Indeed? What an interesting coincidence. There are many from Pry-Ree in this Hundred, Queen Dowager. It is, after all, across the water from us. Traders come and go every day selling goods."

"Traitors, you say?" she asked.

"Traders—those who buy and sell."

"Ah, I see. So what you are saying, Aldermaston, is if I visit every fletcher in this Hundred, I will find others who can make arrows such as this?"

The Aldermaston paused, eyeing her shrewdly. "I presume you already have or you would not be asking that question. What are you suggesting, Madam?"

Her voice fell lower. "I believe you know who murdered my lord husband. Even though you cannot leave the Abbey grounds, you know. Very little, if anything, passes your notice. As an Aldermaston, you are forbidden to lie. But as a wise man, you know how to avoid speaking the truth. That is what I am suggesting. Your missing hunter. You sent him away when you learned we were coming. I *suggest* you did so to protect him."

The Aldermaston's face was hard as stone, but Lia could see the flames of anger in his eyes. Just as softly, he replied, "The cloister is an inappropriate place to hold such an important conversation. We will retire to my study to discuss this further. You are quite mistaken."

Lia heard boot steps on the walkway outside, and then the porter's key jiggled in the lock. As she turned, she stood face-to-face with the Earl of Dieyre. He looked at each of their faces, and then a smirk twisted on his mouth, as if he savored contention. "Please tell me that we are not hunting today. I am wetter than a pup plunged in a moat and do not fancy the treachery of mud."

"The Aldermaston forbids it," Pareigis replied tautly.

"Well I, for one, think he is wise as well as aged. Tell me, Aldermaston. I understand you have a copy of Ovidius here, perhaps even the original tome. Is that true?"

"Not the original, of course." The Aldermaston looked choked with fury.

"I have not read it since my days as a learner. With your permission, Aldermaston?" He bowed gracefully.

"Shall we continue our conversation?" the Queen Dowager asked, her eyes gleaming.

Both were staring at the Aldermaston to see what he would do. Lia wanted to say something, but she had no idea what. It was happening so quickly. There was a reason Dieyre wanted to linger behind in the cloister, and he did not want the Aldermaston there. A glance at Ellowyn's table was all it took.

A thought brushed against her mind. She looked up at the Aldermaston in shock.

Safeguard Ellowyn.

It was softer than a whisper, just a fleeting thought that flitted by and was gone. She was not certain she had even heard it. The Aldermaston stared at her, his eyes boring into hers. Slowly, she nodded, and he looked relieved.

Guerney held the door for the Aldermaston and Queen Dowager and then shut it behind them and locked it. Dieyre was already moving past her, toward the table and Ellowyn Demont.

Wherever there is danger, there lurks opportunity; whenever there is opportunity, there lurks danger. The two are inseparable. They go together.

—Gideon Penman of Muirwood Abbey

CHAPTER FIFTEEN

Billerbeck's Kiss

How does a single hunter, a girl, stop the best swordsman in the realm? Lia wondered as she followed Dieyre into the study room. In her mind, she thought of all the training she had from Martin. She could stomp on his foot. Yank him off balance by clutching his belt or sleeve. A jab to the throat or eyes with her fingers. Her heartbeat surged in her chest, and a sickening chill went through her body at the thought of hurting him. Or *trying* and ending up facedown on the floor herself. She focused her thoughts, crushing the fear that engulfed her. Martin had trained her. That had to be good enough.

Marciana stared loathingly at Dieyre as he approached the table, and she could see by the flush on her face and daggers in her eyes that they knew each other.

"Is that Ovidius?" he said mockingly. "The tome of love, as it is called? Are you not weary of only *reading* about it, Ciana?"

"What would you know about love, Dieyre?"

"Plenty. As I showed you in Billerbeck." He turned his salute to Ellowyn. "So, you are Demont's niece? Not as pretty as I was expecting, given your famous lineage. We are not all equally endowed. It must be the Pry-rian blood tainting you. I am jesting, darling. You had best get used to it, for I am good at little else."

"Hello," Ellowyn said, her face going scarlet with mortification, and she stared at her hands. There was no Colvin to retreat behind.

"I have embarrassed *and* offended you!" he said with delight. "Forgive me, lass! Marciana is quite used to my barbs. We knew each other at Billerbeck, where she wasted far too much time pining over ancient tomes instead of learning about the world."

"What are you doing here?" Marciana said venomously.

"Offending you as well, naturally. We all have talents, it is true. This is mine. I do not have the penchant for reading as you do."

"You never found much occasion to be at the cloisters at Billerbeck. It is a wonder you care to be in one now?" Marciana observed.

"Always ready with an insult."

"You accuse *me* of that?"

"It is a waste of a beautiful mouth to use it in quarreling. Shall I silence you, as I did in Billerbeck, with a kiss? Think of the shock. Think of the lurid stories they would tell." His voice dropped lower, and he stepped toward her.

Marciana's face went ashen. "I bit you then," she whispered defiantly. "You will not steal that from me again."

A little smirk quivered on Dieyre's mouth. "No, I will not steal it. It must be given freely next time. But at least I have the memory to treasure. Especially when I realized you enjoyed it. There is also the pleasant scene of your brother's reaction." He turned and glanced at Lia. "Are you my shadow? Why are you still here?"

Lia stared at him, at his sudden provocation, and then she knew. It was as if she could look into his soul for just a moment. She understood him. "You followed *me* here, my lord."

His eyes narrowed. "You are filthy and soaked."

"So are you. My lord," she added deferentially. "Why did you come here?"

"Are you questioning me?" he asked, his eyebrows arching. A look of anger kindled on his face.

"Yes," Lia replied, moving around the other side of him to force him to twist his neck to see her. She was closer to Ellowyn now. "Your purpose for coming to the cloister? Other than to annoy the learners?"

He looked at her. "How old are you?"

Courage began to seep back into her bones at meeting his challenging tone. "If you will not submit to my questions, then I will not submit to yours but kindly insist that you leave. If you have no reason to be here, that is."

He paused, staring at her so keenly it was unnerving. But she steeled herself and met his gaze, as she had always done with the Aldermaston.

"How much would it cost me to purchase your loyalty?" he asked in a low voice. "Such a maiden as you is worth fifty squires. Maybe a hundred. I know you are a wretched, that you owe a debt of service. But I would gladly take you into my service when your debt is done."

For a moment, Lia was startled, but she did not let it show. She knew his measure. "If you have no business here, then kindly follow me to the door so the porter can let you out."

"You are not to be distracted, are you?" he said, grinning.

"I am a hunter," she replied simply, cocking her head and raising her eyebrow.

"Very well. I will state my purpose before you embarrass me in front of the learners by tossing me out on my ear." He wagged his finger at her. "Do not deny that would tempt you. My purpose then is to persuade these young women both to leave Muirwood."

"Persuade us?" Marciana said, her voice brim with loathing and antipathy. "Or abduct us?"

"As much as I would enjoy trussing you up like a piglet, Ciana, my purpose is as I stated it to be. I have given you my purpose, Hunter, so sheath those glaring eyes, and let me further my cause by asking several questions of great importance." He turned his gaze on Ellowyn. "Your uncle—Demont. Does he intend you to wed the young king?"

Ellowyn's eyes bulged, and her mouth widened with shock. Lia covered her face and sighed.

"*Try*, lass, to control your face. That will never do at court. It will not do at all. Given your blatant surprise, I gather the answer is no. Is he going to hand you over to the Pry-rians then? Those dogs that are baying after you like table scraps?"

Lia's blood flared hot when he called them dogs, but she did not let it show on her face.

"My…my uncle…"

Marciana squeezed her arm. "You do not have to tell him anything, dearest. He is prodding in the dark."

"I swear, I just may shame you with another kiss, no matter how sharp your teeth are," he said with a growl. "Has your brother been practicing his swordsmanship much these days? A good fight would make the most of such tedious weather. This is an Abbey, after all. I am sure they could spare an ossuary for his bones."

"You will not provoke me, Dieyre," she replied, obviously struggling but succeeding to maintain her composure. "Why do you care to know Demont's plans? Ask him yourself!"

"I have, but he is midstream in a river, stuck in a tide pool, and getting spun about so quickly he cannot see his course any longer." He looked at Ellowyn. "If you were wise, you would set your sights on the young king."

"They are cousins," Marciana reminded him.

He snorted. "How many of us are not in some way or another? A decree from Avinion can be easily obtained with enough coin. Think on it, Ellowyn. You are heir to the kingdom of Pry-Ree. A princess by birth, by right of your father. The young king is titular sovereign of Pry-Ree—named its protector as an infant. Idumea's hand, he was born in Pry-Ree, too! You would be a fool if you did not consider it. It would expand his borders and your influence. That is why you should not be here, nor Billerbeck, nor any of the many fine Abbeys in this realm. The sons and daughters of kings study at Dochte Abbey in Dahomey. It does not matter what realm you are from. Your mother could not study there, for she was a traitor's daughter, but her mother—your grandmother—did study there because she was a king's daughter. And so are you, Ellowyn. That is where Demont will send the young king to study, if Pareigis gets her way. And she always does. He does not deserve to be strapped to Demont's side, obeying his whims. Let him be a king!"

Marciana's eyes were veiled. "She is the Queen Dowager, not the king's mother. She has no say over his destiny."

Dieyre smirked. "She *will* get her way. I promise you that. I have said what I came here to say. Just do not linger at Muirwood. Either of you."

"Why?" Marciana asked, her voice betraying a hint of desperation. Lia swallowed.

"I would tell you, but the Aldermaston's hunter is standing too near." He pitched his voice lower, his voice full of intrigue.

"Come see me in my room tonight, and I will tell you. I will leave the door unlocked for you."

"You need not bother, for I will not come."

"You almost sound sure, Ciana."

"I am sure, Dieyre. Go back to your mistress."

"There are so many, which do you refer to?" he asked, smiling broadly. Then rising languidly, he looked at Lia. "Would you escort me to the porter door then? It is warmer out in the storm than in here." He gave a gallant bow to Marciana and Ellowyn and then marched back to the door. Lia rang the bell, and Guerney arrived and unlocked it.

The rain fell in heavy sheets. The fountain basin was nearly overflowing, the surface pockmarked as the raindrops shuddered into it.

Guerney started shuffling back to the porter door, but Dieyre seized Lia's arm and stopped her.

"A warning for you as well," he said in a low voice. "Pareigis has brought a *kishion* as part of her retinue."

"A what?" Lia asked.

He lowered his head, smirking in disgust. "A kishion. Ask the Aldermaston what one is. Be on your guard. He is on the grounds. I have seen him already. He will be left behind when we leave."

With that, he caught up with Guerney without giving her a second glance. She stood still, folding her arms, and tried not to shiver.

***

The Aldermaston's kitchen was warm and smelled heavenly of soup and baked bread. The guests had been served and all were drinking cider back in the manor, except for Colvin, Marciana,

Edmon, and Ellowyn—who lingered with Lia and Pasqua in the kitchen. The other two girls were serving the guests their meal. Lia took another nibble of cheese, pondering the strange tidings she had learned that day. Marciana was pacing, deep inside her thoughts, glancing occasionally at her brother. Lia rose from the bench and joined her.

"I know what you are thinking," Lia said in a soft voice. She noticed Colvin at the other table, next to Ellowyn, was observing them.

"I am brooding." Marciana said with a sigh.

"Let me see if I can arrange the hints. You did not touch your meal. You have not told Colvin about your run-in with his enemy, and you keep looking at the door as if you expect Dieyre to arrive any moment."

Marciana smiled softly. "You are good hunter, Lia. The Aldermaston was wise in choosing you."

Lia shrugged. "You are wondering if you should see him tonight. To pry into his secrets."

Marciana stared at the floor, her face darkening. "You do see through me."

"You are not worried about yourself. You worry about your brother. If you can gain information that will help him, you would do it. But that means putting yourself in danger. You should not go. Colvin would not want that."

"He would be furious if he knew what Dieyre said."

"Which is why he said it," Lia pointed out.

"What do you mean?"

Lia stopped and shook her head in puzzlement. "It is as if he uses the Medium somehow, but in a twisted kind of way. I did not recognize it at first when I met him at the laundry, but he is strong with the Medium. Not in the way you were taught."

Marciana's eyes widened. "Do you think he has a kystrel?"

Shaking her head, Lia replied with a frown, "No. When someone uses one, their eyes glow silver. What I meant by the Medium is he pushes his thoughts at you. He says things to provoke you deliberately, as if he is planting seeds he hopes will sprout. Colvin taught me so much about the Medium, about how it was passed on to him by the Aldermaston of Billerbeck. Dieyre is using the same principles, but toward selfish ends. That is why he asked you to come tonight. He planted a thought in your mind, which will fester and fester until you pluck it out or until you act on it." She squeezed Marciana's arm. "It happened to me when Colvin was hiding. The sheriff put thoughts in my head to influence what I did. He hinted that I was a Demont, that he knew who my father was. He told me what I most wanted to hear, not what was true. Dieyre is doing to same to you. Do not trust him."

Marciana stared at Lia for a moment, pondering. Lia could tell she was wrestling with it. "You are right, Lia. He is using the Medium that way. He has always been a very selfish man. He can be so charming when he wants to be, or angry when thwarted or petty and jealous. He had no desire to become a maston. He mocked the very idea from the first moment he arrived. He never wanted to become one, and I will only marry a maston. There was a time when I believed...that Dieyre loved me. His attentions are flattering. At first, I did not heed Colvin's warning. But Colvin was right. And so are you. You are much alike. You have a way of seeing things clearly."

Lia blushed, glancing over at her brother, who was scrutinizing them with such an intense look that she winked at him for prying on their conversation with his attention.

"Do you really think he wants Ellowyn to marry the young king?" Marciana asked her.

"I do not pretend to understand his motives, other than that he accomplished his desire. He is trying to convince Ellowyn to grasp at that possibility, whether or not it is possible. And he gave you the impression that Muirwood is not safe and that you would be safer in Dahomey, the Queen Dowager's country. I doubt that, for some reason."

"Well, he was not lying that it is a famous Abbey. Dochte is the Muirwood of Dahomey. The princes and princesses of every realm study there. It is a high honor to be invited. It is said that it was founded by Idumeans, that the Leerings left behind can do magnificent things."

Lia was curious. "Like what?"

"You would have to ask Colvin. He is the one who told me. I am not sure I even believe it."

"Give me an example," Lia pressed.

"What he said was that king-mastons who study there become so powerful with the Medium that they…they can command in Idumea's name, and trees obey them. They can bring fruit out of season, for example. Or the mountains obey them or even the sea. Such power…"

Her words brought thoughts to Lia's mind, thoughts so dazzling she could barely understand them. It had happened to her before as Colvin explained the Medium's power. Ideas and thoughts so huge and full of possibilities that her mind quivered with their weight.

Marciana continued, "There have not been many king-mastons in our generation. Most never finish the training because of the responsibilities of state. The regents they leave behind to rule tend to be selfish and disinclined to relinquish power. Long ago, the kingdoms helped each other. Now, they squabble over territory, over privileges and honors, over coin and trading agreements."

"I have one more question for you, Marciana. Perhaps you can help me answer it. What is a kishion? Do you know that name?"

She knew at once that Marciana was familiar with the word. She scowled, her face losing its shine and sparkle. "They are dangerous, Lia. A kishion is a hired killer. A man who murders for coin and guards the secret. They are the opposite of mastons in every possible way. Thank Idumea their kind are not allowed in this realm."

"Thank you," Lia answered, gazing at the door with a spasm of worry. "I need to see the Aldermaston."

CHAPTER SIXTEEN

Xenoglossia

The Aldermaston eased into the chair, wincing as he sat. A stifled breath of pain hissed from his lips, but he straightened himself and then motioned for Prestwich, who looked at him in alarm. "Leave us, but wait outside. I do not want us to be disturbed again. Thank you, my friend."

"Is it still troubling you?" Prestwich asked softly, his brows agitated.

"More so at night. Do not worry. All will be well in the morning. Thank you."

The snow-haired steward did not look convinced, but he obeyed the Aldermaston and gently shut the door. A pent-up breath passed in the hush of the evening. Only the desk lamp offered light. Lia nestled at the window seat, where Martin usually did, and watched the Aldermaston's face, so tired and in obvious pain.

"I am sorry to add to your burdens," Lia whispered.

"You did as you should. Thank you, Lia." He looked at her solemnly. "You do not realize how much I rely on you. Or how much I trust you. Let me see if I can arrange the facts as I understand them. If I miss any, do correct me. The Queen Dowager seeks to lay blame for her husband's death on Muirwood and specifically, myself."

Lia's blood sizzled with anger. "How can she accuse you when it was I?"

The Aldermaston held up his hand. "Let us understand the facts before we discern motives. She arrived at Muirwood earlier than her message indicated. She departs on the morrow for Winterrowd with her retinue but claims she will return to celebrate Whitsunday, which is next week. Martin has not returned. You tracked Scarseth to the Tor where you were ambushed by riders, likely part of the Queen Dowager's retinue. Those riders are probably still in the woods, searching for Martin or perhaps waiting for you to wander out. It is clear they had a description of my hunter before they arrived. The Earl of Dieyre travels with the Queen Dowager and offers a warning to Ellowyn Demont to leave Muirwood, hinting that it is dangerous to be here. He discloses to you that a kishion is part of the retinue, and you have rightly learned that they are hired killers." He stared at his desk. "Did I neglect anything?"

Lia leapt out of the window seat. "How can you sit there so calmly?" She started pacing. "My head is so full! I do not know what to think or what we should do with so many threats. I am at a loss, Aldermaston. Should I take Ellowyn now and flee in the storm? Is there a safe haven that would welcome her?"

He shook his head and gently held up one hand in a calming gesture. "The time is soon, Lia. But not yet. It is brooding with me right now. My feelings tell me we should wait."

"Wait for what?"

"What indeed? For the right moment to act. The Medium will tell us when that is."

Lia folded her arms. "The way the Earl of Dieyre said it, it makes me fear that Muirwood will be destroyed." Just the thought made her furious. It was her Abbey, her *home*.

He smiled sardonically. "Which is why he said it, Lia. Do not trust him, as I warned you not to trust Almaguer. He told you about the kishion precisely because he wanted to put you on your guard. To *make* you worry. It is his purpose for being here."

"Should I not worry, Aldermaston?" Lia said, pacing again. "Who am I against the best swordsman in the realm? Against a kishion? I am barely fifteen."

"You are who you have always been. I told you that yesterday. In this Abbey you are the strongest in the Medium. You have powers of influence, powers of insight and wisdom, and protection that your enemies do not have. You are under my protection as well as the protection of the Abbey. And not just this one, but every Abbey in the realm who stays true to the oaths and covenants that are made here. The Blight has not struck us yet. So remember, child, that there are more with us than with them. Even hosts you cannot see."

"If anything were to happen to the Abbey…to you…" Lia muttered, feeling a surge of protectiveness.

His eyes crinkled. "My fate rests with the Medium's will, Lia. Not a kishion's. Not even the Queen Dowager's, though she would believe otherwise. And so does yours. Remember that. Always remember that."

"What would you have me do?" she asked, looking at him with respect. He had always been so stern. Rarely had she heard such softness in his voice.

"Prepare ourselves to act, as the Medium will soon direct us at the right moment. But it would help us to be wise. The rain will delay the Queen Dowager's departure until later in the day. Many of her servants only speak Dahomeyjan, so they converse with each other in that language, which is foreign to our helpers. Let us change that."

Lia stepped closer. "How?"

"Come here, child. Kneel before me so I do not have to stand. I intend to Gift you."

A thrill went through her heart. Eagerly, she approached and knelt before him. She could feel the power of the Medium radiating from him. His eyes, though red with fatigue, were strong and choked with emotion. She bowed her head and closed her eyes so he could make the maston sign without her seeing. His heavy hand pressed against her head, and a shiver went through her skin.

"Lia Cook," he said in his deep, raspy voice. "By Idumea's hand, I Gift you to hear and understand languages. I Gift you with the ability to speak in any foreign tongue. To be understood and to speak freely. I give unto you the Gift of *Xenoglossia*. May it serve you well in your purpose in life. I also Gift you peace and protection that you will live to fulfill the Medium's will."

As he spoke, the Medium surged within her. She felt it singing in her blood, filling every nook within her. Tears stung her eyes at its familiar, tender presence. The peace of Muirwood descended on her. He finished the benediction and lifted his hand.

Gratefully, she stood and looked at him, feeling a sharp pang in her heart. "Thank you, Aldermaston. I have a feeling that...we will be parted soon."

He smiled. "I feel it as well. Long have I been preparing you for that moment." His voice thickened with repressed emotions. Glancing down, he coughed to clear his throat. "I pray you will forgive me, but I nearly refused another attempt to purchase your freedom. That was selfish of me. I should give you the opportunity to choose for yourself, and so I have."

She paused, looking at him sternly. "I would never serve the Earl of Dieyre," she said.

"No. I would counsel you against that. The Fesit family is coming to celebrate Whitsunday in the hopes of procuring your release so you can marry their son. Apparently, you made an impression on them last year at the dance. They will be arriving at week's end."

Lia's eyes widened with horror. "Duerden?"

The Aldermaston nodded. "It is your decision, Lia. My only request is that when the time comes, you escort Ellowyn Demont to a safe haven. But I will not forbid your happiness. He is a good young man, will make an excellent maston. You could do much worse than him."

"Thank you, Aldermaston," Lia said, trembling with shock as she left.

***

Sowe and Bryn were asleep, the door to the kitchen secured tight, so Lia slept on a pallet on the rush-matting in Pasqua's room, but Pasqua's snores kept her awake most of the night. Her mind raged with thoughts. Duerden wanted to marry her? They had never discussed such a thing before. He had never intimated that it was his desire.

Awake before the dawn, she washed her face with water from a dish, combed some of the tangles out of her wild hair, and then joined the commotion of the manor house that struck earlier than usual. The Queen Dowager was not to be deterred by the rain and snapped orders to her servants to make ready. As the sun rose, her retinue had gathered outside the gates. In a black velvet riding cloak, the Queen Dowager mounted astride a white stallion with a leather harness studded with silver stars. She stared at the Abbey, studying it with an expression of loathing. Lia wanted to spook her stallion and make it bolt. She walked amidst the host and servants, all barking to each other in Dahomeyjan.

"Will the Abbey burn with so much rain?" one muttered savagely, his dark face twisted into a scowl.

"Hush, you fool," another snapped, glaring at Lia as she passed.

"She is a wretched," the man said with a snort. "She cannot understand."

The Earl of Dieyre was not among the riders, so she sought out Prestwich. "Where is Dieyre?" she asked him.

"Still abed, complaining of a stomach ailment. Siara is attending to him, but he says the cramps will not let him mount. He is all but accusing the Aldermaston of poisoning him."

Lia smirked. "It is a pretext. He has another motive and does not wish to ride with the Queen Dowager. Tell the Aldermaston I heard one of them mutter of burning the Abbey."

"I should like to see them try," Prestwich replied grimly, his eyes searing with anger.

In due order, the retinue exited Muirwood's gates and rode toward the Tor, where Lia imagined they would meet up with the other men and possibly even the kishion. If what Dieyre said was true, he would linger after the retinue left. She wondered what sort of man he was. The bulk of the day she spent roving the grounds, looking for signs of Dieyre or any stragglers from the retinue. She missed the midday meal, but came to the kitchen afterward and was grateful Pasqua had finished frying some crispels on a skillet. They were warm and sweet.

"Where were you yesterday?" Bryn asked Lia, twirling around. "It was raining so hard, there was nothing else to do but wait inside. Edmon danced with us."

Lia raised her eyebrows at them both. "Did he?"

Bryn was beaming. "He said he wanted to be sure he knew the maypole dance done in this Hundred. He asked Sowe if she would teach him. When she did, he then danced with me and then Pasqua. He is a very good dancer, Lia. He said he wished you were there so he could dance with you as well."

"He is a cheeky lad," Pasqua said, sitting on a stool with a mug of cider. "He danced with us all to cover his intent, but he wanted to dance with Sowe. He is smitten with you, lass. It is as clear as the noonday sun."

Sowe went scarlet at the attention, but managed to keep her composure. "He is kind and tells amusing stories. But I think you exaggerate his affection." She scrubbed her hands on a towel. "Did Duerden find you, Lia?"

She nearly choked on the crispel. "Was he looking for me?" she stammered.

"Yes, he came by the kitchen after studies. He looked…guilty. Did he do something wrong?"

"I suppose it depends," she replied, her stomach souring. "Did Edmon dance with him as well?"

Bryn giggled, Pasqua poshed, and Sowe just smiled. "Do you know why Duerden was seeking you out? He has never come asking for you at the kitchen before."

"He is a respectful lad, as learners go," Pasqua said. "I was tempted to drive him off with a broom, but I did not."

"I think I know why," Lia replied, twisting another piece of crispel. She brushed crumbs from her skirt. "The Aldermaston told me that his parents sought to purchase my freedom."

Everything went quiet. Sowe and Bryn looked at each other and then at her. Pasqua's mug was partway to her mouth and hung, frozen.

"Do you mean…?" Bryn suggested.

"Lia?" Sowe asked, coming over.

"The Aldermaston said he wants to marry me," Lia said, blurting it out.

It was quiet, awkwardly quiet.

"Has he asked you?" Sowe asked, sidling up next to her on the bench.

"No, I have not seen him in several days." Not since she had shamed him in front of Colvin. The thought made her wince. Had he been working up the courage to ask her then? To tell her his thoughts? She had never considered it.

Bryn's face was still contorted with confusion. "But you do not love him, Lia," she said softly.

Lia laughed at the absurdity. "I did not say I was *going* to marry him. Only that I heard he would ask me. His parents sought the Aldermaston's permission, and he gave it."

"He…he gave it?" Pasqua demanded, her expression bewildered.

Sowe and Bryn glanced at each other, their faces betraying them.

"What is it?" Lia asked, squeezing Sowe's leg.

"You cannot marry him," Bryn insisted.

"Why?" Lia demanded. Pasqua's expression was paler than milk.

"It is secret," Sowe admitted. "Something Edmon told me."

Lia was on her feet, her heart beating faster and faster. It was one thing to be told that Duerden sought her, but the look in Sowe's eyes was of much greater importance. "What is it? If you know something, say it!"

Sowe bit her lip. “It was a few nights ago. Pasqua was asleep. Colvin left to escort Marciana and Ellowyn back to their chamber. Edmon said he was not supposed to know, but he had overheard Colvin and Marciana talking about it. That he was going to ask you soon.”

Lia stared at her hard. “Talking about what?”

It was Pasqua who finally said it. “Colvin wants to marry you, Lia. It is the reason he and his sister came to Muirwood.”

A new idea is delicate. It can be killed by a sneer or a yawn; it can be stabbed to death by a quip and worried to death by a frown on the right man's brow.

—Gideon Penman of Muirwood Abbey

CHAPTER SEVENTEEN

Intentions

Lia needed to think, but the wild pounding of her heart made it impossible. Thinking? What was she supposed to think? How could she stop herself from thinking? Fleeing the Aldermaston's kitchen, she was engulfed by the storm breaking over Muirwood. The wet grass was spongy with mud, but she did not care. She tugged up her hood and walked, trying to fix a destination where she could go and be alone. Away from the manor or the old cemetery grounds, for Colvin might be in either place. Not the laundry, not where Reome would torment her. She needed to sort through her surging feelings, to control her face, her voice. Colvin wanted to marry her? Her? She wanted desperately to believe it, but did not dare summon the hope for fear it would be dashed. He had come to Muirwood to ask her. Colvin Price—the Earl of Forshee. Marry her, a wretched from Muirwood?

She glanced over her shoulder at the cloisters, knowing Ellowyn was there struggling to read and hating every moment of it—hating every moment that Lia craved for. To be able to learn. To have her own tome. But not just that. To spend time with Colvin. To be with him, to study with him. To share ideas and interpretations. To share their hearts with each other. The thought of it—the amazement of it—was more than she could cope with. Tears stung her eyes. Had he shown by his actions that he cared for her? That he valued her opinions? That he was comforted by her presence?

Her boot splashed in a muddy puddle, and she realized she was walking toward the Cider Orchard. A good place to hide in a rainstorm. To hide beneath the boughs, to think about what she suspected and reason it out so she knew what to do and how to react if he asked her. Rain gushed around her, making her shiver, but not with cold. Her emotions could not be controlled.

She remembered holding Colvin's hands in the tunnel. He had not pulled away, had not rejected her as he usually did. She bit her lip, unable to rein in her thoughts. What else could it be? Sowe and Bryn had their account from Edmon, his close friend—close as a brother. There were no words to describe how she felt, how her heart tumbled inside her, bringing quivering feelings of heat and chills at the same time.

The Cider Orchard loomed in front of her, and she slipped inside, moving through the rain and mist to hide herself and calm her emotions. She was soaked and muddy. She did not care. She just needed a moment alone, a moment before she would have to face him. If only her heart would not burst open at the thought. Was there anyone else she cared about more than him? Their shared secrets had forged something wonderful between them.

She found a sturdy apple tree and fell against its trunk, heaving with the effort of walking so fast. She leaned her head back against the firm wood, pulling off her hood to listen to the rain. *Think, Lia. Just think.* A wretched could marry into Family. It had happened before, had it not? The Medium was strong enough.

With her hood down, she realized that someone was calling her name. At first she dreaded it was Duerden, but her heart shuddered in recognition of the voice. It was too soon. How could she face Colvin without crying? Without fainting? It was happening too fast. It was too soon. She was not ready.

"Lia!" his voiced called again, and she heard him trudge through the mud.

She hurried to her feet and had taken only a few steps when he discovered her. Rain ran down his face, his hair a wet mass, dripping from the ends. His breathing was hard, he had obviously labored to catch up with her.

"You walk…so quickly…I was calling after you…"

She shook her head a moment, trying to make her tongue work. "I did not hear you. The rain. I turned around when I did."

"I am glad you stopped. Why are you out here?"

"The Aldermaston…well, he said…well, it does not really matter. Did you stop at the kitchen first?"

"No, I saw you crossing the grounds."

"It is warmer in the kitchen." She felt like an idiot. Her mind was not working.

"Of course it is warmer in the kitchen. Why are you out here in the rain? Is something wrong?"

"No. It does not matter. I can do my errand later. Did you… is there something you needed me for? You usually do not go hunting after me like this." She looked around, seeing how alone they were, and her heart burned so much, she thought she would never be able to swallow. She noticed his hand and hungrily wanted to grasp it.

"Lia, I wanted to tell you something. I have tried, but so much has interfered. I wanted to share something with you from my tome, which I left in my chamber. I had to tell you before we must leave Muirwood." He looked down at the mashed grass. "I wanted to tell you since I came, but I could not. Not until now."

"Tell me what?" she asked, trembling. She could not stop herself from shaking.

"You are cold."

"I am all right."

"I should take you back."

"Just tell me, Colvin." She looked at him pleadingly.

"Here, away from the rain." He moved beneath the canopy of trees, bringing her with him. "I spoke to my sister. She is the one who suggested it, actually, after I told her about you."

Lia nearly fainted. She swallowed, her thoughts blazing. She could not speak. She could only lean back against the trunk of the apple tree and gaze at his face, watching his mouth as he spoke. Her fingertips bit into the bark as she waited breathlessly for him to say it.

Colvin gazed down, then into her eyes. Rainwater trickled down his cheek. "There is a power that the Aldermastons have—a power only they can use. Through the Medium, they can adopt you into a Family. As if you were born into that Family. They do not agree to do this very often. But it does happen." He swallowed, steadying himself. "Lia, my sister and I…we would like you to be part of our Family. To be a Price. To share our Family name."

For a moment, Lia did not understand. Then her thoughts came crashing down around her like stones. "You want…you want me to be your…your sister?" she whispered in disbelief.

Colvin looked at her in confusion. "Yes. Through the Medium, that can happen. That is what I wanted to show you in my tome. The reference to it. Lia, what is wrong? You look ill."

"Nothing," she lied, staring at the ground. The truth stung her as if she grasped for a rose stem without realizing there would be so many thorns.

"I thought you would be…we thought you would be pleased. If you were Family, you could study at an Abbey. You could finally become a learner." His voice was concerned. "I thought that is what you wanted." He stood in front of her, perplexed by her reaction apparently. "You were not expecting this."

Lia shook her head, unable to meet his eyes, unable to free herself from a rising surge of humiliation. Tears betrayed her again, and she squeezed the trunk so hard her fingers ached. She could not stop the tears and turned her face away.

"Do you…do you understand what I am offering you?" he mumbled, and she could hear the anger starting to surge in his voice. "Lia? Were you expecting something else from me? You thought I was going to…to what? Tell me what you are thinking!"

She bit her lip, too ashamed to say the words. She gazed up at him, her eyes blurred with tears and saw the wild look of distress in his face. He was confused, angry, concerned.

He stared at her, his hands slowly clenching. "This is not what you were thinking I would offer. You thought…I wanted to marry you?"

He said it, confirming her worst fears and plunging her into darkness. He said it out loud. There was no going back. There was no way to pretend their conversation had not happened. No way to disguise how she felt about him.

"Is that what you thought, Lia?" he asked in a flat voice.

She looked at him desperately, begging him to leave with her mind.

"Is it?" he said fiercely, his eyes blazing.

Weakly, she nodded. It was the only admission she could make, for not even her tongue would obey her. She had desperately wanted to believe it. Marciana's words haunted her: *We are slow to believe that which, if believed, would hurt our feelings.*

It unleashed a new kind of storm. As thunder boomed over Muirwood, Colvin stood back from her, his eyes blazing with shock and anger. A sharp wind whistled through the grove as he stared at her, understanding for the first time. "I cannot believe this. What do you think would happen if I were to pledge myself to a wretched? I am from a noble Family. My mother was from a noble Family. I have a duty, a sworn duty, an obligation and covenant that has lasted for hundreds of years that binds my family to the Medium forever. I have a duty to marry someone of noble blood. I know you are strong in the Medium, Lia, but I cannot give you that. I could *never* give you that." He shook his head, as if someone had slapped him. "I am the Earl of Forshee. Do you have any idea what would happen if I were to choose someone of your station to be my wife? Forgetting my duty, forgetting the oaths my forbearers have sworn and that I swore myself. Do you have any idea the mockery, the ridicule, the contempt that would bring to me and to my Family?" His face showed outrage, his lips quivering as he spoke.

Lia could hardly breathe. Each word, each glimpse at his eyes was a dagger thrust in her heart. "I am sorry, Colvin. I am sorry I…I just thought…I hoped…"

"I would lose my earldoms," he went on. "I would lose all my lands, save perhaps a small cottage or freehold. Is that what you want? A marriage must be a marriage of equals, Lia. You are my superior with the Medium. I know that and accept it. But you are not my equal in rank. You are a wretched—someone who does not know her ancestors. You grasp at something you just cannot have!"

Lia choked on her tears. "You think that of me?" she said, blinded by her shame as well as the tears and unprepared for the hot surge of anger that followed. "That I was trying to snare you? To *snare* you?"

Colvin's face twisted with anger. "I have never tried to pretend anything with you."

"Nor have I!"

"Then how could you think that I would ever marry you? You know me, Lia! You know me more fully than anyone else. It is my duty to protect Demont's niece, it is not what I desire to do. It is my duty to carry on my family name honorably. Duty is greater than a wish. It is the motive that compels me. That goads me." His voice fell, but his face showed all the fiery emotion still raging inside of him, a look of pure contempt and loathing. "I must go. We cannot be seen like this."

"Please!" Lia said, grasping his arm, but he shook her grip off. "Please, Colvin. I am sorry. I misunderstood."

"How could you misunderstand?" Colvin said, nearly shouting. "Because I did not reject you in the tunnel? I interpreted your gesture very differently from how you intended it, I can see that now."

"No, it is a misunderstanding. I was wrong."

"You believed I could betray my rank, my sister, my duty for someone like you? As a sister, it would be without scorn or shame. As my sister, your world would be expanded without mine being diminished. You could visit the kingdoms we have only talked about. You could learn more than what you know now. As my sister, you could do that. But not more. Never more than that."

His words were like poison. The look on his face devastated her. She had to make him understand. "You are my dear friend, Colvin. What we went through together, in the Bearden Muir... that night at Winterrowd. I cannot tell it to anyone, nor have I. What our...friendship has meant to me. In my heart...you became...even more dear to me. More than a brother."

He looked away, his teeth clenched tightly. "I cannot stay here."

"Please do not leave like this."

His scorching eyes transfixed hers. "I was afraid this would happen. If we spent too much time together, it would make one of us vulnerable. I should have heeded that inner voice. I never meant to injure you, Lia. Your friendship has been valuable to me as well. You saved my life. But I cannot give you what you wish for. I will not betray my Family in that way. It would be recklessly improper, with your feelings, for you to become part of my Family now. It cannot be, Lia."

"I know what I am, Colvin," she said, sobbing. "I cannot help being a wretched. It was never my choice. But if I...but if I was Ellowyn Demont instead? Would you...?"

The look he gave her sucked the breath from her lungs.

"But you are not," he said and stormed away.

CHAPTER EIGHTEEN

Surrounded

Lia ran through the orchard rows with their interlocking branches, through the wet, whipping rain, through the mud and muck until her legs throbbed with pain and her chest heaved with exhaustion. Colvin's words burned in her ears and filled her with such self-hate, she thought she would die of it. The tree line vanished abruptly, and the ground beneath her feet gave way down a small hillside. Down she ran, faster and faster, trying to outrace the wind and her sickened feelings. What had she done! Why had she ruined everything with Colvin? The ground was slick and muddy, and there was no one to catch her fall, so she tumbled headlong to the base of the slope. There, in a crumpled heap at the bottom, she sobbed.

The pain of it—the pain of knowing that she had lost him—no, not lost him for she had never *had* him to begin with. The deception was exposed, her deepest secret was bared as a shell—a husk. That somehow the Earl of Forshee would look past her being a wretched, would love her for who she was and accept her. His hand had always been extended in friendship, but never more than that. And she had ruined it. How could she face him again?

How could she look at him without the searing pain in her heart choking the thought of any words? Never in her life had she felt so desolate, not even in the midst of the Bearden Muir when she feared she would never see Muirwood again.

The storm howled around her, adding a certain delight to her misery. Yes, this was the kind of day to be spurned by a man. The savagery of the storm paled next to her grieving. Sitting up, clutching herself, she let out a cry of sorrow and pain for the injustice of her birth. The shame of being a wretched had never stung so much.

How could she have misjudged him so badly? She was not angry that he scorned her. She was angry that she had let herself believe he would care for her in the way she did for him. The truth of it frayed away, like the dead husks enfolding the core of an onion. Since she had saved his life, the secret had begun inside her, sprouting like a tiny seed. Only now did she focus on the monstrous growth that resulted from her untended thoughts. He had promised to teach her to read, but what hurt more was the broken promise of Whitsunday. How many times had she dreamed about holding his hand as the music played? How often had she lingered on the memory of holding his hand in the tunnels beneath the Abbey—alone, secluded, heeding the forbidden urge to comfort him, warm him, be near him. He had not rejected her then, as she had feared. It emboldened her to believe that his feelings, though masked, matched hers. The mask was gone. In its place, a look of contempt.

Lia opened her swollen eyes at the mud-splattered thing she had become. Mud and grass clogged her hair, mucked her gear, and burrowed beneath her fingernails. Her chest quivered and wheezed from the surge of tears. How could she go back to the Abbey? How could she ever look at him again without blushing a thousand shades of crimson?

"Lia, you fool," she whimpered. "You stupid, stupid fool." How she hated herself!

What would Marciana say? In her elegant gowns, freshly combed and braided hair, with her callous-free hands? Lia looked at herself in disgust. A hunter's life bemired her. The lavenders were always clean and smelled of purple mint. Not Lia. She clenched her teeth to stop them from chattering and hugged herself. Marciana had solicited her friendship, her intimacy. She prided herself on noting hints of love. She would be furious to learn Lia deceived her. Edmon's information was obviously incorrect, regardless of how true he believed it to be.

Then there was the Aldermaston. How could she disguise her feelings from him? Would he pity her? Or would he forbid her to see Colvin again? The thought of never seeing him again tortured her. It would be for the best if he left Muirwood. She knew she would survive it somehow. But the pain—how could she go on with the wrenching ache constantly reminding her of what she had ruined?

She loved him. She loved him more than anything else in her life. Even though it hurt, even though his rejection shattered her, she could not change her feelings for him now that she admitted to herself what they were. He had his faults, but there was so much she had always admired about him. His constant struggle to control himself. His desire to placate the Medium so that it would serve him. His care for his sister and his iron determination to succeed despite his worst fears. He was not driven by the ambition to be rich, had never once mentioned that his actions were motivated by the thought of added rewards. Duty drove him. She admired that.

Lia lifted her chin to the sky and felt the water cleanse the mud from her face. She would endure it. Somehow, she would. But how?

It begins with a thought.

The very concept tormented her because Colvin had taught it to her. Yet she knew she could. If she focused on something else, if she pushed her will and all her efforts, it would bloom in her life. She just needed an idea. Something to hold on to, to give her strength.

The sound of hooves clomping in the mud.

Lia's eyes opened as the black forms of three horses appeared from a screen of trees nearby. Each was mounted by a rider wearing a black tunic threaded in silver. She had seen the design before—the Queen Dowager's men. She rose, for they approached at an even canter.

"She moves! After that tumble down the hill, I thought her ankle twisted," said one rider to another.

"Hush! She can hear us!"

"But she cannot speak Dahomeyjan. She is from the Abbey."

The third rider hissed. "She is the hunter Dieyre warned of. Fool girl to wander this far. Look, she is poised to fly. Calm her, Renart, while we hedge her retreat."

The middle rider was a handsome man and tapped the flanks of his stallion. "Are you well?" he asked in her native language but with the same inflection of the Queen Dowager. "We saw you fall. You are from the Abbey, yes?"

Lia's mind whirled with the danger. She eyed the other two horses as they slowly broke off and started on each side of her. They were backing her toward the hill where their steeds would make it easy to outrun her. If she made it to the Cider Orchard, she would have the advantage, but it would be pointless trying to outrun the steeds when they were so close.

She said nothing, quickly thinking about her options. She had no bow, only the gladius and a dirk. They each had swords belted to their waists, and one had a crossbow dangling from a strap on the saddle horn.

"Do not be frightened," the rider said, his smile disarming. "Did you hurt your leg in the fall?"

Lia took a tentative step backward, away from them and then winced with pain and flinched. It was a ruse to make them think she was injured and could not run.

"She is hobbled," the other said with a wicked grin. "The kishion wanted clothes for a disguise. Let us bring hers."

"The earl said not to harm her," the other warned. They were close to Lia, coming at her from three sides.

"Who cares what he thinks!" the other snarled. "She is our prize. The kishion wants clothes. He will not care what we do with her."

"Give me your hand," the first rider said, leaning forward from the saddle. They clustered around her, the snort of their steeds just shy of her face. "I can take you back to the Abbey. It is a long walk." The smile did not reach his eyes. The look made her stomach squirm with loathing at the lie. She knew exactly what they were planning to do with her.

"Thank you," Lia mumbled, wincing still, and hobbled forward a step.

"Why were you running…?" he started to ask, when Lia lunged suddenly and grabbed his wrist instead of his hand. With her other hand, she seized his tunic sleeve and then dropped to a low crouch. He toppled straight off the stallion and grunted against the muddy earth. He was stunned for a moment, shaking his head as he wondered how he had fallen off the horse, giving Lia time to draw her gladius. She slammed the pommel into the back of his skull, right where Martin had showed her. He did not get up.

The rider's horse screamed and flailed, offering distraction. Lia went for the man with the crossbow next, whirling around and cutting the exposed strap so the weapon thumped harmlessly to the ground.

"Grab her! Grab her!" the other shouted, stamping the horse with his spurs.

Lia slipped around the flank and severed the saddle belt, slicing into the horse's belly with the stroke. It reared in agony, and the saddle slid off his back. The rider clutched the reins still, yanking the stallion's head back farther. It twisted and bucked, and both rider and stallion crashed into the mud, pinning the man's leg beneath it. He roared with pain and Dahomeyjan curses. Lia promptly stomped on his face, silencing him.

The sound of metal clearing a sheath made her look up as the last rider dismounted and cleared the blade from the scabbard. His face was mottled with rage.

"I have you all to myself then!" he hissed in Dahomeyjan, stalking her. "Eh? You feel brave with a puny sword?"

He swung high and then low, slipping in gracefully. She was outside his reach and so did not move to parry or counter. She counted his steps in her mind, struggling to subdue her fear. With her left hand, she slipped the dirk free.

"A trencher knife now! You wish to stab me with a trencher knife!" He lunged at her, extending his reach fluidly to close the gap. The blow was aimed at her shoulder, not her heart. She knew he did not want to kill her. That would ruin his purpose. Lia twisted, using her gladius to separate herself from the blade. She deflected the thrust high and stepped inside and locked their hilts together. He was taller than her, stronger by far. In a test of strength, he would win.

Already he twisted his blade free and grabbed her cloak with his free hand, jerking it hard to wrap her in it. Lia stepped the other way and brought her heel down on his foot. His face crumpled with pain, but he was not finished with her, and she knew it. She dropped low and pressed the dirk blade into his groin.

"I will castrate you!" she warned in perfect Dahomeyjan. "Drop your sword! Now!"

His eyes bulged at the position he was in. She was low, the dagger already in the motion of stabbing. His fingers opened, and the blade thumped into the mud.

"My foot," he gurgled, his body trembling. "It is broken. I cannot…stand!"

Lia swung the gladius up and nestled the edge of the blade against his throat. "On your knees!" she ordered and watched until he obeyed. Then she moved around behind him, keeping the blade against his flesh.

"My foot!" he wailed, his face wincing.

"If you even twitch toward your sword," she warned, "I will cut your throat. How many of Pareigis's men are in the woods? Answer me!"

"How do you speak Dahomeyjan?"

She pressed the blade harder against his skin. "If you do not answer my questions, I have no use for you."

He swore in vexation. "There are a score of us, her personal knights. The rest are survivors of the battle when her husband met his doom. Three hundred, spreading like a net around the Abbey grounds."

Lia swallowed. Three hundred? "How does she keep them in line? That many men, how are they kept?"

"You do not know Pareigis."

"You are not being useful again," she said sharply.

"The knights keep the rabble in line. And the muted one with the tattoos. But only the kishion is allowed to enter the grounds, for he can move unseen."

Lia knew she would not have much time to question him. If these three had seen her fall, others hidden in the woods might be running for help. "Why are you here?" she asked.

He winced, his face creased with pain. "To raze the Abbey if the Aldermaston defies her. You can tell him that, girl."

"I will consider your suggestion. What does she want?"

"I do not know. She only tells the Earl of Dieyre of her plans. We stay in the woods and wait until the sign. And since you will ask me what it is, I will say this. When the gargouelles burn, it will be safe for us to enter the grounds and raze the Abbey."

"Does the muted one make them burn?" Lia asked.

"He does."

She felt it then, the sniffling and mewling around her legs. The Myriad Ones swarmed around them, hissing and baying in the quiet storm. Revulsion swelled inside her. How it was possible, she did not know. She had never felt the Myriad Ones on the grounds before, never within the borders. She looked at the woods where the riders came from.

"The muted one," the wounded knight whispered greedily. "Do you hear him yet? In your thoughts?"

Unable to stop herself, Lia pulled the blade away from his throat. "Tell him to stay away from Muirwood. I will be watching for him."

"No, child. He is watching you. And he will open the borders for the kishion to enter."

No maston can purchase his virtue too dear, for it is the only thing whose value must ever increase with the price it has cost. Our integrity is never worth so much as when we have parted with our all to keep it. Sadly, many will part with theirs for a trifle.

—Gideon Penman of Muirwood Abbey

CHAPTER NINETEEN

Irrevocare Sigil

For nearly seven years, Lia had carried in her bosom the memory of Jon Hunter arriving at the kitchen during the storm, sopping wet and splattered in mud, anxious to bring the Aldermaston a terrible message. She thought it strange how life had the tendency to repeat itself over and over, roles changing but the story being the same. At the cloister, she had learned that the Aldermaston was in the kitchen, so she hurried there instead. She knew Colvin might be there and prepared to face him, but her fight with Pareigis's knights lent her a strength she had never known before. The training had worked. Without help, she had disarmed three enemies, each a man and much larger than her, and interrogated one of them for useful information. There was something satisfying in the act of pulling a man from his horse or watching him go limp with a well-placed blow. In her mind, she could see Martin's fierce, clenched grin of approval.

As she stomped across the grounds to the kitchen, she imagined how wild she looked, all brown and gray with mud, her wild hair hanging in tangled clumps down her back. Her thoughts were spinning wildly with the events of the afternoon, like so many butterflies in a grove, all dancing this way and that in the air, and she was unable to rein in any of them. She was haunted by the look of contempt in Colvin's eyes as he spurned her. Another image—a Dahomeyjan knight leering at her. Yet another—Reome at the laundry, blocking her way, and then something inside Lia cracked, and she saw herself rushing the girl, stomping her foot, and choking her in the water trough. Then Sheriff Almaguer was in her thoughts, his eyes blazing silver as he whispered about her parentage, killed at the battle of Maseve. How she wished she had known back then all she had learned being a hunter.

Thunder boomed over the Abbey, making her want to laugh wildly as the memory of Jon Hunter stabbed her heart again. He was dead in the Bearden Muir because the Aldermaston had sent him to protect her. Each of her steps on the muddy grass brought painful memories. She looked up, the skies darkening with a storm-induced twilight, and there was Duerden leaning against the wall of the kitchen, shivering and soaked.

"Oh no," she whispered. Already his head snapped up, hearing the noise of her approach, and he saw her. His face looked ashen with nervousness.

"Lia?" he asked tremulously, stepping toward her.

"I must speak to the Aldermaston," she said brusquely. "I cannot talk to you now, Duerden."

He looked crestfallen. "I…I see. Another time then, when you have a moment." With a sigh, he stepped away from her path and started back toward the cloisters. She watched his wilting with a surge of remorse, but she could not…she would not want to listen to him at that moment, not with her wounded heart still bleeding.

"Lia?" he called after a moment, as her hands found the handle. She looked over her shoulder at him, amazed he had the audacity to ignore her polite warning. His mouth was drooping in a frown, but his eyebrows looked concerned. "Are you all right? Can I help you?"

She stood for a moment, surprised at his sensitivity. She had a wild urge to kiss his cheek and thank him, but she knew that would confuse him into thinking she felt more than she really did.

"Yes, Duerden, something happened. But this is a problem for the Aldermaston." Again she was tempted to reveal more than she should. *I left three men at the edge of the grounds. One of them may die because I might have hit him too hard. The Earl of Forshee, the man I love, was disgusted with me when I told him how I felt. I am soaked and wet and tired. And how are you this fine day?*

"I will not keep you," he said, biting his lip and wiping rain from his eyes, and then started back toward the cloister.

Lia swung open the kitchen door and entered. There was Pasqua, rubbing her shoulder with obvious pain, and the Aldermaston leaning over her, speaking in low tones. Siara Healer was there as well, mixing up some powder with a pestle. Sowe and Bryn were busy making supper, and both glanced over at her and stopped, gawking at her strange appearance. There was Edmon, lounging on a barrel, and he also rose when she entered.

"Lia, what happened to you?" Edmon asked, his face contorting with alarm.

The Aldermaston turned, his brow also creased with physical pain, and his eyebrows flexed with concern. He said nothing, only waited for her to speak, to share the news that would change the Abbey's situation yet again.

"Dahomeyjan soldiers," Lia said, coming near him and keeping her voice low. "The Queen Dowager left some of her knights in the woods. They have rallied a remnant of the king's army, and it surrounds the grounds, hidden. I believe they will use

Scarseth to set the Leerings afire before they attack us. I encountered three of them, just past the Cider Orchard, and they attacked me. I defended myself, but I may have killed one. They said the kishion is coming."

She stopped, trying to catch her breath, and stared at the Aldermaston.

"We must take Ellowyn away from here!" Edmon said, closing the gap. "We can have horses saddled and be on our way at once!"

The Aldermaston shook his head. "That would play into their hands and forfeit your life unnecessarily. You are a brave lad, Edmon, but allow me to do the thinking." He paused deliberately, his eyes veiled, masking the pain he suffered. "For someone who does not believe in the Medium's power, the Queen Dowager is taking some precautions to ensure her success. That is in our favor. She underestimates us and does not appreciate the Medium's guidance. All afternoon, I have felt a burden. Your news confirms it. They will try and abduct the girl before the Queen Dowager returns. If they have her in possession, it will strengthen their position. She must be safeguarded. Edmon, hurry to the cloister, and summon her and her companion to my manor. You and the Earl of Forshee will guard her during the day. Lia will guard her at night. She must be under watch constantly. I feel it heavily upon me, as certain as I know the moon will rise, even though we will not see it through the clouds. Lia, you are her primary guardian. Stay near her constantly."

Lia frowned. "I can take her away tonight. Even without horses. If we go into the Bearden Muir, they will have difficulty following us."

"She is not ready, nor is it the right time. In this deadly dance we play with Pareigis, we must watch our pace and not stumble over our feet. Our collective wisdom is greater than all the cunning of the Queen Dowager and the Earl of Dieyre. Go, Lia. Go, Edmon. Safeguard her to my manor. The future of the realm depends on keeping Ellowyn Demont safe."

***

Darkness settled over Muirwood with a sullen whisper. Rain-choked leaves burdened the limbs of the mighty oaks surrounding the Abbey. Inside the manor house, Marciana stood at the gap in the doorway of her resting chamber, guarding the scene. "Thank you, Aldermaston. I bid you good night. Tell my brother I will explain everything. He will understand. Thank you, again." Slowly, she shut the huge oak door and settled the crossbar into place.

She turned and looked at Lia gravely. It was the first time they could speak privately since her time in the orchard with Colvin. "You dear creature," she said simply. She sighed and shook her mane of hair. "My first reaction and admission must be honesty. I was surprised when Colvin revealed the nature of your conversation. But how can I blame you, when I esteem him so highly myself? We will speak more on this matter in due course. But first Lia, we must attend to you. A bath, I think, would do your spirits some good."

Lia stared at her in amazement. "You are not angry with me?"

A puckish smile came with the reply. "I am sorry for you. But no, I am not angry. Ellowyn, would you mind if I attended to Lia first tonight?"

The shy girl smiled. "I would like to help. I can…I can wash her clothes after she's done with the bathwater. It is late, after all, and we should let the lavenders sleep."

"That is kind of you both," Lia said, feeling sore and discouraged. The thought of a bath did sound pleasant. "But do not wait on me. I can bathe myself and clean my own gear."

Marciana smiled. "Of course you are able to, Lia. But you are to be our guardian tonight and every night. You give us service in doing so. Please, let us offer this small service in return for yours. It will go faster with help. You let Pasqua and Sowe help you. Why not us?"

"Because you are both nobles."

Marciana shook her head. "It would be a privilege, Lia. Please."

Lia nodded in awkward agreement and went to the wooden tub in the far corner. The changing screen was folded open, and Lia felt the gentle murmur of the Medium as the water Leering set into the wall near the tub flared to life, and water began churning into the basin. Marciana concentrated harder, and a gentle haze of steam followed shortly after. She glanced back at Lia and winked at her. "Is this warm enough?"

Lia had seldom visited the guest wing of the manor house, it being on the opposite side from the kitchen, closest to the main gates of the Abbey grounds. Most of the rooms had high windows set into the thick stone walls, but this room had none. The only way in or out lay through the sturdy oak door. The furnishings were elaborate. A single stuffed mattress, which the two ladies shared, lay against the northern wall, with canopied bedposts made of damask and velvet with golden tassels. Several couches, changing screens, tables and cushions, and a garderobe also complemented the design. Tapestries adorned the walls and rush-matting that was changed daily was green and fragrant. She ran her fingers through the stream of water and nodded.

Marciana treated the bath with scented oil and soap, making it frothy and inviting. She seemed familiar with the vials and stone basins, and Lia figured she did not hire a servant to bathe herself, as many nobles did.

"Let me help you out of those soiled clothes," Marciana said. Lia unbuckled her leather bracers and girdle, which were filthy and damp. She suddenly remembered that she had not brought with her a clean gown. "What is it?"

"I have a spare dress back in the kitchen," she said softly. "I can send Astrid..."

Marciana touched her arm. "I have something you can wear. Do not worry. Here, hang your garments behind the screen."

Lia slipped into the warm water and shivered. The tub was spacious, much more so than the one in the kitchen where she had bathed all her life. Having a water Leering next to it was ideal, for water did not need to be toted in buckets from the ovens. There was a fireplace and chimney with a fire Leering for warming water. But Marciana's trick, learned from Colvin through Lia, had saved much time in filling it. With a soft sponge, she washed her arms and fingers while Marciana cleansed her hair with a dish of water, just as Sowe had always done. The water turned a murky brown.

"You have lovely hair, Lia," Marciana said, and she squeezed the clumps of her tresses and wrung them out. With a sculpted wooden comb, she began untangling them.

"It can only be subdued for a while, never tamed," Lia said wistfully. "It is not straight and beautiful, like yours and Sowe's."

"It is beautiful in its own right. It is darker than mine but not as dark as Sowe's, and it has some lovely hints of copper amidst the crinkles. Here and here." She knelt by the edge of the bath, her flowing sleeves a little damp but pushed up past the elbows. Lia was not sure how much time had passed, but she felt luxuriant and clean, as she had not felt for months.

"The water is cold. Can I dry by the fire now?" Lia asked.

"First something to wear," Marciana said and rose. She went to one of her chests and withdrew a pale chemise with an embroidered hem. Lia had never owned a chemise before, and as she slipped it on, it felt warm and soft against her skin, like a warm breath. It was loose at the shoulders, so Marciana helped tighten the lacings in the front. The sleeves fit her well, but she was taller than the other girl so it did not reach down to her ankles.

"By the fire then?" Marciana joined her, sitting at the mouth of the fireplace, staring into the lapping flames and the Leering's eyes. The scent of the soap against Lia's wrist, the way her hair smelled, even the chemise which had been packed with purple mint to keep away moths reminded her that she was not of their station. For a moment, she wondered what it would be like to be a noble like the other two were. To have more than a spare dress. The chemise was made of the softest material she had ever worn.

Silently, Ellowyn gathered up the dirty gear and went to the tub and commenced washing them.

"You are pretty, Lia," Marciana said. "You will not struggle to find a willing husband when it is your time. But it will not be Colvin." She shook her head, her expression full of pity as well as sympathy. She stroked Lia's arm gently. "I need to explain to you why."

Lia looked into the flames, grateful that Marciana had kept her voice low. She knew that Ellowyn could hear them, but at least the girl had the decency to pretend to ignore them as she scrubbed the leader girdle with soapy water. "He made it clear why I cannot be with him. I am not a simpleton."

"No, you are not. But in his fit of anger, he did not explain something to you. It is important, Lia. Have you ever heard of the *irrevocare* sigil?"

Lia turned, her eyebrows raising. "I have not."

"It is a maston custom. You know so many of them, I was not certain if you had heard of it. The term is an ancient one, a practice that goes back to the First Parents. It is a binding sigil, one that has the power to last perpetually. It lasts forever. Only an Aldermaston can invoke it and only within the most important chamber of the Abbey. It has been the custom for generations, within the order of the mastons, to bind certain things using an irrevocare sigil. Specifically, a marriage between two maston families. When this is done, the power of the Medium flows even stronger with the next generation. That is why maston families tend to intermarry and spurn marriages to those who are not of the order. To the Earl of Dieyre, for example, marriage is a means of growing his already disgusting supply of wealth. But a maston who comes from a long line of marriages bound by the sigil will always seek out another of that station. Always the next generation is more powerful in the Medium because of it." She squinted at Lia. "Am I making sense to you?"

Lia looked down at her hands. "What you are telling me is that your parents were married this way. Possibly back many generations."

"Six, actually. There are some maston families who have tomes recording their lineage back to the Flood." She smiled sadly and touched Lia's arm. "I know that Colvin fancies you. He admires and respects you. If he had deeper feelings than this, he has done well to tame them and keep them hidden, even from me. But he will marry a girl who is a maston, whose parents were married by the sigil. He is concerned about future generations, not just his own feelings. Or yours."

Lia had never heard of irrevocare sigils before. There was no real reason a wretched should be told about them, but that did not stop it from aching inside her. Being bound to Colvin forever? The thought made her blush.

"It is not my fault that I am a wretched," Lia murmured softly.

"I know, Lia. That is why it is so pitiable. I just wanted you to know. Colvin behaved poorly this afternoon. He did not expect your reaction. Likely, you had a father who was very strong in the Medium who fell in love with a girl who was probably a learner herself. Unable to tame their feelings for each other, you became the result. Not because they did not love you. Not because they did not love each other. But there are so few mastons left, and even fewer who will be patient enough to wait for the sigil to be performed. Colvin is qualified for the sigil because of our parents. He is determined to have it."

A bitterness twisted deep inside of Lia. "He is nothing if not stubborn."

Almost as if to answer that thought, a firm knock sounded on the door. She knew it was him. Alarm flashed in Marciana's eyes, but Lia stood and went to the door. "Who is it?" she demanded, hand firmly on the crossbar.

"I need to speak with my sister." Cold, stern, implacable.

Colvin.

CHAPTER TWENTY

Hillel Lavender

Mustering her courage and quelling her self-pity, Lia lifted the crossbar and tugged at the door. The hall was dimly lit, and Colvin carried a candelabra, the flame flickering in his eyes as he stared at her. He blinked, seeing her in his sister's chemise. There was something in his expression, a stumble of some kind, as if his defenses were momentarily breached.

"What is it?" Lia asked, her voice cold.

Colvin swallowed. "Dieyre is in my room. Marciana, I want you to hear what he has to say."

She rose from the fire and advanced, her face skeptical. "What is happening, Colvin?"

"I will explain on the way. He insisted you be there, or he would tell me nothing more."

"What of Ellowyn?" Lia asked warningly.

Colvin nodded to her but looked slightly annoyed. "Under your protection, as the Aldermaston said."

For a moment, Lia had worried that he would suggest Ellowyn come with them. That they would try and steal away from the Abbey that night, with or without her help.

Marciana kissed Lia's cheek. "I will knock when I return, but you can sleep if you like. The bed is soft."

Lia grimaced. "I hold vigil this night, remember? I will be awake when you come." She looked in Colvin's eyes, saw the mask concealing his feelings again. He dipped his head to her and then started down the hall with his sister, whispering to her about Dieyre. She watched a moment as he left, her heart aching at the yawning chasm separating them.

After settling the crossbar back in place, Lia turned and found Ellowyn still scrubbing the clothes clean, humming a little tune to herself. It was the first time they had been alone together. She had no recollection of ever having had a conversation with the girl. Jealousy was the normal feeling she experienced when she looked at Ellowyn. Watching her hum and scrub, she felt the first pangs of gratitude and even a little fondness for the simple girl.

Lia approached Ellowyn awkwardly, wondering whether she wanted to talk or not. Without lifting her head, she heard Ellowyn's shy, reserved voice.

"My parents were married by the irrevocare sigil. It was done by two Aldermastons by a plight troth. My father in Pry-Ree. My mother in Dahomey, for she was living in exile. They loved each other a great deal to risk it, do you know why? If one of them had perished before they could consummate it, the other would never be able to marry again. That is true love, I think. My uncle told me so." She glanced at Lia covertly, and her voice went from simple to sardonic. "But Colvin does not love *me*. Not in any way. He is gentle, thoughtful, and patient. He pats me on the head like a little chick that has just broken free of the shell." She gave Lia a sidelong look and then sighed.

Lia reached the edge of the tub, saw her shirt hanging by a peg on the changing screen, as well as the girdle. Ellowyn scrubbed thoroughly at one of her bracers. "If I had a fortune, the Earl of Dieyre would wish to marry me. He is so handsome. But I do not have a fortune. Yet. Nor good looks. The Pry-rians want me, regardless. Some ancient family speaking a language that would bewilder me, so I could produce an heir and restore their former glory." She scrubbed a little furiously at a particularly muddy spot. "A vessel. That is all that I am to them. Like that water dish to rinse your hair."

Lia saw Ellowyn in a new way, and it startled her a little. "You almost sound resentful of your new life," she said.

"Resentful? No…I am terrified, Lia. I have felt nothing but sheer terror since I left Sempringfall Abbey. I miss it dreadfully." She squinted at the dark leather and scratched out a stain with her fingernail. "Imagine being plucked from your home, then shuttled forth from place to place, Abbey to Abbey. Learn this. Say that. Eat this way. Do not laugh like that. It is not proper. What is taking you so long? We learned that word yesterday, you still have not learned it?" Her face twisted into a scowl. "Never a moment to myself. Never a moment to say what I really feel. Except moments like now."

"I do not even know you," Lia hedged.

"I do not care. If I do not talk, I will burst. This is how we would work at my Abbey. Work and whisper among ourselves. Talk about the boys and which ones liked us and which ones we scorned. I miss that too. Marciana does not understand me. Colvin does not understand me. But you do. How I am jealous of you and Sowe." She kept working, her scrubbing motions looking almost desperate. "There, this is looking much better, I think. I would trade these dirty clothes of yours for mine in a moment. I do not belong in their world. The Leerings mock me. Truly, they do. The Medium will not hearken to me, no matter how I plead with it. No matter that my parents were both skilled. I cannot do it because I am terrified. Every day, I worry that someone is going to try and take me. To force me to do something I do not want to do. To marry someone I do not know just to bear their child. And that in my fear, I will let them. I will do whatever I am asked, because I am supposed to. Not because I want to." She winced, gnawing on her thumb a moment, then put down the bracer and seized the other one. She looked sidelong at Lia. "So…you love him, too?"

There was a double meaning in her words. "You care for him, Ellowyn?" she asked.

The other girl smiled sadly, scrubbing with zest. "How can I not, Lia? He is so different from other men. He never says more than he feels. He is thoughtful and wise for someone so young. He is never rude or conceited. I remember when he and Edmon first arrived at Sempringfall. You should have seen the gaggle of us at the laundry after they rode in. Most of the girls thought Edmon the prettiest boy they had ever seen, but he did not catch my fancy. It was the Earl of Forshee—so stern and poised. A dark beauty. He fears nothing. Absolutely nothing. I fear everything unless he is near me."

Lia sat by the tub, listening closely. She knew what Colvin feared. She knew so many of his inner secrets, his qualms.

"I was elbow-deep in suds…just like now…when he came with the Aldermaston. My name was Hillel Lavender. Did you know that? There was Colvin and the Aldermaston together. He was looking at us, and it was quiet, except a few nervous giggles. Before the Aldermaston said my name, he looked at me. His eyes—how do you describe them? Like smoke and sky together, I thought. He was frowning slightly, as he often does. But his eyes just burned into mine, as if he knew who I was. The Aldermaston spoke my name and beckoned me. You can imagine the jealousy and the whispers when we left. In the Aldermaston's study, Colvin told me my true name. Ellowyn, not Hillel. The Aldermaston warned what would happen if I left the Abbey. He said the old king had sworn to raze the Abbey if I was revealed in any way." She looked sidelong at Lia. "It is a guilt that I carry. And a fear. What would I do if they burned the Abbey...because of me? Colvin swore an oath he would protect me, and that my uncle's knights would protect the Sempringfall. I swear, I fell in love with him as he spoke those words. That he would guard my life with his own."

Lia swallowed thickly. *You are right, though. He does not love you*, she wanted to say, but she could not bring herself to utter it.

"Though I am afraid, I feel calm when he is near. He has tried to help me learn how to summon the Medium, but in truth, it is even harder to try when he is near me, for I cannot concentrate. I keep staring at his mouth, his hands, his eyes. He speaks so passionately, I want to succeed just to please him. But he has never once uttered a breath that he cares about me. He will ask if I am thirsty. Or tired. Or if my stomach ails me. But he does not confide in me, as he does with Ciana. Or you." The last was added with a hint of bitterness. "I wish I could be as outspoken as you, Lia. You never fear to say what you are thinking. It serves you well. I always fear I will be misunderstood, so I say not much at all."

"Until now," Lia said with a smile and a little shove. "I have hardly heard you say five words together since you arrived. I did not realize you were so watchful. Or carried so many concerns."

Ellowyn flushed and smiled guiltily. "I could talk to Sowe or Bryn or you. In truth, I still feel like a wretched, even though I know my birth. You act like a highborn girl, despite your station. Why is that?"

Lia bent her neck and thought a moment. "It is my temperament. I do not like being sad, so I choose not to be sad…as often as I can. I try not to regret what I do not have and enjoy what the Medium has given me. I have much to be grateful for. I have the Aldermaston's trust. I have Sowe and Bryn as friends. I have had good teachers in Pasqua and Martin. And I have enjoyed the torturous pleasure of Colvin's friendship, until today, when my outspokenness, as you put it, ruined it. I swear, I would look miserable right now if I did not feel like laughing at myself for being such a fool. An irrevocare sigil. How could I have known such a thing existed?"

Ellowyn squeezed the final garment and set it down. "You could not have known until you were told. Just as I did not know that my parents were married that way. They are dead, of course. But they are together still outside of this flesh. Someday, do you think we will see them again? Those who have passed on?"

Lia pursed her lips and thought. "Martin believed it. He said there is a fair country after this life, where there are no knaves. I imagine the Earl of Dieyre will not be there then," she added impishly.

Ellowyn laughed. "What do you think he is telling them?"

"I suppose we will have to wait until he finishes before we will know." There was a gentle knock on the door. They both looked at each other in surprise. "That was a hasty conversation," Lia said, rising and going to the door. "Marciana?" she asked through the crack.

"Astrid," replied the lad. "M—message from the Aldermaston."

Lia lifted the crossbar, sorry for the boy since it was so late. She saw his eyes first, quailing with fear.

"What is wrong?" Lia asked. The boy slipped inside the room, his entire body trembling. He walked past her, turned, and looked at her, his face white.

"Lia, behind!" Ellowyn shrieked in warning.

She heard the footfall, so soft it could have been the scuffing of a pillow. A strong arm enclosed around her neck, pressing against her throat. She could not breathe as she realized that the kishion had found them.

A desire to be observed, considered, esteemed, praised, beloved, and admired by his fellows is one of the earliest, as well as the keenest, dispositions discovered in the heart of any maston. These dispositions must all be repressed. In playacting, as in the ancient days of Idumea, the applause of the audience is of more importance to the jongleur than their own approbation. But upon the shabby stage of this life, while conscience claps, let the world hiss.

—Gideon Penman of Muirwood Abbey

CHAPTER TWENTY-ONE

Muirwood Awakened

There is nothing more sacred than air to someone dying. How many times had Martin practiced with her. How many times had he said that protecting her breath would save her life. A year earlier, she would have had no thought how to free herself. There was no time to think, no time when each thudding pulse of her heartbeat would bring her to oblivion.

Lia grasped the kishion's arm with both hands and tugged down. As she did, she twisted and stepped backward, bringing her leg behind his. The motion brought her entire weight against the pressure of his arm, and it was enough to force open an airway, to breathe again. Twisting out of the noose, she kicked at the back of his knee, meeting the hard muscle but bending it. If she moved quickly, she could get his hand and twist it the right way to subdue him. She did not see his other elbow whipping around until it struck her cheekbone.

Pain blinded her. The blow was so sudden, so fast, she had not prepared herself for it. Ellowyn shrieked in warning. Lia back-stepped quickly, trying to find her vision again. She staggered back into the far wall, realizing there was nowhere to run.

Her vision cleared as a forearm rammed at her throat. Lia ducked the blow, and the kishion's arm struck the wall with a shudder. She was frantic. With one hand, she clawed at his eyes and felt skin rip beneath her fingers. She brought up her knee, but he was moving again, her fingers suddenly tangled, and he threw her to the ground.

She knew at once that she could not stop the kishion. He was trained every bit as a hunter, even more so and more deadly. It would have been easier to fight off Martin, and she knew that his experience dwarfed hers. As she gazed up at him, she was amazed by what she saw. The strength of his hands belied his size, for he was shorter than her. Wiry and thin, like a page boy. Had she seen him in a crowd, she would not have looked twice—except his eyes. They were a muddy brown color and devoid of any spark of compassion. It was like staring into a spider's soul. He had killed countless men, dispatched them with brutal efficiency. He had no care that he was killing a girl. Only his assignment mattered to him.

From the corner of her eye, she saw Astrid rush for the door and enjoyed a surge of relief. If she could delay the kishion for a few moments, it would be enough to bring Colvin and Edmon and even the Aldermaston. She kicked up at the kishion, but he caught her foot and buried his elbow against the side of her knee. He kept his grip on her ankle and twisted it, spinning her effortlessly onto her stomach. Astrid seized the door handle and pulled.

Lia did not see the dagger appear in the kishion's hand. She only saw it stick in Astrid's back and watched his legs gave way. Leaving Lia on the ground, he rose and walked to the door, shutting it quietly and then dropping the crossbar in place. Astrid twitched on the ground, gasping in pain. Ellowyn let out a hiss of fear and shrank against the wall, cowering.

By the bathing tub on the stone tile, Lia saw her gladius still in its freshly cleaned sheath. The room was not large, but it seemed as if a chasm separated her from it. She pushed herself to her feet, wishing she had even the feeble protection of her hunter leathers instead of the thin chemise.

The kishion approached her without a word. There was no worry in his expression. He knew how it would end, with her dead on the ground and Ellowyn his prisoner—or also killed. Lia looked into his eyes, his dead eyes. His hair was cropped, not much to grab at. A short beard covered his sour mouth. He could be no older than Jon Hunter when he died, though gaunt as a starving man. Lia wished she had her bow at hand, but wishes were for fools. As he approached her, Lia moved away from Ellowyn, toward the large bed, concealing her true aim. She snatched a blanket from the bed top and hurled it him, but the kishion only stopped a moment and let it flutter to the ground. A small smirk tugged one corner of his mouth. Just a twitch, as if a fish hook snagged him.

"Lia," Ellowyn whimpered, biting her hands. She was terror-stricken.

The kishion came forward again, closing the distance more quickly, backing Lia toward the tub. Her cheek throbbed, her knee ached, but she was not afraid. Seeing Astrid laying there, a dagger in his back, made her furious. The hunter was patient. The prey was careless. Lia saw the tremor of the bathwater from the corner of her eye and realized her blade was somewhere on the floor near her and knew her back would collide with the wall if she kept retreating. She did not look away from the kishion's eyes.

Astrid gurgled, spasmed, and then stopped twitching. Somewhere deep in her mind, it was as if she should hear Astrid screaming, though no more than whispers. She knew at once he was dead.

Hate, a searing bitter hate, filled Lia's heart. She glanced quickly, saw the weapon, and lunged for it as the kishion lunged for her. There was no time to draw it from its sheath yet. After she closed her hand around the hilt, she swung it, scabbard and all, at the kishion's head. He dodged the blow and sidestepped her. Lia sidestepped the other direction to increase the space between them, putting herself closer to Ellowyn. She cleared the gladius from its sheath, throwing the empty leather scabbard at him, but again, he flinched slightly, and it sailed past his ear. It was the only moment she had left.

Lia twirled the blade in front of her, whipping it in large circles, and lunged straight at him. His eyes watched the blade's dance as he back stepped in time with her advance. If she could drive him into the corner, it would reduce his movement.

The thought cost her dearly.

Suddenly, the kishion was moving. Just as the blade swung down, he stepped in on her and grabbed her wrist. It was like trying to touch a puddle of quicksilver—he was impossibly fast. Her arm bent the wrong way, making her gasp. A jerk against her wrist and her fingers opened, and the blade dropped with a thump onto the rush-matting nearby. The next thing Lia knew, the bathwater rushed up to meet her. The kishion's fingers clamped around her neck, holding her head under the water. Her arm was still twisted backward, her shoulder screaming in pain. The waters thudded in her ears, and she felt herself dizzy with pain. Drowning—she had never thought she would die that way. She kicked at the kishion, tried to dislodge him, but there was nothing she could do. The air burned in her lungs. She knew if she breathed in the water, she would die. It would end.

She had failed the Aldermaston and Colvin. She had failed the Abbey.

Muirwood.

The thought rushed to her mind. At the head of the tub was a Leering used to summon water. With all her mind, with all her will, she summoned the water and, with it, enough fire to make it scald. The Medium roared inside her as she opened herself to it. She felt the Leering seethe awake, responding to her thoughts with outrage and fury. A blast of steam engulfed them both, and the kishion screamed.

His grip did not loosen; if anything it tightened.

Lia fed the Leering with her desperate need to breathe. It was no longer scalding water but a blast of steam, like a storm suddenly bursting. The kishion let her go, stumbling backward against the onslaught. Lia pulled herself up, gulping in air and spluttering. Ellowyn's face was white with terror at the kishion's ravaged face. His skin was blistering, his eyes welded shut by the reddening flesh. The Medium surged through her, as if every stone and timber screamed with it. The fire Leering at the fireplace blazed white hot.

The kishion stumbled over a chest and went down, his body twitching with pain. Short, heavy grunts came from his mouth. After clawing back to his feet, he staggered toward the door, avoiding the glare of the firepit as if the waves of heat were excruciating.

Lia blinked the water from her eyes, wiped her mouth, and felt the Medium whisper to her.

Redeem the Abbey.

The kishion turned, as if he too had heard the voice. He faced the flames of the fireplace, his hands held up in agony and protection.

Lia stared into the Leering's eyes and summoned a blast of fire that engulfed the kishion in a sheath of flames. It was so bright that Ellowyn shielded her eyes and slunk on her knees, sobbing. It was so bright that it seemed as if the entire chamber was blazing. Instead of night, it could have been the sun at noonday.

There was a rushing sigh, a brief gust, and the fire tamed and stilled. All that remained of the kishion were ashes.

***

Prestwich choked with his grief, bringing fresh tears to Lia's eyes. His snowy head heaved, his face a contortion of emotions. Lia had never seen him display more than casual displeasure, not the crushing sorrow of a parent over a dead child. Astrid lay still on the only bed in the chamber. Lia sat on the edge of a chest, still wearing the chemise that was now spotted with her blood, but she wore her hunter leathers as well, gripping the pommel tightly as if it were the only comfort left.

The Aldermaston conversed with Siara Healer at the door. "Some yarrow poultice, please."

"Can I see the boy?" Siara pleaded. "Is he sleeping? I do not see him breathing."

"It would be helpful if you would bring some yarrow poultice. And some valerianum for Ellowyn. She is with the earls of Forshee and Norris-York, along with Marciana. Thank you."

"I should be caring for him, Aldermaston. Please, he looks very pale. And the floor rushes are soaked with…"

The Aldermaston's voice was firm. "Please, do as I say," he said and shut the door. He lowered the crossbar into place so they would not be disturbed.

Prestwich turned away from the boy's body, his shoulders quivering in silent sobs.

The Aldermaston approached the bedstead slowly, as if every step caused him pain. He clasped Prestwich's shoulder. "Do you believe, my old friend?"

Lia wondered what that meant.

"I…I loved that lad. He…he was always so obedient." His voice choked away. "Should have been I. I am old."

"Do you believe still?"

Prestwich looked up at the Aldermaston. "Yes. I will always believe. I have seen too much to doubt you."

The Aldermaston smiled sadly, patting the other's back and then faced the bed. He approached the soiled blankets where Astrid lay stiff but peaceful.

"Lia, close your eyes," the Aldermaston said.

Surprised, she obeyed, bowing her head as well. She heard the Aldermaston gasp shortly as he reached toward the boy's head.

"Astrid Page," he said in a pained voice. He said nothing after that. Lia felt the Medium in the room, it was so full. She clenched her eyes shut, believing the Medium could heal the boy. He was like a little brother to her. But there was something wrong with the Medium. Some hesitance to it.

"Astrid Page," the Aldermaston said again, as if his voice were choked with an unspent cough.

Lia added her will to his. Let the boy be saved and recovered. Let him live! She burrowed deep within herself. She was dizzy with the lack of sleep and the terrible emotions of the day. Never had she felt so spent, so drained. Yet she shoved the despair and discouragement aside, reaching deep inside herself for hidden wells of strength.

The Aldermaston's voice interrupted her. "Lia?"

She opened her eyes and saw the Aldermaston looking at her, a peculiar expression on his face. His right hand was resting on the crown of Astrid's hair. The other hand was lifted skyward, as if pointing to the stars nearest to Idumea.

"Join your hand to mine," he whispered hoarsely. "It must be so."

Lia stared at him, then nodded in obedience and approached the bed from the other side. She looked at him curiously, then reached her hand over to Astrid's head. The Aldermaston's was knobbed and warm, his veins protruding like old worms. "Make the sign," he said, and she copied him.

As she did, the strength of the Medium flooded through her and into the Aldermaston's hand. She could not breathe, for it burned. Light dazzled her eyes, appearing all around them. It gave her a feeling of warmth and safety.

"Astrid Page, I Gift you with life. Live until your work is completed. By Idumea's hand, may it be so."

There was a shudder on the bed. Lia glanced down at the boy, and his eyes fluttered open. The Aldermaston lowered his hand, his face like gray chalk with the effort. He seemed about to collapse. Lia had never felt such strength and energy in her life. She felt she could run all the way up the Tor and back without pausing for breath. She stared down at Astrid, at his awakening eyes and the recognition in them.

"I...I was dead," he whispered hoarsely. "I saw you both, crowding around the bed. Just a moment ago. Then there was a light, and I felt my breath coming again." He sat up, and Lia started, for the wound was in his back.

She looked at his ripped shirt, and it was gone—healed.

Her eyes met the Aldermaston's over the nest of hair.

"It is time, Lia," he murmured. "You must face the maston test."

She stared at him, shocked. "But I do not…know how to read."

"You must face it still."

CHAPTER TWENTY-TWO

Whitsunday

News about the kishion's attack in the Aldermaston's manor was hushed, and it was forbidden to speak of it. Word began to spread that an untamed fire had happened in the chamber where Ellowyn and Marciana slept, and Lia's quick thinking had prevented it from being a disaster. Astrid recuperated slowly, but he was ever obedient to the Aldermaston's orders. Only a few knew the truth of the attack, including the Earl of Dieyre, who had looked at Lia the next day with guarded respect. The storm blew over the Abbey, and the days that followed were humid and bright.

She did not speak to Colvin over the days that followed. He neither sought her out nor avoided her. His expression was taciturn as always, and he seemed to brood over the impending arrival of Whitsunday. When Lia asked Marciana about the visit with Dieyre, she was vague in her reply and said that Dieyre had attempted to persuade them to an alliance with the Queen Dowager, who he affirmed would be victorious in the contest for power chafing the realm.

Duerden had not tried to find her after she had rebuffed him at the kitchen. She thought perhaps he was biding his time until the festival.

On Whitsunday morning, Lia found herself trudging toward the Abbey kitchen to break her fast before sleeping. There had been no disturbances to Ellowyn or Marciana since the kishion attack, and she found herself dozing in the stillness. As she entered the kitchen, she recognized the familiar trove of delights that Pasqua had been slaving over for days. Pasqua bustled back and forth, pinching loaves, ladling syrupy treacle, and hollering for the girls who were up in the loft, staring out the window.

"It is the same every year," Pasqua bellowed. She glanced at Lia with a grunt of disgust, massaging her shoulder. "This is your second year dancing. It is still the same maypole, still the same streamers. Good morrow, Lia. I have a bowl of porridge and some cheese over by the bread oven. You must be starving."

Lia smiled wearily and fetched the bowl, seeing a generous dollop of treacle to sweeten it. It was delicious and warm and melted on her tongue. "Thank you, Pasqua."

"It was by and by that you lived here," Pasqua said, patting a loaf and shaping it. Flour dusted her hands. "A year that has gone by so quickly. Do you miss it, Lia? Miss being in the kitchen?"

Lia did not have to lie and nodded with enthusiasm. "There is a smell to this kitchen, especially this time of year. A hundred little smells—of cinnamon, of cardamom, of garlic and onions and sage and pumpkins. This is my home, Pasqua. I will always cherish it."

That earned her a smile as well as a fierce hug that nearly took her breath away. Then she looked at Lia closely, her eyes filled with concern. "So he did not want you?" Pasqua asked softly so the other girls wouldn't hear it.

Lia raised her eyebrows and tilted her head curiously.

"You know who I mean," Pasqua said, stroking her arm and giving her a look full of tenderness with a wince of regret. "It is not that cheeky little Duerden I am speaking of. He is a cute boy, but Colvin is a man. I would have sworn on the stars of Idumea that he cared for you."

Lia wanted to wince, but she kept her expression calm. "As a sister. Nothing more. Edmon was wrong."

Pasqua rolled her eyes. "How freely he talks, it is no wonder then. The lad has only half his brains with him at best when he is around Sowe. She is a pretty girl. He would be a fool to pass her by."

Lia wondered who was being the bigger fool, but she said nothing and finished the porridge before joining Sowe and Bryn in the loft.

"Has anyone toppled the old man off the pole yet?" asked Lia mischievously.

Bryn answered first. "No, but they have tried. This is my first year to dance. They better not knock him down."

Sowe touched the glass gently. "There are more people out this year than normal. They must be very excited. You look tired."

"I feel it," Lia replied, drawing near, hovering above both of the sitting girls, and staring out the panes into the village. Sowe's hair was freshly combed, and she smelled of purple mint. Over the year, she had blossomed even more. Lia could see it now, see how her shyness and soft-spoken demeanor gave her an alluring quality. The other wretcheds of the Abbey adored her, except the laundry girls.

Amidst the crowds swarming the village green, there appeared horses with poles fixed with standards bearing the Queen Dowager's emblem. Lia stiffened at the sight, for they were pushing through the crowd toward the main gates of the Abbey.

"Look at all the horses," Bryn murmured in awe, but Lia was already moving. Her sleeplessness was gone as her heart began pounding in fear. Snatching her bow sleeve and quiver, she hurried out the kitchen and sprinted toward the gate.

***

Pareigis sat astride her foam-white stallion. She wore the familiar black velvet gown, as well as a black headdress and gauzy veil that shielded her face from the warm midsummer sun. The late season storm had turned the entire landscape green, and the starkness of the contrast between the Queen Dowager and her mount was striking. She was surrounded by knights, also astride, their hands resting menacingly on sword hilts or the domes of studded maces. Lia approached the gates just behind the Aldermaston, in his wake but close to him to keep an eye. Positioned at the gates ahead of them were much of the Abbey's helpers and teachers, as well as Colvin, Edmon, and the Earl of Dieyre. Lia was the only girl in the company.

When they advanced within earshot, the Queen Dowager stiffened in her saddle. "Your gatekeeper forbids me entrance, Aldermaston! I, who was your honored guest but a few days ago. I told you my coming was to be expected, yet I am forbidden to enter!" Her voice rang with fury.

The Aldermaston stopped near the gate, his face masking the pain she had noticed earlier. Anger brooded in his eyes. "You may celebrate Whitsunday in any quarter of the realm you desire, Queen Dowager. But you have violated the oath of hospitality and so are refused admittance to the grounds. There are many fine inns within the village to choose from."

"Open the gates," Pareigis ordered, and Lia felt a surge from the Medium at her words.

The Aldermaston stared at her curiously, his eyebrows arching. He kept his focus on her, but Lia searched the faces of the soldiers surrounding her. One of them stood out in the baleful sunlight, for his eyes glowed silver. It was Scarseth, wearing the Queen Dowager's livery. His hand clutched the fabric near his heart, and she knew he was fondling the kystrel. Lia felt the Medium quicken within her.

"I forbid it," the Aldermaston replied.

The white stallion pranced and twirled, and the Queen Dowager adjusted her view of them from her haughty pose. "Open the gates, Aldermaston. I have just returned from the killing fields of Winterrowd. Do you wish me to accuse you so publicly?"

It was a taunt, one spoken with malice intended. Lia stiffened her hold on the bow stave.

"As this was your intent all along, why ruin it? Say what you must and be done with it."

Lia could see the Queen Dowager's teeth. She rose higher in the saddle, her back stiff and straight. With a black glove, she pointed directly at the Aldermaston. "I accuse you of high treason by the name of Gideon Penman, Aldermaston of Muirwood Abbey. For you did willfully and unlawfully bring about the death of my lord husband, the late king of Comoros. I charge that you did aid and abet fugitives of the king's justice, even the earls of Forshee and Norris-York. That you sent your own sworn man, Jon Hunter, to bring them safely through this Hundred to plot my husband's death at Winterrowd. That your sworn man, Jon Hunter, did fell the king with this bloodied arrow!" Her voice had built to a fevered pitch, and she thrust the arrow into the air within the sight of everyone assembled.

"Therefore I arrest you, Gideon Penman, for the murder of my lord husband. You will stand trial for your crimes and be punished in the manner befitting a traitor. I charge the Earl of Forshee with high treason. I grant amnesty to the newly made Earl of Norris-York, for he was not a party to the plot. Now in the name of the young king, I command you to open the gates!"

The surge of the Medium was so strong it rocked Lia back on her heels. The Aldermaston bowed his head, as if bracing himself against an unseen storm beating cruelly upon him. The strain of it showed, but he lifted his head again. She saw his legs begin to the tremble and stepped forward to hold him up, but he glanced at her in warning, his eyes blazing.

Turning, he faced the Queen Dowager. "You have no authority to condemn me," he stated simply. "Surely you know that."

"In Dahomey, traitors are dealt with regardless of their rank," she spat.

"But we are not in Dahomey, nor do we converse in Dahomeyjan."

"Some of yours can speak it well enough," the Queen Dowager sneered.

"As do many in this country. But you overlook that, as an Aldermaston, I can only be brought to trial by the High Seer of Avinion. You have no legal custody over me or this Abbey. I have the charter grants engraved and sealed within the cloister library. The king has no jurisdiction here and neither do you. You come here and flaunt your supposed authority in the hope of cowing me into submission. I refuse to accommodate you. I will answer to the High Seer only."

Her face was beautiful but twisted with fury. "A formality I have not overlooked, Aldermaston. Even as we speak, I have riders brooking to Avinion."

"The term is *breaking*, your highness. Your Dahomeyjan tongue gets tangled at times. I do not fear the evidence you will undoubtedly conjure to support your accusation. My man Jon Hunter was murdered in the Bearden Muir by the sheriff of Mendenhall, and I can summon his bones to prove it. You helped dig his grave, did you not, my lord Earl of Forshee?"

Colvin was as stern as a boulder. "With my own hands, Aldermaston. He was my guide through the Bearden Muir. He was killed by the sheriff, as the Aldermaston says. He was dead prior to the battle."

"You were seen!" Pareigis shrieked. "Following the battle, you were seen with the hunter! I have twelve witnesses who will vouchsafe it."

"Then produce your witnesses," Colvin snapped. "There were many looters after the battle that came to strip the corpses. For the right coin, they would say anything you wished. I demand to face my accusers. I am not a traitor but a member of the king's Privy Council. Your accusation is absurd."

"You are not an Aldermaston," Pareigis said, seething. "You are an earl of the realm. You must face a trial of your peers, as you say. So I arrest you…"

"He is within the protection of Muirwood Abbey," the Aldermaston said, interrupting her. "These grounds safeguard him, as they do any with the rank of maston. You cannot arrest him here. It is contrary to the laws of the realm. I will not grant you audience any longer. Be gone." He turned and started to hobble away, his face grave and wincing with pain.

"Do not turn your back on me!" she commanded. "This is your final warning. Open the gates at once! I cannot hold my men back forever."

The Aldermaston paused and looked back at her, as if she were nothing but a buzzing fly. "I am not concerned for my safety or the safety of this Abbey, Pareigis. You mock what you do not even comprehend."

"No, Aldermaston," she replied in a low voice. "It is you who does not understand. These bars will not protect you from me. And those who mistakenly trust that you will shield them will cower and wail in fear when they discover it is but an empty promise. Even walls of stone can burn."

Like fragile ice, anger passes away in time. Therefore, the greatest remedy for anger is delay.

—Gideon Penman of Muirwood Abbey

CHAPTER TWENTY-THREE

Pareigis's Terms

The Aldermaston walked firmly away from the gates, trailed by Lia, Prestwich, and the knight-mastons. Shortly after, the Earl of Dieyre caught up with them, his stride easily overtaking theirs. His voice throbbed with anger.

"It would not take much to batter down those gates," Dieyre warned. "You should treat with her while you still can. She is merciful. She has spared many from the gallows."

"No doubt to enlist them into her service," the Aldermaston replied archly.

"I cannot believe you are ignorant of the risks you face by opposing her. Do you not care of the lives of the villagers?"

Colvin's voice was cold with fury. "Are you saying she will turn those murderers loose on our countrymen?" His hand closed around the sword pommel.

"No, Forshee, I am not. But I cannot believe the Aldermaston would risk it. She does not suffer fools, and she remembers every slight. Offer to treat with her."

"I will not let her step foot on the grounds," the Aldermaston replied gravely.

"You let her in before."

The Aldermaston stopped and faced Dieyre. "I will not treat with her."

"Why ever not?"

Lia had rarely seen the Aldermaston so furious. His expression blazed with contempt. "Have a care how you mock me, my lord. You are a stripling that has barely seen a score of years. I have seen kings and princes and Aldermastons scheme and plot and kill before you finished your first wet-nurse. Do you think I am a simpleton? That your presence within the Abbey walls at this moment is not entirely convenient for her purposes? Have a care, Dieyre. You are not on the king's land. This is my domain."

The earl's eyes flashed with pent-up anger. "You are actually threatening me, old man?" His hand dropped to his hilt. Colvin stepped forward, his motion timed exactly with Lia's.

Dieyre's voice dripped with mocking. "Please, Forshee. Do not embarrass yourself."

"Neither of you will draw your swords," the Aldermaston said. "There will be no more bloodshed on these grounds. The Abbey will strike down any who lift their hand in wrath."

Dieyre snorted. "I do not believe that."

"It does not matter whether you believe it," came the reply. "I have warned you."

Dieyre did not release his grip on his weapon, as if debating whether he would test the Aldermaston's claim or not. He glared at them with disgust. "For how many centuries have men like you with gray beards warned that some doom or other would happen if we did not listen to your words. It is a web of lies. This Abbey is no more protected by the Medium than is my little finger. If people believe a lie long enough, it becomes truth to them. Let me be candid. This Abbey is surrounded. It is vulnerable. There is no walled keep to lay siege against. This is no fortress that will hold out until Demont can answer a cry for help. If Pareigis wills it, the townsfolk will be put to death, and she will make you watch, Aldermaston. You delude yourself if you think some mystical power that mastons alone control will save you or this Abbey. If you thwart her, she will burst open the gates, round up everyone inside, and set it afire as an example to others that they need not believe the Medium even cares which sides use it. Can your heart cope with that, old man? Can you watch your great Abbey burned?"

Lia felt a swelling feeling of protectiveness surge inside her. She wanted to strike Dieyre across the mouth for suggesting it, but she deferred to the Aldermaston, who gazed at him coldly.

"You never earned the rank of maston," he said. "So you do not understand that you are playing into her hands."

"I refuse to swear blindly to follow the whisperings of dead ghosts. I do not believe in these little mutterings you believe in. It is a lie."

The Aldermaston's gaze turned thoughtful. "What are her terms?"

Dieyre arched his eyebrow. "You will have to ask her..."

"Do not for a moment think that I believe anything but that you are in league with her in every possible way. I will not play this game with you, this bartering for trifles. What are her terms?"

"Ellowyn Demont in her custody."

"To murder her?"

Dieyre looked shocked. "By the Hand, no!" he said as if it were the most ludicrous suggestion. "We need her alive to treat with Demont!"

The Aldermaston smirked. "Is that what she told you?"

Lia could see the discomfort on Dieyre's face. "You are trying to plant seeds of distrust in me, Aldermaston."

"Am I?"

The Earl shifted uncomfortably. "Demont controls the king. Controlling the king gives him the control over the patronage of the realm. Every minor office, every major office. Forshee and York have both benefitted from this."

"And you have not," the Aldermaston stated simply.

"Power must be shared. Demont thinks that because he is a maston," he nearly spat the word, "that his motives should be trusted without question. I am sorry, but I have known mastons who have lied and cheated. Who have violated their supposed oaths sworn in the bowels of an Abbey like this one. Sevrin Demont once held control of a king, too, and it cost him his life. The Medium abandoned him just as it will abandon his son because it answers to whoever wants it the most. It answers to the strongest will. If we have the girl, it can avoid further bloodshed. We can negotiate an ending to the hostilities. Think of how many lives could be saved, Aldermaston."

There was a pause before the reply. "When must we relinquish custody of the girl?"

"You have until the morrow," Dieyre replied. "I do not care how many horses Demont has. He is already being lured north to face the Earl of Caspur. Even if you could get a message to him, there is no way he could get here in time. You must see that she has the upper hand. If you believe the Abbey will save you, that your will in controlling the Medium is stronger than hers, then defy her. At dawn, the Abbey will fall, and the villagers will all be killed. It is within your power to protect them. Release the girl. Do not be a fool."

The Aldermaston looked wary. "I ask for one term."

"What is that?" The earl had a smug look on his face.

"A safe conduct. To anyone who wishes to leave the Abbey. Anyone—learner or wretched. If the Queen Dowager seeks to make an example, let her limit it to those who do defy her. But if I am right, the Abbey will defend us as it did when the kishion struck. Even if there are only a handful of us remaining, let that be your witness that the Medium is on *our* side."

The Earl of Dieyre shrugged. "I will personally vouchsafe their safety, upon my honor. The gates are made of iron. The walls are made of simple stone. It is beautiful and impressive. But it is not sacred or guarded by anything more mysterious than generations of lies. I have given you a chance to see reason."

"Very well. Please present my terms to the Queen Dowager straight away. Any who leave the Abbey grounds are no longer under my protection. But I will hold you accountable, personally, for their safety."

"You are a fool, Aldermaston. But I think you are bluffing. At dawn, we will see who is right."

"We will indeed. My hunter will escort you to the postern gate."

***

Lia said nothing to the Earl of Dieyre as they walked, and he said nothing to her until they reached the gate. The postern was away from the main gate, one of the few other walled entrances to the grounds, a small iron door that provided another means of exiting the grounds.

"If you killed the kishion, as I think you did, then I am amazed at your resourcefulness." He gave her a nod of respect.

"My offer still stands, even though the bruises on your cheek have not fully faded." With a finger, he caressed the skin of her cheekbone. "Come with me, and you will not want for opportunities."

Lia nodded to the doorman to unlock it. "I believe we already had that conversation," she replied.

"Very well, then do me the honor of passing on a word to Marciana."

Lia breathed heavily. "It is time for you go, my lord."

"You are a harsh strumpet, but I like you." He looked her sharply in the eyes. "Tell her that she owes me a dance around the maypole tonight. I will be waiting for her. If she comes, her brother lives. If she does not, I cannot keep that promise. I do it for her sake, not for his. You can tell I despise him. Send her my message." He reached into a pouch at his waist and withdrew a fistful of gleaming coins to give her. Once, long ago, a man had offered her coins for her help.

She refused to take it. "Good-bye, my lord."

He looked at her warily, a confused smile on his mouth. He shrugged and followed the doorman into the inner wall. Then he paused and without looking back, he said, "We know of the tunnels beneath the Abbey." And then he was gone, and the doorman shut and locked the gate behind him.

There was an oppressive pall in her heart that contrasted with the gleaming blue sky and the smell of fresh flowers on the grounds. As she walked back toward the manor house, she fished the ring out of her bodice and squeezed its edges until it hurt. Every word the Queen Dowager and Dieyre said was sopping with doubt and menace. They rattled her soul, yet still she believed in the Medium's power. She had experienced it so vividly throughout her life that she could not deny its reality. Yet Dieyre's warning cast little shards of doubt into her heart. She tried to crush them, but still they poked and stabbed her.

When Colvin and Ellowyn had first arrived, the Aldermaston told her that the time would come when she would need to use the Cruciger orb to find a safe haven for them. She knew that they would leave that night, under the cover of darkness. Only in the dark would they be able to find their way past the wall of Pareigis's men. That was the only thing she could think of. But what if Dieyre was right? What if they had a way to release the Blight on Muirwood, and it would no longer be able to defend itself? There was so much she did not know. There was so much confusion. Glancing around herself as she walked, she saw the frantic scurrying of wretcheds and learners alike. So many had overheard the altercation at the gates. Rumors would be flying to every corner of the Abbey. Doubts and more doubts.

She reached the manor house and found the Aldermaston conversing with Colvin in the hall. "Yes, enough provisions for several days. See Pasqua, she will prepare them for you. I must give other instructions. If you need any additional supplies, see my steward. There is much to do still."

He gripped Colvin's arm to steer him away, but the earl stopped him. "You are wise, as Lia says. I trust your judgment in this, and I am grateful you did not betray us."

The Aldermaston nodded impatiently. "Yes, yes, be gone. I must speak to Lia now. Come, child."

Colvin glanced at her, his expression concerned but hopeful, then left.

Lia approached him worriedly.

"Is Dieyre gone?" he asked in his whisperlike voice.

Lia nodded. "He gave me a warning…"

He hushed her with his fingers. "Of course he did. Speak no more of it. For a moment, I thought my plan would be ruined, that he would never leave."

"Your plan?" Lia asked, a little dazed.

"Oh yes, Lia. And because the Medium is truly with us, I received confirmation of it this very morning."

Lia was excited. "Is Garen Demont coming?"

The Aldermaston smirked. "No, the Earl of Dieyre was well-informed on that point. He is leagues away, heading into a conflict against a superior force. He is betrayed on all sides."

Lia gulped. "But I thought you said…"

He hushed her again and turned and opened the door, beckoning her to follow him. "Yes, the Queen Dowager is well-informed, and they laid their trap very deftly. I commend them for their subtlety. But as we learn in the tomes, be wise as serpents, yet harmless as doves. They have managed to discover and keep watch over many of our secret tunnels. But not all of them. Not all of them."

He motioned toward the window seat.

Martin sat there, arms folded smugly, his teeth showing through his beard in a fierce grin. "By Cheshu, lass. It is good to see you safe."

CHAPTER TWENTY-FOUR

The Wretched of Pry-Ree

With a surge of relief and a half-choked sob, Lia rushed to Martin and hugged him. His face was smudged with dirt, his eyes puffy from lack of sleep but still alert. Some of Pasqua's crumbs were stuck in his beard, but he managed to shoo her back, scowling at her affection, yet his gaze was gentle and warm.

"That is enough, lass, stop smothering me. You thought I had died on my journey? But I am not careless and evaded the Dowager's net. Had to wait most of yesterday to slip past them at nightfall, but it was dark, and they are drenched. The Aldermaston said you did well enough in my absence. I suppose you learned something from me after all."

Lia took his dirty hands with hers and squeezed them. "I learned *everything* from you. Where have you been?"

"Roundabout," he replied. "A hard journey. There is much that has happened in the wide world. I have already told the Aldermaston. We will be parting again soon, but at least you know your own strength now."

She gazed back at the Aldermaston, who nodded slowly.

"You noticed me speaking with the Earl of Forshee just now," the Aldermaston said. "Martin brought ill tidings. Two Abbeys have fallen in the last fortnight. Burned by fire."

Lia felt stricken. "Which?" she whispered.

"Dorset Abbey in Caspur's domain. And Sempringfall Abbey to the east."

"Sempringfall!" Lia gasped. "That was Ellowyn's…"

"Indeed," the Aldermaston said. "Garen Demont is marching northward with an army to confront the Earl of Caspur's forces. Which is why the Queen Dowager is combining her allies here. Martin will take Ellowyn and the others into the Bearden Muir tonight. That will give them a strong lead when Pareigis comes calling in the morning."

Lia was confused, but she still clutched at Martin's hands as she stared at the Aldermaston. "I want to go. You said I would be the one to take them."

He shook his head. "I need you here, child."

"But I have the orb," she insisted. "Where is Martin going to take them?"

"He has not told me, nor will he. He is the only one who knows, and that is for the best right now. I can claim honestly to the Queen Dowager that I do not know where they are."

"It is for the best, lass," Martin said, freeing one of his hands and patting hers. "The Aldermaston needs you here."

She bit her lip, feeling the sudden weight of hopelessness at the thought of Colvin leaving Muirwood without her. She had to see him before he went. How awkward it would be to part without bidding him good-bye. As much as it tortured her to see him ever since their moments together in the orchard, it would even more unendurable *not* to see him.

She looked at the Aldermaston again, who slowly sunk into his chair, his face a mask of twisted pain. She had noticed it growing more severe. "You are sick," she whispered.

He closed his eyes tightly, fighting against a hidden pain. "Not sick, Lia. I am dying. That is why I need you to stay."

It was as if he had slapped her hard across the face. "But you cannot be," she murmured.

"Oh, I am old enough to recognize the limits of my humanity. It may not happen for a while yet. But it will certainly happen. Maybe even tomorrow," he added with a hushed voice.

Lia left Martin's side and approached the Aldermaston. "What is it that ails you?"

"I am old, Lia," he replied with a wincing smile. "I knew this time would come. My keenest desire is the protection of Muirwood, the records guarded in the cloister, and everyone who shelters here. While I am within the boundaries of the Abbey, the defenses will work. It takes great desire and concentration to maintain them. I need...your strength. Especially if the Queen Dowager storms the gates on the morrow. Your strength, coupled with mine, should be enough. If it is not, then I need you to lead the others to safety. Will you do that for me?"

Tears stung her eyes.

"Do not cry, Lia. I knew this day would come. It may not be tomorrow. But it is helpful to be prepared regardless. As is a tale, so is life: not how long it is, but how good it is, is what matters."

The hot tears trickled down her cheeks. All her life, she had known the Aldermaston. She had not even known his real name until Pareigis spoke it that morning. In his gray cassock and robes, he seemed the embodiment of Muirwood itself—built from stone, permanent. His cropped beard and thinning hair were white still, but his brows had always been dark, his eyes even darker and full of strength and will. Even now, as he struggled without complaining against the pain that caused him much suffering, his eyes were fierce and determined, his mouth pressed firmly into a perpetual scowl. Much like Martin's.

"What can I do?" Lia whispered.

He looked at her seriously. "You must pass the maston test. Tonight."

Again, it felt as if he had struck her. She looked at him in shock, almost unable to speak. "Why do you think I will be able to pass it when others more learned than me have not?"

His frown was pinched for a moment into a smile. "Because your thoughts are stronger. I know that you have long suspected your ancestry, at least on one side, is Pry-rian. I have been an Aldermaston for many years and have hosted many visitors from different kingdoms. I once met one of the rulers of Pry-Ree, back when a truce had been declared between our realms. This was before your birth. He was a king-maston and honored Muirwood with a visit during his journey to Comoros to treat with our lords. I asked him how long he had worn the chaen, and he surprised me with his answer. It was a tradition of his Family, he said, to wear it by the age of fifteen. His own grandfather had passed the maston test at fourteen. His grandfather was a great leader and unified some of the warring factions within his realm and became the high king of Pry-Ree. He was exceptionally gifted in the Medium. His grandson, the one I had the pleasure of meeting, had passed the test himself at a young age."

Lia's heart buzzed with desire. "This king-maston that you met. Was he related to Ellowyn's family?"

The Aldermaston nodded, his expression curiously vague. "Very much. He married Ellowyn's mother while she was in exile in Dahomey because of a truce he had made with Sevrin Demont years before. A truce which he honored, even though Demont was murdered, his lands forfeited, and his body brutally mutilated. Those were dark days. The daughter became a woman, and he honored his promise to her father, even though she brought him nothing by means of wealth and certainly nothing by reputation. Ellowyn was the result of their marriage. The mother died during the birthing. This noble prince was so bereft, though he loved the child."

Lia had heard this story before. "Do you think…?" She paused, collecting her thoughts. "Do you think I am from that family somehow?" She was desperate to believe it.

"It is possible," he replied. "I have wondered what signs of your heritage would emerge as you got older. It was last year, when the Medium opened up in you as it never had before. Back when you left Muirwood. The old king, you remember, was the one who crushed Pry-Ree. It was no accident that you were at Winterrowd. I feel that strongly." He flinched again, biting back his words from the pain. "It is no accident that you are here now to protect an heir of Pry-Ree."

She looked down at her muddy shoes, exhausted but excited. "Did this high king have any close relations? Any brothers or sisters?"

"He did indeed. He was survived by a younger brother who became high king on his death. He was rebellious as a child. He never was a maston himself, and so the Medium did not help him. He was captured by the old king and executed."

"Did he have any children?" Lia asked.

"It was common knowledge that he fathered many children, within and without of wedlock."

Lia bit her lip, struggling with her surging feelings. "Why did you not tell me this before?"

"When Almaguer first visited?" he asked, wincing as new stabs of pain afflicted him. He shifted uncomfortably in his chair. "You showed a penchant for the Medium, but nothing more than that. It was after you returned from the Bearden Muir that you told me the orb spoke to you in Pry-rian. When you aided me healing Astrid, the Medium spoke to me very clearly. It was time for you to take the test."

Lia nodded dumbly, amazed at what she had learned.

The Aldermaston's eyes flashed. "There is a mystery here, Lia. You see, there are no wretcheds in Pry-Ree."

She looked at him sharply, then glanced at Martin, who nodded. "It is true, lass, what the Aldermaston tells you. If children are born out of wedlock, they have the same rights of inheritance as a natural born child. We feel it a great cruelty to abandon any child." His voice choked for a moment with strong emotions. He clenched his teeth again, grimacing, then continued. "If one is abandoned, there is always a family willing to claim the babe. Always. Even total strangers. There is no practice of abandoning a child in the gutters of an Abbey. It does not happen."

A surge of feelings went through her. She looked at the Aldermaston seriously. "So you are saying it is a rare thing for me to be here. A wretched from Pry-Ree?"

He nodded slowly. "Indeed, it is rare but not impossible. You were born when Pry-Ree fell. The children of the ruling Family were gathered up, Ellowyn for example. Get some rest now, Lia. You must be fresh if you are to face the test tonight. It will not be easy. Martin will slip away with the others while we are inside the Abbey. Before dawn, you will be a maston."

Lia swallowed and thought about what she had learned. "Do you truly think so?"

The Aldermaston winced again, but he did not gasp or quail. His knuckles were white as he gripped the table. "Passing the test requires a good memory. You must be prepared to remember what you learn inside. I cannot help. I can only teach you. You may ask no questions once we are inside. But if I know anything about you, Lia—you do have a good memory. You always have."

She smiled at him and then started for the door. As she touched the handle, she stopped and glanced back. "Is the Blight coming, Aldermaston?"

His face was grave. "Only the Abbeys hold it at bay, child."

"If Muirwood falls, it will come?"

He nodded slowly. "When you become a maston, you will be hunted. Those like the Queen Dowager will seek your blood."

She gave him a small smile. "I think you suspected that happening when you called *me* to be a hunter."

"Wise…for one so young," he whispered hoarsely.

She gave the Aldermaston a look of sympathy. "I am glad to be taking the test at Muirwood. It is my Abbey. I will defend her."

Perseverance is more prevailing than violence; and many things, which cannot be overcome when they are together, yield themselves up when taken little by little. Many tyrants have sat on a throne, and those whom no man would think on, have worn crowns.

—Gideon Penman of Muirwood Abbey

CHAPTER TWENTY-FIVE

Duerden's Kiss

It was a fitful sleep full of strange, whimsical dreams. Lia awoke gradually, feeling more rested than she deserved, considering the punishment she had given her body in recent days. As she left Pasqua's bedchamber and exited the manor house, there was the feeling of fog in the air, though nothing obstructed her vision. The sunlight came down at an angle, indicating the approaching dusk. The air was thick and humid, each breath heavier than normal. From the corner of her eye, she saw the majestic Abbey, and it seemed to whisper to her, to beckon her inside to learn its secrets. For a moment, it seemed alive, staring at her.

As she rounded the corner to the kitchen, there was Duerden pacing outside, his face flushed. He did not see her, so she darted back around the corner and went toward the rear doors, where she could avoid him. There was a whistling sound and she paused, peering around the bend. In the shade was Colvin, lunging with his sword, swooping and twirling it as if he faced a dozen knights trying to kill him. She bit her lip, wondering if that was the moment to talk to him, but he looked so fierce and determined that she slunk away, back against the wall.

Both doors were blocked.

Muttering to herself at the unfairness of it, she decided to confront Duerden. When he saw her coming, his cheeks flushed.

"Are you going…to the maypole dance?" Duerden asked, stammering in his speech.

She stared at him as if he were ridiculous. "I do not think anyone will be dancing tonight," she answered.

"No! Several have been outside the gates and back again with the news. The Queen Dowager wants the Aldermaston and the earls in custody. Everyone else has been given a safe conduct to come and go as they desire. She announced it at noon and opened up her coffers to pay for cider and bread. Those who approach her knights are given coins. Whitsunday is still going to happen tonight. Where have you been, Lia?"

She was dumbstruck. What was happening? "I have been sleeping, Duerden. The Aldermaston has errands for me tonight." How exactly could she tell him that she was facing the maston test?

"Surely you are not staying here tonight," he said warningly.

"Surely I am. Muirwood is my home," she answered. "Jon Hunter did not murder the old king, Duerden! The Aldermaston had nothing to do with it."

He looked crestfallen. "The other wretcheds are leaving. Reome, Treasa, they are all in the square drinking Muirwood cider! The only ones who have stayed behind are Astrid, Pasqua, and Sowe. They are in the kitchen, eating the treats because Pasqua will not leave, and she will not sell them to the Queen's men."

"Did Bryn leave?"

"I think so..."

Lia shook her head and marched past him to the kitchen doors, but he caught her arm.

"Lia, you cannot stay here!"

She looked him in the eye. "How can you abandon him, Duerden? He is the Aldermaston. Who is the Queen Dowager but a foreigner from Dahomey? When did she earn the right to govern in this Hundred? To threaten us? Go join the others then. I will not abandon him."

His expression was troubled, wracked with pain. "I do not want you to get hurt. I...I care about you."

She scowled at him. "I know. The Aldermaston told me. We are only fifteen, Duerden."

He looked desperate. "My father and mother were both fifteen when they pledged their troth to each other. They did not marry until later, of course. I was not suggesting...what I mean is that I did not want you to think...you are right, we are so young, but I wanted you to know how I felt about you."

She looked at him with a mixture of affection and exasperation. "I care about you, Duerden, but you are a learner. You do not need to pledge your troth to me. I am only a wretched."

"Not to me," he answered firmly. "I have given it much thought, Lia."

"But we see things so differently. You want to join the dancing. I have duties here."

"My parents are out there, Lia. How can I remain in here?"

"You should go to them. Please, go to them! I do not deserve your feelings, Duerden. And we are still too young. You may feel different...after you know me better."

He looked pained. "We have known each other for two years. This is not a mere fancy."

She shook her head. "There are things I cannot share with you. Things that I know...about myself. I will not make any promises to you. I owe the Aldermaston a debt that I must repay. Please, go to your family. Be sure they are safe."

He struggled with his feelings for a moment. Then he took her hand and kissed it quickly. "My feelings will not change, Lia. But I will obey you, as I always have." With a look of despair and sadness, he walked away from the kitchen toward the outer gates.

Lia swore at herself in frustration, with the lingering sensation of his lips on her knuckles alarming her. It was a tender gesture, straight from his heart, and it worried her. She turned and opened the kitchen door and received another shock when she stepped inside.

There was Edmon standing in front of Sowe, his face so close to hers, his voice low and urgent. He was holding her hand. Pasqua dabbed at her eyes as she watched nearby, her face a mixture of emotions.

Edmon's face jerked as she entered, but he looked relieved. "Lia! Thank the Medium. I thought it was the Aldermaston." He looked back at Sowe. "If you are forced to flee the Abbey, you will find a safe haven in Norris-York. My groomsman's name is Jon Orchard. He will offer you shelter until I return. If you can, hire a wagon or cart to take you. Here," he said, fumbling at his belt untying his purse. He seized several coins from it and plopped them into her hand. "This will be plenty for clothes and shelter. Disguises. Only if it comes to that." He looked over at Lia. "For you, as well, if Colvin will not shelter you. But I think he will."

Sowe bit her lip. "You do not have to give me anything. Pasqua and I will be fine. If the Abbey falls, Lia will protect us."

His face looked pained. "I do not doubt it. But Dieyre's threats are haunting me. If they force the gates open, I want you to run.

Hide where you can. Wait until it is safe and then slip away. I will look for you on my estate. Can I trust you to do that, Sowe? Pasqua?"

Sowe nodded, unable to meet his pleading eyes.

Lia stood, staring at them quietly, unable to mistake the pain in Edmon's eyes.

"This may be the only chance I get to say good-bye," Edmon said. "The Aldermaston wants us in his manor house before sunset so that we can be seen entering."

"I know," Sowe whispered, still unable to look up. "Good-bye then." She clutched the coins and fidgeted with her hands. Tears dangled from her lashes.

Sowe looked so beautiful in the fading light that Lia could only stare, her back to the door to prevent anyone from intruding on the moment. She held the crossbar brackets behind her.

"Sowe." His voice was just a whisper.

She glanced up at him, her eyes deep with fear and brimming with longing. He leaned down and kissed her on the mouth. Watching from the doorway, Lia was stricken by its simplicity, its tenderness, and with the crushing sickness of jealousy that Colvin would never do that to her.

When their lips parted, he grasped her shoulders and forced her to look at him. "I can only leave knowing that you will do everything to safeguard yourself." He reached down and took her trembling hands and brought them up to his mouth for another kiss, like Duerden had. "I hope these coins will aid your departure. If not, and nothing happens, then they are a small token of the pleasure you have brought me on my stay at Muirwood. Or you can take them as payment for a kiss, which I did not ask your leave to take." With one finger, he traced the bottom of her chin. "For that, I beg your pardon."

She nodded mutely, struggling to find her voice. Then said softly, "I forgive you."

Edmon enfolded her in his arms, rested his chin against her hair, and then broke away and started for the door.

Lia felt the door tug behind her, but she was gripping the crossbar brace so tightly that it did not open. Coughing in warning to Edmon, she turned and opened the door and found Colvin standing there, sweat glistening on his forehead, his blade sheathed in its scabbard. He looked startled to see her, his face showing the surprise before hardening into impassivity again.

"Edmon," he beckoned, but the other earl was on his way. He looked at Sowe, who trembled like a leaf, and said nothing until after he had exited the kitchen.

"What were you doing?" Colvin asked as they started away, without a single word to Lia.

"Bid the girl good-bye," Edmon said in a tight whisper.

"By her look, you did more than that," Colvin warned.

The whisper was louder, frustrated. "No, I said bid the girl good-bye! Lia! Do not just walk away from her."

Colvin scratched an itch at his neck. "I will do that in my own..."

"When?" Edmon said with a surge of anger. "You are so hard-hearted, I swear. Your way then. Insufferable..."

Lia felt the tiny pleasure of vindication and shut the door so she could no longer hear them. But a moment later, there was a knock behind her, and she turned and found Colvin standing there. He glanced at Sowe and Pasqua within, but then back at Lia again. His jaw was clenched with fury. She knew the look well and gave him raised eyebrows only, saying nothing.

"Can I speak with you?" he asked.

She shrugged and left the kitchen behind, shutting the door slowly. Her heart pounded inside her chest, but she tried to look calm and self-assured. It was a lie, but she tried her best to make it seem natural. They had not really spoken since that day in the grove of apple trees. The fading sunlight turned the gray walls of the Abbey a rich golden hue. Again, she had the feeling of it calling to her, summoning her.

"Walk with me," Colvin said and started back to the manor house. "Even though I cannot tell you where we are going, that would not stop you from finding us."

She said nothing. He knew she had the Cruciger orb and could find him anywhere.

"Marciana told me this afternoon that she wished you were going with us, instead of Martin. He is a stranger to her, but I know that you trust him. You owe your skills to him. He has trained you well."

"Thank you," she replied, wondering what he would say next.

He did not say anything, and they reached the rear door to the manor house. He stood facing the door, as if struggling with the act of extending his hand and opening it. "I do not fear for your safety, like Edmon does. He still has much to learn about controlling his feelings. I trust you to the Medium. If you follow it, you cannot do better." He turned and looked at her. "We are leaving Muirwood tonight. I will not be coming back."

Lia managed to keep her composure, but inside she anguished. "I will worry about you, wherever you are."

He shut his eyes and then looked at her. "You have enough worries here to occupy your thoughts at present. I must go."

She stopped him as he reached for the door. "There is a question I never asked you."

He paused, his jaw clenching, but he kept his temper in check. "Yes?"

She moistened her lips. "Were you afraid to take the maston test? Is it something to be feared?"

His eyes glinted. The shadows around them thickened as the sun went down beyond the distant hills. For a moment, he paused, thinking of his response. "It is something to fear in its own way. There is a weight and risks to the obligation, not the least of which is being asked to sacrifice your life, as happened to Edmon's brother."

She looked at him hard. "The risk of being murdered?"

He nodded subtly, his expression stern. "There are fates worse than murder."

She crinkled her eyebrows. "I cannot imagine that."

"Well, it is clear from studying the tomes," he went on, "that those who do not fight the Myriad Ones may end up becoming like them."

She shrank within herself. The thought was as repulsive as she could imagine. "Are you saying that the Myriad Ones are the souls of the dead?"

He looked her in the eye. "No. The Myriad Ones go by many names. One of those names is the Unborn. They are souls too evil to be born."

She shivered in the twilight.

"They surround us constantly, Lia. In the air we breathe. They worry us and nag at us with their thoughts. They deceive and seduce. If Muirwood falls, it will be because of them and those who heed their whispers. Rather than allowing us to be overrun by them, sometimes Idumea sends the Blight. Even death would be a better fate than to live in a world ruled by the Unborn." He pressed his lips closed. "Perhaps I have said more than I should have. The knowledge is a maston's burden to carry. I am sorry if I disturbed you. Why did you ask?"

Lia looked at his face, tried to hold it in her mind in case she never saw him again. But she did not reveal why. "I always have questions. You know that. Be well on your journey." She turned away toward the kitchen, not wanting him to see the tears that swelled in her eyes at the thought she would never see him again.

CHAPTER TWENTY-SIX

The Essaios

When Lia had crept inside Muirwood Abbey to seek Colvin at the Pilgrim, she had been amazed at the Leerings inside, how they had lent life to flowers and plants that never enjoyed the sun's warmth. On that day, she had stolen inside as a wretched. Now she was invited. Instead of her wretched gown and cloak, she wore the learner robes she had seen others wear and a veil to cover her face and hair and hide her identity. Prestwich walked alongside her the short distance from the manor house to the Abbey door she had entered before. The Aldermaston would be waiting for her within, she was told. She was nervous as she approached.

Prestwich halted before reaching the final steps leading up to the doors. His face flushed with emotion. He was as old as the Aldermaston. How long had he served him? "You will go on alone," he said. "The gates are shut on the Aldermaston's orders. No one will be allowed in or out of the grounds until he emerges. Good luck, Lia."

"Thank you," she replied and turned back to the final steps. As she approached, she experienced the warning feelings of the Leerings inset into the archway, filling her with doubt and dread. But she expected them, and their warnings were but a murmur in her thoughts, easily silenced. She pulled at the thick handles and opened the pewter doors. She left the world under the blanket of twilight. Inside the Abbey, it was as bright as noonday.

At the threshold, she removed her shoes as she had been instructed to do and covered her feet with velvet slippers. Slowly, she lifted the veil so she could gaze at the inner structure, afire with brightness and radiance. Each Leering seemed to be rejoicing to see her, and the feelings of warmth and happiness banished any dread the outer world had threatened her with. It was the essence of Muirwood, and it flooded her. She waited a moment, and then the Aldermaston appeared from the deep end of the Abbey proper, his gray cassock exchanged for one that was buttery in color and threaded with gold. There was no pain in his gait as he approached, as if the Abbey lent him its own strength for the task. He motioned for her to follow him and then took her down the corridor a short distance to the staircase leading down. It was the place where she had found the tunnel leading to the Pilgrim.

The chamber was beautifully carved out of marble and tiles and polished wooden benches set in rows. The Aldermaston directed her to sit on the bench, and he approached the large stone table at the head of the chamber. The Medium was so thick in the air, she could hardly breathe. It thrummed inside of her with its power, filling every crevice. Tears stung her eyes at the feelings surging through her. She remembered the stone table she had seen before. There was something familiar about it. Instinctively, she knew that both of her parents had been mastons. She clung to the hope that gave her.

The Aldermaston stood behind the stone table, his eyes warm and affectionate. “Do you have any Gifts?” he asked her.

She was not sure what to say, but the Medium whispered to her. She nodded her head. “I have the Gift of Xenoglossia and the Gift of Courage. I also have the Gift of Wisdom, I believe.”

The Aldermaston nodded proudly. “You have other Gifts you did not name. The Gift of Firetaming and the Gift of Recollection. These are powerful Gifts. If you pass the maston test, you will earn more. Where much is given, much is required. Do you seek the rights of the mastons?”

She was about to answer more elaborately, but the Medium whispered for her to simply say, “Yes.” So she did.

“Before you pass the maston test, you will be given a Gift of Knowledge. It will help you to understand the test, for you must pass it alone. No one else will be with you. This is the lower dungeon of the Abbey. It represents the world where we live, not the world we came from. Deeper in the Abbey, behind a latticework called the Rood Screen, you will find the Apse Veil. The room beyond is a representation of the world of Idumea. To pass the maston test, you must do everything required to enter the Apse. Before you pass the Rood Screen, you will be given the chance to turn back. If you quit, you will lose your chance to become a maston. If you fail the test, you may try again in one year’s time. If you succeed, you will receive a shirt of chaen and another Gift.”

Lia waited patiently.

“Let me begin with the Gift of Knowledge. I will only speak it this once. You will not be allowed to ask questions, but you will be given the chance to ponder what you have heard after passing the Rood Screen. Listen carefully, and let the Medium impress upon your thoughts the words that I will say. It is truth not to be engraved into tomes. You must engrave it in your feelings and in your thoughts."

Lia listened with anticipation to every word. She was not expecting the truths the Aldermaston taught her. Some she already knew. Most of them were new and filled her with amazement. As the Aldermaston spoke, the power of the Medium surged, filling her mind with thoughts and images. She knew he was standing in front of her, but there was opened to her thoughts a new world that went beyond anything she imagined. As he spoke, she could see in her mind the events he described. Not just words, but she could see their representation.

The vision dazzled her.

All her life, she had heard Idumea described as a world, as a person, as a benevolence in the aether that blessed everything with life and health and joy through the intervening power of the Medium. Now she learned that Idumea was a place, not a person. It was a world filled with a race called the Essaios. They were beautiful and graceful beings, perfect in delicacy and strength. They looked like men and women that surrounded her, only taller, more graceful and beautiful than anyone she had ever seen. Even more, their skin glowed with the power of the Medium, for *it* obeyed *them.*

She saw their beautiful cities, their enormous gardened cities and wept with joy and wonder. To her, the Abbey grounds were the most beautiful place in the world, but the city-gardens of Idumea were a thousand times more beautiful, a hundred thousand times more grand. The enormity of them defied comparison. She realized that the finely sculpted grounds of Muirwood were merely a pathetic attempt to mimic the wonders of Idumea. The Essaios were wise and powerful, and they could never die. From the world of Idumea, they reined as king-mastons and queen-mastons over millions and millions of worlds spread throughout a skein of interlocking worlds that was beyond Lia's comprehension, vast beyond anything she could imagine. Millions of little worlds, like hers, spread throughout the infinite expanse. The Essaios used the Medium to craft worlds, to command the forces of fire and ice and sea and storm to create and to tame the wild elements into obedience. As she watched, she hungered to be like them, to wield the Medium in such a powerful way. Then she realized that she could, someday—that she was already a part of them, and that they had created *her* as well as their worlds.

Lia was amazed to learn she herself had come from Idumea. It was her home, the place of her first life. So many times she had heard of her existence as a "second life"—that she was born as wretched, but it was not her beginning. There was a place before that, a place where she lived among the Essaios. How could she describe herself? A spark? A floating ember? A spider's web of immateriality that lived among the Essaios, so fragile, so delicate. An intelligence. An awareness clothed in a substance as faint as a shadow.

To become an Essaios, she would have to leave Idumea. Her shadow-self would have to come to a fallen world with no memory of her former life. All were equally ignorant. None were given the advantage of remembering their life in Idumea. She was promised—they were all promised—that if they would be calm and listen carefully, they would hear the murmurs of the Medium guiding them back. The Medium would aid them and assist them if they allowed themselves to be tamed by it. In order to tame it, they must first be tamed *by* it. If they followed the whispers of the Medium, it would teach them how to craft buildings of sculpted stone that would become a link back to the world of Idumea and allow their return.

That thought was profound and amazed her. Muirwood, as with the other Abbeys, was a gateway back to Idumea. And not just to Idumea but to any of the other millions of worlds where there were enough mastons to build them. Each generation of maston families grew stronger and stronger with the Medium, until at last a new generation was strong enough in the Medium to banish death. There would come a time when the chain was strong enough that two mastons, joined by an irrevocare sigil, could use the Medium to bring all of their ancestors back from the dead, in bodies remade into the race of the Essaios and together cross the threshold back to Idumea and join the ranks of others who had so done. It had happened in Muirwood already, she suddenly realized. The stone ossuaries that had washed away, revealing nothing but grave clothes and wedding bands. The Essaios cared not for trinkets of gold or cemetery linen. Nor did they want to linger behind on a fallen world. Unseen, they had entered the Abbey and crossed the Apse Veil back to their true home.

That was the destiny of her race, she realized. It was the duty that compelled Colvin—to be part of that grand chain, that link that would make it possible for himself and his family to conquer death. She knew that it was part of her blood as well. Was it possible then that her parents had been joined together by an irrevocare sigil? Or at least someone from their ancestry?

The knowledge she was given went beyond anything she could fully understand. It smothered her with possibilities. Yet she was so happy, so full of the intent of what it meant. But the Aldermaston was not finished. There was more to the history than she had been told so far.

With the burning desire still inside, she listened as the information began to shift into darker tones. Yes, Idumea was a place of beauty and power. But occasionally, rarely, there were those shadow-selves, like she had been, that wanted to become Essaios without delay, without earning it. Beings that learned how to force the Medium to do their will instead of submitting their wills to it. Just as there were millions and millions of stars and worlds shimmering and sparkling, there was a balance, an equal portion of dead things that would not progress, would not grow, would not enter the cocoons of birth and transform. There were those that turned so much inside themselves that every speck of light was smothered, even though they could not die of it. Rather than coming to the world cocooned in a babe's body, they had been flung out of Idumea, cursed for their wickedness and cruelty. They were banished to the very worlds where the scions of Idumea were coming alive.

Lia understood Colvin's comments now. The Myriad Ones were not the dead. They were the Unborn. They were the sparks, the gossamer threads, the shadow-intelligences that were too wicked to be born, too selfish to create, too wild to tame. And they had a Queen.

Lia watched in horror. Yes, the Myriad Ones would never be born, but they were cunning and devious and twisted truths to suit their purposes. They were led by a Queen named Ereshkigal, who hated the Essaios for banishing her and her followers and swore she would destroy the Abbeys, to prevent anyone from returning to Idumea. Anyone. To further her cause, she created an order, just as the Essaios had created the order of mastons to build Abbeys and bring people back to Idumea. They were called the *hetaera,* and they only accepted women into the order. They were taught to hate the mastons, to murder them, and destroy the Abbeys. The hetaera were the hidden power behind kings and emperors who they manipulated all to their ends. In every land, in every realm, they existed—some in secret and some openly.

The hetaera forged the kystrels and used them to entice, through the Medium, others to do Ereshkigal's bidding.

Without being told, Lia realized that Pareigis, the Queen Dowager, was a hetaera. And just as assuredly as she realized that, she knew that it was Pareigis who had driven the old king to murder the mastons. A hetaera was the equal of a maston in using the Medium. It was a frightening thought. Only one of the race of Essaios was more powerful.

Lia realized the risk then. If she chose to become a maston, she could qualify ultimately to become an Essaios. She could also be murdered for becoming one.

The Aldermaston did not make that final conclusion, but she realized it nonetheless. She understood now the risk that she faced. If she proceeded to the Rood Screen, she would get the chance to pass the maston test. Or she could walk away, keeping silent the knowledge she had received and wonder for the rest of her life if she had made the wrong decision.

"Do you seek the rights of the mastons?" the Aldermaston asked her softly.

She remembered when she had first met Colvin, wounded on the tiles of the kitchen. How she had noticed his chaen shirt and recognized his fear of being killed. Somehow, he had managed to live with the fear. Could she do any less?

"Yes," she answered firmly.

***

The Rood Screen was beautifully carved of oak, stained dark like blood. Tall wooden slats ran straight up and down, but the tips were connected into intricate arches. The wood was twisted and sculpted with decorations marked with maston symbols—

the offset squares forming eight-point stars. Each ridge of wood, the junctions and the trim, were all beautifully carved out and polished. Between the slats of wood hung misty white shrouds, preventing any glimpse of what lay beyond, though she discerned there was a light Leering beyond, which made the soft sheets glow brilliantly. Hesitantly, she looked at the Aldermaston.

"You must proceed on your own," he said in a whisperlike voice. "I will wait for you until you return."

She bowed her head and nodded weakly, wondering what would await her. What challenge would test her? What would it mean? Her mind was so full already that she did not know how much more she could endure.

At the center of the Rood Screen was a wide section, a doorway. The Aldermaston motioned her toward it, and she stepped softly toward the gossamer fabric. Her hand trembled a little as she reached and parted the curtain. As she stepped through, she was jolted with the full force of the Medium. It made her knees wobble and tears stab her eyes. The room was beautiful and carved from stone. It was circular in design, with seven stone pillars, each carved into the shape of a Leering. The one directly opposite was of a bearded man, and it gripped her attention. It was more than a man's face, it was a robed body with one arm lifted toward the sky. The image transfixed her, drawing in her eyes, wondering at its meaning, and then she remembered seeing the Aldermaston perform the maston sign while saving Astrid from death.

There were other Leerings as well: one of a lion, another of a sheep. Another of a snake. She looked at the others also. A blazing sun. One of the Leerings was a twisting vine, with flowers and leaves. The last, a bull with horns. Each was sculpted to the smallest detail, with craftsmanship beyond anything she had seen. Between each of the pillars were walls of marble with carved insets with white stones on them. The stones shined brilliantly, illuminating everything in the room. Not every gap between the pillars was stone, however. The one behind her was made of the white linen shrouds. Two other shrouds were on the far wall, between the pillar with the bearded man with the lion on one side and the sheep on the other.

The floor was a mosaic that dazzled her, but in the center of the room, inset into the floor, was the lip and ridges of a stone ossuary that went below the ground. The lid of the ossuary was open and shoved partway aside. In front of the shallow pit was a wide stone bowl and before that, a bundle of white linen.

Lia wondered what to do, but the ossuary drew her eyes, and she cautiously approached it. It was long but not very deep, and inside was a stone slab—a bier. The bundle of linen was the first thing in front of her, followed by the bowl, and then the ossuary. The Leerings stared at her, and she could feel their eyes on her, boring into her. Watching her stand there, gaping.

She advanced slowly. The thought of rushing about was abhorrent to her. There was power in this place beyond anything she had felt before. The ossuary was not deep, but it looked disturbing. What was an ossuary doing in the middle of the Abbey? She looked at the white bundle. Were they grave clothes? What was she supposed to do?

The thought came quickly to her mind, as it always did. Everything was arranged in a certain order. She knew the billowy curtain on the far wall was the Apse Veil. It was her objective to cross it. Before she could, however, there were things she needed to accomplish. The linens were first, so she guessed that it was required for her to put them on. She knelt by the bundle of fabric and unfolded it. There were two pieces, she discovered. A beautiful white chemise with designs along the shoulder as well as the hem. The designs were threaded in silver, more beautiful than anything she had beheld. The other garment was a lacy shroud that was longer than the chemise, like an outer garment. She had to wear them, she realized.

Looking around, with only the Leerings to look at her, she slowly removed the learner robes. She trusted her instincts, but she was still nervous. She fingered the edge of the chemise and realized that it bore the same markings she had seen before—and had seen on Colvin's chaen shirt. Was the maston custom different for women from what it was for men? She did not know.

Anxiously, she pulled on the soft chemise. She still wore the necklace with the ring threaded through it. Images from that night flooded her memory. Grave clothes found near empty stone ossuaries. She stood and straightened the fabric. The chemise was shorter, but the laced garment was full and deep, and it extended down to her wrists and coiled to her ankles on the floor. It fit her like a gown, surprisingly. She folded the learner robes and left them in a bundle by the basin.

Lia stared at the bowl and noticed a Leering carved into the bottom. She knelt in front of it, looking at the simple face carved there. With a thought, she summoned its power, and it filled with clear, cool water. In her mind, she heard it speak—a woman's voice. *Bathe your hands, arms, and face.*

Lia obeyed, cupping the cool water in her hands, washing them and then her arms. She cupped water in her hands and lifted it toward her face, but it felt…wrong. That was not the way to do it. She gripped the edges of the bowl and then pushed her face into the water.

The Leering's eyes flashed with light, and she felt a calm, peaceful feeling. Its words were barely a whisper. *Lie on the bier.*

Lia rose from the bowl, her face dripping, and she felt clean, refreshed. Gazing down into the ossuary, her heart spasmed with fear. It was not deep. It was not menacing. Yet there was something about it that terrified her. She gazed at the bowl's edge, wondering what to do. Would the lid close on her, trapping her beneath the Abbey? What would happen? The fear was so strong, she felt helpless as she stared at it. But a thought murmured through the blackness, reminding her of where she was. Feelings were caused by the Leerings themselves. Gazing into the hole, she saw them, engraved into the walls surrounding it. Fear, uncertainty, strangeness, anticipation—all these emotions blurted out from the Leerings, warning her to go back. They were strong Leerings, but no stronger than any other she had faced. With a thought, she silenced them. The peaceful feeling returned.

Lia approached the edge of the ossuary, staring down at it curiously and then descended onto the stone slab set in the middle. She lay down, crossing her arms over her chest and waited. The Leerings were tamed. An insight struck her. The ossuary represented death. So many fears shrouded it because there was no telling what would happen next. It was the uncertainty of it, the anticipation, that made it torturous to ponder. Yet as she lay there, she realized it was but another step in her progress. And not even the most important one. As she lay still, pondering, she heard the seven Leerings carved into the pillars awaken and begin to speak to her. They each had a different voice, but they blurred together as they asked her questions, repeating them over and over, until it was nearly a babble. The images of their thoughts flooded her, and she struggled against the feeling of drowning. There was no way to untangle them as they rushed her.

Will you live in piety toward the Essaios? Will you observe justice toward all men? Will you do no harm to any one unless the

Medium commands you? Will you always hate the Myriad Ones, oppose them in all things, and assist the righteous causes? Will you live a life of purity and forsake every pleasure except with your husband? Will you show fidelity to all mastons, and especially Aldermastons in authority? If you become an Aldermaston, will you at no time whatsoever abuse your authority, nor endeavor to outshine the learners either in your garments, your speech, or any other finery? Will you be perpetually a lover and speaker of truth and reprove those that speak falsehoods? Will you will keep your hands clear from theft, and your soul from unlawful gains? Will you never discover any of these doctrines to others, even should anyone should compel you so to do at the hazard of your life? Will you preserve the tomes belonging to the mastons? Will you safeguard the names of the Essaios and those who visit your world from Idumea? Will you shun the enticings of Ereshkigal and her hetaera and qualify yourself to receive a new body and return to the world of Idumea?

There were so many pleadings, so many questions, she was frightened by them. Yet as she listened, she began to recognize the pattern of the oaths. She comprehended that each of the pillars was asking her two. As she listened, she could discern their voices through the maelstrom of thoughts. She realized that in order to silence them, she had to agree to the conditions each imposed on her. She started with the vine-shaped Leering.

Yes, she thought in her mind. The Leering fell silent.

One by one, she listened for the thoughts, understood the oath she was making, and then silenced it with a thought of assent. After each one, she felt the Medium more strongly. It blazed inside of her, building her confidence. At last, she faced the final Leering, the bearded one.

Will you safeguard the names of the Essaios and those who visit your world from Idumea? Will you shun the enticings of Ereshkigal and her hetaera and qualify yourself to receive a new body and return to the world of Idumea?

It was an invitation. A trust. She felt the pleading words mingle with her emotions. How could she describe it otherwise? A pleading with her to return to them. To recognize the evil of the Myriad Ones for what they really were and to scorn them. To let nothing distract her from her goal of returning to Idumea.

Yes!

The final Leering fell silent for a moment. *Touch the white stone*, it whispered.

Lia sat up in the ossuary, staring at the billowy curtains of the Apse Veil. The white stones shone like noonday sun, almost blinding her with the intensity. She approached one of the inlets and reached out her hand. It was glowing white-hot, but she did not fear it. Reaching out, she cupped it in her hand and peered at it.

In the midst of the blaze a light and fire, a single word appeared on the stone.

A word she could not read.

There is no anger above the anger of a woman. For her thoughts are more vast than the sea, and her counsels more deep than the great ocean.

—Gideon Penman of Muirwood Abbey

CHAPTER TWENTY-SEVEN

Apse Veil

As Lia stared at the single word, she trembled with panic. She could not read it. She could not read anything. Why had the Aldermaston thought she could pass the maston test? She had come so far, taken so many oaths, only to stumble now at the end. The Leerings she quelled. The white veils of the order covered her. How could she stop when it was so close? A few squiggly lines in a burning stone halting her purpose. She stared at them, amazed and defeated. To have come so far.

Anger and frustration boiled inside of her. This was not fair! She was a wretched. How could she be expected to pass a test that required reading? She stared at the word again, intently, the light burning her eyes. She winced at the brightness. She felt a prickle of discomfort in her hand. The stone was getting hotter.

She realized what was happening. The Medium was starting to retreat, to abandon her. Her thoughts were driving it away. The protection it provided slowly withdrew. She thought a moment, calming her heart and her anger, forcing herself to think. Why would the Aldermaston have sent her if he knew she would fail?

She knew him too well. He would not have sent her unless he believed she would succeed. A memory drifted through her mind of when she first held the Cruciger orb and writing had appeared on its smooth surface. Colvin had stared at the writing, but he could not read it because it was written in Pry-rian, and he did not know Pry-rian. The marking on the stone was not the same elliptical pattern of the Pry-rian language—what she had seen on the orb. What language was it written in then?

Another memory surfaced. When she and Colvin had fled from the sheriff's men, they had hidden in the gardens outside the Abbey grounds and met Maderos. He had looked at the orb and understood the writing, even though he had never studied Pry-rian.

Do not doubt. Never doubt. I cannot read Pry-rian. It is a forgotten language now by so many. Though I cannot read the words, I was understanding what it said, little sister. The Medium whispers it to me as it does with many ancient languages.

Then she understood, as if a stroke of lightning came out of the sky and struck her mind. Even a maston would not know the word written on the stone, for it was written in the most ancient of languages—the language of Idumea, the tongue of the race of the Essaios. The test was whether or not one would despair. No matter how many tomes were studied, none of them were written in this language. It was a language that had to be felt, a language only the Medium could teach her.

It begins with a thought. She knew what she wanted. It burned fiercely inside of her. *I want to become a maston. I need to pass the Apse Veil.* She stared at the stone in her hand. It no longer burned her. She stared at the word patiently, waiting for the Medium to supply the answer to the riddle. She knew it would come. It had always come to her. The name of a spiky weed in the midst of the Bearden Muir. The recipe for tar-

tarelles. The proper way to milk a cow or tether an arrowhead to a shaft. Knowledge had always come to her, whispering to her. She breathed deeply, inhaling the Medium with each sigh. She was patient. She waited, keeping her mind open to thoughts she knew would come.

They came as an image—a Muirwood apple. She saw herself holding it, tasting it, savoring it. Within each apple, a crown of five seeds. Each seed containing within it the potential to become a new apple tree. Each tree containing the possibility of producing thousands of apples, each with the possibility of producing trees, over and over, generation after generation. Never ending. Never beginning.

Fruitful.

The Medium whispered the name to her. What a brief, innocent little word. But the enormity of the thought of it drowned her imagination with its poignancy. She was but a seed right now. In the ossuary, she had been buried below the ground. A future transformation awaited her. A future more impossibly wondrous than she could imagine. A future the Myriad Ones were forever jealous of for they could never enjoy it. They were the very opposite of the word. The white stone blazed violently, stunning her with light and pain. It was so bright, it burned her hand like a hot coal, so she set it back on the inlet of stone. She rubbed her palm. The skin was red and flaming. She looked closer. The burn had left a pink mark on her skin in the center of her palm. She stared at the stone, realizing it was no accident.

The billowy Apse Veil beckoned her forward. There were two portals, one on each side of the bearded Leering. She was drawn toward the one on the left.

She approached it, still rubbing her hand and stood before it, waiting. There was a faint shadow behind the cloth—a person.

A man's voice spoke to her. "Welcome, little sister. What do you seek?"

She knew his tone immediately, the peculiar accent. It was Maderos, the one she and Colvin had met in the gardens with his crooked staff. Had he been there all along? Was there a tunnel beneath the Apse Veil leading to his secret chamber with the tomes? A passageway she had never seen before?

He had asked her a question.

Licking her lips, she answered. "I seek to become a maston."

She could hear the smile in his voice. "What do you desire?"

She wondered a moment, but the thought was quick to her mind this time. Everything she had learned from the Aldermaston's instruction made the answer clear. "My home. I seek Idumea."

His voice was thick with emotion. "What is your name?"

She knew the word in her tongue. *Fruitful.* But as she spoke, she felt the Gift of Xenoglossia work her mouth, and she said it in Idumean. "*Eprayim.*"

For a moment, she waited breathlessly. The smudge of shadow moved, and through the gossamer veil, she saw Maderos's hand reach out to pull her through. With excitement flittering inside her, she grabbed his hand. As soon as their skin touched, the world around her lurched dizzyingly. She was falling, falling off a cliff. The air rushed through her eyes, her hair, her mouth, a deafening roar. She could not breathe. She could not think. The rush of light and sound was more furious than any midsummer storm. She gripped Maderos's hand tightly, squeezing it for fear of losing herself into the void.

Then it was over, she was through. The Apse was huge. It was the highest point, with a domed ceiling supported by enormous stone struts. There were windows set into the walls, thick with veils, but it seemed as if sunlight shone through them, which was absurd since it was only just night. The room was magnificently decorated with soft couches, tables, vases, fresh flowers, and bowls of apples. Around the couches were large lacquered tables. One, near the far wall, had an open tome on it. Above the tome was a curious instrument—silver bows with transparent stones set into them. She knew instinctively that they were positioned over the tome to help in the reading of it.

Maderos was with her, garbed in white as well, a glimmering chaen shirt—like Colvin's—beneath his. His crooked staff was nowhere to be seen. He had not changed a bit since she had seen him a year before, atop the Tor, as he pointed her way to Winterrowd.

"Well done, lass," he said, smiling at her. "You are a maston."

"I am?"

"Why must I always repeat myself to you? You need to listen. Eh? You were born to be a maston. Or a hetaera. It is your choices which brought you through the Apse Veil. It was your thoughts."

Lia smiled sheepishly. "This is a beautiful chamber. I have never felt such peace."

Maderos looked at her oddly. "Nor will you, until you visit Idumea." He looked up at the great dome above. "This is not the finest nor the largest Abbey in this world. But that is not the point of building them. This is a place of refuge. I thought of taking you to Hautland, but that may have confused you."

Lia looked at him, shocked.

"Oh yes, little sister. Hautland or Dahomey. Or any of the other Abbeys throughout the kingdoms. The Apse is but a gateway between them. When you are stronger, you will be able to cross on your own. But for now, your first time, you needed help."

"I have so many questions," Lia said.

He smiled but shook his head. "I may not answer them."

Lia bit her lip. "I will ask anyway. Is the Queen Dowager a hetaera?"

Maderos looked at her shrewdly. "What do you think, lass?"

"I think that she is, but I am not sure."

"How did you come by your suspicion then?" He arched a brow at her.

"The Medium."

He reached and grabbed her chin and pinched it between his fingers, waggling her head. "You think that I would give you any other answer than what the Medium gave you? Think, child! Do not doubt. Do not hesitate. Do not worry yourself over what may or may not be. The Medium always speaks the truth. And what is truth? Eh? What is truth?"

Lia stared at him, uncomfortable. Her chin hurt a little. "Truth is things as they really are. Not what we wish it to be."

Maderos quit pinching her and patted her cheek. "Truth, sister, is knowledge of things as they really are. As you said. But it is not confined to that. You cannot confine truth to those terms. It is knowledge of things as they are, but it is also knowledge of things as they were. The past. Why did the old king fall at Winterrowd? You can ask any number of men, and they will all tell you what they believe to be the truth. But you and I—we *know* the truth. It is also knowledge of things as they will be. What you will become, for example. Your destiny."

Lia shivered.

"Give me your hand, child."

She hesitated, wondering if he would squeeze it too hard, but she extended it to him. He clasped it in between his hands. His skin was warm and calloused, rough as stone. With a piercing gaze, he looked into her eyes.

"I Gift you. With a glimpse at your future. Not to see it clearly, but to see the truth of it when it is time to know the truth of it. There is a Gift that you already possess, child, that you did not name. The Gift of Seering. Your father had it. You have experienced it already, if you remember. Inside your mind, you have seen events unfold that happened in the past. Or were happening in that moment. The night before Winterrowd, you saw the king in his tent. That was the Gift of Seering. When the Aldermaston taught you about Idumea here in the Abbey, you saw the past and the fall of Ereshkigal. Use this Gift well. Only the Medium can bring it to you. So now I give you a glimpse of the future that your Gift may be complete. This hand will impact the lives of millions of souls. Your name will be had for good, as well as for evil. But to those who know the truth, they will always hold you in reverence for what this hand will yet do."

She licked her lips, not feeling any different. "What does that mean, Maderos?"

He grinned at her. "You will see when it is time." He patted her hand. "Let me teach you wisdom, one of the hidden secrets of this second life, just as it was a secret in the first life. Surely, you have already learned that men and women differ. Each has strengths and weaknesses. It must be so, for we are incomplete without the other. Here is wisdom, if you will hear it." His hand squeezed hers gently. "The greatest power over a man is his desire to please a particular woman. This is crucial to understand. So much in this life hangs on it. It is this inherent desire which gives that woman power to make or destroy him. Most men will never confess that they are influenced…easily influenced…by the women they prefer. Wives, lovers, mothers, daughters, or sisters. Many have no idea that they are. This knowledge is the source of the hetaera's power. It *is* powerful, child. So subtle and powerful.

It can and does influence men to murder. It causes men to forsake their sworn oaths and duties. Even mastons. These feelings can shatter mountains into broken pebbles. They can break down the strongest man. Remember this teaching. It will benefit you in the future as you ponder it."

Lia shuddered. "Is the Queen Dowager more powerful than the Aldermaston?" she whispered.

"Of course she is," Maderos answered. "Because he is only a man. She is more powerful than Garen Demont because he is a man. More than your friend, the *pethet,* because he is a man. More than a dozen mastons together with all their fierce wills combined."

Lia's heart froze with fear.

"But," Maderos said, wagging his finger at her. "Is she more powerful than you? That is the question, is it not?"

"Is she?" Lia pleaded.

"What does the Medium tell you?" Maderos asked pointedly.

In the silence of her mind, the Medium said nothing.

CHAPTER TWENTY-EIGHT

Fall of Muirwood

The Aldermaston looked at Lia's expression, and his eyes wrinkled with worry. "Did you fail?" he asked her, his voice cracking into a hoarse cough.

She realized her expression was alarming him. She shook her head slowly. "I am a maston."

He shut his eyes in relief. "For a moment, I doubted. I should not have. What troubles you?"

Lia swallowed painfully, her mind swollen with conflicting thoughts. "I…I did not realize it. The danger, Aldermaston. The Abbey is in grave danger. The war with Demont—it is just a disguise. I understand now, like I have never understood before. She wants to destroy the Abbey. She wants to destroy you. This is not about Demont. This is not about Ellowyn. This fight is about Muirwood. She will kill you."

She gazed into his eyes and saw the truth of it there. He knew it as well. She wanted to bury her face in her hands. What if she was not strong enough? What if Pareigis, the Queen Dowager, could breach the Abbey's defenses? They would all be slaughtered.

The Aldermaston reached out and stroked her cheek, near her eye. "That is my burden, Lia. Not yours. I am touched by your compassion. It warms my heart, truly." He traced his finger across her cheek. "Do you not think it odd…deliberate…even contrived…that you are here just now? Of all the people in the kingdom who I would want standing by my side, it is you who have not forsaken me. A hunter-maston. A wretched of Pry-Ree. You are here for a reason, Lia. I knew that when I first laid eyes on your tiny body, wrapped in a blanket, with a shawl draped over a Cruciger orb." His voice was thick with emotion, a breathy rasp. "The Medium told me then that you would play a role in Muirwood's destiny. You are special to me in ways you cannot understand, in ways you cannot yet appreciate. Thank you for being here, Lia, in this hour when I need you most."

She had never heard more tender words from his mouth in all her life. Instinctively, she reached out and hugged him close. She had never done that before. Never. It surprised him, this stern man, who could rebuke with a glance or a scowl, who could command and even the skies would obey him. He stood stiffly, awkwardly, and then settled his hand on her head tenderly. She closed her eyes. He was family to her, and her feelings were sacred. The closest thing to a father. Pasqua was her mother. Jon Hunter and Astrid Page had always been like brothers. Sowe her sister. Old Martin an irascible uncle. The family of Muirwood.

The Abbey door opened. Lia pulled away from the old man, tears swarming in her eyes. It was Prestwich. His eyes were blazing with anger.

"What is it?" the Aldermaston said.

"I know you warned me not to disturb you," Prestwich replied, his voice thick with outrage. "But I had to tell you. The Queen… the Dowager…she is dancing at the maypole. Her manner…her form. It is shocking. There are learners who want to come back inside the grounds with their families. Can we let them?"

The Aldermaston's eyes burned with fury. "No. They made their choice. Do not look at her, Prestwich. Warn them not to look at her as well." He turned to Lia. "You will change back into the learner robes. The chaen is yours to wear. It will guard you against the Myriad Ones. It will protect you from them, so long as you keep the oaths you made. The Queen Dowager will come at dawn."

***

The Aldermaston was right. She came at dawn.

An unusual midsummer mist cloaked the grounds. It was strange for that time of year, but it was a strange morning. Lia had not slept, keeping a post at the gatehouse. She did not watch the festival through the gate. Only the shadows illuminated by the blazing fires would she look at. It seemed that each dance got more and more wild. Everyone was drinking cider. She could hear the metal cups clanking. The Queen Dowager taught the girls a new dance, a dance without a partner. Some of her men had strange instruments they played. She had never heard such haunting music before. It made her want to look, to see what was happening beyond the gate. Part of her craved to see it, but she held the thoughts at bay with memories of Colvin, Marciana, and Ellowyn. Memories from the time they had stayed at the Abbey. The memories helped her ignore the celebration outside. With the memories, came the pain of losing Colvin again. The subtle throbbing was like an ache that would never fade.

The celebration ended, and it was quiet until just before dawn. She was warm enough with a cloak wrapped around her, but the chaen was warm and soft. It reminded her of everything she had learned inside the Abbey. The knowledge twisted and turned, showing new angles and interpretations. Deep in the dawn mist, she heard the horses before she saw them. The clatter and rattle of hooves seemed to fill the air, advancing like an army.

"Get the Aldermaston," she whispered to Astrid. He nodded and darted through the mist like a shadow.

Lia gripped her bow and tensed the string, bringing the cloak open to reveal the arrow-feathers stuffed in the quiver. She stood near the gate, breathing deeply, trying to calm her nerves.

The white stallion emerged first from the mist, flanked by riders in black. The Queen Dowager was no longer veiled. Her face was beautiful and cold as she gazed down at Lia. Her black cloak was lined with silver fur, open at the throat. Her fingers held the reins tenderly. Gently, she smoothed the dress at her leg.

"Open the gate," Pareigis said. It was said in a low tone, almost a purr. Behind the words, the force of the Medium struck Lia like a hammer. Her mind recoiled from the surge, but she gritted her teeth.

"I do not have the key," she answered truthfully.

Pareigis scowled, thwarted and furious. The Earl of Dieyre chuckled wryly, his horse appeared next to the Queen Dowager's.

"She is wiser than she looks," he murmured. "You sent for the Aldermaston?"

Lia nodded.

"Well done. Ah, he is coming now."

Pareigis's eyes lifted, looking past Lia's shoulder. There were at least thirty riders, a wall of black behind her. The horse stamped and snorted impatiently. Scowls met her on every face. Lia glanced through the crowd until her eyes met Scarseth's. He stared at her coldly, his eyes glowing silver.

The Aldermaston approached slowly, awkwardly, stiffly. She heard it in the way he moved, the pain whistling in sharp puffs through clenched teeth. Her mind filled with anger, and she clenched the bow. It was the Queen Dowager who caused the Aldermaston such pain. It was she who had come and stripped away the loyal people from Muirwood. Better that she was the dead one at Winterrowd instead of her husband. The thought struck her forcefully—it would be over so fast. A quick arrow, through the gate bars and into the Queen's breast. Her other hand twitched toward the quiver, but she clenched it shut, realizing the feelings were not her own. She shoved at the hate, the loathing. The temptation to kill was powerful. It was not her own.

Pareigis's voice was void of any accent. "You are abandoned, Aldermaston. Open the gate."

"I think not," he replied solemnly. "I will not invite you willingly."

A smirk twisted the corner of her mouth. "Then release the girl as you promised. Demont's niece rides with me to Comoros."

"I am afraid that is impossible," came the simple reply.

Her eyes narrowed. "You think you can save her from me? I came here to fetch her, and I will not leave without her in my custody."

The Aldermaston's voice was humorless. "Then enjoy your stay in the village, my Queen. She is not here to give to you. The earls left at sunset, certain I would betray them to you. They escaped during the confusion of the dance."

Her face hardened, her mouth drawing back into a simmering frown. "Where did you send them?"

"You misunderstand me, my Queen. They left on their own accord. I do not know where they went."

"You let them out a porter door!" she accused, rising higher in the stirrups. Her stallion shied and snorted, its tail thrashing.

"I did not," he replied. "The exterior grounds are confined by the Bearden Muir. It is a difficult and treacherous wilderness, made even more so by the untimely rains. They may be lost. I do not know where they are."

"You lied to me!" she seethed.

"You may believe whatever you will," he answered back.

"You are my enemy," she returned. "You are responsible for the murder…"

The Aldermaston's voice erupted like thunder. "Shall we end this tiresome game, your Highness? Your words and accusations mean nothing to me. I care only for the life of the learners and the villagers of Muirwood, not my own. I have the earl's sworn word about their safe conduct, so any massacre this morning will end with his hands bloodied, not mine. They are fled. The earls have a great lead on you, but they do not have horses, for we do not have any to spare, even if I were so inclined. Their fate and destiny is in their own hands now. I care not whether you kill me or let me live. I do not care!"

Her face was livid with fury. She was so beautiful—so dark, yet so beautiful. "You will care, Aldermaston," she answered softly. "There are deaths even you would shrink from. When I see you next, expect my vengeance in full." She straightened in the saddle. "Ten thousand marks for whoever brings me Demont's niece by sundown!"

The fleet of horses surged and then stampeded. It was a ruckus of hooves and shouts and whistles. The hunt had begun.

The riders all cleared away, save one. The Earl of Dieyre stared at Lia, his eyes inscrutable. The Aldermaston turned to shuffle away, stifling his groans again as he walked. Lia stared at Dieyre for a moment and then turned to follow.

"Wait," he called after her.

She turned back to the gate and approached. He slid off the saddle, landing gracefully in the muck.

"Lia, is it not?" he asked her.

She nodded. "You are not riding with the rest?"

"I do not need ten thousand marks," he replied in a sallow voice. He fingered the cold iron bar gently. "So that is it? Your great Abbey's defenses? I must confess I was looking for something a bit more…dramatic. The fog turning into fire. Or the Abbey shattering us into salt." He fingers squeaked against the iron. "Maybe an infestation of weevils at least."

"The Medium is not always manifested in a dramatic way, my lord," she answered. "In its most powerful form, it is often softer than a whisper."

"Indeed," he replied, his voice low and serious. "She is gone? Truly?"

"Yes, Ellowyn left last night. I did not see her go, but I heard that she…"

"Not her, you simpleton. Ciana." His eyes looked haunted. "Forshee left her behind. Hid her in a tunnel?" His voiced begged it to be so.

Lia stared at him in shock, and realized he was being serious. Maderos was right. Men would do extraordinarily unwise things for the women they preferred. "You think he would not take her with him?" she asked, amazed. "You do not know him at all."

His teeth clenched and so did his hand around the bar. His face was so near, she could see the shadows under his eyelids. "I do not care to know him! He is an insufferable rag. I hate the man. But I love the sister." He rested his forehead on his hand. He looked up at the sky. "I thought…I truly thought she would come last night. When she did not, I began to suspect her faith in this Abbey was greater than my doubt. Did she truly, earnestly believe it would protect her? It seemed so. Now I do not know what to think." His voice was bitter.

"Or what to believe," Lia added, feeling a spark of sympathy for him.

His head jerked up, his eyes staring as if she had seen right through him.

She stared into his eyes. "That is your problem, my lord. Your thoughts tell you that the Abbey is only made of stone and glass and fine furnishings. But your feelings tell you it is made of something more than that. Just because an Abbey can be made to burn does not mean it cannot also save. Until you put them together—your thoughts and your heart—you will only see confusion."

A wry smile crossed his mouth. "You almost sound like an Aldermaston."

"I have learned much by being raised in Muirwood's shadow. How long have you ever stayed in one place?"

"One year at Billerbeck Abbey," he answered stiffly.

"Then I pity you," she replied. "You have never known a home."

"Pitied by a wretched," he mused. "I am not sure how to feel about that." His face went grave. "Will you track them for me? I do not care about the Demont girl. She can rot in the swamp. Help me find Ciana."

Lia shook her head. "Good day, my lord." And she turned and followed after the Aldermaston.

The worse a person is, the less he feels it.

—Gideon Penman of Muirwood Abbey

CHAPTER TWENTY-NINE

Sorrow

The bonfires around the maypole had all become ash. Lia was amazed at the wreckage in the village green. Broken casks of cider, torn ribbons from the maypole, garlands tossed and trampled, dashed cups. The mist finally cleared, revealing the debris, and Lia stared at it from behind the slats of the bars. The first family that had defected from the celebration was the Fesits. They were followed by the Chaldwilks and then the Bitners. They were the first families to rejoin the Abbey after the Queen Dowager's men had ridden away. Lia and Prestwich took turns escorting them from the porter door to the Abbey kitchen, where they joined Pasqua, Sowe, Astrid, and some of the teachers who had refused to leave the grounds in the first place. There were so many uneaten treats in the kitchen that they all enjoyed themselves.

After returning from another trip, Duerden took Lia aside, a tartarelle crammed in his fist. "You were right," he told her, taking a bite without enjoying it. "I wish I had never abandoned you last night. I cannot get the memories of it out of my mind."

"What memories?" Lia asked.

He looked stern for a moment. "It felt…wrong to be there. The maypole dancing started as it always does. Even the Queen Dowager joined in and let it go for several rounds. Then she insisted we do the maypole dance as they do in Dahomey. In her country, the girls bind the boys in the sashes until they cannot move. Then they run while the boys wriggle free, and if they catch a girl, any girl, she has to allow a kiss on the cheek."

He took another bite. "I did not join them. It did not feel right to me, but so many others gladly did. The Earl of Dieyre allowed himself to be tied up that way. But I did not feel comfortable…I mean, even if you were there, it would not have felt right. Like it was stealing something from a girl who may not want to give it. Some of the lavenders refused to pay their kisses, even when they were caught. Each dance got more and more wild. Everyone was drinking cider. It tasted a little strange, so I did not drink much of it. My parents are still shocked at what happened. If they had not been here last year, they would have asked if the dance always ran wild like last night. Then the Queen Dowager taught the girls a new dance. A dance…without a partner. Why would Dahomeyjans do that, Lia? What a strange land they come from."

Lia stared at him, understanding what Pareigis had done. In a small way, she had realized the lure as a child, when learners wore jeweled chokers and then the wretcheds all mimicked them. It would not surprise her if the learners began wearing low-cut gowns like Pareigis did. Or practiced the dancing they had but learned the night before. It was new and exciting—and it was different from what their kingdom was used to. The curiosity of it would guarantee it would be passed on. Just the sort of thing a hetaera would do. That way her influence would continue to corrupt everything around her. Lia knew all this but was bound by her oaths not to tell Duerden. It would have to wait until he faced the maston test himself.

"Do you think—" Duerden asked, interrupting her thoughts. "Do you think she will come back? "

Lia looked at him thoughtfully, unable to say what was in her heart. "I suppose she may," she answered. "But I hope not. I do not like her."

She left him to enjoy the tartarelle and snatched a wafer herself and started off on another errand when Sowe caught her wrist.

"Are you going on a walk?" Sowe asked timidly.

Lia nodded. The girl looked miserable. "Come with me," she invited.

Sowe smiled gratefully, and they left the overflowing kitchen. Lia had never seen Sowe so downcast. She seemed neck-deep in her feelings of loss, while Lia had spent as much time as she could keeping busy so she would not mope about Colvin being gone. Every time she saw a shock of dark hair, her heart spasmed with recognition and then disappointment.

"It was so noisy in there," Sowe murmured. "When the treats are all gone, it will be quiet again."

"I am not fancying the treats this year," Lia said. She squeezed Sowe's hand as she used to. "You are sorry he is gone."

She flinched. "Not so much for him being gone. But he whispered a promise in my ear, and I have a feeling he will not be able to keep it. I know he probably will not be able to keep it, and so I am preparing myself for the disappointment and the hurt. Like you have had to bear."

Lia gave her a sharp look, surprised.

"I am not blind, Lia. Did we not grow up together in the kitchen? You know all of my faults, and I know all of yours. Our little habits that make us who we are. I sleep too deeply, and you can hardly sleep at all. You adore treacle over everything else. Whenever Pasqua bakes the pumpkin loaves, you snitch and snitch and snitch. The Earl of…well, Colvin…he is gone, and you wish he were back, but you are not sure you can stand the pain of that thought."

Just saying it like that made it hurt. Lia swung their arms, trying to stay cheerful. "At least Edmon kissed you good-bye. That was not a brotherly kiss."

Sowe reddened but looked even more forlorn. "I wish he had not."

Lia was surprised. "What—you would rather a kiss from Getman? I thought Pasqua would have chased him out with the broom for sure, but she was crying with joy and fit to burst."

Sowe looked mortified. "No! Of course I would not want to kiss Getman. I shudder at it. Think on it, Lia. I will forever have that kiss in my memory. My husband, poor soul, whoever he will be, he must compete with that memory. It was perfect in every way. He has already stolen my heart, but he is an earl, Lia. I cannot believe he will come back for me. He is always one for speaking without thinking first. For dramatic gestures without pondering the consequence. He is gone now. His feelings will cool. He will marry some woman who is the daughter of an earl or the like, and he will never come back." She gripped Lia's arm. "How can it happen any other way? Colvin may have spurned you, but he will keep his word. He does not say much, but you can rely on what he does say. Edmon speaks too much. I fear I cannot rely on his words as much as you can."

As they walked, Lia found they were approaching the laundry. She had completely forgotten the errand the Aldermaston had set her on—Siara Healer and some attercorn to steep in warm broth. She was just about to tug Sowe toward the apothecary, when she spied the Earl of Dieyre beneath the covered awning of the laundry. He was alone with Reome. She felt a prick of unease seeing him on the grounds. Had the Aldermaston given him permission?

"This way," Lia murmured, tugging her slightly along.

Lia could not make out much of the conversation until they got closer. Dieyre spied them coming, and his expression changed abruptly.

"I had too much cider last night, lass. You will forgive me if I am in a bit of fog still concerning my memory. If you said I promised you five marks a year, then it is five marks a year." He rubbed his forehead and winced. "I could use you at my manor in…" he sighed, "in Lambeth. Yes, that would be the place. It is near Comoros. You are a wretched, so you have not been there. I will advance you some wages for your travel." He fished in his purse for some coins and pressed them into her hand. "I will warn my steward you are coming."

Reome's voice was far from excited. In fact, to Lia's ear, she sounded frightened. "But you said…"

"Lambeth," he said firmly. He put his hand on her cheek—a gesture too familiar for such an occasion. "I know you are worried about what the smithy will say. There are many smithies in Comoros. He will follow you. Five marks is more that he will earn hammering shoes on horses." His voice dropped even lower. "You would both be wise to leave Muirwood before the Queen Dowager returns. Leave at once. There is a good lass. Ah, Lia. I have been meaning to speak with you."

At the mention of the name, Reome stiffened with surprise and shock, and whirled. Her eyes were red from crying. Her hands were tangled together, as if she were wringing her own fingers, instead of the soiled garments she was used to. The look she gave Lia and Sowe was mottled with hatred and shame. Her face went white, and she curtsied to Dieyre and then rushed away, wiping her eyes.

Dieyre ignored her and left the laundry with a bold stride. He bowed gallantly to both girls. "My, you are fair," he said to Sowe, bowing twice to her. "No wonder Reome hates you so much. Has the Aldermaston finally let you out of the kitchen? What, is he dead?"

Lia gave him a burning look, and he held up his hand. "A jest. Only a jest. I have seen this fair girl at mealtime only. Never been able to coax a word out of her yet, though I try. The other girl, Bryn, is quite chatty. But Sowe keeps her secrets hidden behind those blue eyes. Ah, she is blushing now!"

"You are contemptible," Lia said, stepping in front of Sowe. "Who let you on the grounds?"

"That shows a lack of hospitality and a greater lack of tact," he replied. "In my Hundred, a servant could be whipped for disrespecting her betters in such a way."

"We are not in your Hundred," Lia countered. "Answer the question."

"I rode in on my horse," he replied, folding his arms.

"Through the gate?"

He shook his head. "Hardly. I rode to the top of yonder hill—the fat one over there." He pointed to the Tor. "From that vantage, I saw a path onto the grounds behind the walls. I will have you know that I did get lost momentarily in the woods but found my way again. And so here am I. Surely, you will not consider imprisoning me?"

Lia looked at him in wonderment.

"You are wondering how I made it past the Leerings," he said. "Since I am not intending anyone any harm, they merely scowled at me. That or they are, after all, only bits of carved rock with angry faces." His mouth twitched with a smile.

"You have violated the Aldermaston's hospitality," Lia said. "He will decide what to do with you."

"I put myself under his authority and guidance," Dieyre replied. "I am not a maston and cannot claim the privilege of sanctuary here. But I request it all the same."

Lia was not sure what to think. Was Dieyre's change of heart sincere? Could he be sincere about anything? "You will have to appear before the Aldermaston then and petition him in person. He is ailing, as you know, and needs to rest. It may be some time before he will see you."

Another unconscious smile twitched. "It would amaze you how patient I can be."

Lia frowned, bothered by his words and some deeper meaning. It was as if the word he meant to have said was *stubborn* instead of *patient*. "Why were you speaking with Reome Lavender?"

"Is that any of your affair?"

"Let me be the judge of that. She was crying."

"That seems to be a curse most women are afflicted with."

Lia waited patiently, staring at him. Silence seemed to work best in these situations.

"There was a misunderstanding last night at the maypole dance. With a local smithy who has been carrying a torch for the girl. Completely besotted with her, you see. Did not take it in a friendly way when I earned a kiss." He held up his hands. "He was acting a bit possessive, and the cider had definitely gotten the best of his wits. I am sure you saw more than one broken cask on the green. One had his head in it. Two of his friends tried to help him and ended up wearing wooden crowns as well." He smirked. "The lad is a fool if he thinks she will pass up my offer in favor of his paltry one. Ask the villagers. I am sure you will. They saw it."

Lia suspected there was much more to the story. But this was not the time or the place to learn it. "Go to the manor house, and ask for Prestwich."

"The balding, aging fellow with a sour spleen?" he asked derisively.

Lia gritted her teeth. "He will grant you audience with the Aldermaston."

"Very well." He started on his way and then stopped, looking back. "The weather is fine. I should like to go hawking today. Please arrange it with your other duties. A falcon or a hawk will do. I am not fond of hunting with kystrels."

The way he said it made her shiver. The look said much more than his words. He turned and left, marching quickly toward the manor house.

Sowe's hand slowly found Lia's. "He is…he is so dangerous," she whispered.

"Colvin said he was the best swordsman in the realm," she replied, watching him go. "But I am not sure if his greater talent is not his ability to persuade. Poor Ciana. He is relentless."

"Let us go back to the kitchen. I feel safer there," Sowe suggested.

"I need to go by the apothecary first," Lia answered, remembering her errand.

"I will go with you."

They walked in silence the rest of the way. As they approached the apothecary, the door opened from the inside, and Getman

Smith came out, holding his head. His eyes were bloodshot, his face wrinkled with misery. But when he saw Lia and Sowe, his wince turned into a dark scowl.

"Sowe," he whispered, his face suddenly burning.

CHAPTER THIRTY

Betrayed

Sowe's sudden squeeze on Lia's hand shocked her with its intensity. Getman shuffled down the stone steps from the apothecary door, his scalp bandaged. Lia had the strong suspicion that he was one of the young men who had tried to punish Dieyre and failed.

"Why did not you come last night?" Getman said to Sowe, ignoring Lia.

"I was with Pasqua," Sowe whispered, so faintly that Getman could not hear it.

"What?"

"She was with Pasqua," Lia said abruptly. "You look terrible, Getman."

"Was I talking to you?" he said with a snarl. Then back at Sowe, he glared. "You did not join the maypole dance last night. It was Astrid, then? He told you? I thought I saw him sneaking. He probably overheard."

"I..." Sowe said, starting to tremble. "I...did not want to go last night. To leave the Abbey."

Lia could see that Getman was bitterly disappointed in the turn of events. He was humiliated, furious, and desperate. He had one more year until he was required to leave Muirwood, and he had counted on the Whitsunday fair to progress his relationship with Sowe. He was completely blind to her feelings, of course. Most men were afflicted with that curse.

"Astrid," he muttered savagely as he walked by them. He shook his head in rage.

Lia felt a pang of concern for the boy. She caught Getman's sleeve. "You leave him alone," she warned in a low voice.

She was unprepared for the depth of his reaction. A lidded kettle frothing so violently inside that the release let out a scaling hiss of steam. His face contorted with uncontrolled rage. In an instant, he was screaming at her.

"Do not touch me! I swear I will thrash you too, hunter or not! You strut around this Abbey with a blade and a bow. I could take you down with one fist. One fist!" His clenched fist quavered high, threateningly. "You are nothing, Lia! You were born nothing, and you will die nothing! Like we all will! All of us, each one! I hate this place." His fist continued to quiver. "If you ever touch me again, I swear I will thrash you until you are black with bruises. You are nothing. Nothing! We are all nothing here. How I hate it."

A red haze of anger swelled inside Lia. The look in Getman's eyes—it was horrific. He was so angry, so humiliated, he was going to lash out at anyone and everyone. In one move, she could have him face first on the ground. Who was he to talk to her like that? He, who had been a bully to her all her life. She had trained with Martin for almost a year. She had protected the Abbey from the Queen Dowager's men—had thrown a man off his horse. She had fought a kishion face to face and nearly been drowned. Who was this blacksmith boy with a cracked skull?

"Lia," Sowe warned in a tremulous voice.

More than anything else, Lia wanted to humiliate Getman Smith. For all the bruises he had left on her arms. For all the tormenting he had done to the wretcheds. What would everyone think when they heard that she, a hunter, had knocked him to the ground? She was not a nothing! She could use the Medium better than Colvin or Edmon. She had defended Muirwood that morning in a way that Getman would never understand. She was not just a wretched, she was a wretched from Pry-Ree. And now she was a maston.

Will you observe justice toward all men? Will you do no harm to any one unless the Medium commands you?

Getman's voice was thick with contempt. "You may dress like a boy all you like. You probably enjoy it! But you will never be the man Jon Hunter was. You will never be as good as him. Why the old man chose you, I have never understood. It should have been me. I should have been chosen. Not you."

Lia wrestled with her anger and the oath she had taken. She could hardly speak through her fury. "Do not touch that boy," she warned.

"Or what? Are you going to stop me? No, you will tell the old man. like you tell him everything I have ever done. I know he hates me. Might as well leave now. I cannot stand another year in this place."

"You have no idea what you are saying," Lia replied, trying to calm herself. "Let us go, Sowe."

She reached for the other girl's hand and started to pull her away, when Getman grabbed a fistful of her clothes at the shoulder, ready to yank her back and insult her again. In grabbing her gown, he also seized her chaen.

The Medium flared inside her, a wall of blazing ice and fire that stunned her with its intensity and fury. To Getman, she imagined it was like gripping a lightning bolt. His eyes went wide with shock, his fingers paralyzed by the feeling blazing through him. As if something huge and heavy collided with him, he stumbled few steps backward, his hand as red as if he had pressed it against the inner wall of the forge. It was the Medium that had struck him, not Lia. She had not called it to bear at all. She had not summoned it or even thought about it. All she had done was cool her temper and trample her instinct to humiliate him.

Getman gaped at her.

Lia smiled warningly. "Do not touch me," she said.

***

After Whitsunday each year, the learners returned with their families back to the manors and castles they came from. Teachers who had not seen their families for the duration of the year abandoned the Abbey for a brief season. The cloister was locked and secured. The wretcheds kept working but had more time to enjoy without the constant fuss of learners. With the Queen Dowager gone like a whirlwind as well, it was quieter on the grounds. A new routine would begin. The end of the season was a quiet time, one that Lia usually relished.

Colvin's departure crushed her with wistful memories.

Before he had returned, there were places she could go that would remind her of him. The forbidden grounds where Maderos's lair existed, for example. The loft ladder or the Pilgrim Inn. She could go to those places and remember seeing him there. But since he had stayed at Muirwood, it felt as if his footprints were everywhere—in the grass, near the majestic oak trees, through the Cider Orchard. Especially the orchard. It pained her to walk there now, remembering the look on his face when he had rejected her. The memories surprised her with their vividness and the intensity of feelings.

He was gone, and he would never return. Did she truly believe it? That they would never see each other again? The Aldermaston was still ailing and had asked her to stay close to the grounds in case the Queen Dowager returned. She did not know if they were still surrounded or not—their enemies could still be lurking in the woods. She wanted to investigate but would not disobey the Aldermaston.

At least once a day, she had to endure the presence of the Earl of Dieyre. He was so different from Colvin. Talkative, witty, shallow—intense. She took him hawking twice, and he was courteous and grateful, yet always pressed her to go farther from the grounds than she thought wise. She refused, and he relented, but he still pushed her. He knew the sport and enjoyed the kills. But she did not trust him. For some reason, the Aldermaston had let him stay.

At dusk on the third day after Whitsunday, Lia checked the perimeter of the grounds as she usually did, always on the lookout for the sign of trespassers. She had passed the grounds on the far side of the fish pond and worked her way around to the far side of the Cider Orchard. The light was beginning to fail, but she saw the matted grass first before she noticed the boot prints.

Lia froze, staring at the ground. Instinctively, she reached for her gladius and drew it. She approached the telltale signs. There was no mistaking it. A man's step, a man's stride walking quickly and deliberately up the hillside and into the orchard. Her heart went wild with uncertainty. The prints were fresh.

She stooped, tracing the edge of the print with her finger, her sword hand ready. What to do? She could go straight to the Aldermaston. But he would have her track the prints. Why the orchard? Was someone stealing apples for food?

Lia started along the trail, following the steps into the Cider Orchard, listening to the wind rustling the branches and leaves. It was silent. No thrashing of limbs. No thumping of falling apples shaken loose from the stems. She crossed as quietly as she could, keeping each step soft and deliberate. She smelled the air, listening to the sounds, hoping there would be something to warn her of danger. How had the intruder made it past the Leerings? Each step brought her deeper into the orchard until his voice came from the shadows on her left, startling her.

"You found me quickly."

It was Colvin.

Lia's thoughts spun with surprise and shock. She turned on her heel, staring as he emerged from around the trunk. His face was mud-spattered. His leather jerkin soiled and damp, his fingers stained with mud. Bits of bark and nettles stuck in his clothes. He looked like she usually did after a foray into the Bearden Muir.

"What are you doing here?" she demanded in a hoarse whisper. "Colvin, what is wrong? Are you hurt?"

"You seem surprised to see me," he answered, his face a mask of intensity and anger.

"Of course I am surprised. Why are you here?"

"You truly do not know?" his voice was thick with disbelief.

"I would never lie to you. You know that. I never have. Where are Marciana and Ellowyn? Are they nearby? I only saw one set of steps to follow."

"I was hoping, Lia, that you would tell me," he replied stiffly. His face contorted with rage. "The Aldermaston betrayed us. Martin led us into a trap."

He may have well punched her in the stomach. She shook her head. "No, that cannot be true."

"Would I lie about this?" he snapped impatiently. His eyes burned with fury and another look—desperation. "Please. I need your help. I did not know where else to go. You can help me, Lia. You are the only one who can."

She shook her head, still amazed that he was standing before her. "I do not understand. The Aldermaston told me he did not know where Martin was taking you. It breaks a maston oath, does it not? To swear falsely?"

He cringed as she said it. "Do not speak of things you know nothing about. I believed him, but would Martin have betrayed him? I was assured of his loyalty, and he led us into a trap. But you can help me, Lia. If you get the Cruciger orb, you can show me the way to them. I must find them." His face looked even more desperate. "They have my sister, too," he choked out.

"What?" Lia demanded, unable to pull her thoughts together. "The Queen Dowager has them?"

"No!" Colvin said fiercely. "The Pry-rians! We were ambushed. We were led right into their midst. Martin said they were taking Ellowyn back to Pry-Ree, back to her true family. They took my sister as a hostage."

"Where is Edmon then?" Lia asked, sick.

Colvin shook his head. "Though they warned us not to follow, I told Edmon to follow after, in case they let my sister go. I came straight here, but as you can imagine, I do not know my way through the Bearden Muir. There are still remnants of the Dowager's men in the woods below the grounds, so I had to wait until dusk to approach unseen. I knew you made your run of the grounds around this time and hoped to encounter you as I did and persuade you to abandon the Aldermaston to help me." He gripped her shoulders with both hands, and it made her shiver. "Please, Lia. I must beg you to help me. Help me rescue my sister. Help me save Ellowyn. I swore an oath to protect her. On my life, I swore it. I promised her I would safeguard her. Please, I will do anything you ask if you help me fulfill my vow."

Lia stared at him, at the panic in his eyes. She could only imagine at the depth of desperation that had driven him back to Muirwood to seek her help. No doubt he remembered his coldness. No doubt he remembered they stood in the same grove of apple trees where he had scorned her. No doubt he remembered that he had not fulfilled his previous promises—to teach her to read or the dance with her. He was a proud man. Yet his determination to fulfill his duty and to protect his sister outweighed the personal humiliation he was enduring.

His fingers burned into her shoulders, as if he clutched her like a drowning man to a rope. His expression was exhausted. He had probably walked without sleeping. Was he hungry? When was the last time he had some water? She looked at his face, his concern, his helpless expression.

A feeling of tenderness and sympathy moved her. Even though he had spurned her, she chose to help. His earlier scorn still stung, and she could not bring herself to try and comfort him with a hug or murmured assurances that all was forgiven. She winced, not with the pain of his fingers stabbing her shoulders, but at the conflict boiling inside of her. Helping him would mean being near him, even if that closeness would make her heart ache.

"Of course I will help you," she whispered, her throat catching on the last word.

No maston ever became wise by chance.

—Gideon Penman of Muirwood Abbey

CHAPTER THIRTY-ONE

The Chase

Lia knelt by the bedside and clasped the Aldermaston's hand. His grip was surprisingly strong, his face flushed. Great drops of sweat dripped down his forehead. The clenched jaw of his mouth shook with repressed anger and unbearable pain.

"What would you have me do?" Lia asked, meeting his gaze. "Colvin is gathering victuals from the kitchen right now. We are to meet in the stables and take his and Edmon's horses."

"Of course," he said with a choking voice. "Use the orb to elude the marauders in the woods. I am sure…" he stiffened with a wince, the pain so severe it stole his breath. When he was able to speak again, his voice was pale with weakness. "They…have… made it to the Pry-rian border by now. Or they are…nearly to Bridgestow and will ferry across…from there. You must…find Ellowyn. She was under…our protection. She still…is."

Lia squeezed his hand harder. "Why did he do it, Aldermaston? Why did Martin betray you?"

He shut his eyes, sighing deeply. "He always felt…he was betraying Pry-Ree by not fetching her. He loves his people deeply.

The Blight that struck…Pry-Ree…was so severe. He could not live there…like a sickness. A cancer."

Prestwich bathed his forehead with a damp rag. The Aldermaston looked miserable.

"Are you going to die?" Lia whispered. "What will happen to the Abbey?"

He shook his head, thrashing it in the effort. "My pains… come and go. When it passes, my strength will return. I am old, but I have work yet to do. The Medium has assured me of that. The pain will pass soon."

Lia bit her lip, watching his suffering with sympathy. "What if the Queen Dowager comes back…?"

"Hush," he interrupted. "Would you bring her to us…with those fears…so soon? The Medium controls my destiny. I told you…that. Go, child. Help the Earl of Forshee find his sister. And Demont's heir. I was certain…several days ago…that you would be going. Now I know why. Prestwich…I am going to be sick again. Fetch the basin. Go, Lia…leave tonight."

Once more, she squeezed his hand, kissing his sweaty forehead and hurrying from his sickroom. Astrid was just beyond, pacing nervously.

"Will he die, Lia?"

She shook her head. "I do not know. You must help him while I am gone. Search the boundary each night. Warn him if you see any riders." She gripped his shoulder firmly, gave him a stern look, and then hurried to the kitchen. Pasqua and Sowe were fussing over the stores they had gathered and tied into linens and leather rucks. She had already fetched the Cruciger orb and tied it to her waist. While Colvin shouldered the burdens, she took her bow sleeve and three quivers of arrows. Pasqua stifled a sob and gave her a crushing hug. Sowe was more gentle and whispered in her ear, "Keep Edmon well for me."

Lia promised she would and then left with Colvin into the dark. They crossed the Abbey grounds afoot, their stride marking their urgency to reach the stables.

"What did he say?" Colvin asked brusquely, his eyes unreadable in the gloom.

"That Martin was convinced Muirwood would fall. That Demont will as well. He has lived through this season before—when the Abbeys are destroyed and the Blight comes. He has always been loyal to his native land. Maybe Martin thought that because of her birthright, she will be able to reverse the Blight that has plagued Pry-Ree."

"I should have foreseen this," Colvin muttered darkly. "It is dangerous whenever there is a conflict of loyalties. You were right to confer with the Aldermaston. I am glad you did."

Lia smiled in the dark. "I regretted I did not the last time I ran off with you. I have learned a little wisdom since that day." Then she saw it. "There is a light on in the stables."

"The groomsman?"

"No, he should be abed by now." Again, her hand went to the hilt of her gladius. Must everything be so difficult?

"Let me see who it is," Colvin said, increasing his pace, but Lia held out her hand and blocked him.

"This is my duty, Colvin. We go together."

Without trying to disguise her approach, she walked straight to the stable doors and thrust them open. Inside, she found two saddled horses—Colvin's and Edmon's. The third was being fitted by a crouching figure who rose when the door opened.

It was Dieyre. He glanced at them, his face flushed from the exertion of saddling the horses so quickly. "Where are we riding?" he asked, cinching the harness and adjusting the bridle.

Colvin stared at him in surprise and loathing.

Dieyre peered over his shoulder, snorting when he saw the look on Colvin's face. "Please, Forshee, do not take this amiss, but I *am* coming, too. You can draw your blade and get humiliated again in front of the girl, or you can recognize that I am a better fighter, a better rider, and equally interested in what happens next. I had a suspicion that if I lingered, one of you would wander back. Or she would lead me to you if I watched her like a kystrel. Do not start, Forshee! I am not speaking of amulets, I am talking of birds! There are two of you, you say. Fair enough. But why waste time fighting about this? I can help get you past Pareigis's traps."

"Why?" Lia demanded, approaching Edmon's horse and stowing her gear in the saddlebags.

"Not for the ten thousand marks," he replied snidely. "You already know the reason, Lia." His heavy lidded eyes flashed at Colvin. "You are either here because the plan was botched or returning for the horses was part of it. Care to enlighten me?"

"Not really," Colvin replied. He mirrored Lia by unloading the foodstuffs into the saddlebags.

"Then let me see if I can help you," Dieyre continued, tightening the final brace before swinging himself up by the stirrup. "We received word that the Pry-rian council was plotting to kidnap the Demont girl. Some of our informants in this Hundred spied your hunter…the bearded one…meeting with emissaries in some villages northeast of here. We have been fairly certain that he is allied to the plot. What you may or may not know is that he fought during the Pry-rian wars. There are men who have sworn testimony that he participated in some massacres after the fall of Pry-Ree. He is not just a simple woodsman, he is a soldier. There are many who say he was at Winterrowd with Demont. That he was part of the massacre there. Can you vouch for that, Forshee?"

Colvin looked taciturn. "I never saw him. The Pry-rians helped Demont cross the sea. That is all. There were none in the camp."

Dieyre looked skeptical. "I have heard otherwise. They were there, Forshee."

"So was I," Colvin answered defiantly. "And I was there when the old king tried to lure Demont to his death by sending false knight-mastons in the middle of the night." He also mounted the horse boldly, sitting straight-backed in the saddle. "Lead the way, Lia," he said, without taking his eyes off Dieyre.

"I want to believe you," Dieyre said in a low voice.

"I do not care whether you do," Colvin replied sternly.

"The king had an arrow in his back. It had Pry-rian fletching. The same fletching in the arrows the girl carries. How did it happen if it was not murder?"

Colvin leaned forward, his expression full of loathing. "Edmon's brother was the Earl of Norris-York, and he was murdered because he was a maston. He could have been arrested for high treason. He could have been tried by a court of his peers as per the law. But he was butchered because of the markings on his sword. If you crave justice so much, why do you ride with a woman who flaunts the law and twists it to her own ends?"

Dieyre also leaned forward in the saddle. "Because I know she wants to kill you, too. I did not think your sister would like that. I have tried all along to warn you, to help you, to win your trust. Think of it, Forshee. All of my lands, all of my wealth—on your side. On Demont's side. All I want in return is your sister."

Colvin's jaw clenched. "You think I would barter her to someone like you?"

"Do not be naive, Forshee. Of course I think that. Despite your pretty speeches about the Medium and fate and thoughts and old, tarnished tomes, we are still men of blood and bone. You are afraid to let her choose on her own because you know she would choose me. Imagine what we could do if we *joined* instead of bickered at each other."

"I have imagined it. You would want me dead as well," Colvin replied. "I have seen how you treat other women. I have witnessed it, Dieyre. I will not put my sister through the misery of being your wife."

Dieyre smiled at the rebuke. "Well said, Forshee. Well said. You have been *practicing* that insult, I imagine." He twitched at the reins and made the horse snort. "You do not trust me. I can understand that. Trust must be earned, and I am no maston. We can both agree on that. But let us also agree that I can help you. Obviously, I am here instead of with Pareigis. I am my own man, not her vassal. So many of her plans are still coming together. There is time still to thwart them."

The only light in the stable was a single lantern dangling from an iron ring on the wall. Lia could see the dancing flame mirrored in Dieyre's eyes. He was anxious to ride. The thought of plunging into the darkness was thrilling to him. The thought of betraying Pareigis seemed to give him a glimmer of delight.

She had to admit that having the best swordsman with them when they caught up to the Pry-rians was tempting. She fastened her foot into the stirrup and hoisted herself up. The beast shifted beneath her, but she knew and was known by the animal.

"If you would betray her like this, you would also betray us," Colvin pointed out.

"Very astute."

"You are not promising that you will not."

"Would it do any good to waste words that I know you would not believe?" He eased back in the saddle. "I am coming with you, Forshee. Whether you like it or not. You may as well use it to your advantage, as I am using your helplessness to mine. I have a feeling this is a hunt we will all remember the rest of our lives. Lead the way, girl."

She looked at Colvin, saw the set in his jaw, the defiance in his eyes. Every instinct within him warned that they could not trust Dieyre. She could see it plainly written on the crisscross of his eyebrows, the frown so deep on his mouth.

"You do not need to look to him for permission, love," Dieyre told her. "He has already decided. He will do anything to save his sister. As will I. Do you need my help getting past the watchmen guarding the road? We are on horseback, so I assume we are not using the tunnels."

Dieyre was right. Colvin had decided. She could see it plainly on his scowl.

"No, I think we can manage well enough," Lia replied. She needed to use the orb to find Ellowyn and Marciana. In the dark, it tended to glow rather brightly, and she knew it would be difficult hiding it from him. She did not relish the thought of him knowing that she had it or that she could use it. The less she said, the better.

She opened the pouch at her waist and withdrew the golden orb. His eyes widened with surprise when he saw it. He looked at her questioningly.

"The Aldermaston gave it to me," she answered, which was true in a real sense. In her mind, she thought of Ellowyn's face. She imagined how worried she was, how much she had feared being abducted by the Pry-rians and forced to marry someone who did not even speak her language. She saw her frightened eyes, the dull color of her hair and let herself be drawn in to the need to find her. A safe road that would help them catch her.

The orb began to whir, and then the spindles pointed clearly. Lia gave Dieyre a challenging look. "Try and keep up."

CHAPTER THIRTY-TWO

Shrewberries

Lia could not believe her good fortune in finding a thicket loaded with ripe shrewberries. The patch grew wild and was thick with thorns, but plentiful with dark pink fruit—surprisingly so, considering its remote location in the Bearden Muir. It was late in the day, and she was hot, weary, and soaked with sweat. Colvin and Dieyre kept up with the punishing pace, but she could see Colvin swaying in the saddle, exhausted by the hard ride and lack of sleep. Muck and mud spattered their mounts, which foamed at the mouth with the efforts.

"Rest the horses," Lia suggested, pulling short of the thicket and dismounting.

"There is daylight left," Dieyre countered. "Ride on."

"We have tortured the beasts enough for today," Lia said. "Some of us need rest as well." She crouched by the thicket and began plucking buds of fruit from the thorny stems. They were juicy and fat, and she tasted their sweetness, finding only the hint of bitterness. The patch was in a well-lit spot, so the sun had ripened them. They were delicious.

Dieyre's horse snorted and wheezed, but he looked around distastefully. "What are those? Thimbleberries?"

"We call them shrewberries in this Hundred," she replied. "You are like as not to prick your fingers on the stalks, so be careful. They are very soft. You have to eat them right away." She stuffed another one in her mouth. Each had hard little seeds that contrasted with the softness. "They will not keep, so eat your fill."

Colvin slumped off the saddle and approached, his face haggard and weary. She recognized the expression—saw the tight, tired lines around his eyes. He was irritable when tired, so she did not speak to him.

"We are wasting daylight," Dieyre complained.

Lia felt impertinent. "No, you are wasting an opportunity to fill your belly with something better than mushrooms. It is always wise to stop and savor what the wilderness puts in your path, like a coney or a deer. Always be ready for the gift, and be grateful."

Colvin pricked himself on a thorn and snatched his hand back. She had picked enough to fill her palm and offered them to him. Her fingers were quick and more dexterous than his. He took them with a grateful nod and started eating them ravenously.

She picked more, eating as she went, searching for the easiest fruit. Dieyre studied her a moment, scowling, and then swung off the saddle and joined in the feast. He also pricked his hand, but he did not accept any of the morsels she offered. After eating several, his expression changed.

"How far do you think they are from us?" he asked her.

"I do not know," she answered truthfully. "We are not going the same way they did."

"That is what I do not understand," he returned, bristling as he had many times that day. "We are not following their trail, but we are going to where they will be. That does not make any sense to me. How can a ball made of gold know where they are going to be?"

"I cannot explain it, for I do not understand it myself. It just works."

"But how? It could be leading us anywhere. Or nowhere. How do you know it is not pointing the way to Dahomey?"

Lia looked at Colvin and saw the muted smile on the other's mouth. The amount of doubt and disbelief in Dieyre's voice—he would never have gotten the orb to work.

"Dahomey is south," Colvin replied testily. "We are headed north."

Dieyre looked exasperated. "I know that well enough, Forshee. What I am saying is you are putting all your faith in a trinket. A bauble. You do not even know how it works."

Colvin stuffed another cluster of fruit into his mouth. "I do not need to understand it to believe in it. You do not believe in the Medium, so how can any explanation satisfy you? Let it alone."

"I did not say I do not believe. Only that I have never had the patience for it."

Colvin gave him a hard look. "You are welcome to find your own road." He looked back at Lia and nodded gratefully to her, rising to his feet stiffly. He offered her his last shrewberry. "I will feed the horses."

She stared at him pointedly. "You need rest."

He nodded, not disagreeing. "Let me help first. I will take the third watch, if that is all right."

"Weary, Forshee?" Dieyre asked with a smirk.

"I have not slept in three days. It was all I could do to stay on the saddle this long." He touched Lia's shoulder. "Do wake me, Lia. When it is my turn."

"I will," she promised, wishing the Earl of Dieyre would stop smirking at them.

***

Lia blinked awake in the middle of the night, shivering beneath her cloak. No one had wakened her, and it was quiet, save for the creak of gnarled oaks and the hiss of the wind through the leaves. In the distance somewhere, a frog croaked. She glanced up at the stars to see the patterns and knew at once that it was well past her turn for a watch. Was Dieyre being generous, she wondered? Rising on her elbow, she glanced around and found Dieyre asleep, head pillowed on his arm. She moved closer to him and heard his distinct breathing and was sorely tempted to kick him sharply in the ribs for falling asleep on his watch.

Rubbing her arms for warmth, she moved around the makeshift camp, grateful to see the three horses still tethered. It would be dawn before long, so she decided to let Colvin sleep. She nestled near him, on the ground, so that she could look at his face in the dark. Being with him in the Bearden Muir was so different now. Before she had been such a child, whimpering with fear in the dark, easily upset by his gruffness and impatience. She was of little use to him once her fears had mastered her and the Cruciger orb stopped working. They were memories that shamed her. Here he was, asleep next to her, his breathing so faint and shallow. She yearned to smooth the hair away from his forehead but dared not touch him. A flood of emotions came with the thought, and she almost reached out before catching herself.

Folding her arms tightly, she turned away from him and gave thought to their course. Knowing the terrain better, she had determined the orb was leading them northeast. She half expected to wind up on the Bridgestow road, for that city was a two day ride from Muirwood—a major port town that traded with Dahomey and Pry-Ree. She had been there once during the year, on an assignment from the Aldermaston to purchase supplies that could only be found in such a place. But if they were going to Bridgestow, had the orb led them into the moors to avoid the Queen Dowager's men? Surely they would not be able to travel as fast. Or was their quarry taking a different path to Pry-Ree, knowing that the major roads would be watched?

The hunter is patient. The prey is careless.

She wanted to be careful in their pursuit of Martin. He knew about her orb. He was probably expecting her to hunt after him. He would be cautious and deliberate. She knew in her bones that instead of hunting after Scarseth, he had made a foray into Pry-Ree and plotted to kidnap Ellowyn. Having her so close to the borders of Pry-Ree must have proven a temptation he could not resist, for all his loyalty to the Aldermaston. Or had he made up his mind after leaving? She thought back on the moment when he left to hunt Scarseth. She had hugged him with affection, and he had looked as if he wanted to tell her something but could not. Was his betrayal festering in his mind?

She was so disappointed in what he had done. Loyalty was something the Aldermaston treasured and expected. But surely he had justified the actions in his mind. If Muirwood were to fall, then in what Abbey in the kingdom would she be safe? Why not disappear into Pry-Ree where her own people would shelter her and hide her, even though she herself was terrified of that prospect? Lia clenched her jaw, shaking her head. The girl was probably beside herself with worry. Her greatest fear had just been realized. Hopefully, Marciana was keeping calm and watchful, looking for a way to escape their captors.

Lia plucked up an oak twig and twirled it between her fingers. She did not want to hurt the Pry-rians, for they were *her* countrymen as well. How could they free the girls without bloodshed? She did not know, just as she did not know how she was going to free Colvin when Almaguer held him at the Pilgrim Inn. She only knew that she had to try. Her best hope, she felt, was in persuading Martin to release her willingly. To assure him that the Abbey had not fallen to the Queen Dowager or her minions.

Colvin's voice whispered like a ghost behind her. "Is it my watch yet?"

She turned and looked down at him. Gently, she touched his shoulder. "Dieyre fell asleep. I only awoke myself a short while ago. I will wake you at dawn."

Colvin snorted in the dark. "He slept?"

"He was probably more tired than he realized."

"Do not defend him, Lia."

She gave him a playful look. "I have no intention of doing that. He will get the last watch from now on. Go to sleep. I am sure you are still tired."

He slowly sat up, twisting himself around to face her. "I feel much better. Besides, with him asleep, we can speak more freely. Do you know where we are?"

"I believe so. I think we are still in the Bearden Muir." She said it with all seriousness.

"How can you joke," he muttered darkly.

"Teasing is different from joking. We are threading the Bearden Muir toward Bridgestow."

He brought up his knees and rested his arms on them, then lowered his chin on his arms. He sat very close so he could whisper. "Bridgestow has always been loyal to Demont. Years ago, during the civil war, Sevrin Demont was in negotiations within

Pry-Ree when the old king mustered an army to threaten him. He tried to cross back into the realm, but the bridges were all destroyed. Bridgestow sent ships to ferry him back, but they were caught and burned. Shortly after that, the battle of Maseve. I doubt the city leaders are part of this plot. I believe they are loyal to our side."

Lia shifted into a more comfortable position. Their backs slightly touched. "Would they help us free her?"

"I think so."

"That is good to know. We need allies." She chose to be quiet, not wanting to interrupt his thoughts or annoy him with banter. She sat still, listening to the desperate frog croaking in the silence and said nothing.

His voice was even softer. "Why did you help me?"

She was expecting a question like that. She had puzzled over the possible question all day, turning it this way and that in her mind, as if trying to determine the best way to free a nut from an unripe shell. She was not sure if she had a suitable answer. "Because you needed it," she replied simply. She felt a smirk color her next words. "You require a good deal of looking after, my lord Earl of Forshee. Member of the Privy Council." A gentle nudge to his shoulder.

"That is true," he said, the hint of amusement in his voice. He cleared his throat carefully. "Have you thought of what you wanted from me? I did promise to reward you."

She was quiet in response, deliberately so. She could not say what was brimming up inside her heart. Could not ask for what she wanted most to hear and knew he could never say. So she waited in silence, letting it stretch out. Sometimes silence was more meaningful than words.

Apparently it was torturing him.

"Lia?"

"Yes?"

"Did you…did you hear my question?"

"Yes," she replied simply. Did he remember that he had once accused her of being too talkative? "You owe me nothing. Not reading or engraving. Not a dance around the maypole. I release you from all obligations. I was childish when we first met. You were bloodstained and vomiting in the kitchen. I did not see you as a person, but as a means of getting what I wanted." She sighed deeply. "What I came to realize is that what I wanted more than anything was just to be your friend. That was enough. I thought I lost that a few days ago. But when you came back and asked for my help, I realized that a true friend is not easily offended. If you could swallow your pride and ask for help, I could swallow mine and give it without bartering for something. You need me, and I am fond of Marciana and Ellowyn. And besides, you are not nearly clever enough to outfox Martin. I know how he thinks. Maybe that will help. Maybe not."

It was his turn to be silent. She let it flow past them, like a brook of sweet water.

Another voice broke the stillness. "Is it almost dawn?" Dieyre asked. "With all your whispering, we may as well saddle the mounts and ride. I swear, you two are the kingdom's greatest fools." He rolled over and glared at them, his eyes digging like knives. "How can anyone sleep with all that whispering?"

Lia glanced at Colvin, saw the anger flaring in his eyes. She did not know how much he had overheard.

"If anyone deserves to be scolded, it is you," she said, rising to her feet. "You slept through your watch. In a war, you would be flogged, I believe. Instead, I will withhold your rations. Enjoy the shrewberries, my lord. When you have a duty, you must fulfill it. Or you will ride alone after this."

She said it pointedly, wanting him to question whether or not she was sincere, but inside she did worry how much Dieyre had overheard.

The Blight is not to be feared. It is only a manifestation of the thoughts prevailing in the world. Where weeds are sown, weeds grow. We are more wicked together than separately. If you are forced to be in a crowd, then most of all, you should withdraw into yourself.

—*Gideon Penman of Muirwood Abbey*

CHAPTER THIRTY-THREE

Vengeance of Pry-Ree

There was no way around the bog, so they went through it. The horses struggled against the mire, straining to pull their burdens through the fetid waters rising up to their flanks. Swarms of gnats and mosquitoes tormented them, and she could hear Dieyre and Colvin bickering in low tones behind her. The oak trees were sickly and stunted, the branches black instead of brown. There was a new smell in the air, heavy and spoiled and vaguely familiar. The farther they went, the more it became distinct—pungent—and then it revealed itself. They were near the sea.

Dieyre's voice rose in tone. "But you are a *man* as well as a maston. Best if you realize that someday."

Colvin's horse suddenly plunged faster, churning through the mud as he caught up with Lia. Her eyes were trained on the expanse ahead of them—a building knot of oaks so thick, it rose on a chain of hillocks that would hopefully lift them out of the deep wetlands.

His voice was thick with suppressed anger. "If I asked you, would you shoot him with your bow? The man is insufferable."

Lia glanced over her shoulder, smirking. "Are we that close to murder? Maybe I could shoot his horse instead. What is he troubling you about now?"

Colvin's eyes flashed darkly. "It is of no concern. He merely presumes every man is like himself, and it is his sworn duty to help them realize it. His conscience must be searing him again—if he has one."

She nodded and kept prodding her beast forward. "Do you smell it?"

"We are near the waters separating us from Pry-Ree. Do you think we are far from Bridgestow?"

"I do not know," Lia replied. "I was hoping the hills ahead of us would offer a view, but they seem rather crowded with trees. We are going east, that is all I know, and Bridgestow is east."

"Damnable flies!" Dieyre roared behind them. "This is the most loathsome place in the kingdom."

Lia glanced at Colvin and shook her head. "There is a certain beauty to this wilderness that I had not recognized until Martin trained me. Ah, the ground is firmer."

With solid earth beneath them, Lia dismounted to rest the weary animal and led it by the bridle. She withdrew the orb and summoned it again, watching the spindles whir and point. In a moment, she was surrounded by the Myriad Ones. They engulfed her, drawn to her thoughts or to the orb, and began snuffling and mewling around her. The orb flashed once, and writing appeared on the smooth surface, thin filigree letters that had always haunted her. She stiffened with panic.

"Do you feel it?" Colvin whispered, pulling his horse next to her. His eyes met hers.

She nodded. "They are thick. I am…not sure if the orb summoned them or we did."

"Put it away," Colvin instructed. He calmed his horse, which turned fractious the moment the Myriad Ones swarmed them.

Lia did and withdrew her bow, getting an arrow ready.

"What is it?" Dieyre said, riding up behind them. He scanned the woods, his eyes suddenly wary.

"I must scout ahead," Lia said, handing her reins to Colvin.

"No, let me," he returned, but she shook her head.

"I am better at this work than you," she said. "You two are not very quiet."

Colvin frowned, hesitating a moment, but he took her reins and nodded mutely. With her bow ready, she continued up the hill, amazed at the thronging smoke shapes around her, the Unborn. It felt unclean when they sniffed at her, hissing in the invisible realm they came from. She realized something as she walked. Until that moment, she had felt the comforting presence of Muirwood all around her. There was something about wearing the chaen that had captured its essence. Every other time she had wandered the Bearden Muir with Martin or by herself, the moors had felt dangerous and unruly. Since becoming a maston, it was different. Regardless of where she went, Muirwood's peace was with her. Until now—until the Myriad Ones had found her.

The oaks were overrun with scraggly vines with bronze-colored leaves. The brush around her was thick with it when she noticed it. The vines were everywhere, dozens and dozens of leagues from where she had last encountered them, near Jon Hunter's grave. Every direction she looked, except where she had come from, the poisonous growth choked the oaks. She was careful—very careful—not to touch it. But it covered the ground as well. With cautious steps, she bounded this way and that, until she felt the burning Leering ahead on the hilltop. She sensed it before she saw it.

Crowning the hilltop was a stone boulder, enormous in size, like that of a mountain, where the earth had worn away from it. The Leering was carved into its eastward side, but it was so blackened and crumbled that she could not tell whether the image was of a man or beast. The eyes were pockmarks of molten stone, blazing red with furious flames. The growth of the poisonous leaves smothered it. Every nearby tree had succumbed to the tangled vines. The Leering drew her nearer, whispering for her to touch it. Lia approached carefully, listening for sounds—searching for the trample marks of men. There was nothing but the primeval woods. The rock shimmered with heat.

Every sound in the forest stilled except the beckoning whisper from the Leering. She fought down an urge to be sick. The Myriad Ones crooned at her in delight. Slowly, she approached the ragged scorched face.

The urge to touch it became desperate.

She stared into the blazing eyes, into the depths of an excruciating agony, a torture beyond anything she could imagine. The Leering was pleading with her to end it. To heal the burning. The Aldermaston's words drifted through her thoughts, reminding her of the maston training, of her Gifts. Firetaming.

Reaching out, she pressed her palm against the stub-nose of the Leering, confident it would not scald her hand. There was heat and warmth, but nothing that scorched her. In fact, in all her years in the Aldermaston's kitchen, she could not remember a single time she had ever burned herself. The stone was rough and scarred.

"I release you," she whispered, invoking the Medium.

In her mind's eye, she saw Scarseth turn and look at her. She could see him clearly in her mind, hunched over one of the Leerings that protected the Abbey grounds. He stared at her, knowing where she was as she knew where he was. For a moment, they were connected within each other's mind. His thoughts thrusted against her violently.

There you are!

Even with all the distance between them, he used the Leering as a sort of bridge to connect with her. To push all of his deep, filthy thoughts into her mind, to surround her with fear and despair and hopelessness. To force her to do his will. But he had not counted on something. She was a maston now.

"I release you," she whispered again, more forcefully, quenching the fire that raged in the Leering.

The cracked and pitted stone began to cool as the fire guttered out, obeying her. There was no rigid defiance, no angry throb of regret. With a sharp crack, the stone split apart, sheared into huge slabs and slices. With it went the bond with Scarseth. She took a breath of relief, grateful that the Leering had not defied her as the other one had. There were no blisters on her palm or fingers. She turned and looked down the other side of the hill. The woods were thicker, rich and green with ferns and catmint.

A sick worry bloomed in her stomach. Scarseth was still in the woods outside Muirwood, and now he knew that she was gone.

***

After warning Dieyre and Colvin about touching the poisonous plant sap, she led them over the ridge and into the lush lowlands on the other side. The rich and fertile land was a stark contrast, and she knew they had exited the Bearden Muir. They rode forward hastily, knowing it would be a hard ride to reach the town before twilight. A hard ride perhaps, but possible.

The orb led them through the tangled woods, north instead of east, which surprised Lia. Low-hanging branches clawed at them, the growth so heavy in places it was difficult to see far. Treacherous ravines were abundant, but the orb guided them to narrow crossings or makeshift bridges constructed by local woodsmen.

In the deep woods ahead, a woman's scream rang out.

Lia started. The scream was followed by the shouts of men's voices. Sharp commands, barked orders. She held up her hand, motioning the other two to stop. Slipping off the saddle, she threaded an arrow in the string. Whose voice was it? Ellowyn's? Marciana's? There was no way to tell, but the orb was pointing in the direction of the sound.

"Have we caught up with them?" Dieyre marveled, as if truly surprised.

Colvin grabbed her arm. "The Queen's men? Or the Pryrians?"

"I need to get closer to tell," she said. "Wait for me here."

His grip tightened. "Not this time. We go together. All of us," he added before Dieyre could snort his objection.

She sighed. "You can follow me, but let me go on ahead of you in case there is a trap. We do not know how many there are and do not want to stumble in the midst of a fight."

"Actually." Dieyre said with a wicked grin. "I do. Let me go on ahead. If they are the Queen's men looking for the girl, they would listen to me."

"Which is why I will not let you do that," Colvin rebuffed. "I am sworn to protect her."

"That scream may have been your sister, Forshee. I am not going to stand around here arguing with you. My interest is Ciana's safety. Ellowyn can be hanged, for all I care. You have not trusted me this entire trip. It is time I earned it."

"Lia goes first," Colvin demanded.

"Very well, but she cannot have all the fun. Go, girl. Save some of them for me." He jerked his sword loose in the scabbard, his face dotted with mosquito welts.

Lia darted ahead, and they began to follow after securing the horses to some branches. She moved swiftly, low to the ground. There was a screen of bushy ferns everywhere, providing good concealment for her movements. She held her bow in front, ready to be used. The sound of voices grew louder, and she could make out the Dahomeyjan accent.

"Search the house! Up in the rafters as well. Quit wailing, woman, or I will strike you! Move on. Go on then. Inside."

The woods began to thin, and Lia saw the first sentries, set back into the woods closer to her, watching. They were garbed in the black and silver tunics of the Queen Dowager. The two directly in front of her were looking at the scene with interest. Beyond them, she saw a small clearing and a thatch-roofed dwelling. There were at least a dozen or more soldiers tramping the grounds surrounding the wattle-and-daub abode. It had a single door and no windows. Beyond it, she saw the sun glimmering off the waters of the sea, interspersed with thick pine.

Not wanting to be heard, Lia went away from the sentries, moving toward the rear of the house. The fern was even thicker there, and taller, which made it easier to hide as she hunched low. There was enough of a breeze to sway the leafy boughs, helping to conceal her.

To her left, she heard a soft whimper, a child's and then it was stifled. Changing her course, she headed toward the sound, gliding through the mess of fern toward a copse of witch hazel.

A gentle hushing sound.

"I hear them," another girl's voice murmured, throbbing with worry.

"Sshhh, it will be all right," soothed another voice, which Lia recognized at once.

She parted the first bough of green hazel leaves and found Marciana crouched with three small children, huddled tight together. She realized that the children had been speaking Pryrian.

Marciana started when Lia appeared, her eyes wide with fear and then gaped with recognition. "You found us!" she gasped.

"The bad men!" one of the little children said, a girl, tugging at Marciana's gown and pointing back toward the house. "The bad men are coming!"

Lia risked a look, and it was confirmed. Two of the watch were heading toward them, following the trampled grass to their hiding spot. Lia noticed a huge chunk of thatch was missing from the roof, leaving a gaping hole on that side. Someone had obviously seen it.

"Where is Ellowyn?" Lia whispered, clutching Marciana's shoulder and squeezing her firmly. "In the house?"

Marciana shook her head violently. "No, she left by boat this morning. Edmon is in the house! If they search the rafters, they will find him. Did Colvin find you?"

Lia smiled comfortingly. "Behind me. Take the children and flee deeper into the woods. Find a place to hide. I will come for you."

"Lia, I am so grateful…"

"Go!" Lia said, cutting her off. The soldiers were so near, she did not want them hearing. She gripped Marciana's gown and tugged her to get her moving. She clutched a small child, probably two years old in her arms, covering his mouth. The other two were little girls, probably five and eight, and they looked at Lia with surprise and wonder.

"You will be safe," Lia murmured to them in Pry-rian, and their gapes turned into grins.

"Here he is!" bellowed a voice from inside the dwelling. "Up in the rafters, hiding in the thatch!"

"Bring him down!" ordered another voice. "Bring him out here. Where is the girl? Did you find the girl?"

The sound of sudden commotion in the house caused a lot of attention, except the two soldiers approaching were not deterred. They were following the footprints closely, moving into the fern and looking at the trampled leaves. She could see their shadows and hear the crunch of their boots as they closed in on where she was hiding. Her mind raced through the options. Where were Colvin and Dieyre? How close were they behind her? Had they seen Marciana moving deeper into the gorse?

The commotion in the house turned louder, and something crashed and cracked.

"He has a maston sword!" someone roared. "He stabbed Kelton!"

"A maston?" shouted the other man. The one she assumed was the leader. With a voice full of hate and bitterness, he said savagely, "Fetch him down, and kill him!"

Lia's blood ran cold. The Medium surged inside of her. She felt strength and calm flooding her.

"There!" rang a voice just beyond the nest of witch hazel. "I see her! Running with the children!"

There was no more time to plot and plan. There was only time to act.

Rising from her crouch, Lia lifted her bow. The first sentry was hardly five paces away from her when the arrow sank into his heart. It nearly went all the way through him. As he collapsed without a grunt, she had another arrow on the string. The Dahomeyjan knight looked shocked, his sword coming up to try and ward off the blow as the second arrow loosed, and he too crumpled to the ground.

With blood pounding in her ears, Lia drew another shaft from her quiver and rushed into the clearing.

Most people ebb and flow in torment between the fear of death and the hardship of life; they are unwilling to live, and yet, they do not know how to die. Rehearse death. To say this is to tell a maston to rehearse his freedom. A person who has learned how to die has unlearned how to be a slave to fear. He is above, or at any rate, beyond the reach of all political powers.

—*Gideon Penman of Muirwood Abbey*

CHAPTER THIRTY-FOUR

Distant Shores

The two knights had fallen without a sound. Lia rushed across the clearing to the house in a moment of pure confusion. She heard the clang of metal on metal inside, the grunt of fighting in close quarters. Edmon was outnumbered. She knew they would hack him down because he wore the sword of a maston—just as the sheriff's men had killed his brother.

"From the woods, an archer! A Pry-rian!" came a cry of alarm.

Lia rounded the side of the house, into a mass of soldiers clustered near the door to witness the execution. Lia could tell who was the leader—his hair was shocked with gray, his beard peppered with black. He had the comfortable poise of a man who was used to killing and butchery. Her next arrow brought him down.

Complete chaos ensued.

"Get her! Kill her!"

"No, it is the Abbey hunter!"

"Watch her bow!"

Two of the men broke and ran. The rest raised their swords and rushed at her. Lia sent another man to his death. There was a swarm of black tunics and glinting blades. She had to run. There was no way to stand against so many. What was she thinking, running into the midst of them? All she knew was she had to get to Edmon before they killed him.

The thud of running boots behind her and she whirled, ready to bring down the other knights she knew would be closing in behind her. Before she loosed the arrow, she recognized Colvin and Dieyre. Behind them, the two sentries at the fringe of the woods were sprawled on the ground. Colvin charged like a crazed wolf, sword high in the hand, his eyes terrible with anger, his face contorted into a snarl.

"Back to the woods!" he snapped at her as he rushed past, thrusting himself into the midst of the knights, his weapon scything through the mass of bodies. Dieyre's look was equally fierce, his step just slightly behind as he too charged into the mass of men. Lia backed away from the conflict, the sudden flail of bodies and spatter of blood. For a moment, she watched in horror and awe. Colvin and Dieyre fought like madmen, their blades whipping around so fast and deadly, the surprised knights stumbled back, desperate to save themselves, even though they had more numbers. Another ran, and Lia shot him down before he could reach the horses.

Then she remembered Edmon.

Colvin and Dieyre's charge thrust the mass of men away from the dwelling, leaving a gap in the doorway. She nearly tripped over the corpse of the leader, and went inside, which was blackened with soot smoke. One man was crumpled on the ground, clutching a bleeding wrist. Edmon was face-first on the ground, stunned, a knight above him with a naked sword.

Lia raised the bow and felled him with an arrow. There were three more men, including the wounded one. As she reached in the quiver, her fingers met nothing. The rest of the arrows were gone, still attached to her saddle. Furious, Lia screamed at them, a cry of rage and hate, and drew her dagger and gladius.

One of the knights thrust his sword down at Edmon's back. She watched the blade strike the ground. Edmon had twisted away just in time. His boots kicked out at one of the knights, snapping his knee, and the man roared with agony.

The room was so small. Lia ran at them, spinning around once while she ducked and thrust her gladius into the man's belly. As she twirled, she deflected a blade with her dagger and pulled her weapon free, loosing a gush of blood. Edmon wrestled with the wounded knight and took away his sword. It was two on two. The knights attacked, slicing at Lia and Edmon, but Lia felt the Medium coursing through her, strengthening her. Blocking the blow, she stepped in, stomping on his foot, crippling him. Catching his sword guard with her gladius and locking it, she thrust the dagger into his navel and jerked the blade, killing him. Edmon's blade whirled around, and the last man sagged to his knees, headless.

Lia pulled her weapons free and whirled at the creeping movement in the corner of her vision. The knight with the wounded wrist was carefully sneaking toward the door. When their eyes met, he quavered with fear and babbled for mercy in Dahomeyjan.

She raised her gladius and pointed the blade at him. "Stay there. If you even twitch, I will kill you."

Edmon mopped blood from his nose. "Lia!" he gasped with relief. "You speak Dahomeyjan? I cannot believe it! You came…I had almost given up hope…but I did not. I knew the Medium would protect me, as it did during Winterrowd."

A body filled the doorway, and Lia spun around, ready to fight again, but it was Colvin.

"I heard your scream," he gasped to Lia, the sweat from his face mingling with his opponent's blood. He planted his hand on the doorframe to steady himself. He looked at the shivering knight on the ground, glaring at him.

"Mercy!" the man squeaked in a trembling tone.

Lia sheathed her weapons and then picked up her discarded bow. "Did you see your sister?" she asked Colvin. "She is in the woods."

He shook his head. "No, I saw you charge. There you were, one little girl charging into the midst of Dahomeyjan knights. Lia, what were you thinking!"

Edmon stepped forward, breathing heavily. "If she did not, I would be dead right now."

"Yes, a *great* loss," Dieyre murmured from behind Colvin. He looked sardonic as usual. "Lucky the lass was here to save your neck, York."

Edmon stared in surprise. "What are *you* doing here?"

"Murdering my allies," he quipped. "Do not look so shocked. I have my reasons, as you may well suspect. Ah, one of them lived. Are we going to question him or just dispatch him?"

"Let him go," Colvin said bluntly. "He is of no use to us." His eyes narrowed and fastened on Edmon. "Where is Ellowyn?"

Edmon frowned, crestfallen. "The Pry-rians took her this morning. There is a dock on the other side of those trees. She is gone to Pry-Ree already."

***

For a long while after the battle was over and the bodies of the dead were removed, Lia leaned against a tree outside the family hut, breathing deeply, struggling to control her emotions. After Winterrowd, she had been haunted by the images in her mind of the dead. But that was different, since she was the cause of only one of them and that was done at a distance, and she did not have to look into the lusterless eyes of her victims. Her feelings were conflicted and raw, and she wiped her eyes and nose, trying to subdue her feelings. Martin had warned her that death brought many emotions. There was the thrill of battle, a sense of being aware of every breath and every murmur of sound, of using skills to stay alive. There were sounds and sights that would never be sponged from her memories. Even though the Medium had wanted her to save Edmon, it still shocked her how efficient she had been in killing others and how powerful it made her feel. Part of her had even enjoyed it, and that knowledge made her shrink inside herself and cringe with remorse.

The remaining horses, save one, were set loose to wander the Bearden Muir. Lia thought with amazement at the short work of the battle. The three of them had killed nearly twenty men. Two had escaped by horseback at the beginning of the battle. The wounded man was let go, and he slinked away after Lia had paused to treat his wound, much to Dieyre's disgust. He was just as well leaving the corpses to litter the grounds, but Colvin had insisted they clear away the dead.

Colvin found Lia in the woods, his expression grim and hardened, and asked for her help communicating with the mother of the children, who gibbered at them in Pry-rian.

Lia dried her eyes and met with the mother and was able to determine much from the woman about the family they had discovered. They lived in the wilderness, and her husband rowed a small boat back and forth to Pry-Ree once each day. They ferried goods to trade, occasionally travelers, and did well enough to support themselves year to year. All goods brought in to Bridgestow were taxed by the king, so her husband's business was small but prosperous as a way of circumventing the taxes. After much hard rowing day after day, the husband had determined their specific location was the shortest distance between Pry-Ree and their kingdom, and thus the least amount of work for a man who earned his living by rowing. He had built the thatched cottage himself in that spot and the pier to dock his boat. He would return by nightfall from having taken Martin and the visitors across the narrow strip of sea that separated the two kingdoms. The family was not involved in the plot to abduct Ellowyn. In fact, they did not know who she was, other than some highborn guest. There were eight men, including Martin. Just enough to fit in the boat for the journey there and back. And because they had not crossed at Bridgestow, the sheriff of the Hundred had not known they were there or when they arrived.

It was just like Martin, Lia realized. He had planned the escape perfectly, knowing how many men he would need and how to avoid the places where he might be accosted. They had traveled on foot, which slowed their progress. She wondered whether they would have caught up to them if they had not slept during the night.

"Those soldiers discovered the smoke from our chimney," the woman explained to Lia. She cuddled with her children, grateful to be alive when so many had been butchered on her doorstep. Her name was Aerona, and she had introduced her two oldest daughters, Blodyn and Dilys, and her infant, Cowan. "They arrived without warning, we only had time to hide the children in the loft. I was so frightened. Edmon helped the little ones escape from the thatch, but the knights shoved their way in and saw him in the light. I was so fearful my little ones would be hurt. I speak very little of your language. You speak our tongue very well. What clan are you from?"

Lia evaded the question by explaining her remarks to the three earls. Nightfall was approaching, and Aerona was anxious for the return of her husband.

Dieyre paced as she listened, absorbing the information. Lia noticed that Marciana glanced at him surreptitiously. All of their horses were saddled, in case they needed to escape quickly. Edmon stood watch.

Dieyre muttered under his breath. "The last thing Pry-Ree needs is another war. This makes no sense."

"Perhaps not to us," Colvin agreed, "but their motives are different from ours."

"They are a rash and faithless people. They got what they wanted without Demont's help. The heir of Pry-Ree has returned. Now the entire country will burn for it."

"Why do you say that?" Edmon asked from the doorway, still watching the woods.

"Do not be stupid, York. I know that is difficult for you, but try and keep up."

Lia bristled at the condescending attitude, but Colvin's voice was patient. "She is a prize that many will fight over. I am sure a reward will be offered for her return. One large enough to tempt even Pry-rians to betray her. No matter where they keep her, someone will tell. Or someone will try and kill her." He shook his head and sighed.

Lia felt a twinge of pity for him, but she had already decided on the best course of action. "That is our advantage," she offered quietly. "They are not far ahead of us." She rose and folded her arms. "I will bring her back. I speak Pry-rian. I can cross tomorrow morning, after the boatman has rested, and find her."

Dieyre looked at her, startled. "There are eight soldiers. I know you are clever and brave, but you are still but a girl. Their leader is the master who trained you, if I remember it right. You will be caught."

"I have to try," Lia said.

Colvin looked up at her, eyes wide with amazement. "You would go?"

She looked him in the eye and nodded curtly.

"I was not going to ask that of you. I had already made up my mind to go."

"What?" Dieyre said with a choking laugh. "You cannot be serious, Forshee!"

"Colvin, no!" Marciana said, her face suddenly flaming with worry. "It is a wild country. The Blight is there. I have heard stories. Serpents and other poisonous things. The land cannot be tamed."

"Ciana is right," Dieyre went on. "Brave, yes, but also the height of foolishness. Our kingdom subjugated theirs. They have not forgotten it, you know. When any of our knights fall into their hands, they are murdered cruelly. They *hate* us, Forshee. I am not sure that word is strong enough to describe their feelings. Even with your personal allegiance to Demont, they would see you as less than a dog in their home country."

Lia was not aware of the hatred, but she agreed with Dieyre. "I will go. If there is any way I can bring her back, I will. Catching her now will be easier than it will be later. I can find her with the orb. I can do this alone."

Colvin looked at her. "Yes, you can do it. I have no doubt. But I will go with you."

She shook her head. "I cannot accept that."

Dieyre watched them with fascination. "He is considering it. I cannot believe it! You are daft! This is as close to Pry-Ree as I would ever dare go without ten thousand soldiers at my back."

Colvin rose to his feet, his face flushed with anger. "I know it means little to you, but I swore an oath to protect her. To guard her life with my own. It is my obligation. How can I go back and face Demont? I must do everything in my power to save her, use any means available to me. That is what loyalty means, Dieyre. Loyalty binds me. I must go after her. If Lia can find her, I can help free her."

"Colvin," Marciana said in a pleading voice. "I do not want you to go. Think of the danger. I know you feel your duty here, but please. You are an earl of the realm. You have duties to Demont. He needs you right now."

"Listen to her," Dieyre said, folding his arms. "You will not last two days in Pry-Ree. They will kill you." But his expression made it seem that he secretly wanted Colvin to go.

"I must try," Colvin said, looking at Marciana. "Edmon can take you to Bridgestow. I will meet you there when this is done. It is a stronghold for Demont. Either way, he needs to know what happened to his niece." He sighed deeply. "If I am only to survive two days there, then we must go and return that quickly." He looked into Lia's eyes hopefully. "Will you take me?"

Lia wrestled with her feelings. Should she insist on going alone? She knew how stubborn he could be. He had already made up his mind. If anyone could keep him safe in Pry-Ree, she knew that it was her with the orb. Just as she had done before.

"We had better rest now," she replied. "We will get little there."

CHAPTER THIRTY-FIVE

Blight of Pry-Ree

The boatman's name was Pen-Ilyn. He was strong but not as hulking as Lia expected him to be—about the same size and build as Colvin. He was talkative in a way that made her seem as tight-lipped as Sowe. He and his wife shared in tales and business as he rowed, back straight, muscles churning the oars with regular repetition. After learning his family had been attacked by Dahomeyjan knights, he was in no mood to leave them behind, but brought the family on board as he rowed. Better to lose any of the trinkets in the house than to lose any of his precious brood. He spat and cursed the Queen Dowager's name and her foreign ways.

Lia and Colvin sat in the prow of the boat as it sliced through the waters toward the distant shore of Pry-Ree. With Pen-Ilyn unable to stop talking, they had no time to speak quietly among themselves. Her rucksack was propped next to her, bulging with food and a blanket. Colvin had purchased clothes from the boatman and looked more like a commoner than a noble from court. He had not shaved in several days, so he wore the beginnings of a beard, reminding her of their trek to Winterrowd. She even studied the puckered scar at his eyebrow and felt the forbidden urge to touch it. Blushing, she looked away.

Pen-Ilyn turned his head and spoke louder. He had an accent, but he spoke both languages well. "There is a little island called Steep Holm in the waters over yon. Some think it is on Pry-rian shores, but it is not. If I am getting weary, or if there is a storm, I shelter there until it passes. If I wanted to, I could row to Pry-Ree and back twice each day. It is not so much as being strong as it is not getting tired. If you keep a steady pull on the oars, it becomes a rhythm, like a flute. I wish I could flute and row at the same time, but I cannot."

"If you fluted, Papa, who would pull the oars?" asked his oldest daughter, Blodyn.

"Which is an excellent question. How about you blow the flute for me, lass, and I will do the pulling. Sometimes my girls make the journey with me, if their mother can spare them. I usually only make one trip each day. There are folk who know the Bridgestow road, and they know where I am. The sheriff calls now and then, but he thinks I am fishing. Even though I do not have any nets. I could buy some nets. I wonder if the fishing is any better?"

Lia looked at Colvin, who looked as if he had a headache from the constant talking.

"Where are we going?" Lia asked. "Is there a town?"

"I cannot say with any certainty which direction they were off to, but the hamlet across the water is called Enarth. The larger town is Caerdeth. It is the port that trades with Bridgestow. There is a garrison castle where the sheriff lives. He stays indoors mostly, because he fears an arrow lodging in his neck. That happens sometimes in Pry-Ree. Maybe they went to the castle first. It is not a far walk from Enarth."

Colvin smirked. Lia doubted Martin would take Ellowyn to one of the king's castles in Pry-Ree. Pen-Ilyn talked more about flutes, the wool trade, tax collectors, sheriffs, the price of Muirwood cider, fishing, storms, as well as family members. Before long, Lia's mind wandered back on the morning as they departed. The images of the moment were still fresh in her mind, her feelings powerful. Marciana clutching Colvin in a tight hug, tears running down her cheeks as she said good-bye. She had received a hug herself that nearly choked her with intensity and a whispered, "Do not let anything happen to him!" Edmon was not his usual self. The acid tongue of Dieyre had frightened away his amiable nature. Edmon stood resolutely on the shore, promising Colvin he would see his sister safely to Bridgestow. As they left, Marciana was crying on Edmon's shoulder, Dieyre regarding them with a mixture of odd sympathy and jealousy. He waved to Colvin, offering thinly veiled advice on how to stay warm at night. Lia blushed with rage, but she held her tongue, recollecting just how tactless Dieyre was. Lia watched them mount horses as the oars dipped into the choppy water, saw them pose near the shoreline and wave. Edmon would return with fresh mounts and men from Bridgestow and await their return after Marciana was safe away.

Colvin touched her hand to get her attention, and she nearly flinched at his touch. She smiled and looked at him.

"How do you speak Pry-rian and Dahomeyjan, Lia? Has Martin been teaching you?"

She shook her head subtly. "Actually, it is the Aldermaston's doing. He Gifted me with *Xenoglossia*. When I need to understand something, it just happens. When I need to say something, it just comes out. It is not something I really think about."

Colvin nodded. "A powerful Gift of the Medium." He looked over his shoulder into the horizon. "This is your country, I think. Your parents are not alive. But I think they were from Pry-Ree. You will have an advantage there. It is probably wise if I do not speak much."

"I am sure that will be difficult for you," she teased.

He ignored the thrust and went on. "With the orb, we will not need to ask directions or track their steps. I only hope we can make good time and head them off on their escape. Have you any thoughts about outwitting Martin?"

Lia looked out across the water. "I am sure he will be watching for us to follow. If we can get in front of him somehow, that will be a surprise. My guess is that they will not stay in towns, but sleep out of doors. He would not want too many witnesses, and bringing someone like her would cause talk. I know that he will keep a watch during the night, but that may still be the best chance to free her. I might be able to make the guards fall asleep."

"Like you did at the Pilgrim."

She nodded. "It was valerianum, of course. But I do not think it affects someone so quickly. I think it was the Medium. If that does not work, then I may try talking to Martin and explaining the situation to him."

Colvin shook his head. "He has already committed to this act. He will not be persuaded. But if you could lure him away from the others, I could subdue him."

Lia bit her lip. "I do not mean to be offensive, Colvin, but I doubt that. He…he is very good." She could see she had offended him. She reached out and touched his leg. "I think Dieyre was right about him in one way. I do think he was soldier. I think he trained other soldiers. He taught me many ways to kill or disable a man. Though I do not think I have the heart to hurt him." She frowned. "Please do not kill him, Colvin."

He snorted. "It is more likely that he would kill me, it seems."

"I am sorry if I hurt your feelings."

With a shrug, he waved her off. "Was he the one who suggested to you that it was safe strategy to charge into a mass of enemy knights with only a gladius and a bow?"

She stopped short and looked at him quizzically. "In a way, yes. Are you criticizing me?"

"Ah, I have offended you now. I wondered what possessed you to charge in like that. You were assuming we would rush in behind you? You communicated nothing. I saw you rise up and shoot down those hapless men, then rush into the thick of them. It frightened me out of my wits. The one advantage to your action was it surprised them and drew their focus to you. The second is that it forced Dieyre to make a stand, one way or the other. I do not see how the Queen Dowager will forgive him for killing her men. So you may have committed him to our side without intending to. It was bold, Lia. But never do that again."

She gave him a curious expression. "You were worried about me?"

"You should have worried more. Have a care next time."

Lia felt a flush of pleasure at the words. "One of the things Martin did teach me is that war is about surprising your enemies. Doing something they cannot anticipate. Throwing dust in their eyes. Stomping on their foot. A man cannot fight if you cut off his thumb. Being unpredictable is your best weapon. If you can get them to react to what you are doing, it gives you more choices than reacting to what they are doing. To be honest, my only goal was to thwart a murder. To draw the attention from inside the hovel to outside. I knew you and Dieyre were behind me. We did what had to be done."

His frown was not stern, just troubled. "Just warn me next time," he insisted. "Before doing anything rash."

When they looked back, there was land.

"Ah, there is Steep Holm," Pen-Ilyn said. "We will take a short rest there."

***

The hamlet of Enarth was smaller than the village of Muirwood. Perhaps a dozen small dwellings, a muddy road, and a single dock with fishing boats tethered there.

"It is a humble place, but we will stay with my sister who lives a short way from here," Pen-Ilyn said. He clasped their hands, one by one. "Per our agreement, my lord, we will wait on this side of the shore for you to return. You paid for two days, so we will wait for two days, despite other business that may be lost. If the Dahomeyjan cowards return, they will find our place desolate. If we wait any longer, our livestock may all be gone when we return. We get our milk and cheese from cowherds in Enarth anyway, so that will not trouble us. Be careful. The land is treacherous. Mind the snakes and scorpions."

Lia thanked him for his advice, and the two headed off into the woods where she could use the Cruciger orb discreetly. As she cupped it in her hands, she thought of Ellowyn's face, how terrified she must be, and focused her intent on where they would be and if there was a path that they could safely take to head them off and away from Pry-rians who would challenge them. The orb was cool in her hand, then it started to spin and pointed clearly. Colvin looked relieved and secured his rucksack against his shoulders. His sword dangled from his belt. Together, they followed the direction and forsook the muddy road.

Pry-Ree was a wild and untamed land. The trees were different from the ones that grew in the Bearden Muir. They were taller, thicker, more ancient. The ground was rugged and mottled with boulders and stones. The greenery was sickly with weeds, and Pen-Ilyn's warning about snakes was soon justified. There were snakes and voles everywhere. The serpents feared their passing and slithered away as they tromped through the brush, but their very presence made Lia shiver with revulsion. They crossed a wild lowland valley, but on the other side rose an imposing crag of mountains with giant trees. There was a haunting familiarity about the land, like a song that had once been sung, its echo dying on the breeze.

About midday, they came across a small cabin in the midst of the valley. There was no smoke from the chimney, and the fence was in tatters. They approached cautiously, but there was no sign of anyone living there. The garden was spoiled, there were no animals in the pens. All life had been scrubbed clean. After passing the property, they found other similar dwellings, abandoned or forsaken with no trace of fire or harm. As if the owners had simply abandoned them and walked off.

"It is strange," Colvin muttered, looking at another abandoned dwelling. "Not a soul."

Lia nodded. She searched for any sign of what had happened, but the homes had been abandoned for several months. Each step brought them closer to the shadow of the mountains. The ground became more rugged, and the boulders were enormous, as if huge slabs of rock had broken off above and tumbled down the mountainside to rest on the valley slope. The ground became steeper, the journey more difficult as they ascended into the region. The sky was clear of any cloud, but it did not make the mood cheerful as sunlight usually did. Lia felt oppressed by the stones around her. Their massive, jagged cliff faces seemed to mock her with her insignificance.

The look of Pry-Ree began to alter before their eyes. The brush was thinner higher up, more verdant than down below in the valley. The trees were enormous, taller than a castle wall, tall enough to rival the stars. The mountains were thick with huge pine and redwood trees. The wind became more fierce. It was not like climbing the Tor. This was a mountain, not a shallow hill. Each step burned as they walked and pushed themselves higher into the crown of trees. The day began to wane, but they ate as they walked, trying to crest the mountain before the sunlight gave way. It was colder, and Lia was glad to have brought a blanket.

"Do you see that one?" Colvin asked, his voice hushed in wonder. "I have never seen a tree so thick. It would take ten men to clasp around the trunk."

Lia saw it and marveled. The redwood was enormous, so thick around the base it would take an axeman a year to cut through it. There were no branches lower down, but high near the top, the branches grew as thick as trees she had seen. It was enormous—greater even than the Sentinel oak in the woods near her home. They approached the wonder, and as they did, discovered that it was not the only giant living in the forest. More trees could be seen farther off, some even bigger.

"I have never seen the like," she whispered in awe. She rubbed the bark with her hand, wondering how ancient the tree was. Ferns grew thick in the area, but nearly all the other growth was stunted compared to the formidable trees.

Higher into the mountains they went, and the trees got bigger and bigger. One was so wide at the base, it would have taken thirty men to encircle it. They also discovered the skeletons of trees that had been struck by lightning and eventually collapsed. She could only imagine the crashing noise they would have made when they fell. Surely the earth would have shaken with the impact. After falling, the roots were splayed and wide open, revealing black tunnels made of soot and charcoal. It smelled familiar, like the kitchen ovens after a heavy day of baking. That same smell of ash she had grown up with. The roots of the giants were wide enough to fit them both and then add more. At last, they reached the peak, and the ground began descending the other way. The peaks of the mountains extended on both sides still, but the orb had led them to a hollow in between the rugged pair and then led them down the other side, where numerous fallen giants littered the woods, along with boulders and a stream.

There was one giant where the exposed roots were so deep, it was like a cave. Using the orb for light, she explored the depth and discovered that it was not the den of any animal. The burned inside of the tree was probably not a place animals cared to dwell, but it was tall enough to stand in until the very end.

"It will be twilight soon," Lia said, rubbing her hand against the charcoal interior. "If we go down the mountain at night, we will need the orb for light. We will probably be seen by anyone lower down. To be honest, I am tired. We covered a lot of ground today, most of it uphill." The little den was about as comfortable a shelter as she could have hoped for.

"I am tired as well." he said, unslinging the rucksack and setting it down. He stared at the tangle of exposed roots, his expression curious. "This is truly an ancient land. I have never seen the like and probably never will again." He looked at her. "I have never slept inside a dead tree before. I suppose they would make good shelter."

Lia agreed and withdrew the orb and summoned its power again. Sometimes lettering appeared when it was trying to warn her. None appeared now. The orb had not changed directions for a while. "Weather in the mountains can be treacherous. Even though it is summer, it can snow or rain up in the highlands. At least we have this as shelter if that happens."

Colvin agreed, and they set about making a small camp in the hollow of the roots. They did not want to risk a fire, but just in case the temperature fell severely during the night, it would be smart to have dry wood ready and nearby. With the fallen segments, it was easy to gather enough kindling and logs, so they were gathered in before the darkness swallowed them. Sitting in the pit of the tree, they shared their meal. The wind was cool, but the giant tree carcass still clinged to the sun's warmth.

"They might be riding around the mountain," Lia guessed, acutely aware of how quiet Colvin was. "I do not know how wide this range is, but if they are traveling around it, we may catch them tomorrow. I wonder where they are camping tonight. Or if they stopped for shelter at an inn."

Colvin said nothing, and she wondered if he was asleep. It was strange being in Pry-Ree, even stranger being with him. The land was more wild and untamed than she expected. Not as savage as the Bearden Muir, but harsh and alien. There were plants she did not recognize, and the air had a different smell to it, a musk from the redwoods that was different from the oaks she was used to. She settled on top of her blanket and pulled her cloak over her shoulders, sitting up and leaning back against the ridged inside of the trunk, not sure how she should feel about her homeland. It was not familiar, but it was part of her still. She was a daughter of the land, even though she had no memories of it. She glanced down at the shadow of Colvin's body and decided she would take the first watch while he slept. The wind rustled the air, and the towering limbs of the giant trees creaked as they swayed.

"Lia?" His voice was soft, almost a whisper.

"Yes?"

Another silence.

"There is something I must tell you. A confession I must make."

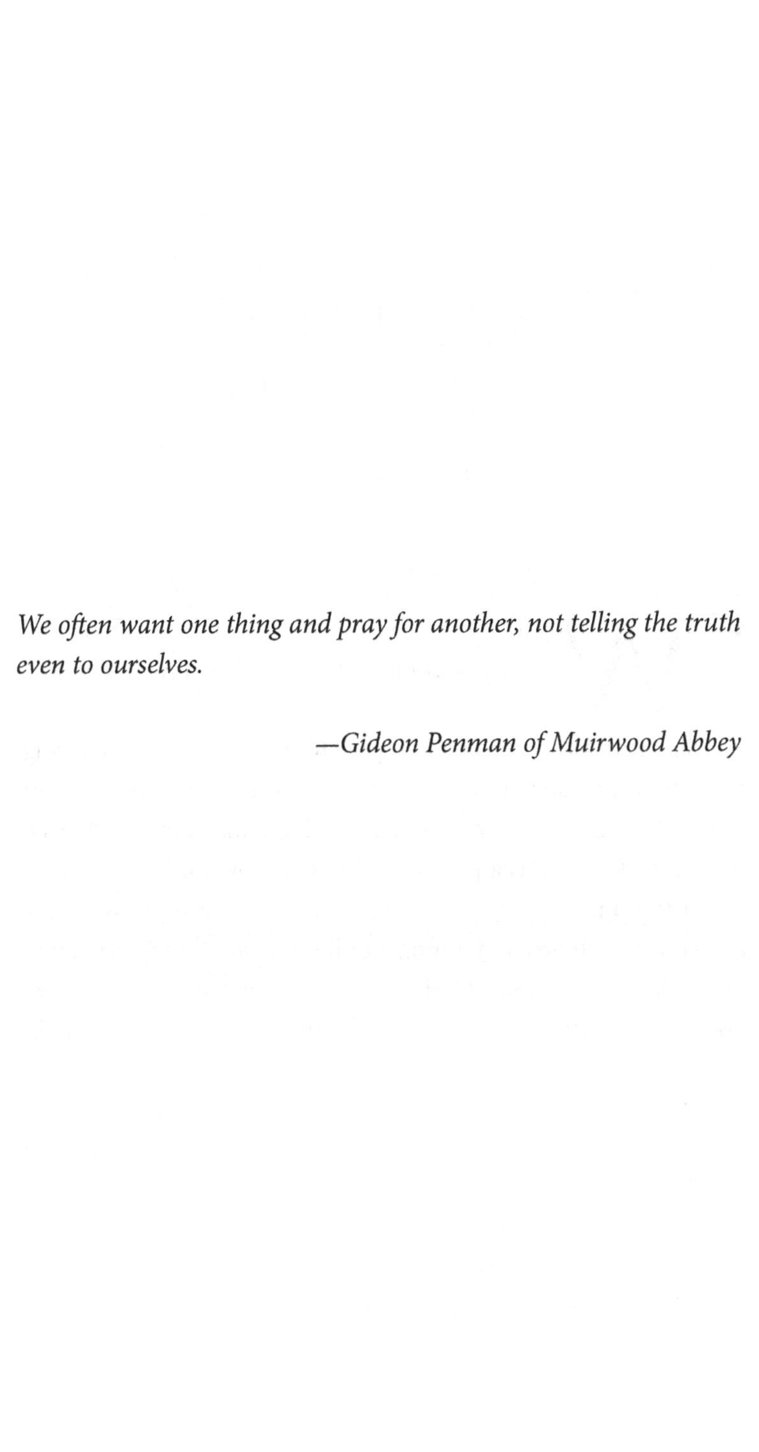

We often want one thing and pray for another, not telling the truth even to ourselves.

—*Gideon Penman of Muirwood Abbey*

CHAPTER THIRTY-SIX

Fallen Giants

"What is it?" Lia asked, turning around to face him. She could not see his face, it was so dark.

"Light the orb please."

She withdrew it from her pouch, and it shone, enclosing them both in a sheath of light. She set it on the ground in front of her. The air was musty with charcoal, getting colder with each moment. Her breath came out as a fog as she breathed. She moved closer to him, studying his serious face. His expression was restless and eager to say something, but his eyes were dark, reflecting one of his somber moods. He struggled with the words, looking down at the orb and then at her. She noticed a slight tremble in his hands.

"I was laying here," he began, "trying to escape my thoughts in the dark. But I cannot escape them. Not anymore. I have been in misery since we spoke in the orchard when it was raining. Up to that moment, I had persuaded myself that you were fond of that boy, Duerden, that only my feelings were at risk. I was determined to master them. To control them." He looked down at his hands and then up at her. "For the life of me, I cannot. I have wrestled against them. I have fought them. I have tried to burn them out with fury. To scald them out with regrets. Every verse in every tome I have ever read is flat and meaningless against what I am feeling. Ovidius comes the nearest, but his words only torture me. They do not comfort. I have lied to myself, and I have lied to you. I cannot do that any longer. I must tell you the truth."

Lia's heart was hammering so wildly, she did not know what to think. She hugged herself, but it was not the cold that made her shiver. It was giddiness, hope, fear, and longing, all boiling and seizing inside her at once. She could only nod for him to go on, unable to trust herself with words.

Colvin looked down at his hands again, as if ashamed to meet her gaze. "I am not afraid of succumbing to a blind fit of passion. As a maston, I have made oaths that I will not break. I value the presence of the Medium, though I cannot hear it right now. Should I even be telling you this? My head says I should trust you. My heart is nearly bursting with the words." He looked up at her again, his look more desperate. "My biggest fear was hurting you. Disappointing you. Now I must risk that, though it pains me. It is so difficult…finding the words. The poets always could. But that is not my way." He looked away, she could see the frustration by his clenched jaw muscles. She wanted to reach out to him, to comfort him, but she did not move. She waited until he was ready.

"You have a strange power over me, Lia. No one else has ever impressed me so deeply. In your presence, I have been my worst self as well as my best self. I have retched all over you. I have shouted at you, scolded you. I have wanted to clamp my hand over your mouth more than once. But I dare not touch you, because when it happens, it makes me feel things so intensely. It makes me forget who I am and what I want to be. When I was a learner at

Billerbeck, there was a girl who tried to win me, despite my efforts to shun her. I am sure she was a worthy prize—from a good family. She knew languages and had the patience for engraving. But I did not care for her. My heart was secretly longing after Demont's missing niece, even though I did not know who she was." He chuckled darkly. "But now that I do know her, I cannot love her. She is too simple. Too biddable."

Colvin looked her in the eye, his mood shifting again. His voice was grave. "When I care for someone, it runs deep. It becomes a firm part of me, like a stone. When I awoke in Muirwood in your kitchen, when I saw you peering at me with worry and concern, it brought out feelings that I had never experienced before. They were so powerful and so overwhelming to me that I thought it must be a kystrel…that you were some het—some girl who had found one and was using it to control my emotions. When the Medium obeyed you, and you lit the fire, I believed violently that I was right. How could a wretched be so strong in the Medium? Especially as young as you. But the thread around your neck only concealed a ring, not a kystrel. I wanted to be away from you as quickly as possible, because the feelings were so impossibly strong. The way you savored life…even mocked its unfairness by taking such pleasure in simple things." He laughed at himself. "I cannot hold an apple without thinking of you. In my mind, I see you smelling it before taking that first bite." He leaned closer, his hand resting near the orb…near her fingers. "I do that myself now. Every time. The flavor of apples reminds me of you. The smell of purple mint. So many little things in my life remind me of the time we have shared together. The memories are *cutting* me apart like knives."

He sighed in frustration, squinting at the light coming off the orb. "I am still not being plain enough. Your very presence here tonight is a torture *and* a comfort to me. Part of me wants to tell you that we cannot leave each other again. Never. That I cannot live without you being near me. But at the same time, I know we cannot. That if we are near each other, it will cause irreparable harm to us both. All my life, I have had duty prescribe to me the appropriate action to take in any circumstance. But right now, my feelings compel me to tell you that I love…" he swallowed, his voice thickening, his eyes seeking hers again, "that I love you. That I have concealed it from myself since you sheltered me in the kitchen and cured me. I did not recognize what the feeling was then. I thought I had mastered it by staying away. I let myself believe that when I returned to Muirwood, I would be able to control my thoughts and feelings as I should. That I would *grow* to only love you as a sister. I have failed miserably. I should not even be telling you this—not now when we are alone in the mountains. But we are not alone. It must be the Medium that pushes me to tell you, to trust you with my feelings." He stared into her eyes deeply, full and unguarded at last. "To trust you with a most dangerous secret. To trust you with my heart—my whole heart. Not holding anything back. We cannot be together, Lia. But I had to tell you how I truly feel. And trust that you will not use it to harm us."

He had said it. Lia was so relieved to hear the words, to understand she had not been imagining his feelings all this time. She trembled, knowing she would savor his confession for the rest of her days. It brought a strange feeling of calm over her. A feeling of safety and warmth.

She looked back at him with an impish smile. "What were you afraid of, Colvin? That I would throw myself at you? Twist a promise of marriage out of you if you told me that?"

He looked at her, bemused.

"Thank you for telling me your true feelings," she continued. "They are sacred to me. I will treat them so. Yet I am troubled by something. You say that we can never be together..."

"We always have a choice in our actions, Lia," he answered blackly. "But we cannot choose the consequences those choices will produce. I can forsake my heritage. I can forswear my oaths. But I would be miserable if I did. The part of me that longs to live out my days with a brood of children, away from wars and violence, clashes with the fact that every maston is being killed, and it would only be a matter of time before we were discovered. In giving you the key to my heart, I am asking you to set me free. To not bind me in any way that prevents me from fulfilling my oaths or my duty. You will always know, to your last moments, that it was *you* that I loved. No one else."

It was gratifying to hear the words, but Lia was nothing if not stubborn. "But why, Colvin? Why must the future be as you say? I do not want you to forsake your duty. Not for me. Why insist that it must end like that?"

He sighed heavily and gazed down at the floor.

"Look at me," she said. He obeyed. She met his gaze. "You are right about something. I am not a hetaera."

The look of shock that crossed his face almost made her laugh.

"Be at peace, Colvin. Let me explain how I know that word and what they are. The Queen Dowager is a hetaera. But I am not. I am a maston, too, you see." She smiled at him, pleased at the reaction on his face at her revelation. "I took the oaths after you left with Edmon and your sister. The Aldermaston conferred them. Many of my...my family passed the maston test when they were young."

Colvin's eyes bulged. He sat straight up, his eyes flooding with hope. "Truly, you are a maston, Lia?"

She nodded. "I crossed the Apse Veil. I wear the chaen." She timidly held out her palm and showed him the scar that the white stone had burned there. He reached out, staring at it intently, but would not touch it. His expression was full of contradictions—hope, fear, longing, joy, the realization of the possibility that her ancestors were mastons. "You should see yourself. Why are you so shocked? Is the thought of a wretched maston so horrible to you?"

He shook his head. "But what of your family? You never knew about them. It is almost too much to hope that you will discover who they are."

"The Aldermaston has given me some clues. You and I—we both know they are dead. I tried to use the orb to find them, and it did not work. Remember? The Aldermaston said that many of the nobles of Pry-Ree passed the maston test when they were young. He implied that I may be related to the royal house. A cousin of Ellowyn, perhaps." She looked at him keenly and gently took his hand in hers. "So before you continue with your thoughts that we can have no future, would you leave a little portion of your mind open enough to consider that we just might? You said before that you will only marry a maston. That is my goal, too. You also said that you would only be married with an irrevocare sigil. Since we do not know for certain who either of my parents were, perhaps there is just enough reason to hope that one of them came from a line which was bound that way."

He looked doubtful. It was plain on his face.

She let go of his hand and glanced down at the orb with a flush of timidity. "I imagine there would need to be evidence before an Aldermaston would willingly perform a binding ceremony. There is time. I am only fifteen. What I am trying to ask of you, as delicately as I can, is that you give me a chance to prove my lineage."

"But what if—?"

She put her fingers on his mouth to hush him. His breath was warm. His lips were soft, except for the stubble. "*If* there is a tome in an Abbey somewhere in this realm, or any realm, that can prove my parentage, then I *will* find it." She let her hand fall and blushed at the promising look he gave her. "I am very motivated to try, at least."

He was quiet and thoughtful.

"Now it is my turn," she said, looking down.

"What?"

"It is my turn to make a confession."

He moved a little closer, his eyes curious and guarded. "There is more? You surprised me already with your news of being a maston."

She reached around and fetched the bow sleeve and laid the weapon across her lap. Looking down at it, she smoothed the woolen fabric. "The Aldermaston did not want me to tell anyone. Only he and Maderos know the full truth. You have shared a secret with me that could ruin you. I do the same in return." She looked up timidly. "The morning…of Winterrowd. The king was watching the battle from a small hill, surrounded by his knights. It was…*near* to my hiding place. He was in disguise, clutching the standard of Pry-Ree." She bit her lip, pausing. "I am the one who loosed the arrow that made him fall. The Medium warned me to do it." She stroked the hard curve of the bow beneath the sleeve. "I do not think I could have hit him from that distance without the Medium guiding me. When it was done, I fainted. Maderos was there when I awoke, engraving in his tome what had happened. I do not think it was an accident that I was there, Colvin. You were supposed to bring me."

His look was thunderstruck. "I never suspected you."

"Why would you have? I have received all of my hunter training after returning to Muirwood. The Medium wanted justice for all the dead mastons, for the dead of my people. It was no mistake that you were dragged to the Aldermaston's kitchen unconscious that night. All along, Pareigis has been accusing the Aldermaston of plotting the king's murder. He has done everything he can to shelter me since then, to keep the secret hidden from the world. That is my last secret. Now you know more about me than anyone else."

She wanted to confess her love, but found her feelings surged so intensely, she could not find her voice. She shook her head, trying not to cry. She always cried in front of him. It took several deep breaths to calm herself.

Glancing back at him, she said, "You look tired. I will take the first watch."

"Should we light a fire?"

She shook her head. "Not yet. If the cold gets unbearable, I will light it. This is a good shelter."

"Very well. Then good night, Lia," he whispered, looking at her with warmth.

She smiled in return and revoked the light from the Cruciger orb. The darkness was thick and intense. She could hear the sound of him shifting, the stretching out on a blanket on the hard charcoal ground. As the wind whispered outside, the groaning of the limbs, she waited thoughtfully, patiently, until she heard his breath come in an even, shallow measure. He was asleep. She knew the sound, and it was comforting to her.

Reaching out to the orb, she thought about candlelight—just a little. Just enough to see him. The orb glowed faintly, like the moon. He was facing her, his face relaxed—at peace. The hint of a smile was on his mouth.

Leaning over him, she bowed closer, listening to the sound of his breath. She touched his eyebrow with the scar, as light as a butterfly. “Good night, my Colvin,” she whispered.

CHAPTER THIRTY-SEVEN

Gray-Rank

Colvin's hand squeezed Lia's shoulder, and she came awake. She blinked quickly, wondering why the ground was so black, and then the events of the night returned. Rolling on her back, she looked up at him, watching him fumble through her rucksack until he withdrew two Muirwood apples. He looked at them both, chose one, and handed the more pock-marked one to her. The one that would be sweetest.

She accepted the apple as she sat up, brushing some of her wild hair from her eyes. "How long have you been watching me sleep?" she asked him pointedly, noticing it was light enough to see. He should have woken her earlier.

He did not answer, only gave her a smile that made her insides lurch.

She raised the apple to her nose and smelled it. She breathed in deeply, closing her eyes, grateful that their conversation was not just a dream. Everything in the world felt fresh and new and exciting. It was as if a thousand butterflies battled inside her. Opening her eyes, she bit into the fruit, and it was as delicious as she anticipated. "I never grow weary of Muirwood apples," she said. "I have eaten hundreds over my life. They *must* be from Idumea."

Colvin raised his apple to his nose, his eyes scrutinizing hers as he smelled it. "I will never tire of watching you enjoy them."

They ate in silence and then shook out their blankets and rolled them up tightly. They each pondered how much farther they would have to walk before finding Ellowyn, and what dangers they would face. Even with so many questions, they were comfortable enough with silence, sneaking glances at each other as they stowed the blankets and slung the rucksacks over their shoulders.

As Lia reached for the orb, a roar sounded in the woods that stopped her cold. It was a keening sound, a sound that went straight down her spine and made her shiver. In all her wanderings in the Bearden Muir, she had never heard a beast make a sound like that.

Colvin stood bracingly, staring into the woods, his hand on his sword hilt. "What sort of creature was it?" he muttered.

Lia's heart froze with fear. The sound was enormous. She had heard the growl of bears and wolves. She knew the piercing cries of elk that sounded so much like a screaming child, as well as the shrill noise of falcons and eagles. This was something different—a keening wail broken up by a coughing chuckle, like dogs on a hunt. The throaty sound of some large animal.

"I do not know it," Lia said. "Best if we leave." She withdrew the orb and summoned its power, seeking a safe path off the mountains to find Ellowyn. Again she pictured the girl in her mind, focusing on where she would be.

The roar sounded again, closer. Her heart leapt with fear, and the orb faltered for a moment. Then the spindles showed the way.

"Quickly, Colvin," Lia murmured. She strung the bow, noticing that her hands were shaking. She readied another full quiver of arrows against her leg and brought one out and rested it on the string, holding it firm with her finger. They left the barren cave made of tree roots and started down the mountainside. It was much faster going than the previous day. Mist shrouded the mountaintop, not as thick as in Muirwood, but thick enough to hide the immediate surroundings from them, giving the beast a good amount of cover.

"I pray it is not a gray-rank," Colvin said, his hand still on his hilt. They walked swiftly, watching the ground for broken rocks that would trip them but glancing backward into the mist.

"What is that?" Lia asked, for she had not heard of them.

"They are beasts that live in the high country. They are big, like bears, with gray fur and claws. They walk like men. I have heard the rumors, but very few ever see them. I did not remember the myth until I heard the roar."

As Lia listened to Colvin's words, her ears picked out the sound of crunching steps, heavy and spread wide apart, coming down the mountain behind them. She swung to a halt, spinning around with her bow, and pulled the shaft back to her ear. Colvin's blade rang as it cleared the scabbard.

The following footsteps silenced.

A spasm of fear shot through her, primal—like the Myriad Ones—except she did not sense their typical mewling around her body. The feeling was in the fog.

"What is it?" Colvin whispered.

"I heard something following us." She waited, gazing into the mist. Studying the trees for any sign of a shape. It worried her even more that the sound had stopped. Beasts reacted by instinct. A bear intent on attacking charged straight ahead. A beast could not reason.

Something moved in her vision on the right. There was no sound. She spun and aimed, but she only saw the shadow of a giant redwood.

"Let us go. And listen," she warned, turning around and heading down the mountainside. Colvin followed, but he kept his sword in his hand. As they walked, the sound of crunching steps began to follow again.

"It feels like the Medium," Colvin whispered. It was cold but his face was wet with dewdrops. "Does not it?"

"Yes, like a Leering," Lia admitted. "But it is behind us and following. A Leering cannot move. As we get farther, the feeling should be fading."

"A warning then," Colvin said. "Check the orb."

She was afraid it would not work. She was terrified. "I better not," she whispered. "I cannot control my feelings. I think we should run."

"Run?"

The feeling of dread was so intense, it made her sick. She grabbed his hand, and together they ran down the mountain. Each bony step jarred at her legs and knees, but she did not care. They ran hand in hand, as they had off the Tor. No horsemen in black this time, but something huge and menacing. She could hear it now, the crunch and crack of it as it rushed down the mountain after them. The mist grew thicker.

"Stop!" Colvin warned, squeezing her hand and pulling her. They had almost ran into a tree. Her chest was burning with the run, but the fear had not diminished. It was getting worse. Even after they stopped, the sound of crashing and stamping continued. There was a growl and a huff in the fog behind them. The size of it sent shudders through her.

Colvin spun around, sticking his sword tip into the dirt at his feet. He raised his arm in the maston sign. It brought back all of her memories of the Abbey—the feelings of safety, the chaen that she wore. She set down her bow and mimicked the sign.

"We are mastons, Lia," he said hoarsely. "We hold dominion over this world and any creature from it. Do you believe that?"

"Yes," she said, almost sobbing with fear.

Colvin jutted out his jaw. The sound of the pursuit slowed. A snuffling noise came through the mist. As Lia watched, a hulking shadow could be seen in the fog.

"We are mastons," Colvin told her bracingly. "We will leave the mountains in peace. It will sense that, Lia. It will sense our intentions. Hold your hand steady. Show no fear."

She clenched her teeth, wanting nothing more than to pick up her bow and send a shaft into it. But what damage would her arrows do to something so big? Even Colvin's sword seemed like a pitiful weapon.

Lia struggled to subdue her panic. The creature hesitated just beyond the pale of vision. A low growl came from its mouth. A snuffling noise that disturbed the air like a wheezing hiss. The mist concealed it, showing only a shadow of its bulk. A smell of rottenness and decay flowed into her nose and mouth. She gagged.

Colvin stood firm, hand in the air, willing it to depart. She could feel his thoughts pressing from his eyes, exuding from his entire body. He was the master of the situation, not the beast. It must pay homage to him. Lia's courage was bolstered by his. She also sent her thoughts at it, demanding it to depart. Together, their intent shuddered the air.

All at once, the mist began to lift. It did not reveal the creature. It was gone.

Relief swelled inside her chest. After waiting a moment more, they fetched their weapons. When they turned, they saw the mountainside ended abruptly off a jagged cliff, not a dozen paces more from where they had stopped. Lia gasped and clutched at Colvin's tunic. Had they continued their blind charge down the mountain, they would have run directly over it. The clearing mist revealed the danger.

It also revealed an Abbey nestled in the crags below.

***

It was an Abbey hidden in the mountains. It was not the same size as Muirwood. It was more squat and square, rising with a steeple toward the jagged cliffs that dwarfed it. They approached from the rear, and from the mountainside, Lia could see the cloister hidden in its shadow, with several small buildings connected with stone and mortar, representing the different abodes for crafts. What struck her eyes immediately was the fact that she could not see anyone roaming the grounds. There were no learners walking in the cloister. In fact, it looked overgrown. The grounds were lush and thick, not trimmed by sickles. Wildflowers grew throughout the expanse. It looked abandoned. There was, however, smoke rising from the hall of the main manor, outside the Abbey walls. There was also a small garden, blocked off by rings of stone where vegetables and fruit trees grew. It was a small patch, though. Quail and deer trespassed across the grounds. She studied the scene, watching closely.

"The ruins of Tintern Abbey. This *must* be Tintern. What do you make of it?" Colvin asked, crouching low next to her.

"My first thought was it is abandoned like the farms from yesterday, but there is a small garden that looks as if it is tended.

And the smoke. This does not make sense. Look how the ivy has crawled on the walls. Normally, the servants would have cut it down. Perhaps this is where Martin has taken her, a place hidden where people would not see her. I want to see that garden up close before we decide what to do. It does not make sense to me that there is a garden here. Who would be tending it if the Abbey is abandoned?"

Colvin nodded, and together they stayed low and crept down the final incline, moving from tree shadow to tree shadow to disguise their approach. Other than the thin plume of smoke from the main chimney, there was no other sign of life manifested. How curious, Lia thought. Tintern Abbey itself was carved out of a reddish stone, and it was probably half the size of Muirwood. The thick woods of the mountains provided the necessary cover, and they both approached the garden from the outside. The wall was high enough that deer would not be able to vault it. Colvin helped Lia over first, and she dropped to a low crouch, watching for any sign of movement. Colvin followed with a soft thud, also dropping low.

The garden was thick with vegetables, cut into even rows and tethered by stakes and strings. The earth was a rich black loam, and Lia pulled a massive carrot from it that was nearly as thick as her wrist. A small patch of strawberries, shrewberries, and blueberries grew along the wall, each with full, ripe fruit. Lia snatched one of the strawberries and bit into it. The juice was sweet and tender—perfectly ripe. She stared around, amazed, for the harvest season was over. Juice dribbled down her chin, and she mopped it with the back of her hand.

"Look," Colvin pointed out in a low voice. In the center of each wall segment on three sides were Leerings carved into the stone. They exuded such quiet power, she had not recognized their presence. They were ancient stones, worn away by storm and snow. "Do you recognize the feeling?" he asked her.

It took a moment, and she did. "The apple tree in Maderos's garden. I remember it now. Even though it wasn't the right season, there were apples growing on the tree. I think the purpose of these Leerings is to preserve food."

Colvin nodded. "So maybe the Abbey is truly abandoned. What does the orb do? Does it point toward the manor house?"

She withdrew the Cruciger orb and held it in her hand. The orb spun lazily and pointed directly at the manor house. Writing appeared on the orb. Excitement burned inside her. Ellowyn was inside. She was certain of it. Looking up at the sky, she noticed the sun starting its downward slope. She did not relish the thought of returning to the mountains in the dark.

"Maybe they are sleeping," Lia suggested. "Now might be the right moment to free her."

He sat down and snapped a few blueberries off the bush. He ate them slowly, his eyes deep and serious. "I wonder how many men there are."

Lia sat next to him, grabbing a few of her own. Their shoulders touched. "I wish there was a way we could find out."

Almost as the thought left her mouth, she heard something. It was the sound of a door shutting. The garden had a low wall, but it was not low enough that they would not be seen if someone walked nearby. Thankfully, there were several fruit trees in the enclosure, and Lia and Colvin moved quickly through the growth and hid behind the thick mass of leaves and apricots and plums. She snatched a few and stuffed them into her rucksack, listening to the sound of approaching footsteps. She heard two sets. Craning her neck, she stared toward the manor house.

The first person she observed was a tall, thin man wearing the gray cassock of an Aldermaston but with a dirt-smeared smock over it. There was a pocket in the front of the smock and some wooden-handled objects protruded from it. He was much younger than the Aldermaston of Muirwood, and like Martin, had plenty of gray in his dark beard. His hair was thicker, combed instead of untidy. He walked with a serious step, heading toward the gardens, speaking softly to the person beside him. There she was, head slightly bowed—Ellowyn Demont.

The mind that is anxious about the future is miserable.

—Gideon Penman of Muirwood Abbey

CHAPTER THIRTY-EIGHT

Aldermaston of Tintern Abbey

Colvin approached so quietly, she was startled when she felt his breath against her ear.

"I can hardly believe it," he whispered. "The Medium has brought her out to us."

As the Aldermaston and Ellowyn approached, their voices could finally be heard. The Aldermaston had a soft voice, one that was slow and rich and full of tenderness. "Are you cold? Do you need a shawl?"

"No, I am quite comfortable," was Ellowyn's meek reply.

"I told you, child, that no one will make you marry against your will. You fear something that will not happen. You looked so uncomfortable in there, I thought some air might do you good. Or would you rather be back inside with the men?"

"No," Ellowyn said, a bit hastily. She glanced back at the manor house and hastened a step. "I would rather be with you. You speak my language. At least I can understand what you are saying."

"I would like you to see my vineyard. The fruit is not ripe yet, so it needs pruning. Will you help me?"

"I do not know what to do," Ellowyn demurred.

"I will show you. It is this way, past the garden." Their voices faded as they passed the wall and trailed off as they crossed a screen of overgrown alders. Lia could not imagine their luck. No, it was past luck. It was the Medium, as Colvin said. They looked at each other.

"We cannot take her by force," Lia said.

Colvin nodded. "I agree."

Lia rubbed her mouth thoughtfully. "Then I will try and persuade him to let her go. It will be dark before long. This is our chance to free her. I feel…I must be the one to speak to him." She looked down at the Cruciger orb, at the writing still shimmering on its surface. "He will be able to read this."

Colvin reached out, touching her hand. He nodded in encouragement.

Holding the orb before her, she silently crossed the garden and slipped over the wall, following the direction they went. As she drew closer, she could hear their voices again, deep in conversation. After crossing the sentinels of alder trees, she saw row after row of stakes and trellises of a vineyard. The vines were thick, the broad leaves fat and green, the grapes a deep purple color. The sun was slanting down in the western sky, retreating toward the mountain peaks.

"Why do you cut away so many grapes?" Ellowyn asked.

Lia could not see them, but she could hear them well enough and saw the vines trembling with their movement. She crept forward soundlessly.

"The vines produce more fruit than they have strength to ripen," the Aldermaston answered. "Slice along the stem, like this.

Let me show you. See? A little nick is all it takes, and the fruit falls. Collect them in your apron."

"But which ones do I cut? Which do I spare?"

"You can guess, of course. That is one way to do it. But I use the Medium to tell me which to cut. It knows which fruit will be the sweetest at the time of harvest. Those are the ones we want to save. Look at this cluster. See how tight they are together? If we did nothing to prune it, the ones in the middle will become misshapen. There are too many here. The whole cluster will be sour. But if we cut, here and here…" Lia edged closer, and she could hear the fruit fall with little thumps. "Then the rest will grow, and all will be sweet."

"You prune the entire vineyard?" Ellowyn asked timidly.

"Yes. The harvest is worth the work. You could eat these now, but they would not be sweet enough. Culling is an important process. Look at this grape. It will be a strong one. Like you. When it fully ripens."

"The Medium does not listen to me," Ellowyn said softly. "I mean…I cannot even hear it. It is my fault."

"Why do you think that is?"

"Because I am always fearful. Everything I have been told, the things you have told me, it frightens me to death. I did not realize how severe the Blight will be. I wish I could have warned my friends before it was too late for them. Before all the Abbeys have fallen."

"Have you ever seen a forest burn, child?"

"I have not."

"There is nothing left but char and ash. Everything left behind is soulless and void. There is nothing living—or at least that is how it seems. But from the ashes and from the char, new seeds sprout and grow. The forest renews itself. It takes time, but it happens.

There is both good and evil in this world. If we did not intervene here, the grapes would all turn wild. They would all become sour, you see. The Blight is merely a culling. A chance for a rebirth. Let me compare what I told you about the Abbeys burning to the vines that have grown so wild and unruly, so untamed that only fire will cleanse the land to begin anew. The Medium curses and blesses. The Blight that is coming…it will destroy everything, much like the fire in the woods I mentioned. After the Abbeys are razed, the Blight will come. That is why you must go far from here—to a land of safety. In the ships."

"Where the other Pry-rians have gone," Ellowyn stated simply. "It is far across the sea. Do you know where?"

"No. I will not be going, you see."

"But why? If you know the Blight is coming, why cannot you leave as you warn others to?"

Lia could hear the little snips and cuts and fruit fall into the apron. "Because I am an Aldermaston. Tintern is my Abbey, my responsibility, my home. Until another comes to release me, I cannot leave it. One who has authority to do so. And I must stay to warn others. To give them a chance to escape before it is too late. Before the last ships sail."

Ellowyn was quiet for a moment. "So you will…die?"

There was a short little laugh. "We will all die eventually, child. I am worth no more than this little grape. As long as I try to be a sweet one, that is all that I care to do. All the servants and learners have gone already. I would not keep any one of them behind, not when they could save themselves. The final ships are being built, and the rest of the Pry-rians will be told. They will walk away from their lands, walk away from their plows, walk away from their corn. When the time comes, they will all leave."

"Except for you?"

"And the other Aldermastons who will not forsake their oaths. So much is changing in the world. So much attention on the rights and duties of rank. It may be several years before the Blight destroys everyone. It may happen much sooner. Those Aldermastons who have spoken of it, have seen it in vision, have called it the Black Death. A plague that cannot be stopped. A plague that will kill everyone touched by it. A plague with no cure. In another world, Idumea even, it was a flood of water. Only eight souls believed in the warning. The rest were killed by water. But that was a very wicked world. There are many who believe the warning now. Many who are hewing wood to build ships to sail away. As it gets closer, fewer will believe. That is the way of things."

Lia's heart was pounding. She could see the Aldermaston and Ellowyn through the gaps in the vines. Her heart was burning inside her chest, and tears stung her eyes. She knew that what he was saying was true. The Medium burned its truthfulness into her heart.

The Aldermaston stopped. She saw his head bow in concentration. Then he turned and looked her way. "There is someone listening to us." His voice shifted to Pry-rian. "Who is there?"

Lia rose from her crouch at the same time as the Aldermaston did, and their eyes met over the row of plump grapes. His eyes were gray and curious, wary. His bearded mouth was frowning—not with anger but concentration. He stared at her hard, his eyes blinking rapidly when he saw her.

His language remained Pry-rian. "Who are you, child?"

Ellowyn rose as well and looked at her with shock. "Lia!" she gasped.

Lia replied in his language, the language of her ancestors. "I must speak with you, Aldermaston. The Medium has brought me here. Brought me to you. I needed to hear what you were saying. I think you are the only one who can read this for me? Will you?"

Lia ducked beneath the vine leaves, joining the aisle where the other two were. She held the Cruciger orb before her.

His eyes widened even farther. He was stunned. "Where did you get that, child?"

"It was with me, as a baby, when I was abandoned. The writing is Pry-rian, but I cannot read. It brought me here. To you, because of Ellowyn. But I think it brought me here to learn about the Blight and what form it will take. So I can warn my people about it. I serve an Aldermaston too, in Comoros. The Aldermaston of Muirwood."

He stared at her, his eyes suddenly filling with tears. He brushed them away. "Let me see it."

Ellowyn looked so relieved, her face was bursting. Tears streamed down her cheeks, and she pressed a fist against her mouth, trying to control her sobbing. She was murmuring Lia's name.

"What does it say?" Lia whispered, holding forth the orb. It glowed brilliantly.

The Aldermaston wiped his eyes again and looked at the writing. He studied it closely, his face intense. He shook his head in wonderment. "I can read it," he said, his voice choked with emotion. He glanced at her. "You had this orb…as a child? In Muirwood?"

Lia nodded. "What does it say?" she asked desperately.

His expression paled. "It says…it reveals quite plainly that Ellowyn Demont must go to Dochte Abbey in Dahomey. She must warn them of the coming of the Blight. It will happen before anyone realizes it. This is her task. The Medium wills it. Her name will be spoken of for good and for evil for generations because of it." The Aldermaston shook his head, stunned. "What is your name, child?"

"I am Lia from Muirwood. I am…I am a wretched, but I am of Pry-rian birth. This is my homeland. I was sent to protect Ellowyn."

The Aldermaston looked even more surprised. "How did you come here? I know the road was being watched."

"We came over the mountain."

"But the Fear Liath…how did you get past? The Fear Liath lives in the mountain. Only a maston can pass unharmed."

Lia swallowed. "Yes."

"You are a maston?" he said, clutching her arm in complete surprise.

"I am," she answered.

He squeezed her so hard it hurt. Tears trickled down his cheek. "You must go then. I cannot keep you here."

In the distance, a door opened and shut. Voices came from the manor house, speaking Pry-rian. She would have recognized Martin's voice, but the men were not him. The Aldermaston looked back and then at her. He pulled her down amidst the vineyard. With his other hand, he pulled Ellowyn down, too. He took their hands and clasped them together. He spoke in their common language next. "I will delay them. You must go at once. They will not listen to reason. They will try and follow you. Hasten to the mountain. The orb will give you guidance. If the Medium protected you on the mountain, it will do so again. You must go with all haste."

Lia looked at Ellowyn and then back at him. "Do you know who I am?" she whispered.

The Aldermaston blinked back tears. "Yes. I know you, child. I know you. When your task is complete, I will tell you all. Go, child" He grabbed Lia's cheeks with both hands and kissed her forehead. Then he kissed Ellowyn's as well. He clutched the surprised girl's hands with hers. "I Gift you with courage," he said to Ellowyn. "You will need it in the mountain and on your journey. Now, go. Go!"

Lia hooked her arm around Ellowyn's and tugged her with her, staying low so that the vines would shield them. They moved quickly down the row, their footfalls softened by the earth. Voices carried as they approached, the warbling tongue of that country. They were easy in their banter, comfortable.

"Did you see which way they went, Kieran?" one asked.

"Nathen said they were going to the vineyard. I think it is over there."

"No, that is the garden."

"Let us check there first. I want some strawberries."

Lia panicked. Colvin was still in the garden. She was not sure what to do. The end of the row of vines led up to the woods at the base of the mountains. The garden was off to their left, past the low stone wall.

As Lia poked her head above the hedge of grapevines, she saw the two Pry-rians enter the garden. They wore leather hoods and vests, and each had a gladius at their belt. They approached the cropping of brush where she had left Colvin hiding.

CHAPTER THIRTY-NINE

Fear Liath

Lia bit her lip and held her breath. Sidling up behind a thick pine, she glanced through the maze of trees at the garden at the two Pry-rians. Both were wearing woodsman garb, like Martin. Both had gladiuses belted to their waists and leather tunics with hoods. She stared at them and pressed the thought at them: *Find Ellowyn. She is missing.*

"Do you see the size of these? I've never tasted one so sweet. Here, try one."

"No, I want a plum. They are rare. I want to take a few with me when we go to the ships. I have never seen one so big." The branches hissed as they were disturbed for the fruit.

Find Ellowyn. She is missing. Lia pushed the thought again.

"Do you see the Aldermaston or the girl?" one of them asked. "Do you think everything is all right?"

"What is wrong?" Ellowyn whispered in Lia's ear.

Lia raised her hand to silence the girl, focusing on the two men. She stared at them, directing her thoughts fiercely toward them. *Go look for her!*

The two men plucked at fruit from the garden. One looked toward the alder trees. "I do not hear them."

"Hear what?"

"I do not hear the Aldermaston or Ellowyn. Where do you think they went?"

One spoke with a mouthful of fruit. "The vineyard. I told you."

"Are you sure?"

"Why are you worried?"

"I do not know. I just am. Let us go see where they are."

The other grunted noncommittally.

"No, we should go see. Come on."

"All right. Let me grab one more."

Lia watched with growing dread each moment they lingered in the garden. Then they went out past the main ledge of the garden and walked toward the trees. Lia closed her eyes, grateful. When she opened them again, Colvin had slipped over the wall in front of her, landing in a crouch. She was relieved to see him. After fetching a pinecone, she tossed it toward him, drawing his attention to their location. He kept low and joined them in the woods.

"Colvin!" Ellowyn gushed, throwing herself at him and hugging him fiercely. She pressed her cheek against his chest, her eyes squeezed shut, and the look of pure delight and relief on her face. He stared at Lia helplessly, his hands opening and clenching awkwardly, looking at her with bewilderment. Lia gave him an exasperated smile and mouthed, *embrace her*, as if he were the biggest idiot in the world. One of his hands patted her back gently. She was much shorter than him. She gazed up into his face adoringly. "You came for me," she whispered. "You came, just as you promised!"

He nodded, still looking conflicted about her surge of emotions. "I promised you I would. But I could not have done it without Lia's help." He glanced at Lia. "Where is the Aldermaston? You did not…harm him, did you?"

Lia grinned at the question and shook her head. "No, he let her go. The daylight is fading. We must climb the mountain even in the dark. We cannot stay here." Lia grabbed Ellowyn's arm. "I hope you are you ready for your task. This is not the only mountain we must climb together. There is so much I have to tell you both."

***

The moon was bright in the sky, and Lia was exhausted. Sweat drenched her face, even though the night was cold. She used every trick she had learned from Martin. Backtracking to disguise their trail. Crossing over rocks when possible, to not leave a mark. Leaving false trails in another direction. When the darkness closed in, she stayed near Colvin and Ellowyn, retreating often to mask their passing as they ascended the mountains.

It was clear they were being pursued.

The glow of torches shone as pinpricks in the dark, moving and wending up the mountain pass behind them. Lia knew they would not stop. When she needed to use the orb for direction, she would shield the light between their bodies, or go inside a hollowed-out trunk of a giant redwood. It seemed that no matter what they did, the train of torches was never far behind.

Lia puffed with the exertion, weary to the bone, but knowing they had to race Martin and the others back to the village where Pen-Ilyn waited with his boat. With water separating them, it would ease their pursuit. Martin would not know of their plans, though he might guess at them. She looked up at the moon and saw it ringed with frost. She could see the breath coming out of her mouth as she panted. Cold settled in around her. Fog began to form in the air, gathering in wisps.

Oh no, she thought with dread. It was starting again.

Hurrying forward, abandoning her makeshift broom, Lia caught up with Colvin and Ellowyn. It was not difficult, for Ellowyn was staggering with weariness, and Colvin had a hold on her arm to keep her on her feet. He soothed her with encouragement and looked at Lia as she advanced.

"The mist," he said flatly.

"I know," she replied. Fear began to squirm inside her. The moon was veiled in gauzy vapors that seemed to rush in from every direction.

"I am cold," Ellowyn whimpered.

Lia was not, so she released her cloak and covered the other girl's shoulders with it. She gave Lia a grateful look and hugged herself.

The mist descended over the heights of the trees, weaving through the woods in every direction, concealing even the light from the torches behind them in the gloom. The woods were thick and oppressive. They still had not reached the summit yet. It would be a while before that happened still.

"How far behind are they?" Colvin wondered.

"I have tried to throw them off our trail, but nothing has worked so far. They are moving faster than we are, but are closing the distance more slowly. My tricks are giving us more time, but not much. It will be easier on the way down. We may reach the valley floor by dawn and then cross the valley by midday if we do not stop."

"I need to rest," Ellowyn said. "I can scarcely breathe."

From behind them, the Fear Liath roared. The trio stopped at the sound. It was the same as before, and it struck terror inside them. Ellowyn's eyes were as wide as dishes, and she quailed with fear. "What was that!"

Colvin stared down the mountain. "It is behind us?" he said in disbelief.

Lia understood. It was not hunting them at all. "Martin," she whispered.

Ellowyn grabbed Colvin and buried her face against his tunic. "What is it?" she said, her voice quavering.

"A gray-rank," he answered. "It cannot hurt us."

Lia swallowed, her throat tightening. "But it will hurt them."

"Keep walking," Colvin ordered, pulling Ellowyn with him. Lia froze. "What can we do?" he demanded. "If we help them, will they help us? If the Aldermaston told them we were bound for Dahomey ultimately, why would they have followed us so swiftly if not to stop us? If they are wise, they will go back down the mountain to the safety of their Abbey. They cannot pass."

Lia struggled with her feelings. They were her countrymen. She did not want anything to happen to them. Even Martin, who had betrayed her. She could not explain her feelings. They surged in her so strongly, she hesitated, not knowing what to do.

"Come, Lia," Colvin said, pressing forward in a hard walk. "There is nothing you can do."

They heard the screams.

Lia choked with the sound. The cry of pain, warning. Panic. Another roar sounded, blasting from the slope farther down. A trumpet of rage and anger. More screams. Horror-filled screams. Tears burst from Lia's eyes.

Colvin grabbed her shoulder and pulled her close to him. He squeezed her as the sounds of the night intensified, as a cry of agony was suddenly ripped short. He buried her head against his chest, covering her ears from the sound—a sound of slaughter. A sound that would haunt her the rest of her life.

He squeezed her hard, and she clutched at him, weeping. His expression showed his disgust with what they had heard. The Fear Liath was master of the mountain. Silence followed. A croon of delight sounded from the stillness. It was long and loud and throbbed with triumph.

"Come," Colvin whispered in her ear. "There is nothing we could have done. Those hunters chose to follow us. They chose to pursue. It sickens me what happened to them. Come, we must get off the mountain."

There was no use hiding the trail now. Onward they walked, pressing up the steep slope of the mountain. Tears fell down Lia's cheeks. She looked back, searching for the glow of a torch. Even a single torch. The fog had lifted, revealing a snowy moon once again. But there were no pinpricks of light following. Nothing but blackness behind them and the silhouettes of massive trees all around. How old were the trees, she wondered. How many deaths had they silently witnessed over the long years atop the mountain? A place where no woodcutter dared harvest. A place where the things of the wild reigned as kings.

First Jon Hunter.

Now Martin.

She wished there was a way to leave a Leering there, as she had with Jon. But she knew nothing about it, nor did she trust their safety where the Fear Liath made its home. She wept as they walked through the treacherous woods.

***

They straggled into the hamlet of Enarth just after midday. Ellowyn's face was smudged with dirt and tear tracks. She wobbled on her feet, barely able to keep upright through her exhaustion. Her hair was matted with twigs, her fine gown in tatters at the hem. Lia's feet were throbbing, her legs sore, but she did not stop. Colvin seemed unaffected, his jaw firm with determination. He did not speak as they entered the hamlet. Lia peeked at the orb, which pointed the way to Pen-Ilyn and his boat. He was pacing back and forth by the small dock, rubbing his hands together. A stack of goods were already loaded, and he turned on his heel and started with surprise when they appeared.

"What is this?" he said, a smile brightening his face. "You did it? Well, I ought not to be so amazed, but here you are before me. Hello, lass. We meet again." He walked up to them, his eyes wide with excitement. "You have been in the backwoods, then? Have you had any news in your travels? Do you know what happened?"

Lia was not sure whether he meant the Blight or not. "What have you heard?"

"Word from Caerneth," he said, waving them toward the boat. "You remember, it is the trading town farther north. Word arrived for the castellan. Well, secrets do not keep for long. Especially when he raised the drawbridge. Someone smuggled the word out though, and now everyone is talking of little else."

"What is it?" Lia pressed.

"Word came that Demont's army has fallen. It was led into a trap by one of the earls, and there was a battle. Not a survivor. They were all killed. Every last maston."

Colvin grabbed his arm. "When did this news come?"

"Yesterday," the boatman replied. "That was when the castellan raised the drawbridge. He is expecting a revolt, no doubt.

With turmoil on the other side of the sea, he may as well expect a siege on this side. He will not be the castellan long, I fear. One of our archers will make a target of him. I will ferry you across now, but I will be coming back tonight. I have sent my family to stay with my mother until I return. I only stayed because I promised you I would. But I will not risk my hide living in Comoros now."

Colvin's eyes burned with anger. So many complex emotions played across his face. She understood too well some of what he was feeling. With Demont dead, everything had changed. A man he had admired and respected was gone. Also lost was his position on the Privy Council. Ellowyn's surviving relation was dead. She was the last Demont now. And the ones who had wanted him dead would want her life as well.

"Uncle…?" Ellowyn started to ask, but Colvin shook his head at her forcefully to silence her. Why reveal too much to the boatman?

"Come now," Pen-Ilyn said, walking toward the boat. "There is only some little sunlight left in the day, and I will be rowing hard. I know the tidings are bad. Just be grateful you were not there when all the mastons fell. I am sure it was a butchery like at Maseve. It is a dark day when mastons die."

Ellowyn gasped, the information finally seeming to sink in.

Exhausted, they followed Pen-Ilyn into the craft, catching his hand for balance as they boarded. Not only was the boat rocking treacherously, it seemed everything else in Lia's life was bobbing, too.

To the person who does not know where he wants to go, there is no favorable wind.

—Gideon Penman of Muirwood Abbey

CHAPTER FORTY

Escape

The three were exhausted from their flight over the mountains of Pry-Ree and slept in the boat as Pen-Ilyn braced himself against the oars and rowed. He wanted to return before dark, so he put his muscles to the labor, and the boat sliced through the choppy waters. Lia wavered in and out of sleep, lulled by the motion. No sooner had she drifted off, when the boatman's voice rose over the din.

"The shore. We moved faster than I thought, though the wind was behind us. It has been a lonely trip with the three of you snoring. But I have done my duty. I am sure you are weary from your journey."

Lia blinked awake and sat up. Rubbing her eyes, she gazed at the bend of land looming in the distance. The thatched dwelling was there somewhere, but she could not see it through the screen of trees. The little dock was a spur against the gray waters. It was empty of craft or person.

She stared at the dock, her mind in a fog of weariness and lack of sleep. Should not Edmon be there? And horses left to escort them?

Lia turned to Colvin, who was brooding, gazing at the shoreline. "I do not see anyone waiting for us. Do you?"

He shook his head. "That concerns me."

"Bridgestow is not far away," Lia murmured. "He could have easily gone and returned with horses. If news of Demont's defeat reached Caerneth, it should have reached Bridgestow first. That town was loyal."

Colvin looked back at her, his eyes narrow and distrustful. "What if he never made it there?"

A stab of worry bloomed in her stomach. It made her sick inside. "Dieyre?"

"What did he want more than anything else?" Colvin said in a low voice. "He already knew Demont was going to fall. He already knew the powers within the kingdom would shift. He knew it was happening all along. Even if he had convinced us to join his side, it was already too late."

Lia's hands trembled as she reached into her pouch and withdrew the Cruciger orb. *Where is Edmon?* she thought. *Is he alive?* The spindles spun and then pointed the direction of Muirwood. *Where is Marciana?* she queried next. The spindles pointed a different way—to the east. Away from Muirwood. Away from Bridgestow. Her hope crumpled. She had one last question for it. *Where is Dieyre?*

The spindles straightened, pointing directly in the path they were going.

Colvin studied her face, saw the flush in her cheeks.

"We are sailing into a trap," Lia whispered. "Dieyre awaits us."

The woods looked empty, but she knew it was a deception. Once they left the boat, the trap would spring.

Colvin turned back to Pen-Ilyn. "We cannot go this way. Follow the current, but keep clear of the shore."

He looked at them, confused. "What are you saying? We are almost there."

"We will die if you leave us there. Follow the water, along the shore."

"But..."

"Just do it!" Colvin snapped at him. He pointed. "That way!"

Pen-Ilyn frowned and gritted his teeth, pulling even harder on the oars. He had not changed direction. The dock was getting closer.

"What are you doing?" Lia demanded. "Pen-Ilyn?" She saw the determination in his face.

His voice was dark. "You paid me a great deal to wait for you and row you back. But he will pay even more to bring you back to him. What happens to you then is not my concern." His eyes leveled at Colvin. "If you think you can knock me down, you might be mistaken. If you stand, I will jerk the boat, and you will end up in the water. Believe me, you will. I know you are a maston, too, and it is against your kind to murder. He did not want you dead, only captured. Ah, I see them now."

Lia looked back at the shoreline and saw the horses emerging from the trees. They came as a wall, at least fifty mounted knights lining the shore. It was easy to spot Dieyre, so loose and confident in the saddle. The men bore the standards of the Queen Dowager.

"Please," Lia said, crossing one of the benches to get closer to Pen-Ilyn. "You do not understand what is happening. You do not know who we are."

"I do not have to know," he said back simply. "Simply put, I would rather not. Come no closer, lass. If you reach for your blade, I will jerk the boat. Then you will be swimming."

Lia clenched her teeth. "If he betrayed us, he will betray you as well. He promised you a reward, but did he pay it? Did he trust you enough? Please, Pen-Ilyn. I am Pry-rian, as you are. So is she. You cannot betray your own blood."

He snorted, but he did not stop pulling the oars. "I am not an honest man. I help people avoid the taxes. I will ask for my coin before we berth. But if your knight tries to stop me, I will swear you will…"

Lia lunged, smashing the heel of her palm into his nose. Blood spurted as he flailed backward. He choked and moaned, and she jammed her elbow into his gut and wrenched the oars away from him. Colvin was stumbling past Ellowyn to help, and she thrust the oars at him.

Pen-Ilyn wailed with pain, unable to speak through the blood. He tried to sit up, but Lia shoved him down again. "If you try anything else, it will be you with the fishes," she threatened. "Then you can swim back to Pry-Ree. Row westward, Colvin. Keep going west. They will follow us along the coast, but once we reach the Bearden Muir, their horses will be a disadvantage to them and the boat a help to us. There are waterways that criss-cross the swamp."

The look of adoration and gratitude Colvin gave her nearly made her blush. She reached for her bow and pulled in an arrow from her quiver. She stood up to her full height on the swooning boat and looked at the Earl of Dieyre, who watched them intently. Raising the bowstock, she let the arrow fly at him.

It stuck in the earth right in front of him. A warning. As Colvin pulled on the oars and shifted the direction of the boat westward, she remained standing, the bow held in defiance. Dieyre did not move. He only watched. But she knew he would hunt them.

***

Lia knew all the rivers within the Bearden Muir. The first one was called the Comb, and they passed it, knowing it would be the first boundary that would seriously challenge Dieyre's men. The second was called the Brent, and it was wide and shallow. During the winter, it flooded the lowlands the most, creating little islands that could only be connected by rafts or on horseback. She wanted something wide, something that would make it easier to move quickly. However, its greatest benefit was that it connected to the Belgeneck, the largest river in the Hundred—the one that formed one of the borders to Muirwood. If they could pass the Comb and make it to the Belgeneck, there would be no way that Dieyre could reach them fast enough. Their horses would need rest. A boat did not.

Pen-Ilyn pressed a blood-soaked rag to his nose. "Why did you hit me so hard?" he complained to Lia.

She ignored him.

"It is broken, to be sure. I need a healer."

"You did not leave me with many choices," Lia pointed out. She raised her arm. "That way, Colvin. There is the Brent. We made it before dark." She consulted the orb, asking for the direction of where Dieyre and his men were. They were farther behind.

"You are not used to rowing," Pen-Ilyn said with his muffled, nasally voice. "Let me row. I do not have any fight left in me, and this boat is my livelihood. Let me steer in these waters. I do not want you breaking it on a rock."

Colvin nodded, his face slack with exhaustion. "By all means," he said. "But I will not be as generous as Lia if you betray us again."

Pen-Ilyn scowled. "I know it is not an idle threat. There is a shortage of honest work these days. A man must feed his family, even if it is a brood as large as mine. Here, let me have the oars."

He settled onto the bench and began rowing. "Ugh, the Bearden Muir. I suppose we will get lost in there."

Lia studied the flow of the water. They were rowing against the current, which would make things difficult. The snarl of oaks and willows blotted out the fading twilight sky. If she used the orb, it would give them both direction and vision. But it would also make them visible to Dieyre's riders.

"What are you thinking about?" Colvin asked her, gazing into the gloom.

"Trying to think clearly with so little sleep. We need to deliver Ellowyn to Dahomey. This little boat will not get us that far. Not across the open seas. If we can get to Muirwood, we can warn the Aldermaston about the Blight and the ships in Pry-Ree. That would give other helpers a chance to escape, too. We can get provisions there and maybe horses to ride across the land to another port city. Dieyre will be expecting us to go to Muirwood. If he is smart, he will not try and follow us, but instead, get between us and Muirwood. If we try and get through his line, he will collapse on us from both sides." She shook her head. "There is safety there. And supplies. We cannot make a journey as far as Dahomey without equipping ourselves. It is the closest safe haven we have…if we get there first."

Colvin touched her arm. "How do we know Muirwood has not already fallen?"

She had been dreading the question. "I think Edmon is there."

He looked at her pointedly. "Is the Aldermaston?"

Lia looked down at her hands. But he was right. Before risking the journey, they needed to know. She turned her back on Pen-Ilyn and withdrew the orb. Ellowyn nestled next to her on one side. She was afraid of what it would say. Closing her eyes, she thought of the Aldermaston's stern face.

The Medium soared through her, flooding into her soul. In an instant, she could see it all before her. It was the Gift of Seering. The Abbey stood proud against the fading sunlight. The Aldermaston was crossing the grounds to the kitchen, where Sowe was nursing Edmon on a cot, his face feverish, with bloodstained bandages wrapped around his waist. The Aldermaston stared at the Tor, his eyes fierce and defiant. It was as if she went along his sight and could see from his perspective, could share in his knowledge. The Medium was brooding on him heavily. The Queen Dowager was coming. She would be at Muirwood by dawn. Then he would die.

Lia opened her eyes and saw the spindles pointing toward Muirwood.

"He lives?" Colvin whispered.

Lia's heart spasmed inside her, and tears pricked her eyes. "Yes, but the Queen Dowager is coming, and he is not strong enough to defend it. Not by himself."

"Can we reach Muirwood before dawn?" Colvin asked.

She nodded. "If we reach the Belgeneck, we can follow it to Muirwood. It will be faster than going by land."

"Then we go by boat," Colvin said.

Ellowyn squeezed her shoulder. "If I must go to Dahomey, I want you both to go with me. I do not see why the Medium needs me to do it. I have no power. I am nothing." She was quiet for a moment. "But I will try. If you are both with me, I will do my best not to be afraid."

Lia turned and gazed at her, seeing the courage in her eyes. "I do not understand it either. Why that Abbey? Why you? I do not know the answers. But I do know that it is what the Medium wills. I know it with certainty."

"So do I," Ellowyn said. "I felt it as he was talking to you. I could not understand the language, but I felt it in my heart. I do not know why."

Colvin's voice was patient. "It is because of who your ancestors were. The Medium could rely on them when there was a difficult task to be done. I think I can explain it. There is a pattern in the tomes. It has always repeated itself. Before the Blight, there is a warning. A warning to those in danger that their thoughts have become corrupted. When I heard what the Aldermaston told you, that is what came to my mind. This is the warning to Dahomey. And to the rest of the lands. It is the Abbey where the children of all the rulers study. It is the place where king-mastons and queen-mastons are crowned."

Water sloshed against the hull of the boat. The night sounds churned to life around them, the croak of bullfrogs and the cry of owls replacing the buzz of mosquitoes and the hiss of cicadas.

Ellowyn's voice was very small. "In the tomes, what happened to those who gave the warnings? What became of them?"

Colvin turned away, looking deep into the night. He said nothing.

"Please tell me," she said.

Colvin glanced back at her, pityingly. He shook his head.

"Are they often killed?" Ellowyn asked in a whisper, shrinking. "Like my grandfather?"

He nodded slowly.

She was silent for a while. "It must be important then. If it required someone to give their life." She breathed heavily. "I think…I could do it."

Tears stung Lia's eyes again. She touched Ellowyn's hands and squeezed them. The other girl clung to Lia, as if she were the only solid thing in her life.

"I think I could do it," she repeated softly. "If you were there, Colvin."

Pen-Ilyn rowed against the sluggish water. The darkness was a massive wall in front of them. He guided the boat by sound, going slowly enough to maneuver. Sometimes mud grabbed at the bottom, sometimes tributaries tried to lead them on false paths. The orb would point the way clearly.

Around midnight, the way ahead grew brighter, as if an early dawn was greeting them. But it was not the color of dawn, it was the color of fire.

"What is it?" Pen-Ilyn mumbled, resting his weary arms for a moment, letting the boat drift toward the light.

Lia heard the rush of more water. It was the Belgeneck, the main waterway that would take them to Muirwood. But on the opposite shore, there were torches lining the bank, spread like a curtain across the river as far as could be seen in both directions. Close enough that there was no way to cross without being exposed by the light.

As they approached, the light revealed even more. A fleet of small fishing boats, each loaded with soldiers, rowing down the Belgeneck toward Muirwood. The river was choked with vessels—some large, some small.

"If we enter the river, we will be seen!" Pen-Ilyn whispered harshly. "We must turn back!"

But Lia already knew that there would be no safety that way either. Certainly, Dieyre would have sent boats after them, knowing the river ahead was being used to transport soldiers silently through the wetlands.

She looked at Colvin and Ellowyn, saw their faces now in the faint glimmer of torchlight. She had to get them to Dahomey. It was up to her to get them through the Bearden Muir safely. But against an army? Against so many enemies?

Goosebumps went across her arms, and she realized she was cold.

CHAPTER FORTY-ONE

Bleeding River

Pen-Ilyn and Colvin hauled the boat out of the river and dragged it up the muddy embankment. Lia came off next and began searching the woods for signs of soldiers. Ellowyn stumbled as she came off, but Colvin caught her before she fell and lifted her away from the mud. Then with heaving muscles, he and Pen-Ilyn hauled the boat into the brush to hide it. The Belgeneck could be seen through the screen of trees ahead, the lights flickering every time a vessel passed in front of the torches. How many had they seen already, fifty? More?

Lia went back to the boat and found Colvin tugging on his padded shirt and leather jerkin. Pen-Ilyn had stored the clothes with his gear.

Ellowyn shivered with cold, clutching herself, her eyes gazing at the river ahead. "What will we do?" she whispered to Lia.

Pen-Ilyn hocked and spat. "Are you sure this will work?"

Lia was tired and weary. She was not sure of anything. "If I were you," she said, "I would hide apart from the boat and get some sleep. The army will have passed by dawn, and you should be able to row back up the river to the sea. If they are searching for us, they will find your boat easily. Even if I wanted to hide the trail you just gouged into the mud, and I do not, it would not be hard to find. They will look for our boot prints and see that ours go one way and yours another. I doubt they will follow you. They want us. It is the best we can do for you, Pen-Ilyn."

"And where will you go?" he asked, chafing his arms and rummaging in his belongings for something to eat.

Lia scowled. "If I told you, you would have information they would want. Best if you know nothing more. Good-bye."

He looked nettled but said nothing. He started away, murmuring as he gathered his things. "Broke my nose and abandoned me in the middle of the accursed swamp. We will probably all be eaten by snakes before dawn. Or drowned in a bog. Lovely."

Lia ignored him and led Ellowyn and Colvin into the swamp. The ground was muddy and soft. They had no horses, no way of crossing the fenlands quickly. They had pulled the boat off on the eastern bank of the river. In her mind, she tried to remember the crisscrossing of the rivers in relation to the Abbey. The Bel-geneck emptied into the sea due west, after arching away from Muirwood. It had surprised her to learn that Winterrowd was the fishing village at the end of the river.

The insight came to her again through the fog of fatigue. "Colvin, we have been blind," she muttered. "When the Queen Dowager first came to Muirwood, she said she was on the way to Winterrowd to investigate her husband's murder. That is not what she was doing. She was hiring boats along the coast to ferry her troops. This was her plan all along."

He sucked in his breath. "You are right," he said. "Lure Demont to the north, Dieyre said. Pull him away from the south, leaving Muirwood unprotected. The oldest Abbey of the realm." He sighed with resentment. "Stay near, Ellowyn. The ground is treacherous. Let me hold your arm."

"Thank you," Ellowyn mumbled. They were all exhausted. "How far is it to the Abbey?"

"It is not the distance that is the problem," Lia said. "It is the obstacles. We are two leagues away, if that. We could easily walk there before dawn if we could cross the river. But it looks like they put torches along the shore to guide the boats in the dark. The river is very wide. You remember crossing it, Colvin? Even with a horse, the current was strong. It is cold, and we are tired."

"But we must cross it," Colvin said. "The Abbey is on the other side…eventually."

"Yes, but the Belgeneck floods often and forms a lake at the bend. Those waters are to the north of Muirwood. With all the rain this season, the lake will still be there. We could skirt around the lake on the other side. Two other rivers empty into it, but they are smaller. One has a stone bridge. It is called the Doe Bridge because deer often use it to cross the river. The other river…well, we will be getting wet for that one. But it is not as deep as the Belge, and maybe the orb can help us find a shallow ford."

They walked in silence then, their breath coming out in little plumes of mist from the cold. Colvin broke the silence. "Can we reach the Abbey before dawn?"

"We must," Lia said, her thoughts as dark as the woods.

***

The hunter is patient. The prey is careless. Martin's words teased her and tortured her. She was so tired. Her legs ached. Her boots were soaked through. Ellowyn's teeth chattered with cold, and she stumbled more and more, but she did not complain. She clutched the cloak with one fist and Colvin's arm with the other, willing herself to put each foot ahead.

Lia glanced behind and saw the flicker of many torches drawing nearer. They were gaining ground. She had not bothered hiding their trail. There was only one way they could go, and deceiving the pursuers would do little to help. If Lia led them away from the river, what then? It would only put their enemies ahead of them instead of behind. No, she would need to hold back and fight soon, and she was not looking forward to it. There were six torches. That meant twelve to eighteen men. She sighed. The ones carrying the torches would be her targets. If she shot them down, one at a time, it would cause confusion. By shooting them, no one would want to hold the torches then. It would cause squabbling. If they abandoned the torches, so much the better.

Was that the right way to think? Was she missing something else? Her mind was weary. She had not slept in two days. Her stomach ached with hunger, but they ate as they walked. There was enough water to last, but still she was thirsty.

She remembered Jon Hunter and how he had tried to help them against Almaguer. This was different—almost impossible. There was an army in the Bearden Muir led by Dieyre and the Queen Dowager. What would happen when they reached Muirwood? Would she be strong enough to summon the Abbey defenses? She was so tired. Heartsick. Would she be strong enough to summon the Leerings? She knew the Abbey could defend itself. Had not Maderos once said that an Aldermaston had dropped a mountain on an invading force and left it there? What would it take to summon the defenses? Would she be strong enough to counter the will of Pareigis?

A memory came to her suddenly, unbidden, of the time she had faced the kishion. She was helpless against his skill. He had twisted aside all of her attempts to injure him. It was only after Astrid lay dead that the Medium had commanded her to redeem Muirwood. Blood had been spilled before the power of the Medium was there to save her. Blood spilled. Astrid's blood.

The thought brushed against her mind.

Blood would redeem the Abbey. That was what was needed. Not her skill in the Medium. Not her devotion to the Aldermaston. It was her blood. Or the Aldermaston's. A price to be paid for the power to save them all.

Lia cringed from the weight of the thought.

Was it true? Was it her tiredness speaking, or was it the Medium? How could she be sure? Ever since her experience in the Bearden Muir with Colvin, when she learned about the Medium, it had whispered to her and given her insights and thoughts. It helped her remember the things she learned. The Medium was a close friend to her. Would a friend send her to die?

She swallowed, feeling her heart burn inside of her. Was this what the Medium was asking of her? The thought struck her like lightning. She felt it through her bones. In her mind, the image of Colvin and Ellowyn on a boat crossing a stormy sea. Foam crashed against the hull. She could smell the salt in the air. But just as assuredly as she could see them, she knew that she was not with them. Colvin steadying Ellowyn as the vessel pitched and lunged in the sea. She would not be journeying to Dochte Abbey with them.

The Gift of Seering struck her like a mountain, the irrepressible weight of the Medium confirming her thought. She would not be going to Dahomey with them.

Pain. The thought brought a wrenching pain inside her heart. Being separated from Colvin would be agony. In her mind's eye, she remembered as the two of them had stacked stones on Jon Hunter's body. Instead of that, she saw Colvin and Ellowyn standing there, clutching stones, burying her.

No!

Lia nearly sobbed with the thought, the pain that it caused her. Tears stung her eyes, and she brushed them away. This was the Medium's will for her? To die as a hunter protecting Colvin and Ellowyn? Was this what the Aldermaston had foreseen? The reason she needed to be trained? The reason he had used her?

Each step was terrible. She was cold, wet, miserable. All of the feelings she had experienced in the Bearden Muir a year before came crashing down—loneliness, despair, abandonment. The Medium was abandoning her to die. To save the lives of others. To save...

She wrestled with her thoughts. She struggled against them. How could the Medium expect this of her? She was so young—her life unlived. But had she not, once before, offered her life to save Colvin's? At the fields of Winterrowd, had she not bargained with the Medium to save him? To take her instead? She remembered the moment. She remembered the Medium being satisfied with her offering. Then its powers had come. The power that saved Demont's men from falling in battle. Not just Colvin, but all of them.

The power to save them all.

Even though her heart was nearly bursting with pain, she summoned thoughts of Muirwood again. The faces, all of them. Pasqua. Sowe. Bryn. Astrid. Prestwich. The Aldermaston. Even Getman and Reome and Treasa. All of the wretcheds she had grown up with. All of them helpless at the Abbey, surrounded by soldiers bent on destroying their master. They had no one to defend them. No one but a girl who was feeling sorry for herself.

Lia clenched her jaw. Had Jon realized he was going to die before it happened? Had the Medium prepared him as it was preparing her? How brave he seemed. Or was it better not to know? Not to understand the Medium's will until it was too late. That was the necessity—to surrender oneself to the Medium's will. That was the way of invoking its greatest powers. Holding back, even her thoughts, was enough to send it flying away. She did not do that. She turned the information over in her mind. The Leerings that defended the Abbey borders were in the woods beyond the Cider Orchard. They were hidden amidst the oaks. To be protected, one had to be inside the circle of stones.

Determination filled her. She had to get Colvin and Ellowyn inside that protective ring. She did not know how she was going to do it. But she had to. If her blood was required, then she would do it. She would not shrink from it. Something squeezed her heart with pain, and she glanced back at Colvin. His face was a mask of fatigue and impatience. He looked furious as he walked. Was he hearing the Medium as well? Or was his anger blotting out the murmur?

Seeing his face in the darkness, his scowl and expression made the pain even more intense. Ellowyn looked exhausted, her eyes nearly shut as she stumbled after, trying and failing to keep up. She remembered his confession in the mountains of Pry-Ree. It was such a relief to have heard it. To die knowing that he loved her. She would set him free at last. Did the Aldermaston of Pry-Ree know? When he read the writing on the orb, tears had come to his eyes. He had looked at her with such sympathy and compassion. He had kissed her forehead. Did he know what she was facing? The choice that would be only hers to make?

Would she die for Colvin? Yes. It did not require thinking or reasoning. If she could save him, she would. He would not let her.

Not willingly. No, he was too proud and stubborn for that. He would try and stop her if he knew.

She could not tell him then. Glancing back, she saw the torches were even closer. Soon they would be overrun. How far was Doe Bridge? Somewhere ahead, in the blackness.

"Keep going," she whispered to Colvin. "They are getting too close."

He stopped, tugging Ellowyn with him, waking her from the dreamlike walk. "We stay together."

She shook her head. "I am not going to fight them all, Colvin. Just need to scare them a little. Keep going ahead. I will catch up with you."

His jaw was like a block of stone. He looked frustrated, upset. He shook his head as if to cast away his thoughts. "We will wait for you."

Lia touched his arm. "You are the Earl of Forshee, and she is the last heir of Demont. Your duty is to see her to safety. My duty is to help that. Now do as I say. I will not be gone long."

His face pinched with doubt. "Do not do anything rash," he threatened.

Lia watched as he took Ellowyn roughly by the arm and started off into the woods again. Soon, they would reach the lake at the river's bend. Soon. It was nearly midnight. Lia tested the pull of her bow and walked through the woods the way they had come, toward the bobbing torchlight. Her mind was cool and focused. All of the training rushed back to her. She found a nice, twisted oak to hide behind. She would attack from the side where they would not be expecting her. She would wait until they had passed her and strike from the rear.

Breathing slowly, she waited until the torches became distinguished. Black tunics appeared, the arms of the Queen Dowager emblazoned on them. Dahomeyjan knights. Her heart felt like flint. Twelve men. Six with torches. Dieyre underestimated her. That was a mistake.

They were tired from their long march. They were not paying attention. The lead was not a knight, but a hunter. He scowled and stared at the footprints often, nodding as the trail was clear to his eyes. She watched and waited, silently bringing herself around the trunk of the oak. Slipping an arrow from her hip quiver, she set it in the string. Waiting. The prey is careless. The hunter is patient.

The man stopped, holding up his hand. He found the place where they had stopped. His head lifted up slightly, listening. Lia pulled the string back and let the arrow loose. Before he crumpled to the ground, she had another one out and dropped another one of the torch carriers.

Gasps of alarm. Swords ringing from their scabbards. Another one went down, also carrying a torch.

"Over there! From the trees!"

Lia shot another one, bringing him down with a single shaft. She darted away from the tree and slunk behind another one. They were panicking. Good. Someone grabbed one of the fallen torches, and she dropped him, too. Moving to the other side of the trunk, she sighted another one and let loose another arrow. He went down without a sound. There were six left.

"No, it came from that way!"

"No, I saw it! Over there! There!"

Lia waited two heartbeats and came around again, sighting another torch carrier. She did not miss. The last man with a torch was wiser than his friends. He dropped it and scampered into the woods. As the torches hit the wet marsh grass, they hissed and smoked and quickly burned out. A final one still was aflame, crackling and hissing. No one tried to fetch it. Lia stared at the dark, seeing several cowering behind trees.

She stepped away from the oak and started off the way she had come. Her heart was heavy for having killed so many. As she walked, she raised her voice and spoke in Dahomeyjan. "If you follow me, you will die, too. Go back to your masters."

For a moment, she wondered if she should go back and shoot the rest. It would be more difficult in the dark. They were afraid. Their hunter was dead. They could run to the shore and cry for help. But she knew she needed to save her strength. The greater battle was still ahead.

The soul attracts that which it secretly harbors; that which it loves, and also, that which it fears. So often we bring into our lives that which would ruin us merely by thinking and fearing it.

—Gideon Penman of Muirwood Abbey

CHAPTER FORTY-TWO

Firetaming

Doe Bridge was tall, built of stone and bricks and a double arch. One of the arches was round and narrow and a little higher than the other, to guide the overspill of the river through it when the flood season came, rather than eating away at the banks of the shore. The other arch was thicker and peaked in the middle, straddling the main body of the river. Scraggly oak trees grew along the thick, mossy banks. Despite the recent rains, the secondary run beneath the shorter arch was dry. An outcropping of mossy stone was revealed in the moonlight, where the column of brick and stone met to form the middle of the river, and supported it. That junction formed a little bend in the bridge and connected both sides of land. Lia, Colvin, and Ellowyn were grateful for the mossy rock, for it muffled their steps as they crept toward the base of the bridge.

Dahomeyjan knights were posted at each end, their horses tethered. There were easily twenty men, guarding both approaches of the bridge. Lia knew that dawn was coming, and they would probably need to fight their way through the Queen Dowager's army to reach the safety of Muirwood. Getting past the soldiers without a fight was her first choice.

Lia led the way, her bow ready, an arrow nipped in the string. She moved slowly, carefully, trying to reach the shadow of the bridge that their torchlight could not expose. She heard them speaking in Dahomeyjan as she advanced, complaining of the cold and wondering when they would abandon the bridge and join their fellows in the woods surrounding the Abbey.

"We will be warming our hands soon enough," one of them said. "Over the burning stones of the Abbey. This land is cursed with cold and mist."

Lia reached the block of stone at the base of the bridge, midstream. She could hear the soldiers above her, but no one had heard her approach. Ellowyn, watching the bridge, nearly stumbled off the rock into the water, but Colvin caught her and kept her near him. She trembled and shivered. Lia sighed in relief and listened. There was the loud rumble of horses approaching from the north in the darkness. She motioned for Colvin and Ellowyn to hurry.

Looking down at the black waters, Lia shuddered. How deep was the river? She could not tell. It looked absolutely frigid. The far end was not near enough to jump. She wished that the bridge was not guarded. She was not counting on having to cross two rivers. How would they cross quietly enough? They had to cross directly under the bridge, or the knights might see them, and then it would all be over. She rubbed her eyes, trying to think.

Colvin dragged Ellowyn up to the hiding place, clutching her hand as she shook, her teeth chattering. The girl was too cold. A dunk in the river might kill her. It was looking like they would need to fight their way across.

"It is Dieyre," came a muttering voice. "He looks vexed."

Another chill swept down Lia's spine but not because of the water or the breeze. How she wanted to reward him with the arrow for his treachery. The sound of advancing horses closed in, and the soldiers clustered along the banks. There were probably a dozen riders in all, the mounts panting and snorting. Hooves dashed in the dirt.

Dieyre's voice was unmistakable. "Any sign of them?"

"Of who, my lord?"

"Of anyone, you idiot. I had men coming down the river this way. They should have reached you by now. No sign of Forshee or the girls?"

"Believe us," said a tired voice, "If there were womenfolk wandering about tonight, we would have noticed. Some warm flesh would be appreciated on a such an accursed night as this. Would you agree, my lord? I do not see your prisoner with you. Where is she?"

Lia and Colvin faced each other, their eyes mirroring the same thought. *Marciana.*

"Safe and quite warm, I assure you. I left her on a fur coverlet with cider and meat. You can pay for *your* pleasures when the work is finished. Some of the lasses at the Abbey are pretty. Stay here until the next watch, then ride hard. I want you at Muirwood by dawn."

"We will not be late, my lord."

The clop of hooves started across the stones above them, each one thundering. With a dozen or so knights, riding one at a time, it would be a noisy crossing. She whispered that in Colvin's ear. He understood. Dieyre's arrival would help them cross undetected.

"How deep is the water?" Colvin whispered to her. She shrugged. Nodding, he held her shoulders and ventured into the river first. He scowled with the shock of cold water, but he was tall enough he could stand. It was up to his waist. Motioning for Ellowyn, he reached out to her. She looked confused, but Lia helped lead her into his arms. He turned, adjusting her weight and then looked back at Lia. "I will come back for you," he whispered.

She shook her head. "No, I will follow. I am not that cold."

He shook his head violently. "Wait for me." Then he stepped deeper into the river. The clatter and clash of hooves overhead was like thunder. Ellowyn squeezed around his neck, burying her face against his cheek. He struggled with her weight and his footing. Lia clenched her teeth, willing his feet to find safety. The water was deeper in the middle, rising up to his chest. He hoisted Ellowyn higher, teeth set, and then the worst was over, and they were in the shallows on the other side. He deposited her on the mossy rock in the shadows and then came back swiftly, crossing the river again to the midway point where Lia crouched, shivering with cold and terrified by the proximity of the soldiers above.

He beckoned for her to come to him. Stepping off the rock, she lowered herself into his arms. As he clutched her tightly to him and braved the tug of the river again, she held her bow with one hand and wrapped her other arm around his neck, her mouth near his ear. He stepped deeper into the cold depths, his entire body shuddering with the cold. His teeth rattled, despite his tight clenching. With his face so near, she could almost see the puckered scar along his eyebrow, though all was deep with shadow. He nearly stumbled but managed to hoist her higher, to keep her away from the grasp of the current.

She whispered in his ear. "I am worried about Ciana, too. She is a brave girl. I know she has resisted him. Dieyre's words… so much chaff. He does not believe half of what he says. Neither should we."

He nodded, but said nothing. As they emerged up the other side, he looked into her eyes with cold rage. "I wanted to kill him. But it passed."

She squeezed his neck with her free arm and whispered her thanks as he deposited her on the mossy stone bank on the other side. Reaching out to him, she grabbed his hand and helped pull him out of the icy waters. He was cold. So very cold. The thunder of hooves retreated off the bridge and into the gloom. How many soldiers were between them and Muirwood?

They still had one more river to cross.

***

Lia gazed into the stars with despair. Many had already passed the horizon, and the eastern sky was starting to blush a faint violet—the advent of dawn. She knew there was a bridge somewhere to the east, but Muirwood lay directly to the south, and the orb had led her to the easiest ford. She was also certain that the other bridge would be guarded as well. These waters were much more swollen than the previous river, churning with foam. However, stones in the midst jutted out in intervals. With relief, Lia crossed from rock to rock, followed by Ellowyn and then Colvin, each taking a turn. Some steps were treacherous and slick. Each hop, a danger. Lia wanted to summon light from the orb, but that would attract the eyes of anyone in the moors beyond who happened to look their way.

After crossing an especially slippery boulder, she turned to warn Ellowyn just as the girl lost her balance and pitched into the river. She knew Colvin would try and save her, but he was still shivering from his last crossing. Lia tossed her bow the rest of the way to the far bank and lunged into the shocking grip of the river. The current was dragging Ellowyn swiftly, but Lia caught up with her and seized the hem of her gown and yanked hard. The girl spluttered and choked and grasped at Lia, her face contorted with panic, unable to scream from swallowing so much water. Lia hooked her arm around Ellowyn's neck and struggled to reach the shore. Each pull sapped her already fading strength. The cold made her mind foggy. Which way was the bank? Had the current turned her around? Then she saw Colvin running after them on the far side, and she kicked and struggled until the river slammed them both into a boulder, and she could not see for several moments. She heard Colvin's hiss of breath and clutched Ellowyn tightly, feeling her body limp. Lia struggled against the darkness and groped her way around the water for the boulder and kicked against it.

Again, the current started to tug her away, and she opened her eyes and saw a shaft of wood reaching out to her. Colvin extended the ash bow to her, and she grabbed at the end, and he hauled on it with his strength. Climbing into the river himself, he helped drag Ellowyn to the bank and away from the river's icy grip. Lia was soaked through and hugged herself.

"Put her down, on her stomach," she said through chattering teeth. "Quickly! She's swallowed too much water."

Colvin obeyed, and Lia knelt beside the girl and pushed her lower back hard. She repeated the motion, pushing and pushing, trying to force her to breathe. Ellowyn hiccupped and then started to splutter and choke. After struggling for her air, she started to sob violently, curled up in a ball, and trembled.

Lia stripped away her own leather girdle, which was soaked and wrung out her shirt. Her mind was still fogging, and her fingers did not feel like her own.

"Fire," she whispered. "We are too cold. Without warmth, we will die. Help me with her cloak. Wring the water out."

"We cannot build a fire, Lia," he warned. "They are near. They will see it."

"If we do not do something, it will not matter. She is freezing to death, Colvin. So am I. If we do not warm ourselves soon, we will start wandering aimlessly. It is…so cold. So cold. We need fire."

"I will gather some wood," he said, but she knew there was not enough time.

"We need it now," she said, pulling out the orb. She stared at its smooth surface, cold from the plunge in the river. She had summoned light with it. She had summoned directions with it. Opening her eyes, she stared at its face, pleading with it for warmth.

The orb began to glow. Not with light but with warmth. She opened herself to the Medium, drawing in fire as she had with the Leering at the laundry. Firetaming, it was called. The orb glowed red hot in her hands, but it did not burn her. Ellowyn rose from her swoon, staring at her. It gave off some light, like staring into a bed of hot coals. Waves of heat wafted in the air. Colvin and Ellowyn both gathered around her, trying to block its light with their bodies. Each held out their numb hands and rubbed them, bathing them in the warmth. Warmth prickled through Lia's body. The cold was driven out of her completely. Their clothes gave off steam.

"How is it that you can use the Medium so well?" Ellowyn whispered, her eyes searching Lia's face.

"I will answer your questions later, Ellowyn. Warm yourself. Both of you."

Colvin stared at the burning orb, at Lia's hands, then into her eyes. He looked relieved and grateful. She could almost see his thoughts on his face. Using the Medium in a way that was not normally permitted. He looked bemused.

"Do not complain," she told him with a half smile.

"I am not," he replied.

In silence, they enjoyed the heat from the orb until their shivers subsided. Lia felt warm throughout. The plunge into the river had shredded her weariness. She felt rested, ready to face what lay ahead. To face her death without flinching.

She felt the presence of Myriad Ones, drawn to the power of the Cruciger orb in some malignant, hateful way. Drawn to the power of the Essaios. The smoke shapes sniffed around them, mewling and hissing. Lia started to tremble again when she felt them. Their thoughts crammed against her mind, trying to daze her. Fear, despair, hopelessness.

The first pink of dawn appeared in the east.

"It is time," Lia whispered, opening herself fully to the Medium's power and its will. *Do with me as you may. I will sacrifice whatever I must to see him safe from here. Guide me.* Then as she looked down at the cooling orb, the spindles began to whirl.

CHAPTER FORTY-THREE

Dieyre's Revenge

Dawn awoke over the valley, bright and cloudless. If there could have been an ideal day for fog, it would have been this one. But the cool morning air was devoid of any breeze, and Lia tromped through the high grass toward the mass of oaks forming the base of the grounds. Muirwood rose up in front of them, beautiful and calm. They had walked all night and still could not reach the higher ground before the sun exposed them.

There was an army nestled in the valley to the west and to the east. She could see the soldiers and horses already beginning to form their lines. As they crossed the lush valley, she knew it was only a matter of time before they were seen. It would be a race to the woods, which she suspected were already thick with knights. They would have to fight to break through the line. She should have been worried. Instead, she was thrilled. The orb led her toward the Sentinel oak, threading a needle between the two masses of men who had converged. She could see its massive branches towering over the others in the grove. There was an underground tunnel entrance there. If she could get Colvin and Ellowyn inside, she could return to one of the Leerings hidden in the woods and summon the defenses. So much depended on how many foes they faced.

"Horses," Colvin warned, just as the sound reached her ears. A row of mounted knights had detached from the columns and bore down on them across the field. There was no mistaking them.

"We run," Lia said. "Remember the gully by the big oak? That is the way in. You remember the word to open the Leering?"

"Yes. Come, Ellowyn." Colvin unsheathed his sword and grabbed the girl's hand with his other, and they started at a run.

Lia followed, bow in hand. Her heart pounded with excitement and fear. There were twenty horsemen, all wearing black. The mounts gained in speed, causing a thunder of hooves that grew louder and louder.

Colvin ran hard, the younger girl barely keeping up with him. The forest loomed ahead, drawing closer, but so were the charging knights. Lia's breath came heavy and fast. As the knights bore down on them, she stopped, dropped to one knee and fired an arrow into the lead stallion. It shrieked with pain and went down, and the other riders had to veer to miss it. She shot again, bringing down another horse, then another. Colvin and Ellowyn were almost to the trees. She sprinted hard and fast to catch up. Crossbow bolts whirred through the air at her, but most overshot. The knights were so close, and she could see another group closing in from the other side.

Swords clanged and battered. Lia looked ahead and saw Colvin spinning around, cutting down a man who emerged from the woods. Ellowyn backed away from him as his sword whipped around again, slicing through another soldier. There were more behind them, and Lia shot as she ran, amazed to hit even one, who crumpled and went down. Colvin and Ellowyn entered the woods, and she could hear his sword clashing as it struck and parried the attacks against him. Lia sprinted harder, beating the charging knights before they reached her. The oaks would make it impossible to gallop. A soldier charged at her from behind a tree, and she sent an arrow into his leg without slowing. More swordplay ahead. She could see Colvin and Ellowyn through the twist of trees. Dodging the trunks, she caught up at last, just as Colvin cut down another man. Three more faced him, snarling and yelling to their fellows for help. Lia took one down with an arrow and then slung the bow around her shoulder and drew her gladius and dagger. Colvin parried two separate thrusts against him and stabbed one through with his sword. Lia did not slow, she ran up to the last man who was swinging down at Colvin's exposed back and blocked his swing with her gladius, stomped on his foot, and slit him with her dagger. His face twisted with pain as he collapsed, writhing to the ground.

"Which way?" Colvin gasped, his face streaked with sweat, his expression showing his barely tamed rage. The woods were impenetrable. The Sentinel oak was near, but what direction? Lia recognized the woods and pointed and then ran, listening to the sound of the knights dismounting and charging into the woods after them. A crossbow bolt thudded into a tree by her ear, and she ducked. Glancing at her quiver, she saw that there were only five or six arrows left. The knights charged through the woods, shouting out loudly to draw others to them.

"This way! Over here! Over here!"

Lia heard the crashing of limbs and foliage, the crunch and crackle of dried leaves and snapping branches. Another crossbow bolt hissed at her, glancing off a tree and spinning wildly aside. She could not think of it. Colvin and Ellowyn dodged ahead of her, reaching the towering oak tree with its sagging branches. The ground was clear around it, without obstruction, making it easy to run past it. Lia risked a backward glance and saw several knights had reached the clearing as well. Shouts echoed throughout the grove, coming from every side.

"Which way?" Colvin shouted.

"The gully! Right there. Get the Leering open!"

Lia struck her gladius into the massive oak branch, sheathed her dagger in her belt, and swung the bow off her shoulder. The men's eyes bulged with anger and fear as she shot the first down. She stood firmly, without flinching, drew another shaft back to her ear, and sent the second man down. The third rushed at her even faster, screaming with rage, raising his sword high to cut her down. She did not have enough time to draw another arrow. As he rushed her, she sidestepped his blow and jabbed the point of her bow into his throat. She could hear him gag and choke, and she swung the bow around against his temple, stunning him. Grabbing her gladius, she sheathed it and started after the others as the fallen knights all twitched and groaned.

Reaching the edge of the gully, she stared down as Colvin's eyes met hers, his face an expression of shock.

The cave had been filled in with earth. She could sense the Leering still, but it would take too much time to dig their way through. Not with so many pursuers—not with so many so close. The sound of crashing in the oaks. The screams and hoarse cries of vengeance. This was the moment. She realized it instantly, felt a cool pang of satisfaction for recognizing the Medium through the chaos.

"That way," she said, nodding toward the gully trail. "Maderos's lair is that way. The ossuaries. Go!"

The ossuaries. The place of the dead. The place where all the rings had been found. She knew it was the end. Her final moment with him. Reaching around her neck, she pulled off the string that held the gold wedding band. It flashed in the sunlight, the ring that reminded her of the Medium. It was something she had clung to since she was a child. She tossed it to him, staring into his eyes as he caught it.

"I love you—always," she said, and before her courage could melt, she ran the other way, where she knew the Leering was that would summon the Abbey defenses. She heard him shout her name, but she ran, bringing her bow around as the knights saw her.

"Run!" she screamed, waving her arm ahead of her, pretending Colvin and Ellowyn were ahead of her still. "I will hold them off!"

The knights rushed at her from three sides. Lia pulled an arrow back and brought down one. Three arrows left. One swore at her, cursing her weapon. She dropped him next, his face a spasm of pain and frustration. Two arrows left. Lia ducked the blow aimed at her head, spun around, and hooked her boot around his ankle. Grabbing his empty scabbard, she yanked hard and tripped him over her, letting him crash on the ground. She did not stop to kill him; she just ran as fast as she could, rushing to the Leering she knew was ahead of her.

From that very direction appeared four men, swords drawn. She changed course, using the trees to separate them from her. A crossbow bolt slashed against her shoulder, splitting her skin and sending a searing line of blood against her flesh. Her breath was so hard, she barely felt the sting. A knight grabbed at her, missing. She smacked him across the face with her bow.

They missed her again as she surged past them. There was another knight now, blade ready, waiting for her. Behind him, she saw the Leering—a boulder about waist-high and carved with the face of a fierce-looking man, a bearded man. It was the Aldermaston's face when he was younger. Another man knelt by the Leering, head bowed, one arm out, his palm on the stone. The eyes on the Leering were beginning to burn, to flame.

Lia shot down the last knight opposing her, leaving her a final arrow. The man bowing before the Leering turned an rose, looking back at her with familiarity.

Scarseth, his eyes glowing silver.

She had one arrow left and yanked it roughly from her quiver. Her fingers started to tremble as she nocked it and lifted the bow. Everything seemed to freeze around her. His eyes burned into hers. His thoughts whispering in her mind.

Release me! I beg of you!

She pulled the arrow back. It felt like pulling a bucket rope full of stones. His shirt was open, revealing the gleaming kystrel. The reddish brown matt of chest hair did not disguise the whorl of black tattoos on his chest that snaked up to his throat and across his shoulders. A sign that he was fully in its thrall.

You are strong enough, girl! I can help you!

She hesitated, wanting to let the arrow fly. Then she experienced the full force of the Medium slam against her. All her desire gutted out of her. She was tired, exhausted, wasted. The bow string was so heavy, so very heavy. She could not let the shaft loose. Her fingers would not obey her.

Pain.

The crossbow bolt stuck into the side of her leg, deep into the flesh, into the bone. Every thought turned into fire, and she cried out in agony and crumpled. Horses crashed through the expanse of oaks, and then she saw him—the Earl of Dieyre—with a mass of knights. He was garbed in mail, a brown tabard fluttering as he reined in his mount. His eyes were livid, his face a contortion of delight and vindication.

"Caught you at last!" he crowed, swinging off the saddle, sword in hand. Three knights had crossbows trained on her. The fourth was reloading a bolt.

On her knee, her leg throbbing with agony, she stared at Dieyre with hatred. She brought up her last arrow and aimed for his throat. She saw the crossbowmen fire, but she was faster. Pulling back, she let the arrow loose and then twisted her shoulders and collapsed on her back, hoping some of the bolts would miss her.

With reflexes honed by battle, Dieyre swung and shattered the arrow with his sword. Gracefully, his sword arm lowered, his grin defiant. One of the bolts struck her hand, impaling it. The others missed. It was worse agony than the first, and she screamed in pain. On her back, she dropped her bow.

The pain made tears swim in her eyes. She could hardly see Dieyre as he approached. Shoving with her legs, despite the pain, she pushed herself closer to the Leering. The entire face of it was burning. If she could only get close enough to touch it. Close enough to touch it with her blood. Mastons' blood screamed when they died. She could hear the sound of her own in her mind. A cry for help, for vengeance, for justice. The cry of one about to be murdered.

Dieyre's voice was mocking. "You should have joined me when I offered, girl. It was quite a chase, but I am persistent. It would amaze you how patient I can be."

One of the knights kicked Lia savagely in the ribs. "Can I kill her now, my lord?" he demanded.

"Not yet," Dieyre answered curtly. "Let her watch Muirwood burn before she dies. Fire the Leerings."

When I first saw the child, that babe in a Pry-rian shawl, I knew that she would be my death. Over all these years, as I have watched her grow, steal, tease, and laugh, that knowledge has whispered to my mind many times. That little girl, so full of life and affection, would bring about the fall of Muirwood Abbey. Yet even knowing this, despite how it pained me, I could not resist loving her or honoring the request her father had made me vow.

—Gideon Penman of Muirwood Abbey

CHAPTER FORTY-FOUR

Burning

Lia couldn't breathe through the pain. She tasted blood in her mouth. Determined to fight to the last of her strength, she pulled her dagger free with her uncrippled hand and jammed the blade into the boot of the knight who had kicked her. As he wailed with agony, she struggled on her elbows toward the Leering. It was so close, but not close enough. In her mind, she willed the fire to cease. The flame spasmed and guttered out.

Scarseth swung around violently, staring at her. His eyes were still glowing.

"Summon the fire!" Dieyre ordered.

The two wrestled for control of the Leering. Lia shoved his thoughts as hard as she could, willing the flames to die. If she could only touch it, she could summon the defenses. A boot struck her in the small of her back, and she could think of nothing but blinding pain. Her concentration snapped, and the fire bloomed again. She could not get a grip on her thoughts, could not collect them past the haze of suffering. She was going to die.

Another kick would do it, another crushing blow. She was so tired, so weary. The Leering was too far.

"My lord, a maston!"

"No crossbows. He is mine," Dieyre said in a low, greedy voice. Then louder, "So you *do* care for the girl! A true man after all. Her suffering will end quickly. I will not let them play with her first. But you have just wasted her sacrifice. Not that you could have hid for long with all the tunnels blocked."

Lia opened her eyes. She could not see through her tears, but she heard his boots approaching, heard the stiff rasp of breath. Blinking quickly, the scene opened like a flower before the sun—Colvin walking toward them, maston sword gripped in hand. Thumping against the leather jerkin on his chest was the ring she has tossed to him. The sword tip pointed down, but she could see the angry clench of his fist, the cool hate mirrored in his eyes.

"Forshee!" one of the soldiers whispered gruffly but with grudging respect.

"Where's the Demont girl?" said another. All attention seemed to be facing the two noblemen who clearly hated each other. Lia started scooting slowly, so slowly toward the Leering. The blood in her mouth was choking her.

"I have been waiting for this moment," Dieyre said, closing the ground that separated them. "Ciana has sworn to be my wife as long as I spared you. But you know how good I am at keeping my promises." There was a grin in his voice that made Lia sick. "I know she wanted to be married in an Abbey. But after today, there will *be* no more Abbeys. It ends here. It ends today. Your lands are mine. Your sister is mine. Even your curly-haired wretched is mine. You have nothing left that I want."

The soldiers had not seen Lia slinking away. The ground was rough against her back, the trampled oak leaves and twigs dragged against her. The pain was beyond anything she had experienced. It took biting her tongue to keep from whimpering with each fervent twitch. Closer, closer!

"I am not afraid of you," Colvin said, his voice hoarse.

"Of course not. You are too stupid to be afraid. Everyone who has relied on you is in my hands. Your poor, useless friend York—I left him in a puddle of blood. Demont is dead and every maston with him. You are the last, I think. The last to fall. You should have fallen at Winterrowd. Let us end it here."

The swords clashed with a shower of sparks. Dieyre came again, faster than a lightning strike, and again it was parried. It was a whirlwind of blows, sweeps, and cuts. Lunges and stabs, as if a thousand iron shields clattered down stone steps in a moment. Dieyre was wearing armor, and Colvin had none. They traded blows and cuts, shoving and stomping and grappling at each other, then moving back and circling, feinting, only to charge and rush again.

Lia gasped as a ribbon of blood appeared on Colvin's cheek from Dieyre's sword, one that nearly took out his eye.

"She is crawling! Look at her!"

They had seen her.

A shadow fell across her body. Scarseth, a dagger in his hand. His eyes were glowing fiercely. She could see the tattoo marks expanding across his throat as he maintained the power over the Leerings, his teeth clenched, obviously wrestling with the Aldermaston in his mind to keep the flames going.

Save me! he screamed at her in his mind. *I do not want to hurt you! Pareigis is making me!*

But what could she do? *Fight it!* she screamed back at him. *Fight her off!*

The clash of steel stopped suddenly. The two knights circled each other, sweat dripping from their faces. Dieyre sounded impressed. "You are better than you were. You have been *practicing*, Forshee!" The swords met again, clash after clash. Lia could not bear to look. She was angry at him for sacrificing himself. He was supposed to take Ellowyn to Dahomey. Who was left to carry out the Medium's will?

Scarseth's hand suddenly closed around her throat, squeezing it. The dagger came down next. Lia caught his wrist with her good hand, arresting the stroke. He was so strong with the Medium's power. Her eyes went black for a moment, then she focused. Dangling over her, loose from his shirt, was the kystrel.

Dieyre continued his taunting. "I wish you could have seen her beg, Forshee. The way she begged me to spare York's life and yours. It would have cut through any other man, especially the tears. I made her promise and seal that promise with a kiss." The blades struck harder and harder. Faster and faster. "Not just any kiss. She had to mean it. She had to want it! And she did, Forshee. I will cherish that memory. Her arms around my…"

And then Dieyre's sword whistled, arcing in the air, end over end, until it landed with a thump on the heath.

Colvin's boot stomped hard on Dieyre's foot, his elbow snapped Dieyre's head back, and Dieyre flopped on the ground. The point of Colvin's sword came down on his chest and stopped.

The soldiers were shocked. A hushed silence fell.

"Kill me," Dieyre growled. "If you are a man then kill me!"

Lia shoved against the wrist, but the blade was getting closer to her ribs. Her whole body trembled with the agony and effort. She could not hold him. Her strength was going to fail.

"Kill me!" Dieyre roared, craning his neck. "You are a man! I spoiled your sister! I ruined her! Do not show me mercy. Do not you *dare* show me mercy, Forshee! You defeated me. Now end it! End my life!"

The kystrel dangled right in front of her. One of her hands was transfixed by a crossbow bolt. She could not even move the fingers. If she let go of Scarseth's wrist, she could snatch it.

Colvin's voice was full of anger and loathing. "I will not, Dieyre. I can see your thoughts. You ordered that she be killed if you met your death. I will not be her executioner and yours."

Lia's strength failed.

She released Scarseth's arm and grabbed the snail-shaped medallion, which was the source of his power over the Leerings. The edges were hot in her palm as the dagger plunged into her ribs. She closed her eyes, summoning the Medium's power to help her in her final moments of life. All the flames from all of the burning Leerings, she summoned into her hand. She could feel the light and heat from her fist blazing. She made it hotter and hotter, a forge fire of intensity. The kystrel melted in her hand, and the binding on Scarseth was snapped.

"Then you will die for me," said the Earl of Dieyre. "A thousand marks to the one who takes off his head!" he shouted at his soldiers.

She could not move. It was over for her as the blood welled up from the dagger wound. Lia felt arms draw underneath her and lift her. Opening her eyes, she saw Scarseth's face near hers as he carried her toward the Leering, his face a mixture of guilt and desperation. He staggered, almost dropping her, and then placed her gently next to the Leering. He took her hand to touch the cooling stone. He was helping her save the Abbey.

"Please!" he whispered. "Save us…"

The Gift of Seering opened up her true eyes, and she saw it all at once. Twenty knights rushing at Colvin, weapons bare. He stood in the midst of a storm, surrounded by blinding golden light. Ellowyn hiding in an ossuary as soldiers searched the rubble for her. The masses of soldiers were marching toward the Abbey, but had halted, confused since fires were no longer burning. What did that mean? She could feel their confusion. Was it safe to go farther? Where was their master?

Lia?

It was the Aldermaston's thoughts. The Aldermaston, who stood alone at the Abbey gates in the hurricane of power that Pareigis unleashed on him. Her guards battered on the gates, which were twisting and bending and shaking, nearly down. That was the moment. That was the instant when things began to tip. The Leering thrummed with power.

Lia, I am the one meant to die! It is my blood! Please! Not you!

But she was already fading, already slipping past the mortal coils that bound her true self to the body of her second life. The Aldermaston could sense her death, and it overwhelmed him with grief. Pareigis was exultant as the gates tottered down, clanging to the paving stones. The Aldermaston crumpled, his heart giving way. Then his thoughts were shielded from hers as he succumbed to the blackness.

Lia felt the tug, the pull of Muirwood Abbey. She drifted in the wind toward it, summoned by it. The Abbey stood on the gently sloping hill, and it seemed as if it were already afire. But not with crackling orange flames—it burned with light brighter than the noonday sun. She could feel the Abbey defenses building, seething, throbbing. The Leerings that were once blazing turned white. As her shadow-self rose toward the ancient structure, she saw it happen. The twin rivers that enclosed the highland on two sides leapt from their banks. A flood of water thundered into the valley floor. The Abbey was encircled by the rivers completely. The soldiers halting in the fields below raised a scream of fright at the waters converging around them, flooding the entire valley floor.

The weight of Pareigis's will tried to stop the floods, to send them back, but it was like shoving the moon. As Lia drifted near to the Abbey, toward the Apse Veil, she watched in delight as maston after maston, wearing the collar and spurs of Winterrowd, emerged from inside. There was Garen Demont in front, rushing with his men toward the gates, swords drawn. Lia felt a rush of joy. Pareigis and her knights were outnumbered completely. The Apse Veil drew her inexorably toward the Abbey. She was returning to Idumea. Instead of sorrow, she felt warmth and peace. There was no pain, no suffering now. Only peace.

But there was something behind that beckoned her. Glancing back, she saw Colvin shining in a ball of light. All around him were dead Dahomeyjan knights. One by one, they fell as they tried to kill him. The feeling was familiar and haunting. Yes, it was the feeling she had at Winterrowd. The power of the Medium in full force. She had summoned it again to save his life. To protect the man she loved. The Apse Veil drew her nearer. She longed to go back to Idumea and see the garden-cities. Part of her wanted to stay. Something was not quite finished. But it was like a tiny leaf trying to pull itself away from the wind that was blowing it. She was incapable of going back there, no matter how much she willed it. The power that drew her own was inexorable.

She passed through the Abbey walls as if they were made of clouds instead of stone. More and more knight-mastons were coming, one by one, from the Rood Screen. It was an army! It was

Demont's entire army! They had not been killed in the north? She did not understand it. But even though she could not, she discovered that it did not matter. She was safe and warm, comforted by the Medium's power. Safe from all harm and from all tears.

She was nearly to the Veil when something snagged at her. It stuck to her and halted her. She was aware of a feeling of discomfort and pain. She did not want to feel that again. She shrunk from it. The feeling was persistent. She was falling…falling down a well shaft into an icy bath of water full of knives and bones and teeth. There was pain and agony and then a warm, calming glow. A calming glow that suddenly flared white hot and bright.

A voice spoke through the light—Colvin's voice.

"Lia Cook, I Gift you with life. Come back to me. You will live. By Idumea's hand, you will live. Come back."

She blinked. There was the pressure of his hand on the crown of her head. There was the sound of water and waves sloshing against her, and she realized she was cold and soaked. She blinked again and again until she was able to see. Looking up, she saw Colvin's face, saw the tears running down his cheeks as he lifted her in his arms and started to carry her up the hill.

Lia could see over his shoulder. Where there had been a meadow full of soldiers, she saw a vast lake. The Tor was tall enough not to be covered, but everything else for leagues was submerged. Muirwood rose like an island, protected on all sides.

"You brought me back," she whispered in his ear. There was so much pain in her side and leg that she could hardly think.

"The price was paid," he answered. "It was enough."

She nodded, smiled, and rested her cheek against his neck and fell unconscious.

CHAPTER FORTY-FIVE

Farewell

When Lia awoke from the draught that Siara Healer had made her swallow, her eyelashes fluttered slowly. She did not know where she was. The only light was the gentle glow of fire from a hearth. Lia blinked again, trying to clear her vision. When she tried to move, to sit up, her body coiled with pain, and she gasped. Her left hand was so bandaged that she could not wiggle her fingers. She wondered if she would be able to use it in the future, if it would ever heal. It took several moments to realize where she was—the room in the manor house where Marciana and Ellowyn had slept. There were no windows, so she did not know whether it was day or night. She rested on the feather-stuffed bed beneath a thick coverlet.

"Do not move," Colvin said, coming from the shadows. He approached and sat on the edge of the bed. She tried to sit up again, but winced with pain as every movement reminded her of her injuries.

"Here, let me help you," he offered, arranging the pillows for support and then lifting her slowly. She wore the thin, soft chemise that Marciana had given her over her chaen.

"The Abbey is safe?" she asked, but she knew that it was. She could feel the warm, peaceful feeling in the air.

"Yes, because of you," he answered.

She was grateful. A great sadness welled up in her heart when she remembered the Aldermaston collapsing at the gate when his thoughts went black. He was dead, she was sure of it. She could not bring herself to ask, though. She blinked back tears.

Opening her eyes, she stared at Colvin again, noticing the difference. "You have shaved," she whispered hoarsely, seeing his face in the firelight. There was a red scar on his cheek. As she cleared her throat, he fetched a cup of water to soothe her thirst. He held the cup to her mouth, and she drank deeply. "Better," she said after. "Is it very late?"

He shook his head. "The sun will set soon. You slept most of the day."

"Where is Ellowyn?"

Colvin looked down at her and smiled, his expression a quirk of interest. "With her uncle. No, she is not dead. And neither is Garen Demont."

Lia closed her eyes, remembering the vision she had seen. "I remember," she said. "He came through the Apse Veil with all of his knights. I remember seeing him…after I died." The thought made her shiver, despite the warmth of the hearth and Colvin so near. She opened her eyes again and looked into his face, which was tender and conflicted. "You brought me back, Colvin. How?"

His lips pursed in a struggle with a smile he tried to prevent. "Your gratitude overwhelms me," he said blandly, then scratched his hair and gave her a pointed look that said she was ridiculous.

"Do you think that I could *force* the Medium to do anything?" With one hand, he touched the ring dangling over the leather jerkin from around his neck. The motion drew her attention to it. He lifted the ring and looked at it and then at her. "When you tossed this at me, I was conflicted. I could not bring myself to let you die to save us. But I also recognized that the Medium might expect it. That was an awful moment for me. A terrible moment. That I might lose you forever." His weight shifted, and she felt her throat constrict, feeling him so near. His face was so unguarded, so exposed it made her tremble. "I wanted to believe that it would not end that way. So I waited as you ran off and pled for the Medium's direction. I could follow the gully the way you pointed, to Maderos's cave. Or the other way, which was the direction you went. Very clearly, I knew what I should do. I told Ellowyn to go the other way and hide amidst the ossuaries. All of the soldiers were following you like moths. I was there in the gully, near you, when they caught you at last. The Medium commanded me to save you." He gently reached out and brushed a lock of curly hair away from her face. "It was a command I was pleased to obey. I knew I could bring you back. I was there so that I could, even though I am not an Aldermaston."

Lia shook her head slowly, feeling grateful and confused and tired and hungry and a dozen other things all at once. "The Medium told me that I was going to die. Why? I saw you and Ellowyn putting stones over me, like we did to Jon Hunter. Was it wrong?"

Colvin's face hardened. "When did you see that?"

"Before dawn. I realized that I would not be going with you two to Dahomey. I have the Gift of Seering. It happened like at other times. I believed I was going to die. That is why I gave you my necklace." She reached out with her good hand and touched the hard edge of the ring. "I wanted you to remember me."

His face flushed, his eyes so intense with emotions that she blinked and discovered tears in her eyes.

"How could I ever...*ever* forget you? When you are in my thoughts constantly, every day and every night. You mean more to me than anyone else in my life. Do you understand that? I am worried about my sister because I do not know where she is. But I cannot go to her. My duty compels me to bring Ellowyn to Dahomey to warn them of the coming of the Blight. Wherever I go, I will be thinking of you. I do not need this thing to remind me."

Lia breathed out deeply, resting against the soft pillows. "That makes me feel much better. And worse. But I want you to keep it. I want you to wear it in Dahomey. How I wish I could go with you...but it hurts to move."

He smiled at her tenacity. "The healer said it will be some weeks before you are strong enough to walk. The bolt broke the bone in your leg. Your hand will heal, she tells me. It will be painful, but the damage will not be permanent. The knife wound was fatal. You lost a lot of blood and could not breathe. But when I called you back, it started to heal. The sound of your breathing has grown stronger all day."

"Have you watched me sleep then?" she asked, a little concerned at the thought of him watching her when she was so vulnerable and unaware.

He smoothed some of the hair from her face. "I was going to hold a vigil for you tonight until you awoke because I wanted to say good-bye. Sowe has been tending you. So have Bryn and Pasqua. They helped the healer tend to you. I was only allowed to see you after you'd been bathed and clothed. Pasqua's bed has been carried into the kitchen. You will rest there where they can look after you night and day. I am sure you are very hungry."

She nodded slowly, still full of questions though. "When are you leaving?"

"At dawn. Pen-Ilyn will row us across the water."

Lia twisted her head and gave him a puzzled look.

Colvin nodded. "When you summoned the defenses, it drew water from several rivers around the Abbey. He was trying to leave when the current suddenly pulled from the other way and drew him back toward Muirwood. All of the ships that the Queen Dowager used were smashed or have sunk. He has the only boat in this Hundred right now. All day he has been ferrying knights back and forth across the huge moat, filling a bag full of coins if I am not mistaken. He will bring us to Bridgestow and continue to ferry for Demont until the waters recede. If they recede."

Lia smiled at the thought of seeing Pen-Ilyn again. "Is his nose broken still?"

"The healer set it. It is purple, but it will heal."

"Was it another one of Dieyre's lies that Demont's army was defeated up north? We all thought he was dead."

"It was not a lie. He truly believed Demont was dead. You will find the story interesting, I think. Remember that everyone in Demont's service is a maston or a knight-maston. They were marching north to deal with a rebellion of the Earl of Caspur. He had control of all the approaches. His men were waiting to trap Demont and prevent escape. Demont knew he was outnumbered, and his men were weary and Caspur's were fresh. There was an Abbey in that Hundred where Demont's men sheltered. He knew that Caspur would not recognize the rights of the Abbey to safeguard them as he was burning the Abbeys within his lands. The Medium told him to cross the Apse Veil to Muirwood. They left their horses. They left the young king behind with a small guard to sneak away. Anyone who was not a maston was told to depart in the night. When the morning came, there was a great fog, like the kind that happen here. Caspur stretched his line so that Demont would not slip away in the mist. There was confusion, and his men started attacking each other, thinking they had stumbled across the mastons. By the time the fog lifted, Caspur learned that his army had nearly destroyed itself. Demont's men, meanwhile, crossed the Apse Veil to Muirwood."

He paused, looking her keenly in the eye. "They crossed two days ago. But they did not arrive at Muirwood until this morning, when you summoned the defenses. Not only did they cross a bridge of distance, they crossed a bridge of time, arriving when they were needed. The men are a little confused at having lost two days unexpectedly, as well as hearing the reports of their death. But they defended Muirwood and have taken the remnant of Queen Dowager's soldiers into custody."

Lia shook her head in amazement. "I believe it. When I crossed the Apse Veil, Maderos hinted that he could take me other places and other times as well. So, what have you done to Dieyre? You just mentioned having spoken to him."

Colvin folded his arms, his face growing severe. There was the anger again, just beneath the surface, implacable and intense. Not fear—only anger. "He is alive, though he will not reveal where he had my sister taken. He knows that is his only coin to bargain with, and he is being greedy with it. I think she was taken or is being taken to one of his manor houses in his lands, with orders to kill her if anyone tries to free her. She is his hostage."

Lia sat forward suddenly and winced with pain at her side. He gripped her shoulders and pressed her back against the cushions. "That is a secret he cannot hide for long. When you are feeling better, then I would like you to take some knight-mastons and save her. With the orb, you can find her."

"Yes," she replied reluctantly. "I wish you had killed him. When there is a poisonous serpent about, it is not wise to let it slither. But for her sake, I am glad you did not. I heard what you told him, that you could perceive his thoughts and knew the trap he had set for you. What a cruel man, plotting her death as a consequence for his. What is being done with him? Please assure me that he is not roaming free."

"Indeed he is not. His mood is surprisingly buoyant for a man whose plot has just met with unmistakable disaster. He is not as glib as he was, nor is he repentant. He demands a trial in Comoros. Demont is willing to oblige him, and he will be taken to Pent Tower after Demont has secured the city. It is a prison for nobles. And as you may guess, he will be under guard constantly, as he is very rich and will likely try to bribe his way out of punishment. I am sure you will want to know about the Queen Dowager as well? I thought so. She is under guard and being kept in a room here in the manor house. When Demont arrested her, he took away her heirloom necklace. There was a kystrel embedded in the jewelry."

Lia was not surprised. "She did wear a lot of jewelry. But I thought kystrels leave a mark on those who use them? Scarseth…his skin was ravaged by tattoos. Does she disguise it somehow?"

"You are right about the effect, but strangely, her skin was not marked. She does not hide it. She said, rather haughtily, that in Dahomey, her family's line does not suffer the marks for using kystrels. They claim that it is the only true way to use the Medium and that we are corrupted in our use. After her failure, she railed against Demont, the Aldermaston, against us all and promised she would see every last maston killed. She ordered us to return her to her brother, the king of Dahomey, which we will not do until our mission to Dochte Abbey is finished. She did not take defeat…gracefully."

Lia grabbed his arm, her heart surging with hope. She had not brought herself to ask the question fearing what the answer would be. "What? The Aldermaston…he lives?"

Colvin smiled and patted her hand. "His heart did fail him, and he collapsed at the gate, but he is still alive. And unconscious. Every time we try to Gift him with healing, the Medium forbids us to utter the words. His steward has not left his side."

Lia was filled with relief and gratitude. "In my mind, I saw him fall. I am so pleased…so pleased we came in time."

"Barely in time, Lia. Only barely. If Scarseth had not carried you to the Leering when he did, then the Queen Dowager would have won. For that reason alone I did not kill him, even though he stabbed you. But we do not know what to do with him. He does not want to be with the few survivors of the flood, but we have no other confinement available. Nor do I trust giving him back his power of speech. He knows too much…especially about you. He was under the Queen Dowager's thrall, there is no mistaking it. Demont thinks the Aldermaston should decide what to do with him after he awakens."

Lia nodded. She felt a mixture of revulsion and compassion for the man who had killed her. What a contradiction. He stabbed her and then carried her to the Leering. She would not have been able to summon the defenses without his help. And she remembered his thoughts—his wild and pleading thoughts to help free him from the Queen's grasp.

There was a gentle knock on the door. Colvin rose and went to it and unlocked the crossbar. In walked Pasqua with a tray of food, as well as Siara, carrying a bundle of fresh linen bandages and a dish of powdered woad.

"She is awake?" Pasqua said suddenly, her voice rising. "And why did not you bother to tell us, you unthinking clod? She must be famished. Famished! I brought some broth for her and something for you to eat, but now I think I will not let you have a bite of it since you did not come and get me right away. Do not just stand there, young man, take the tray! I hope the soup sloshes on you." She shoved it into Colvin's hand and hobbled over to the bed where Lia winced with pain, expecting a hug that would hurt.

"Be gentle," Colvin warned, carrying the tray over.

Pasqua took Lia's good hand with both of hers. "Look at you, child." She swept part of her hair back and caressed her cheek. "When that filthy man carried you up the hill, you looked a corpse, though you were breathing. So much blood and injury. I do not think I can bear to let you out of my sight again, hunter or no. Are you hungry? Can I feed you?"

"Just the broth," Siara said. "Anything stronger she may not be able to handle. Broth first. How is your pain, Lia? Do you need more valerianum to help you sleep?"

Lia shook her head violently. "No, I do not want to sleep." She looked at Colvin, her heart aching with the thought of him leaving with Ellowyn in the morning.

"You need rest," Siara said. "But even more, you need friends with you. Should we move you to the kitchen? There are many who want to see you."

Lia wanted to see everyone, but she also wanted to be alone with Colvin. Maybe her conflict showed on her face, for she saw him approach with the tray and set it down. "I am not leaving your side until dawn." He touched Pasqua's shoulder deferentially. "With your permission, of course."

Pasqua looked up at him grudgingly and then nodded.

Lia sighed, her thoughts painful. She nodded at him as well.

Colvin pulled away the coverlet and gently scooped Lia into his arms. Even the slow and tender motion made her wince with pain, but she clenched her jaw to keep from crying out and tried to breathe through her nose as he started to walk. The kitchen was a short distance, and Siara Healer led the way to pull open the doors, while Pasqua followed with the tray. Lia rested her head against Colvin's cheek as he tried not to jostle her. The pale sky was turning black outside, the smell of the sea hinted in the air. There were knight-mastons walking the grounds with torches, patrolling the borders, keeping them safe. A feeling of protection had settled over the Abbey. All was calm and quiet.

The smell of the kitchen greeted her, and she blinked with the light and the rush of voices and sounds. Pasqua's bed had been installed beneath the awning of the loft and barrels and chests, and baskets had been relocated elsewhere in the room. She saw Pen-Ilyn sitting on a bucket with a tray of sambocade in one hand, shoveling the dessert into his mouth like a starving soul. He smiled and nodded at her, hurrying even faster now that Pasqua had returned. Colvin crossed the tiles to the bed and helped set her down after Sowe turned the sheet and stacked up the pillows.

Sowe took her hand, smiling warmly, and then kissed her. Edmon was her shadow. His face was drawn and pale. He had the look of a slight fever about him, and he moved with a visible wince.

"I am surprised to see you on your feet so soon, Edmon," Lia told him, giving him a look of compassion.

"Not as surprised as I am. Sowe could have been a healer instead of a cook. Blue woad is an amazing plant, though the skin around the wound is a little blue, but the bleeding stopped, at least. And I will have a lovely scar where Dieyre stabbed me. I am sure I will never tire of telling the story of how I got it."

Lia sighed, seeing the flash of old humor in his eyes. "You are lucky to be alive."

His eyes became serious. "I do owe that to you in a way, Lia. Forgive me, but my emotions are a bit close to the surface, seeing you like this. Seeing what you have suffered. I can bear my lot. But it grieves me to see you in such pain. I lost what I was going to say…"

Sowe gave him a bashful look and prompted him, "How you survived. How Marciana saved you."

"Ah, there it is. It is a short story. Do not worry, I will not make it longer in the telling, but I wanted you to know. When you and Colvin left on the boat, Dieyre wasted no time and drew his sword and said he would take Ciana with him. I was shocked and angry, though I should not have been. I was a fool thinking I could stop him—and Ciana for trying to stop me—but I am rash, as you know. He disarmed me with hardly any effort, a fact which still wounds my pride. He cut me here"—he gestured to his torso with a wince—"and then smashed his fist into my face to knock me down, and I am certain he was going to run me through and murder me. Colvin told me that in the Bearden Muir, when the sheriff's men attacked him, you stood in the way. Well, Marciana protected me with her own body and spoke so earnestly with Dieyre that she talked his temper down. He made her swear she would go with him peacefully if he did not slay me. I could see he was tempted. His eyes told me that he wanted me dead. But I was bleeding, and maybe it was good enough. Maybe he thought I would just bleed to death. Ciana honored her part and rode off with Dieyre. I managed to stuff a rag into my wound and lurch on the road. The Medium saved me then, for I found a horse, one of the strays from the Dahomeyjans, and rode to Muirwood. A great, big black. Beautiful animal. I do not know how I made it on the saddle, but I did and collapsed outside the gate and was carried here." He reached out and stroked Sowe's hair absently.

"You should be resting," Sowe said timidly, and he nodded his surrender and hobbled back to a floor pallet where she helped him lie down.

Lia watched them for a moment and then gratefully took the tureen of soup from Pasqua, who clenched back her tears and stared at her injured girl with all the protective looks of a mother.

***

Dawn came too quickly, its arrival a torture Lia had been dreading. Colvin had waited vigil all night long, and they spoke softly to each other, talking of their lives, sharing little stories that they had not told each other before. Sowe and Bryn were asleep in the loft above. Edmon lay still on a pallet near the bread oven. Pasqua entered quietly, before the first cock crowed, and stoked the fire in the hearth, pinched some salt into a cauldron after tasting the broth, and brought another bowl to Lia. She set some loaves near the oven to warm and gathered some fruits and nuts for the journey.

Colvin sat at the edge of Lia's bed still, studying her face, his expression unreadable. "When we returned to Muirwood, I had been looking for a gift or reward for Sowe for her help when I was injured. I think I know what to give her now."

Lia smiled, pleased that he remembered. "What then?"

"You saw the way they look at each other. Edmon is bedazzled by the girl. I cannot blame him. He told me yesterday he plans to stay at Muirwood and pass the maston test when he has recovered from his injury. When I am gone, I would like you to tell her that I plan to adopt her as my sister. The same offer I came here to make to you. She will have a marriage portion to bring.

With all her years serving at the Aldermaston's table, I think she would come to understand her new station. Would you present my offer to Sowe?"

Lia's throat constricted with joy, and she nodded, blinking back tears. "That is generous, Colvin."

"She is your friend. I do this regardless of Edmon. If he changes his mind, which I do not expect that he will, she will still have rank and position. She is a good girl, and I admire her. So does Ciana."

A knock came to the kitchen door, and Pen-Ilyn entered, but held it wide to admit Ellowyn and an older man. The last time Lia had seen him, it had been on the battlefield of Winterrowd, blood-spattered and leaning wearily against a wagon as he spoke to the survivors. She could hardly tell his face through the grime that day. But she knew him at once. Garen Demont.

Something burned inside her heart seeing him, something fierce and tugging. It made her eyes brim with tears. Demont was probably fifty, but he looked younger, with a boyish face—clean-shaven, like Colvin's—and a mess of untidy dark hair streaked with gray. He wore a chain hauberk and splotched tunic with all the comfortable grace of an experienced soldier and had his maston sword buckled at his hip, his gloved hand resting on the pommel. Colvin's hand was on the edge of her bed. Her fingers itched to snake out and snare his, to keep him from going. She knew the moment was coming, but it still hurt.

"Are you ready, my lord of Forshee?" Demont asked Colvin sympathetically. "Though I myself loathe parting with you. If you leave now, you will reach Bridgestow before dark. There are many ships that anchor there, bound for Dahomey. You can make it to the island Abbey by the time we arrive in Comoros with the prisoners, I should think. Dochte Abbey is on the northern coast, if you recall. It will only take you and Ellowyn a few days under sail if the weather is fine, I am certain of it."

Colvin gave her a mournful look, his eyes dark and sad. He stood slowly, as if some heavy burden were fastened to his shoulders. He gave her one final look and then started toward the doorway. "I am ready."

There was creaking in the loft above, and Sowe and Bryn hurried down the ladder. Edmon was awake, as well, and rose, wincing with pain, clutching his wounded side. Pasqua stuffed the food in a new rucksack and handed it to Colvin at the door.

"Be you safe," she said gruffly. "Come back to us when your duty is finished."

Lia ached. She felt the tears sting her eyes as she saw her friends smothering him with attention. It was painful beyond enduring. Who would protect him if not her? Who would guide him when the way was lost? It was agony thinking about being in Muirwood without him. No more walks in the Cider Orchard. Not to see him at the laundry while she scrubbed clothes. His fierce gaze turned back to look at her, his jaw clenched with visible pain.

Edmon saw the look between them. He whispered something in Sowe's ear, and she nodded, wiping tears from her eyes and taking Pasqua by the arm. She and Bryn pulled her outside the kitchen into the fresh morning air just as the sky began to shine. Edmon said something to Demont and Ellowyn and escorted them outside as well, leaving Colvin alone on the threshold. Edmon glanced back and shut the door after himself.

Colvin stood rooted in place for a moment, rucksack dangling from his shoulder. Then he let it fall with a thump, and he marched across the room and pulled Lia into a fierce hug. Lia swallowed with pain and pleasure, ignoring the little jolts of agony that came, and hugged him back, sorry that she was losing him again. She smelled his hair, his leather jerkin, the scent of his skin—inhaling him all in one final memory, squeezing him until her hand throbbed and her side ached and her leg moaned with the motion.

"How I love you," she whispered to him, feeling him tense at the words. "Please come back to me. Please take care of yourself. Every day, you will be in my thoughts, and I will be pleading for your safety. The Medium will protect you both. I have faith in that."

She felt his sigh, his body tremble. Then pulling away slightly, he looked at her with inexpressible pain and longing in his eyes. It was the look of a man being tortured. "This is a hard thing," he whispered. "Leaving you like this. I can hardly bear it. Will you help me? Will you…Gift me, Lia?"

A smile creased her mouth. "If you want me to."

He knelt at the edge of the bed and bowed his head so she could reach it. She made the maston sign while she touched his hair. What could she say? It was her first time pronouncing one herself. What would the Medium require of him? Her thoughts were a jumble, all confused. She knew what she wanted to say, but she knew it had to come from the Medium and not her.

"Colvin Price," she said in a tremulous voice. "I Gift you with…I Gift you with…" She paused, searching through her contorting feelings for the right words. Then she felt it—a spark of warmth and assurance. An insight into his needs. "I Gift you with Wisdom and Knowledge. That you may discern through the illusions and see things as they really are. As they really must be. By Idumea's hand, make it so."

The Medium was a warm blanket that fell around their shoulders. It was comforting and peaceful. She took a deep breath, trying to calm the sobs that would come later. He raised his head and stared in her eyes. His iron will had asserted itself again. He rose slowly from the bed and stared down at her. "I will come back to you. That is my promise. I will not break it this time."

She smiled at him, feeling the tears burn in her eyes as she watched him leave again.

While the Medium reveals itself in many forms and can come as a dramatic manifestation, it usually does not. Some mastons think they need to experience the full, raw power of the Medium before they are convinced of its possibilities. If we have unrealistic notions of how, when, or where the Medium reveals itself, we risk missing the tokens which come as quiet, reassuring feelings and thoughts while we are doing something else. These simple manifestations of the Medium can be equally convincing and powerful as the dramatic ones. Over time, we learn how this works. It is something each maston learns for himself.

—Gideon Penman of Muirwood Abbey

CHAPTER FORTY-SIX

Scarseth's Voice

The Aldermaston revived after three days. Word traveled through Muirwood as fast as the birds in springtime. Pasqua rallied the kitchen to begin its work of feeding him, and Lia was secretly relieved for the news. The kitchen began to hum and thrive, with Sowe and Bryn bending over balls of dough or brushing butter around the edge of a crust. Lia watched with jealousy, wishing she was active again. Each day was less painful than the one before it, though her heart was heavy. Word had come that Colvin and Ellowyn were bound on a ship for Dahomey out of Bridgestow. Garen Demont was still a guest at the Abbey, and he treated his stay there as such, asking for permission from Prestwich, instead of giving orders as if it were his own earldom. He deferred to the Abbey's authority in all things.

"Sowe, can you slice the apples? He likes it in chunks. Bryn, up the ladder with you. Fetch a pumpkin. Go on, girl. Make haste! I am sure the Aldermaston is very hungry. I would like to have something ready quickly. Oh, that I had a spare shank to roast. Maybe I should send for the butcher."

The kitchen door opened, letting in the blinding sunlight. Pasqua turned to bark in annoyance and stopped when she recognized the Aldermaston. Prestwich was there, gripping the old man's arm to help keep him up.

"Aldermaston, we will bring the food to you," Pasqua said, looking rattled at seeing him too soon. "We are working as fast as we can. Sowe, Sowe!"

"I am not hungry," the Aldermaston said, his voice choked and low. He coughed into his fist, his whole body wracked with spasms. Prestwich clutched him to keep him on his feet, whispering soothingly to him. "Please…I must speak with Lia. If you would all leave us for a moment. I must consult with her."

Lia stared at him. He looked even older, and his eyes burned as if he had a fever. Prestwich helped walk him toward the bed.

"But…" Pasqua hedged, obviously distressed about being dismissed from her own kitchen.

But the Aldermaston did not speak further. Slowly, step by step, he approached, his eyes fixed on Lia's. Prestwich helped him sit and then stood away.

"Even you, old friend," the Aldermaston whispered. Prestwich nodded with a surly look and left the kitchen, as did the others. Pasqua grumbled indignantly, but soon the door was shut, and a hush fell over the kitchen, except for the snap and crack of the fire.

Lia reached out and took the old man's hand with hers. She squeezed it, giving him a look of warmth and respect. Her throat choked with tears. It was such a relief to see him awake, his dark eyebrows arched over his fiery eyes. "What is it you would tell me?" she asked hoarsely.

He looked at her intently. "I have learned what happened three days ago. I have learned of your injuries. I know that Colvin has taken…her…to Dahomey because of the writing on the Cruciger orb. How were you able to read it, child? What did it say?"

She swallowed, leaning back against the pillows, and told the story of their journey through Pry-Ree and the arrival at Tintern Abbey. He listened carefully, waiting with great curiosity, great interest on his face. She spoke of their return, Dieyre's betrayal, and the flight through the Bearden Muir. He listened carefully, saying nothing until she was finished.

"The Aldermaston of Tintern," he whispered, his eyes gazing down at the bed. "He knew you? He…recognized you?"

"Yes, but he would not say who I am. When I am well, I should like to go back and speak to him. I wish he had told me what he knew."

The Aldermaston grunted. "He cannot, child."

Lia looked at him, confused. "What do you mean?"

"I am sure the Medium binds his tongue. So they have gone to Dahomey." He sighed deeply. "That is where it will begin. That is where it will start."

"What?" Lia asked, her stomach coiling with worry. "The Blight?"

He nodded. "I saw it in a vision. I saw what Aldermastons in many countries have been seeing. We have all seen the colors of the leaves changing, predicting the passing of a season. But I have seen the result. I have seen the skeletal trees remaining when all the leaves have fallen. It is a Blight greater than any other we have known. A sickness and plague that will destroy everyone. Everyone. Not a man, woman, or child will survive it when it comes. Its devastation will be complete. Total. It will be the end of all kingdoms." His look burned into hers. "I have seen it in my mind. There is only one way to save ourselves and that is to abandon these shores. The exodus has already begun. The Aldermaston of Tintern told you of it."

"Yes," Lia said. "There are boats. They are building ships. Some have already departed. But why Pry-Ree? Why were they given the warning first? Why is it that you did not see it coming?"

He rocked slowly back and forth, his expression pained but thoughtful. "Pry-Ree was a proud kingdom. Too proud. You have heard Martin speak of it. That they succumbed swiftly to their fate, and their princes all were killed. I would disagree with part of his assessment. Many of their princes were strong with the Medium. They knew what was going to happen. The people did not heed their leaders, and so the leaders were taken away. The people focused on earning coins through trade and bringing in the latest spices and metals from other realms and not on learning from tomes. So the Medium abandoned them in their hour of need. As a result of their humiliating defeat, they have learned humility. Only by being broken were they able to see that their aim was fixed on the wrong course. The humility of their people gave their Aldermastons vision. Some pine for the old days of glory. But in the end, it is the fall of Pry-Ree that will save us all."

Lia shivered with the thought. "What must we do then?"

"We must ask them to save us." His face twisted with pain and regret. "But do you see the trouble, Lia? We are too proud ourselves. We, the conquerors. Can you imagine someone like the Earl of Dieyre asking that forsaken people for help? Begging aid from a nation so humbled? They who hate us, and we hate them? Some would rather die. Most will not even believe the situation is so dire. They will not believe because they do not want to believe. Because it would alter their view of the world."

She remembered something Ciana had told her once. *We are slow to believe that which, if believed, would hurt our feelings.*

He shook his head with sadness. “I will do what I can to tell the other Aldermastons. With our kingdom on the cusp of war, there is much to distract us from this threat.”

“Have you told Demont?” Lia asked.

“No, I wanted to tell you first,” he said. “You know the way to Tintern Abbey. With the orb, you can lead a remnant there. Perhaps that is your purpose.” He smiled at her fondly. “Have you felt your strength returning? Muirwood is strong with the Medium. You will heal faster here than anywhere else you could go. Not because Siara is such a good apothecary. The Abbey itself strengthens the mastons who swore their oaths here. You will be walking again soon. And you must. Your journey has not ended here.”

“You said the Blight would begin in Dahomey?” she asked. “Do you know where?”

He nodded, his face grave with inner pain. “Yes.”

The insight struck her like a blow. “It begins in Dochte Abbey, does not it? It will begin when that Abbey falls?”

The Aldermaston said nothing for a moment. His face hardened like stone. “But they will be warned first. They will be warned.” He sighed deeply.

“You know something that you cannot tell me,” Lia whispered.

A half smile was her reply. Slowly, he rose from the bedside.

“What will you do with Scarseth?” she asked curiously. “Will you send him away with the other prisoners?”

He paused. “What do you think I should do with him?”

“I do not know. Maybe we should keep him here.”

“And his voice?” the Aldermaston asked, his expression inscrutable.

"He may know where Colvin's sister is. There is much he could tell us. If we showed him mercy." It felt right to her, even after all he had done. It felt right to show him mercy.

He looked back at her, his eyes piercing. "You would show him compassion? He who has betrayed you and tried to kill you? Who may betray you again?"

Lia swallowed, realizing the Aldermaston's question was more toward himself than her. Had not Scarseth done both to him as well? There was a history between the men. A history of anger and distrust. "That is what I think we should do. If he seeks forgiveness."

The Aldermaston gave her a wary smile. "Very well, Lia. For your sake. The Medium presses heavily on me now. You are unfit for your duties. There is time to heal and rest. Do you know what position he always craved when he was a wretched here?"

She shook her head.

"He wanted to be a hunter," came the reply. "Maybe it is time he had the chance."

***

Lia stood at the edge of the hill, looking down at the vast lake in front of her. Muirwood and the village were completely isolated from the roads. Trees were submerged. Water lapped on the grass lower down. A few hawks swirled in the sky, drifting on a lazy wind. It looked so different from what she had seen all her life, and she said as much to her companion, Seth.

"Even without the lake, it was different from when I was here," he offered, pointing toward the forbidden portion of the grounds. "There was a cemetery there. Some were dug into the hillside, even." He grinned and then winced at the memories. "When I was a lad."

Lia had difficulty walking fast, but at least she could put her weight on her leg again. It was sore every night, but she tried to walk farther and farther each day. When she gained her strength fully, she wanted to be ready to cross the Apse Veil to Dochte and Tintern. A bandage wrapped her palm, and it hurt when she clenched her fist, but her fingers worked, and the pain lessened each day.

She called him Seth now, instead of Scarseth, which is the name he was known by in the Abbey during his time as a wretched. Seth Page.

"I have been meaning to ask you something, Lia." He looked down at the grass, uncomfortable. Since the Aldermaston had restored his speech, he was more soft-spoken than she remembered. More observant. Sometimes, his expression looked tortured.

"What is it?"

"How is your leg feeling?"

"You wanted to know how my leg is feeling?" she asked, confused.

"No," he said, shaking his head. "I was asking if you wanted to rest a bit. The kitchen does not seem very far, but you were starting to limp more back there. I wanted to talk to you."

She nodded and slowly sank into the grass on the edge of the hill, staring out the expanse of water. He joined her, but did not look at her. Wrapping his arms around his knees, he also stared toward the setting sun. "The Aldermaston said you knew how Martin died." His voice was stiff, controlled.

There was a pain in Lia's heart at the mention of him. "I did not see it happen," she said.

"But you heard it." He sighed deeply. "I did not think anything could kill that man. I remember the first time I saw him. It made an impression, I tell you."

"The Aldermaston in Pry-Ree called the creature a Fear Liath. Colvin called it a gray-rank."

Seth hissed at the word. "Ssssttt. A gray-rank. Of course. Worse than a black bear. Fast, too, so I have heard. I was surprised to learn he had died. But a gray-rank could do it."

Lia turned to look at him. "I also remember the first time I saw Martin. In the kitchen."

He smirked. "No, you do not remember the first time, Lia. You were just a baby. But I remember that night."

Something chilled inside of her. "What do you remember about it?"

"I remember it because Martin cried. Never saw that old buzzard cry before. It was not long after the fall of Pry-Ree. That was sixteen years ago."

"But I am only fifteen," Lia said, confused.

He looked at her. "Really? I remember it very well. But maybe I am wrong. It was a long time ago."

"Why did Martin cry when he saw me?"

Seth looked back out at the lake. "What do you know about him?"

Lia thought for a moment. "He is Pry-rian obviously. A hunter. He was working for the Aldermaston for years before I was abandoned here. Pasqua told me that. He had been in Muirwood for…I do not know…say four or five years before that?"

"I remember when he came," he said softly. "He was the captain of the Prince's guard. The Pry-rian ruler's guard. They rode down from Bridgestow to Comoros, but they stopped at Muirwood with their retinue. All of the guardsmen had the same uniform. Leather girdle and bracers, like you wear. A gladius instead of a long sword. They all had bows as well. Dangerous men, all of them. The Prince and the Aldermaston had several long conversations together. They went into the Abbey, too, for the Prince was a maston."

Lia's heart surged with fire. The flood from the Medium was choking her breath. Pieces of the story began to fit together in her mind, interlocking like sculpted stones. "I did not know he was part of the Prince's guard." The Aldermaston had already told her the story of the Pry-rian prince who had come to Muirwood on the way to Comoros.

"Yes. But it was odd that he left Martin behind. I mean, as captain of the guard, why stay behind at Muirwood when your master is treating with his enemies in Comoros? I do not know why it happened. Only that Martin became the Abbey's hunter and sought an apprentice." His look darkened. "A position which I felt should have been mine."

"But you were the Aldermaston's page instead? You delivered his messages…"

"And carried his laundry to the lavenders and fetched this and fetched that." His voice was thick with resentment. "How I hated it! Always being told where to go and what to do. But Martin was free to roam the Bearden Muir. He would be gone for days at a time, and I could not wait until he returned. When Jon was named as the apprentice, I was sick with envy. It was the Aldermaston's choice, of course, and he knew how much I wanted it. But he would not give it to me. But still, I took every advantage I could to befriend Martin. He…he was like a father to me. He taught me little skills and tricks. Not as much as he taught Jon. After he was chosen, I scorned him, though we used to be friends. When we were younger, I would thrash him because I was bigger and stronger." His eyes focused on nothing at all, lost in the memories and the feelings. "But when he turned thirteen, I could not hurt him anymore. He grew strong and quick with all the things Martin taught him. The fights we used to have ended badly for me. My best weapons were words. How I would spit them at him! But he learned to keep tight rein on his feelings. That was something I could never do."

Lia listened with enormous interest. "I never knew you two were rivals."

He shook his head. "He never told Martin about what I did to him. He was quiet, that one. Always kept things inside. He adored Ailsa Cook, but he never told her. She was my age, but he was daft over her. Do you remember her working in the kitchen when you were little? She was taught by Pasqua and helped tend you and Sowe. She was always good with babies." He sighed. "I should have been as wise as Jon. Ailsa was a good girl. She was a friend to everyone. But I loved one of the learners. My one advantage of being the page was delivering messages to the cloisters. I was teased, of course. Makes my ears burn to remember some of the things they said to me. But there was one who I would have done anything for. She and her friends sighed about Jon. Every month he seemed to sprout more and more. But he was so quiet. He would say nothing to *any* of the girls. I had always been a good talker. If I were the hunter, if I were the one who wore a gladius and leathers and roamed where I chose, things would be better. I believed that. But I was wrong. I was so hateful, so angry with the Aldermaston for not choosing me. I blamed him for my own failings. Every snub was his fault. Every mocking look by the girl I craved was because of him." He sighed. "I will tell you the rest. I already confessed to the Aldermaston. When he asked me to be his hunter now, all these years later...well, you can imagine I hardly feel worthy of the privilege. But I need to have it out. I have been carrying it so long."

He looked down at the grass.

"Tell me," Lia whispered, touching his back comfortingly.

He looked at her, his face burning with shame. "The Aldermaston was right not to let me be the hunter. I was already disloyal to him as a page. He should never have trusted me, yet he did." He rubbed his eyes and stared back out over the lake. "I would wander around the Abbey at night, stealing things. A treat from Pasqua's kitchen. Something from the learners. I got very good at keeping quiet, at skulking around in the dark. At night, the grounds were mine—to wander where I chose, like a hunter. As I got older, I began to do worse things. Spy on people. I would break little pieces of the window so that I could listen in on conversations. I knew when all the learners were studying, and I would go through their belongings. Sometimes, I would steal from them. I wondered if the Aldermaston suspected, but he never accused me. No one ever caught me, I supposed. But it did happen eventually. The night I left Muirwood."

Lia swallowed, waiting patiently for him to reveal himself.

"As I told you, I used to wander the grounds at night. I knew what happened after dark. I knew which learners stole away into the cemetery to kiss each other…and worse. I knew the secret habits of the Abbey. Who was brought in to see the Aldermaston at night to face punishment for their offenses." He closed his eyes. "I knew many of their offenses and felt smug that I was never caught for mine. You grew up in the kitchen. You know that nearly everyone uses the main door. I used to climb the ridge of the rear door and look in the windows. You and Sowe were little, but I would try and catch glimpses of Ailsa. I was bored, nothing more. That night, she was bathing." He shook his head, his face grimacing with shame. "And Jon found me. He thrashed me. He thrashed me good. I had never seen him so angry. He said he had seen me on other nights. He knew all along what I was doing. I thought I was being clever. He would tell the Aldermaston, he said. Worse, he would tell Martin. Martin, who I admired more than any man…who I loved as a father. I was sick with shame. I could not face them. So I left Muirwood, bleeding. I left with its scars on my face and in my soul… and hence my nickname."

He clenched his hands into fists and trembled with the pent-up emotions. "Of course, I turned the shame into accusation. I could not live with myself. It was the Aldermaston's fault. If he had let me train with Martin, then Jon would not have found me out. The more I thought about it, the more I hated him and then everything about the Abbey. I left without completing my years of service."

Lia felt pity for him. She had never known. No one had ever breathed the story, least of all Ailsa. "Where did you go?"

"I wandered the Bearden Muir a little. But I was good at sneaking around and stealing. I went from town to town, earning my coins with my fingers but mostly with my wits. I had a good memory, you see. I could hear something once and remember it. I mingled with the dregs of this kingdom and then took it into my head to sell what I knew to the sheriffs. I worked for Almaguer, who was always looking for a way to disgrace the Aldermaston. He hated Muirwood. So did I. Anytime a maston passed through the country, he would pay handsomely to know about it. I did not care about what happened when I told. I tried to ignore the whispers that they were being killed, one by one. I knew the sheriff was a part of it, and I hoped that someday he would be strong enough to bring down Muirwood."

His teeth clenched, and he shook his head. "Before Winterrowd, I was pretty good at my games. I was always looking to turn a profit. Sell information to Almaguer and then try to sell freedom to one being hunted. Or to deliver a message for the condemned. The night I dragged the Earl of Forshee...I knew I had someone important, though I did not know who it was. He was not just a maston...I knew he was a nobleman, as well. They were starting to gather in this Hundred. I abandoned him at the kitchen, ready to earn my fee again. But somehow, you were the fox, and I was the cub. When Almaguer arrived to claim him, he was gone. Oh, I was nearly killed for my treachery. I searched the grounds but could not find where you had hidden him. I was so afraid Jon would find me, I had to be very cautious. So I went back to you, to trick you into revealing him. Do you understand what the curse did to me? I could not speak! That was the way I earned my bread. The way I deceived people. I have spent a year not being able to speak. The medallion was the only way I could communicate, but only those who used the Medium could understand my thoughts."

"When we met in the tunnel beneath the Pilgrim, you wanted me to open it. I thought you were going to kill me."

"No!" he said, shaking his head violently. "I knew you could free me! When I discovered the Leering in the woods, the one you used to destroy Almaguer, I knew you were powerful with the Medium. Very powerful. You would be strong enough to destroy the medallion. I knew that. And so did the Queen Dowager. When she discovered me with the remnant of the king's army, she took control of me. She is powerful, too. I was forced to do her bidding. She wanted me to bring you to her. I never wanted to hurt you, Lia. Not when I knew how much Martin cherished you.

I knew he did because he cried that night. The night you were brought to him."

Lia seized his arm, staring at him intently. The Medium blazed in her mind and scorched her heart with the truth of it. "Brought to him?"

"It was after Pry-Ree's fall. Not long after. He was the captain of the guard, remember? That night, I was roaming the Cider Orchard, stealing apples. There was a man with a basket. He was dressed like Martin. I thought it was him at first, when I saw the gladius. But he was younger. Wore the same leathers and hood. I followed him through the orchard, quiet as could be. He took you to Martin, who was walking the grounds at dark. I was not close enough to hear everything that was said, and I could not understand it because they spoke in Pry-rian. Martin wept bitterly, but he called you his granddaughter. I understood that much and hid in the shadows as the other man stole off. Martin stared at you for a time, teasing you in the basket. Then he dried his eyes, turned all gruff and serious again, and went to the kitchen and gave you to Pasqua to tend." He sighed deeply. "He did not claim kin with you. I never knew why. He let you be raised as a wretched, even though he knew who you were." He gave her a long and serious look. "That is why I never wanted to hurt you, lass. That is why I regret having stabbed you and deceived you. I must ask for your forgiveness, however long it takes me to earn it."

With that, he slowly rose and wiped his nose. "Someday, I would like to visit the mountain where Martin died and ask his forgiveness as well. Maybe you will take me there…someday."

Lia was stunned. Her feelings swam and churned. But it was not right. It was not settled. There was something wrong in what Seth had revealed to her. Nodding to him, she also rose, and they walked in silence back to the kitchen. Thoughts spun through her mind. She sorted them out, putting them together, one by one. As she fit each thought in the right place, she felt the comforting throbs of the Medium reassuring her. It whispered that her insights were true. The Prince had visited Muirwood and left Martin behind. Traits of the Medium were often passed on to the next generation. Lia had the Gift of Seering. She must have had it from her father. Her father, who had visited Muirwood and walked the same grounds. He had visited the inner depths of the Abbey and seen the altar. She had felt his presence when she first entered the Abbey. The memory of it had whispered over the intervening years.

She tried to keep each foot straight. Tried not to walk too hard, to wear herself out, but her heart hammered in her chest. Her thoughts blazed and arched and struck each other, causing more sparks of insight in her mind. Her father had seen what would happen. Had known that a protector would be needed. Why else would he leave the captain of his guard behind at the Abbey when he would be needed most in Comoros? Unless he knew that the captain was needed to protect his unborn child. To train those who would protect the child. To train the child.

Lia shuddered, and Seth asked if she was cold. She shook her head, unable to speak through the lump in her throat. The sky was darkening quickly, and she could see the light from the kitchen windows. He did not question her again, but left her at the door and sulked into the night, likely wondering if she was harboring bitter feelings.

She yanked open the door and walked inside the kitchen. Pasqua looked over at her worriedly. "There you are. You were gone longer than I expected. Is…Lia, are you all right?"

She still could not speak. Scarseth had found his voice, but she had lost hers. Pain throbbed in her leg from the hard walking. Ignoring it, she went beneath the loft and pulled loose the brick that concealed the Cruciger orb. The orb that was left with her as a child. Her father's orb! She stared at it, already knowing what would happen. In her hunt for Ellowyn Demont, she had always pictured the girl in her mind. She did that with most people, thinking of their face instead of their name. Thinking of them as she knew them.

She stared hard at the orb. She was facing south. Dahomey was to the south. *Find Ellowyn Demont*, she thought fiercely. The orb glowed, the spindle spun lazily around once and pointed at her. Writing appeared on its surface.

Lia—Ellowyn—stared at it as the tears burned in her eyes. She knew it all, as the knowledge flooded inside her mind, and her heart felt as if it were on fire. It was the Medium, confirming her knowledge. That the girl sailing to Dochte Abbey with Colvin was not Ellowyn Demont—*she* was Martin's granddaughter instead. A girl the Medium would not respond to. The truth crushed against her feelings relentlessly. Colvin had known of the missing Demont girl as a young boy. He had determined to be the one to find her.

And he had, without knowing it, when he was abandoned on the kitchen steps.

"What is it?" Sowe whispered, looking at her in concern, squeezing her shoulder.

She found her voice at last, though it came out a choked sob. "I know who I am, Sowe. I know it. The Aldermaston knows it, too." Her heart blazed with emotions. "He knows it, too!"

AUTHOR'S NOTE

In *The Blight of Muirwood*, the reader gets to experience the rituals of the maston order. Many early readers wondered where the details came from, so I would like to point inquisitive minds to the works of the Jewish historian Josephus. I read many of his works during my master's program at San Jose State University and found his account of ancient traditions to be quite fascinating. He describes the rituals of the Essenes, one of the various Jewish sects of his day, and you will find that I even used the Greek version of their order (*Essaios*) in the book as well. I did try to focus the world building on ancient traditions that are documented in the sources and in religious texts. All of the oaths Lia makes, for example, come directly from Josephus. The concept of "oath magic" is a theme I have used in my other books as well—that one can harness great powers not through deep study and training but through deep covenants to handle power with restraint.

Of the trilogy, *Blight* is my favorite for many reasons. It was fun to write, first of all, and allowed me to expand on the relationships introduced in the first book. I have always been an admirer of the middle parts of series. *The Empire Strikes Back* is my favorite Star Wars film, and *Elfstones of Shannara* is my favorite novel of all time. Both were the middle stories of a trilogy. I especially enjoyed writing the scenes with Lia and Colvin as their relationship became more complex. There are some moments in the book that were taken from my own life—memories that my wife and I shared as teenagers—such as running down a hill in Rancho San Antonio County Park in a rainstorm in February our senior year in high school. The monastery there is my own personal Muirwood. Others were more recent, such as a family excursion to Calaveras Big Trees State Park in California, which inspired scenes in Pry-Ree.

ABOUT THE AUTHOR

Photograph © Kim Bills

Jeff Wheeler is a writer from 7 p.m. to 10 p.m. on Wednesday nights. The rest of the time, he works for Intel Corporation, is a husband and the father of five kids, and a leader in his local church. He lives in Rocklin, California. When he isn't listening to books during his commute, he is dreaming up new stories to write. His website is: www.jeff-wheeler.com